THE ICARUS CODA

THE ICARUS CODA

TIMOTHY ZAHN

BAEN

THE ICARUS CODA

This is a work of fiction. All the characters and events portrayed in this book are fictional, and any resemblance to real people or incidents is purely coincidental.

Copyright © 2025 by Timothy Zahn

A Baen Books Original

Baen Publishing Enterprises
P.O. Box 1403
Riverdale, NY 10471
www.baen.com

ISBN: 978-1-6680-7235-6

Cover art by Dave Seeley

First printing, April 2025

Distributed by Simon & Schuster
1230 Avenue of the Americas
New York, NY 10020

Library of Congress Cataloging-in-Publication Data

Names: Zahn, Timothy, author.
Title: The Icarus coda / Timothy Zahn.
Description: Riverdale, NY : Baen Publishing Enterprises, 2025. | Series: The Icarus saga ; 6
Identifiers: LCCN 2024050766 (print) | LCCN 2024050767 (ebook) | ISBN 9781668072356 (hardcover) | ISBN 9781964856063 (ebook)
Subjects: LCGFT: Science fiction. | Novels.
Classification: LCC PS3576.A33 I27 2025 (print) | LCC PS3576.A33 (ebook) | DDC 813/.54—dc23/eng/20241210
LC record available at https://lccn.loc.gov/2024050766
LC ebook record available at https://lccn.loc.gov/2024050767

Printed in the United States of America
10 9 8 7 6 5 4 3 2 1

THE
ICARUS
CODA

CHAPTER ONE

As my father used to say, *You'll never know how far you can go until you push the limits. When you reach that point, make sure you have a good exit strategy ready.*

In this case, the limit for Selene and me turned out to be exactly two steps out the back door of the Mycene Ammei enclave's export center and approximately three meters short of the two tall, armadillo-armored Ammei soldiers currently pointing lightning guns at us.

"Is there a problem?" I asked, making sure to keep my hands visible. I'd seen what those weapons could do, and had no interest in a replay. "Isn't this the way out?"

Neither of the soldiers answered. Most Ammei we'd encountered had at least a modest grasp of English, but these two might be exceptions to that general rule. It could also be that they weren't supposed to engage potential corpses in conversation.

Or maybe they just didn't like us. The expressions on their wide, long-snouted faces were a mix of suspicion, irritation, and contempt.

In another place and time I'd probably have congratulated myself on that quick analysis. Ammei faces were similar enough that most of the non-Ammei species they interacted with relied on their wide array of clothing choices to distinguish between

1

individuals. But after three months of quietly investigating the culture, politics, and technology of the Dulcet, Lassiter, and Mycene enclaves, I'd learned how to read the subtle patterns in their full-body scale coverings and the slight variations in snout width and length.

Selene had spent those same three months learning how to read the identity markers present in Ammei scents. She'd also started a mental library of emotional indicators, though a full reading of the species was still a long ways off.

None of that expertise was needed right now, of course. There was a universality to aimed weaponry that superseded cultural barriers.

Behind us, the door we'd just exited slammed open and the export clerk we'd been negotiating with charged out. "What do you do here?" he demanded, his voice and expression agitated. "You cannot be out here."

"I'm so sorry," I apologized profusely, taking one final look at the landscape behind the soldiers. Ten meters past them the flagstoned pedestrian path we were standing on curved out of sight behind a section of the forest that filled this side of the export center. There was no indication of anything special about the path, or that there might be anything more interesting than a Grove of Reflection at the far end. But a single glance at Selene's pupils was all I needed to know that sneaking out the office's back door had been worth the risk.

Somewhere along this path, somewhere very close, was the Mycene end of the Nexus Six Gemini portal.

"I thought this door led back to the main parking area," I told the clerk.

"It does not," he said stiffly. His agitation was quickly turning to anger and suspicion. "Come inside. Come inside now."

"Of course," I soothed, taking Selene's arm. "I'm afraid I get turned around easily."

"Come," he said, pulling open the door. I gave him an embarrassed smile as Selene and I walked past. He strode in after us, the two armed soldiers close behind him.

"Have you had a chance to consider our offer?" I asked as the clerk led the way back toward his office. "We believe the terms to be very fair."

The clerk didn't answer. He led the way to his office door,

but instead of ushering us inside, he continued along the hallway toward the reception room. We reached it, he opened the door, and we walked in.

I winced. Earlier, the room's total occupancy had been a single greeter behind an ornate desk. She was still there, but she'd been joined by two more soldiers and a third armed Ammei wearing the distinguishing hat of a junior officer. "You will explain your actions," the officer said, his voice and expression flat and determined.

"I understand, sir, and I'm extremely sorry for my carelessness," I said. As my father used to say, *Nothing in life is free, and the cost will usually come out of your wallet, your ego, or your hide.* Considering the other options, I would be more than happy to sacrifice whatever pride was necessary to get us out of here. "I know you think me a fool, and you're absolutely right."

I might as well have saved my breath. "You will provide identification," the officer ordered. "*Correct* identification," he added, having apparently concluded that what we'd showed the greeter earlier was false. Which it was, of course. "Afterward you will be brought before First Dominant Prucital for investigation and judgment."

I suppressed a sigh. So that was that. We hadn't yet had the honor of meeting Prucital, but as the leader of this enclave he was certain to have regular contact with First of Three and the rest of the Nexus Six leadership. That meant he would have heard about Selene and me, and had probably seen pictures.

When you reach that point, make sure you have a good exit strategy ready.

Fortunately, I had such an emergency trapdoor at hand. Unfortunately, it was a single-use ploy that I'd hoped to save for later.

But it couldn't be helped. The export center was only a couple of hundred meters inside the enclave, but with three soldiers in front of us and two more behind it would be suicide to make a run for it. There was equally no way I could afford to let First Dominant Prucital get a good look at us.

"You want correct identification?" I asked, letting my voice go cold and hard. Probably a waste of time, given that the officer probably hadn't bothered to learn human mannerisms and vocal tones. "Fine." I pulled my wallet from my pocket and flipped it open toward him. "Major Thomas Aquinas, EarthGuard Special

Investigations," I continued in my most authoritative voice, making sure to angle the gold ID badge so that it sent the ceiling light into his eyes. "We're looking for this man"—I slid out the picture that had been pressed up behind the ID—"and it was thought he might have taken refuge in your enclave."

"No humans hide within our borders," the officer said, his expression suddenly cautious. "What standing does EarthGuard have here?"

"I agree," I said, voicing approval of his comment while ignoring his question. "We've seen enough to confirm he's not here."

Which wasn't even remotely true, of course. We'd walked from the main gate to the export center, plus those two meters out the back door, and that was it. But the officer didn't necessarily know that, not without working through whatever security cameras the enclave had in play. "We appreciate your cooperation, and will now be on our way. I assume your soldiers will provide proper escort to the gate?"

The officer stirred, as if he'd just remembered there was procedure for a situation like this. "Your identity must be verified before you will be permitted to leave." He produced a compact scanner and held out his hand.

Silently, I slid the ID out of the wallet and handed it over, my heart picking up its pace a bit. Depending on what kind of authentication the scanner checked for, we could be out of here in two minutes, or we could end up seated in a locked room for as long as it took for someone with *real* EarthGuard credentials to arrive from the Commonwealth diplomatic station.

Though even that worst-case scenario wouldn't necessarily be the end of the world. Like every other bureaucracy, EarthGuard had its share of organizational blind alleys, deep-black secrets, and the normal social friction inherent in one person not knowing the next guy's job. On top of that, my years as a bounty hunter had garnered me an extensive repertoire of excuses, misdirections, innuendoes, and flat-out lies suitable for any occasion. No matter who the Ammei persuaded to look us over, I was pretty sure I could talk our way out of it. "But be quick about it," I warned as the officer inserted my ID into the slot. "We have three more locations to clear before the end of the week."

"I will be as quick as assurance allows."

He peered at the display, poking at the keys, and I found

myself mentally crossing my fingers. I'd been assured the ID would pass any standard scrutiny check with flying colors. If we were lucky, this would be the end of it.

For once, we were. "Yes; Major Aquinas," the officer said, removing the ID from his scanner and handing it back. "Your identity is confirmed."

"Good," I said briskly, tucking the card back in its wallet. "If you'll now escort us back to the gate?"

"We shall do so," the guard said. "Do you wish to first consult with your colleague?"

Long practice kept me from the sudden freeze that might have brought down the entire house of cards. Someone from EarthGuard was *here*? "No need," I told him, taking Selene's arm. "We're running separate operations. The gate, please."

It looked like we'd gotten away clean. But as my father used to say, *When you're trying to get away from something or someone, bear in mind that horseshoe rules don't apply.* Still, I could sense no unusual scrutiny or suspicion from the Ammei we passed on the walk back to the entrance, and if Selene smelled anything disquieting she didn't signal me. We passed through the gate into the wide strip of farmland that lay between Ammei territory and the minor Drilie city to the north, and I turned us toward the parking area where we'd left our runaround—

Abruptly, Selene's hand squeezed my arm. "Gregory, he's here," she murmured tensely.

"Who?" I murmured back, flicking a quick look across everything I could see without doing something suspicious like spinning to look behind us. There was nothing obvious.

But as my father used to say—

"Hello, Gregory. Fancy meeting you here."

I closed my eyes briefly, the utter ridiculousness of such a coincidence flooding over me. "Hello, Dad," I said, not bothering to turn around. "Or should I be formal and address you as *Sir Nicholas*?"

"*Dad* is fine," he assured me as he caught up with us and settled into step beside Selene. "Nice beard, by the way. Your new hair looks even better, Selene."

"Thanks," I said, glancing at the coal-black wig currently covering Selene's blazing white Kadolian hair. "So how does that go again? *Of all the gin joints—*"

"—*in all the towns in all the world, she walks into mine*," my father finished the quote. "Sadly, Rick didn't know to reference the Spiral in his complaint."

"Sadly, indeed," I agreed, wondering who Rick was and what he was complaining about. My father had a vast reservoir of quotes and sayings to draw from and seldom bothered to explain any of them. "Can we give you a lift somewhere?"

"Better idea," he said, offering a genial smile that didn't fool me for a second. "How about I buy you lunch?"

"Not hungry, and on a very tight schedule."

His smile turned frosty. "Work me in. You're going to want to hear what I have to say."

"Let's try the edited version."

Beside me, Selene stirred. "Gregory, he's serious."

"Never known him not to be," I said, my resolve wavering a little. Whatever Selene had picked up in his scent, it had clearly made an impression on her. That was always worth paying attention to.

On the other hand, we needed to make tracks out of here before some Amme took another look at whatever they used for wanted posters and realized Gregory Roarke, Public Enemy Number One, was still within spitting distance. And as my father also used to say, *Another definition of spitting distance is that you're close enough to be mounted on their rotisserie.* On top of which, I frankly wasn't feeling all that cooperative right now.

"Edited version it is," my father said. "You and Selene have both picked up posts."

Once again, I passed up the guilty starts. But it was a closer thing this time. "*Bounty* posts?"

"The good news is that both of you are on live-detain bounties," he said. "The bad news is that they're two million commarks each."

I swallowed a curse that had once earned me a three-minute scolding. "So someone wants to talk to us," I concluded. "Or else wants the privilege of killing us himself."

"And is *very* invested in exercising one or both of those options," my father confirmed. "There's a nice, out-of-the-way barbeque place about ten kilometers north of here."

I sighed and gestured to the runrarounds. "Lead the way."

❖   ❖   ❖

"The good news first," he said when we were seated in a back corner of his chosen restaurant and had sent in our order. "Whoever's behind this, it probably isn't General Kinneman. I'm pretty sure it isn't First of Three, either."

"Reasons?" I asked, taking a small sip of my Dewar's scotch. I had no intention of getting my mind fogged, especially not this close to enemy territory. But human rib places had a reputation among the Drilie locals for the liberal use of alcohol, and I didn't want to draw attention by standing too far out of expectations.

"For Kinneman, it's budget considerations," my father said. "I've had a look at the Alien Portal Agency's finances, and much as he'd like to throw a net around you there's no way he can pull two million out of petty cash without it sending flags from here to Earth and back again. First of Three has the same budget restrictions plus logistics. Not only would he have to dig up money he hasn't got, but he'd also have to navigate his way through the Commonwealth political and social structure, not to mention the hunter protocols."

"I assume he has agents here in the Spiral he could use for all that," Selene pointed out.

"I'm sure he does," my father agreed. "*If* he trusts them, which is the likely centerpiece of his logistics headache. As I'm sure you noticed while you were on Nexus Six, the Ammei have a lot of internal politics going on."

"We might have spotted an indication or two," I agreed, deliberately keeping it vague. "So what's your analysis? I assume after three months you have the whole thing down cold."

He snorted. "You give me way too much credit, Gregory. All right. The data we've assembled suggests there are five Ammei enclaves in the Spiral, though one is so small it really doesn't count. Officially, they all answer to First of Three and the Nexus Six leadership. Unofficially, there are at least two major factions—one each centered on Nexus Six and Juniper—with threads from both groups weaving through the other enclaves."

"That was our conclusion, too," I said.

"That same political stress also exists within each enclave's leadership," Selene added. "Here in Mycene, for example, First Dominant Prucital is a strong supporter of First of Three. But—"

"Which is why First of Three rewarded him by naming him *Fourth of Three*," my father put in, "and adding him to—"

"Wait a minute," I interrupted him right back. "Prucital is Fourth of Three?"

"You didn't pick up on that?" my father asked, frowning. "No, of course you didn't. Prucital generally prefers to stay in the background when he's here on his own world. You probably never saw him."

"No, we didn't," I said sourly. Fourth of Three had been an elderly Amme who had played translator between Second of Three, Selene, Huginn, and me during our first visit to Nexus Six. "Interesting. As I believe you used to say, *If you can secure someone's loyalty with a fancy title or a few flattering words, you've gotten off cheap.*"

"Yes, that does sound familiar," he agreed. "At any rate—"

"Hold it," I said. "It's still Selene's turn."

"Oh. Right." My father turned to her. "Sorry. I sometimes slip into lecture mode. Bad habit. Please continue."

"As I said, First Dominant Prucital is a supporter of Nexus Six," she said, the brief flicker of annoyance fading from her pupils. She hated when people acted as if she wasn't there. "But Second Dominant Nibagu and his faction are allied with First Dominant Yiuliob and the Juniper Glory political group."

"Really," my father said thoughtfully. "Prucital didn't mention that part. I didn't pick up on it, either."

"You haven't spent as much time poking around the enclaves' edges as we have," I said. After talking over Selene, he deserved a little dig. "Kinneman probably keeps you on a pretty tight leash. What's that old saying about serving two masters?"

"Point taken," my father conceded. "Let's get back to your posts. Interesting that you bring up dualism, given that it appears your bounties originated from two different sources."

"So we're not being hunted as a pair?"

"Apparently not." He nodded to Selene. "You, Selene, are the easy part. The only people who want you that badly are the Ammei, which leads me to suspect First Dominant Yiuliob is behind your post."

"If First and Nexus Six don't have that kind of money, what makes you think Yiuliob and Juniper do?" I asked.

His eyebrows went up a fraction. "You're the ones who've been digging into the depths of Ammei society. You tell me."

"If you insist," I said. First his lecture mode, and now his pop-quiz thing. "We only saw Yiuliob's distribution center for a few minutes, but it was pretty impressive. It looks like most of the exotic foodstuffs go straight there, where they're treated and processed and then distributed back to the other enclaves via the Nexus Six portals."

"Do you know where any of it comes from?" my father asked.

"No," I said. "But Nexus Six has twelve portals, and we've only accounted for five of them. Plenty left for secret farms."

"True." My father took a sip from his glass. "Somewhat inefficient running everything through Nexus Six to Juniper and back, but that may be Yiuliob's influence."

"Or it may have just evolved that way," Selene suggested. "We found indications that Juniper began as the main enclave, with Nexus Six the only other point of the distribution system. As the other enclaves grew and joined in the project, they were looped in."

"Still rather inefficient," my father said with a shrug. "But history and tradition are notoriously hard ruts to break out of. My point is that if any Amme is involved with Selene's bounty post, it's probably Yiuliob." He gave me a speculative look. "Which brings us to you, Gregory. Who have you offended lately?"

"*And* who has that much spare cash to burn?" I shook my head. "No idea. You're sure they're from different sources?"

"The posts have different references and contact information," he said. "Though that might not mean much in the hunter world. Any reason the Ammei might be after you, too?"

"Not that I know of," I said, freshly aware of the two stolen pages from the Ammei enhancement serum formula book hidden in my artificial left arm. "Unless they think I'll be leverage to make Selene do what they want. Or, like I said, it's someone who wants to watch me die."

"Or just wants us neutralized," Selene put in, her pupils showing heightened concern. She didn't like casual talk of death.

"Could be," I agreed. I didn't much like talk of death, either, especially when I was the proposed guest of honor. "In that case, you can probably add Nask or various other Patth to the list."

"Do Patth sub-directors have that much disposable income?" my father asked.

I thought about the ten hundred-thousand-commark certified bank checks tucked away in a fold of heat insulation in the *Ruth's* engine room. I'd borrowed that money from Nask a while back and never found a way to get it back to him. Maybe this was his way of jogging my memory. "I don't think that's something they talk about publicly," I said. "But the prevailing rumor suggests that's a yes."

"Interesting," my father said thoughtfully. "So we have the Ammei, the Patth, and a sprinkling of targets you hunted back in the day. At least you can't complain that your life's been dull. Speaking of dull, I don't suppose you'd care to share what exactly you were doing back there in the enclave?"

"Just more of the same," I said. "I hoped we could get a look past the public areas and see what they're doing behind the scenes."

"And did you?"

"We got two steps before we were stopped," I said. "But we're reasonably sure those steps pointed us to their Gemini portal."

"About two hundred meters behind the export center?"

I stared at him. "And you know that *how*?"

"Same way you did," he said. "Observation and inference." He paused. "Plus, I've been talking with First Dominant Prucital."

"On whose behalf?"

"General Kinneman and First of Three are both eager to work out some understandings," he said. "I've been asked to serve as liaison." He raised his eyebrows a bit. "Speaking of official inter-actions, as I was leaving I overheard something about an Earth-Guard special investigator. That wasn't you, by any chance, was it?"

"You don't seriously think I've joined EarthGuard, do you?" I asked, giving him my best innocent look.

"No, of course not," he assured me. "Perish the thought. I trust McKell and Ixil didn't get their hands caught in the cookie jar getting you that ID."

"I have no idea what you're talking about."

"Of course not," he said again. "Tell them I said hello next time you talk to them."

"I tell everyone that," I said. "What kind of understandings are we talking about?"

"Preliminary ones," he said. "At this point it's mostly just mak-ing the rounds of the various enclaves and introducing myself."

"I trust the Ammei are properly impressed by you?"

"Some more than others," he said. "I'm also poking at the edges the same way you are. The general wants to know how Ammei society is put together."

"I'll bet he does," I said. "Speaking of edges, did you manage to get a look at any of the gossamers' tethers?"

"Really, Gregory," he said with mild reproach. "A man's home is his castle."

"I thought your most relevant saying was, *People who live in glass houses should get their walls frosted.*"

"There's that, too," he conceded. "Though to be fair, gossamers weren't nearly as big a rage back when I said that."

I shrugged. "Blame the intrusive society."

"Not saying it's wrong. Just saying they weren't as popular."

He was right on that count, anyway. The long rise of surveillance capabilities, whether from governments, companies, or general busybodies, had been a thorn in the sides of champions of privacy for decades. The invention of gossamer air shields seven years ago, which had given people the ability to protect anything they didn't want other people looking at, was slowly but steadily reversing that trend. The spiderweb-thin sheets floated on the breeze over whatever territory needed protecting, their faintly glistening surfaces letting nearly a hundred percent of sunlight reach the ground while simultaneously reflecting just enough the other direction to mess with surveillance cameras.

There were rumors that the Patth were the gossamers' true inventors, and that they owned the company that made the stuff. Given the Patth history of interesting and unique technologies—not to mention their obsession with secrecy—I wouldn't be surprised if those rumors were true.

"As to your question, no, I didn't spot any tethers," my father continued. "You?"

"I could just make out the northern edge of the eastern gossamer, but the route we were taken on didn't bring us within sight of anything useful."

"Probably by design." My father huffed out a breath. "Ten years ago we could have mapped every square centimeter of every Ammei enclave. Found their Geminis and everything else of interest. But back then, nobody cared enough to bother."

"Plus, we also didn't know about Gemini portals back then," I pointed out. *We* didn't, anyway. "Even if we had, I doubt anyone would have thought an enclave of obscure aliens might be home to any of them."

"History is full of missed opportunities," he said philosophically. "What's next on your agenda?"

I looked at Selene, saw the caution in her pupils. Now that

we had a better handle on what we were dealing with, our plan was to head to Juniper and start digging in earnest into the links between the Ammei, the Patth, the Kadolians, and the still-mysterious Gold Ones.

Which wasn't to say I should tell any of that to my father. Not just for our safety, but also for his.

"Not sure," I said. "There's still a lot we don't know about the Ammei, and I'm wary of going up against Yiuliob without a complete tool kit. You said there was a fifth enclave? I thought there were only four."

"The fifth's on Belshaz," he said. "It's very small, more like a neighborhood social club. They own about five square kilometers at the southwest part of Rirto City that stretches into the Suzem Desert."

"Maybe we'll look in on them," I said. "Exotic sand sculptures are still pretty popular on Skriff. Maybe the Belshaz Ammei would welcome some fresh buyers."

"Assuming they even do sand sculptures," my father said. "At any rate, be careful. Watch your back and Selene's. Selene, ditto."

"Yes, Sir Nicholas," Selene said, a hint of amusement in her pupils. "You, as well."

"Count on it," he promised as he fished four twenty-commark bills from his wallet and laid them on the table. "Enjoy your meal, and have another Dewar's if you'd like. I'm sure we'll bump into each other again soon."

"Inevitable, I'd say," I agreed. "Enjoy your frying pan, Dad."

"Thank you, Gregory." He gave me a tight smile. "Enjoy your fire."

CHAPTER TWO

Juniper had originally been colonized by the Saffi, who'd been impressed enough by the Vesperin experiment of multiple-species cooperation that they wanted to try it for themselves. Their venture had been somewhat less successful than Vesperin's, partly because the living conditions on Juniper weren't as attractive as those on Vesperin, and partly because the colony started out in the shadow of two larger and better established worlds nearby. Still, over the years Juniper had built up a decent and diverse population, a healthy economy, and had showed a willingness to take the risks inherent in branching out into new areas.

The system was an eight-day flight from Mycene. Selene and I filled the time by going over every bit of data our info pads had on the planet, its people, and its culture. We also studied and discussed everything we'd learned about the Ammei, and worked out our plan of action once we touched down.

The big question, and the reason we'd scheduled Juniper for the end of our to-do list, was whether or not the Gemini linking Juniper to Nexus Six was the only portal on the planet. First of Three certainly seemed to believe there was a full-range portal buried somewhere, or at least he'd pretended he believed it when Selene told them it was there.

Complicating the hunt was the need to make our search as invisible as possible. At the moment, the competition for the things was fairly well contained, with the Icarus Group—I refused to think of it by Kinneman's new title of Alien Portal Agency—the Patth, and the Ammei the only players. If the portals' existence ever leaked to the rest of the Spiral, the number of players would go through the roof.

Especially if the Easter egg in question was indeed a full-range portal. Geminis were dyads, linking a single pair of portals together, while full-range portals like Icarus, Alpha, and Firefall could connect to any other full-range portal anywhere. All a prospective passenger needed to do was punch in the proper eighty-digit number, and the sky would literally be the limit.

Unfortunately, the only known directory with lists of those numbers had come in two pieces: General Josiah Leland Kinneman and the Icarus Group had one half; Sub-Director Nask and the Patth had the other. As my father used to say, *A draw in chess is interesting only to statisticians.*

Unless the Ammei on Nexus Six had another directory.

It wasn't impossible. The planet had been a major Icari travel center once, a full-range portal surrounded by a ring of twelve Geminis. More intriguing was the fact that *Imistio* Tower, the centerpiece of the Nexus Six cluster, had a library that held thousands of books. If someone had wanted to hide a backup copy of the directory, he could search far and wide without finding a better place to stash it.

"Have you decided where we should start looking?" Selene asked as we cleared the dinner dishes off the dayroom table our last night in space.

It was a question we'd pondered in one form or another since leaving Mycene, and we still didn't have a definitive answer. "I'm always partial to forests and jungles," I told her, sitting back down and pulling up my set of Juniper maps. "Any sign of visitors or other tampering gets quickly grown over. You still favoring one of the deserts?"

"I was," she said, sitting down beside me. "Low activity means less chance of someone stumbling over it on their way elsewhere. But you're right about the tampering aspect. And of course, in a desert any traffic at all automatically stands out."

"There are also plenty of lakes, rivers, and small oceans down there," I reminded her. "And we now know portals do just fine under water."

She nodded, a sudden thoughtfulness coming into her pupils. "It's so hard to extrapolate when we only have data points from three full-range portals."

"At least we know Yiuliob hasn't found it," I said, sitting hard on my curiosity. I wanted to ask what that look meant, but it would be better to let her bring it out in her own time. "Maybe our best bet would be to figure out where the Ammei have already searched and look somewhere else."

"Yes," Selene said, the thoughtful look deepening. "I was just wondering...do we *know* Yiuliob hasn't found the portal?"

"Actually...no, I guess we don't," I said slowly. "On the other hand, if he *has* found it, why hasn't First come charging in to take it away from him?"

"Maybe he doesn't know," she said. "Or maybe he knows Yiuliob's found it, but doesn't know where on the planet it is."

"Which would put him in the same boat we're currently floating in," I agreed. "So...?"

She seemed to brace herself. "Maybe First doesn't know where it is physically," she said. "But what if he *does* have its address?"

"Oh, wouldn't *that* be interesting?" I muttered, my brain spinning with a whole new range of possibilities. "That could explain the half-finished launch module on Nexus Six, too. *And* why they haven't bothered building a receiver module to go with it. All First needs is a single one-way trip to Juniper."

"At which point all his team has to do is go outside and set up a location beacon."

"At which point First launches an attack through Yiuliob's Gemini, rips through his soldiers, and hotfoots it over to link up with his advance team at the full-range."

"Or he doesn't launch an attack at the enclave because his soldiers have already infiltrated Juniper and are ready to go directly to the full-range."

"Even better," I agreed. "Avoids the bottleneck problem at the enclave. First could work a leisurely infiltration over a period of weeks or months, sending his troops there via regular commercial transport."

"Assuming Yiuliob doesn't spot them," Selene warned. "Everything we've seen of the Ammei indicate they generally stay close to home. A group traveling across the Spiral could be conspicuous."

"True," I said, trying to think it through. There was no way

Selene and I could sift through all the traffic in and out of Juniper looking for something like that. But Kinneman probably could.

Assuming he was interested in taking suggestions from me.

"You going to contact your father?"

I gave her a crooked smile. Her real-time awareness of my shifting emotions and thought patterns really *did* save time. "Not yet," I said. "He warned us to use that private number sparingly, and I don't want to abuse the privilege. Besides, even if Kinneman agreed to track Ammei movements, it would take just one ham-handed EarthGuard bureaucrat to accidentally tip off First that we're onto him. But we'll keep that plan as a backup."

"All right," Selene said, her pupils suddenly frowning.

"You disagree?"

"No, I think you're right," she said. "It just occurred to me that we never asked your father how he got in to see First Dominant Prucital on Mycene."

"He said he was introducing himself around the enclaves."

"Yes, but introducing himself as what? An official Commonwealth representative? An *unofficial* representative? Did he have a fake ID like ours?"

"Good questions," I said, frowning. "You're right. We never asked, and he never said. Though there's a fair chance he'd have lied about it anyway."

"Maybe," she said. "Maybe not."

"Well, it's long past now," I said. "Let's concentrate on the future. We've currently got three options for getting into the enclave. I'd like to come up with at least one more before we land."

By the time we settled onto our landing pad on Juniper we had the four sets of plans that I'd wanted.

After all that effort, it was almost a shame that, two hours after our landing, every single one of them vanished into thin air.

It was, I'm sure, pure coincidence that the purportedly best Earth barbeque place on Juniper was at the western edge of Pikwik City and only twelve kilometers from the Ammei enclave's main entrance.

As my father used to say, *If you're planning to poke the bear, it's best to work your way in from about ten kilometers out, not start right at the mouth of the den.* Generally good advice; but in this case, it didn't really apply. For one thing, we'd spent three months with preliminary investigations and I had the feeling that our time was starting to run out. That behooved us to start moving as quickly as possible on this final phase of the operation. For another, I hadn't yet met an Amme who liked human barbeque, so the odds of running into one before we were ready to proceed were extremely low.

For a third, the ribs my father had treated us to on Mycene had been very disappointing, and I was hungry.

"I still don't like this," Selene said quietly as the waiter left with our order. Her pupils, I noted, were heavy with anxiety. "There must be bounty hunters out there who know your taste for barbeque. Maybe we should have gone somewhere else."

"We have to get out in the public eye sometime," I reminded her. "Might as well test the waters here and now. Anyway, Juniper should be relatively safe."

"That assumes the Patth didn't put out either of the posts."

"Point," I conceded. "On the other hand, if Nask or one of his people are involved, they have easier ways to find us than a search of Juniper's barbeque hotspots."

"I suppose."

It was a pretty lackluster response. Still, I couldn't blame her. Tipster boards were a bounty hunter's best friend, chock-full of sightings, hints, and other subtleties that could aid a hunter in zeroing in on a target, often before other hunters even knew that target was on a particular planet. The services were extremely pricey, but for that outlay the hunter got up-to-date information from sources that had been vetted and certified by the boards' overseers.

Unless the tipster in question wasn't certified at all and had gotten into the system solely because a helpful Patth sub-director had given him a set of mid-level access codes to supposedly secure sites.

That still meant that only the hunters with enough cash to buy into the boards were currently burning the spacelanes toward our home base of Xathru, where my bogus tip had placed us. But since those hunters tended to be the best and most dangerous, I figured it was worth the effort.

Though as Selene had just pointed out, that was only if Nask wasn't involved with either bounty. Not only was he unlikely to fall for my wild-goose ploy, but he had a better set of backdoor codes that would presumably let him track the *Ruth* with relative ease. Not to mention that the false IDs we were running under had come from him.

"Don't worry, we'll be fine," I assured Selene, looking around the taverno. This was a predominantly Saffnic part of Juniper, and even in a place that specialized in human food and drink there was a sprinkling of Saffi scattered among the predominantly human clientele.

I was doing a second, more leisurely survey of the room, looking for reactions that might indicate we'd been recognized, when the door opened and a disheveled, twitchy alien stumbled in.

At first glance I thought he was just an overly scruffy human. A closer look revealed the more subtle differences: a flatter nose, more prominent brow ridges, the straggly mop on his head composed of something thicker and more yarn-like than human hair, and a subtle wobble in his walk that indicated a slightly different joint structure. He had a pair of what looked like tattoos on his cheeks, thin silvery lines starting at the outsides of the eyes and branching into a confused jumble of other lines as they reached his jawline. He was a bit bulky around the middle and about half a head shorter than me, and was dressed in a nondescript outfit of tunic and trousers. On the first finger of his very humanlike right hand was a thick black ring. As far as I knew, I'd never seen any of his species before. "Selene?" I murmured.

"I don't know," she said. "I've never seen anyone like him. Does he seem...right...to you?"

I winced. "Not really."

It was an ancient bit of folklore that an insane alien could always be recognized as such even if the observer was unfamiliar with that particular species. A questionable conclusion, in my opinion—I'd dealt with enough greedy, frightened, or furious aliens to know that those emotions could easily be mistaken for mental illness.

But I had to admit that this one was doing everything he could to support the theory. He came to a sudden stop, just far enough inside to let the door close behind him. His eyes darted restlessly around, as if wondering if he'd walked into a snake pit, while he made small brushing motions on his chest and arms with his hands as if trying to clear off invisible spiders. His visual survey paused on a table of three men and two women, shifted to another table of Saffi, stopped briefly on Selene and me, went back to the five humans, then started around the room again.

I watched him closely, an unpleasant tingle on the back of my neck. As my father used to say, *People usually underestimate those who are sick or in pain.* While I'd never used that particular gambit in my hunts there was nothing that said it wouldn't be effective. Playing an oblivious lunatic would be a perfect way for a hunter to lull a target off guard and get himself in range. "Stay sharp," I warned, shifting my hips to bring my plasmic into easier grabbing range. "He could be faking."

"I don't think so," she said, her eyelashes going full flutter. "I think I smell dysthensial on him."

"Which is...?"

"A drug that helps alleviate the symptoms of several chronic diseases," she said. "It's also known to aggravate some mental problems."

"Wonderful," I growled. Bad enough when I thought Yarn-Top might just be a crafty hunter. Worse was someone whacked out on an exotic drug drawing attention to the taverno and everyone in it. Maybe Selene was right about our coming here being a bad idea. "Okay. As soon as he clears the doorway, we're gone."

"We already ordered."

"I'll leave money to cover it," I said. Yarn-Top was still surveying the room, and the low hum of conversation was faltering as people began to notice him. I watched him, keeping a peripheral check on everyone else...

His eyes widened. "No no," he gasped, just loudly enough for us to hear from our table. "No no no *no.*" Without warning, he broke from his position and all but sprinted past us toward the bar at the back of the room, trailing a string of frantic *no-nos* behind him.

"Here we go," I said, touching Selene's arm. "On three—"

"Wait," Selene said, grabbing my hand. "There's scent of Ammei on him."

"*Ammei?*" I echoed, swiveling around in my seat. Yarn-Top had reached the bar and was leaning half over it, talking urgently but indistinctly to a bartender who looked like she wished she was somewhere else. "How much?"

"Not much, and not fresh," she said. "A few days ago, or maybe more recent but from a distance—"

"Hold on," I cut her off. A well-built man with long brown hair and a scraggly goatee had stood up from his table and was walking wearily toward the bar. His gait was that of a man who's seen everything, been disappointed by most of it, and was just trying to make his way through life. He came up behind Yarn-Top and laid a comforting hand on his shoulder—

A second later, Yarn-Top staggered him back with a violent backhand blow across his chest.

And as Long-Hair flailed in an effort to hold onto his balance, I knew what I had to do. Sustained violence meant badgemen, security camera scrutiny, and special attention to anyone who left in the middle of the confrontation, especially anyone the badgemen thought looked furtive about their exit. Our best chance now for keeping whatever anonymity we still had was to defuse the situation before it reached that point.

"Wait here," I told Selene, standing up and heading toward the other two. Long-Hair had recovered his balance and was leaning on the back of a chair, talking quietly and urgently toward Yarn-Top. Yarn-Top, for his part, was staring straight back at him, his gaze a mix of angry, frightened, and confused.

"It's all right, Bubloo," Long-Hair was saying as I got close enough to make out the words. "I'm your doctor. Remember, Bubloo? Dr. Robin?"

"You all right?" I asked, coming up to Robin.

He twitched at my sudden arrival. "Oh," he said. "Sorry—didn't hear you come up. What did you say?"

"I asked if you were all right."

"I'm not hurt, if that's what you mean," he said. "But—" He gestured to Yarn-Top. "This is the third time in ten days Bubloo's gotten away from me. One more, and the clinic may decide my services are no longer required."

"Well, we can't let that happen," I said, resisting the temptation to tell him I knew *exactly* how it felt to not be wanted. "You say your name's Robin?"

"Yes. Dr. Chrisopher Robin, xenopsychiatrist." He gave me a wan smile. "Yes, I know. Blame my parents."

"Come again?"

He waved a hand in dismissal. "Sorry. Character out of old Earth literature. Somewhat unflattering for anyone older than ten."

"I'll take your word for it. How do we help him?"

"We start by getting him outside," Robin said, pushing himself off the chair and back to full vertical. Maybe he was thinking about the security cameras, too, and his clinic's view of his current performance. "After that, we take him to my apartment where I can get him proper treatment."

"More dysthensial?"

He threw me a startled look. "How did you—? No, no dysthensial. Anything but. Bubloo's been self-medicating with that. You see where it's gotten him."

"But you *do* have something to calm him?"

"Yes, but I can't treat him in here," he said. "We have to get him to my apartment."

"Okay," I said, eyeing him. As I'd already noted, he seemed well-muscled. But I could also sense a hint of frailness there. "Bad back?"

"Bad back, bad hips, iffy knees," he said, studying me with new interest. "Controllable with meds, but my daily dose hasn't kicked in yet. Are you a doctor, too?"

"Just an observer of the human condition," I said. "Okay, let's see if we can corral him."

We started forward, moving slowly and carefully. Bubloo just stood there, watching us but making no move either to attack or escape. Now that I was up close, I saw that his cheek tattoos weren't so much a jumble as a delicately woven combination of musical clef and breaking ocean wave. I could also now see a meshwork of wrinkles crisscrossing his face and hands, like his skin was half a size too big for his body. "It's all right, Bubloo," Robin said soothingly. "We're your friends."

"Will you help me find them again?" Bubloo asked. There was still a strangeness to his voice, but the frantic nervousness had faded away. Distantly, I wondered if that mood shift was coming from the dysthensial or from Bubloo's own brain chemistry glitches. "I need to find them again."

"Who do you need to find, Bubloo?" Robin asked as he reached tentatively out to him.

"Them," Bubloo said. He was watching Robin closely, but this time he allowed the doctor's touch without fighting back. "You know who they are. Them. The ones they all fear."

He shifted his gaze to me as I stepped up to take his other arm, and I saw for the first time that his pupils were slitted like

Selene's, except side to side instead of her up and down. "*You know*, don't you?" he asked. "The ones we want. The ones we need."

"Who are these people, Bubloo?" I asked as Robin and I got him in a firm double grip. "Can you tell me?"

"You know them," he insisted. "Of course you know them.

"The Gold Ones."

CHAPTER THREE

"Every time he runs he eventually winds up in there," Robin said as he and I eased Bubloo through the doorway and out into the night air. "I don't know whether it's the background music, the décor, or the aromas, but I've learned that if I sit there long enough he'll show up."

"Human barbeque is a great soother," I said, peering down at the top of Bubloo's head. The alien's temperament had shifted again, this time to an uncertain calmness and a lot of mostly dead weight. Considering the alternatives, I was more than happy to call it even. "Or maybe he was looking for these Gold Ones of his," I added casually. "Any idea what that was all about?"

"Not a clue," Robin said. "He's mentioned them once or twice during sessions, but I've never been able to get anything more out of him. Best assumption is that they're another of his delusions."

"A shame," I said. "He's already a species I've never met before. Sounds like these Gold Ones would be a second. Not every day you get your horizons broadened in two different directions."

"I know what you mean," Robin said. "Every time I think I've got a handle on the Spiral and its people, someone like Bubloo comes along." He nodded toward the runaround stand where Selene had gone on ahead to get us a vehicle. "Or someone like your friend there," he added. "What is she, if you don't mind my asking?"

"She's Kadolian," I told him. "They're pretty rare—"

"*Kadolian?*" Robin gave me a startled look over Bubloo's head. "She's *Kadolian*? Really?"

"Yes, really," I said, my gun hand moving a bit closer to my plasmic. "Is that a problem?"

"No, no, not at all," Robin said, shifting his eyes back to Selene. "It's just ... I think Bubloo may have mentioned her species once, too. Sounds like he messed up the pronunciation, which is probably why I was never able to find anything in the data listings. I just assumed it was a hallucination like the Gold Ones."

"No, she's real," I assured him. "You said we're going to your apartment?"

"Yes," Robin said. "It's not far—about ten blocks north—and I've got everything there I need to treat him. You want me to drive or give directions?"

"You can give directions," I said, frowning. The street was relatively dark, but there was a good cluster of lights above the runaround stand and we were close enough to Selene for me to see a fresh layer of tightness in her pupils.

I gave the area a casual scan. Selene had left the taverno only a minute before Robin and I got Bubloo outside, so whatever had happened to trigger that response must have occurred during that window. "Which one's ours?" I asked as we came up to her.

"This one," she said, opening the back door of the vehicle she was standing beside. It was roomier than the ones she and I usually rented, with enough space for our newly expanded party.

"Looks good," I said, gesturing around the back. "Doc, you go to the other side and get in. I'll ease Bubloo in from this side, then get in next to him. We don't want him to bail the first time Selene stops."

"Good idea," Robin said. Letting go of Bubloo's arm, he headed around the runaround's rear. Selene stepped close to me, as if getting ready to help me get Bubloo inside.

I leaned my head close to hers. "Trouble?" I asked quietly.

"Mindi's here," she said.

For a second the name circled my brain looking for a landing spot. Then it clicked: Bounty hunter Mindi, badly wounded on Vesperin a year and a half ago when a group of hunters tried—and failed—to corral the legendary assassin Nicole Schlichting. I'd had a brief encounter with Mindi an hour before that debacle, and had gotten an even shorter look at her afterward as she was hustled off to the hospital.

I'd checked the various info networks a few times during the next couple of months, and had learned she'd pulled through. But since her release from the hospital she seemed to have dropped off the edge of the Spiral.

Until now.

"Did you see her?" I asked.

"No. But her scent's here."

"Ready," Robin called from inside the runaround.

"Here he comes," I said, easing Bubloo through the doorway, grunting a little as he went back into dead-weight mode. "Recent?" I added more softly to Selene.

"No more than a few hours," she said. "Does she use the tipster boards?"

"I don't know," I said, pausing for one final look around as Selene headed around to the driver's side. "Haven't heard from her since Vesperin. Keep an eye out while you're driving, okay?"

"I will." She looked at me over the top of the runaround, her pupils holding a determined expression. "Just don't expect me to be very good with his directions."

As it turned out, she wasn't just not good, but absolutely awful.

She sometimes turned too soon instead of waiting for the street Robin had indicated. Sometimes she turned too late, and had to go around an extra block before getting back on track. Twice she turned into a small parking lot and had to weave her way through the other vehicles to an exit at the other end. Once, she misunderstood what Robin was telling her so badly that we ended up down a narrow alley.

Robin seemed surprised by her general ineptitude, but with most of his attention still on Bubloo he came across as more resigned than frustrated or angry. For my part, I kept my attention on the streets around us and quietly enjoyed Selene's skill at making sure we weren't being followed.

And with the small part of my brain that wasn't otherwise engaged, I tried to figure out what the hell was going on with Bubloo.

Nask had told me—rather disdainfully, in fact—that only the Ammei referred to the portal creators as the Gold Ones. The

Patth called them the Builders, Selene and I called them the Icari, and I had no idea what Kinneman and the Icarus Group called them these days.

So how and where had Bubloo picked up that name?

Selene had said she'd smelled Ammei on him, which suggested he'd interacted with the Juniper enclave. But it was hard to believe any of Yiuliob's people would casually drop the Gold Ones' name where a non-Ammei could hear it. Even less likely was that Bubloo's confused mental state would allow him to pick up or remember such a dropped cue.

Unless what we'd seen in the taverno wasn't his usual state. But that still left the problem of the Ammei name-dropping, especially the name of a people they didn't like.

Unless...

I looked sideways at Bubloo, hunkered down beside Robin like a five-year-old cowering beside his mother. Dark brown hair, pale skin, blue-gray eyes with horizontal slits for pupils. There was nothing there that could remotely be called gold or gold-colored. Ixil had once suggested that the name might refer to wealth, but if Bubloo's clothing was any indication he was about as lower class as anyone I'd ever met, certainly anyone I'd ever shared a runaround with. Besides, whatever the Icari called themselves, it probably wasn't *Gold Ones*.

So how exactly was he tied into Yiuliob and the local Ammei?

I huffed out a silent sigh. All the plans Selene and I had cooked up had started with us infiltrating the Ammei enclave and finding out where they might have looked for the theoretical Juniper full-range portal. Now, apparently, our first task was going to be to find out everything we could about Bubloo.

As my father used to say, *The best laid plans of mice and men usually involve cheese. Be aware that such cheese often comes with a trap.*

But there was nothing I could do about that until we settled down for the night. Readjusting my back against the seat cushions, I continued my watch on the city around us and cultivated my patience.

As part of our mission prep, Selene and I had done a lot of research on Pikwik City, and according to the maps Dr. Robin's building seemed to be in one of the mid-level neighborhoods. The appearance of the third-floor apartment matched that assessment: nice enough and roomy enough, but less upscale than I would expect for a professional doctor.

Still, as we got Bubloo inside and onto the common room couch, it occurred to me that a xenopsychiatrist working a still developing world like Juniper would probably not exactly be rolling in commarks.

Bubloo fell asleep practically before his head hit the cushions. I watched as Robin got a medical bag from the bedroom, set it on a rolling drink tray beside the couch, and pulled out a syringe, a packet of antiseptic wipes, and a vial of clear liquid. Selene stayed beside him, helpfully rolling up Bubloo's sleeve while Robin drew a couple of CCs from the vial. She held the arm to make sure it didn't move as Robin cleaned a spot with one of the wipes and injected the drug. As he withdrew the needle she was ready with another wipe, handing it to the doctor and taking the syringe from him, sliding the tip protector back on the needle as he wiped the injection site. She picked up the syringe and vial and handed them to him, taking the used wipe from him for disposal.

The whole operation was so smooth and natural that I doubted Robin even noticed her giving the vial a close look as she picked it up from the tray. A quick check of the data listings back on the *Ruth*, and we would know exactly what he'd just given his patient.

"So what exactly do you know about him?" I asked as Robin set the bag aside and gestured us to chairs in the conversation circle.

"Precious little, I'm afraid," he admitted as he settled heavily onto a chair facing us and Bubloo. "A few weeks ago he appeared on Juniper, more or less out of nowhere. No one knew who he was, and the authorities are still trying to figure out where he came from."

"Do they at least know his species?"

"Their best guess is that he's a Pakenrill," Robin said. "They're a primitive tribe living in one of the northern mountain regions of Belshaz."

I flicked a glance at Selene, saw my own sudden interest reflected in her pupils. Belshaz was also the planet my father had told us was the site of the fifth and smallest Ammei enclave.

Not that that necessarily meant anything. Planets were huge chunks of real estate, with lots of room for any two groups to lose each other in. Still, if it was a coincidence, it was certainly an interesting one. "Never heard of them," I said, looking back at Robin.

"No reason you should have," he said. "They're classified as sapient, but primitive enough to have a protected-species interdiction."

"Bubloo doesn't seem especially primitive," Selene pointed out.

"Which I assume is why the species identification is still tentative," Robin said. "If he *is* a Pakenrill, someone in the Commonwealth needs to reassess their data." He made a face. "Of course, the Spiral also has a long and sordid history of people kidnapping so-called protected species for study and experimentation."

"Sad, but true," I agreed, a sudden chill running up my back. I'd always assumed the Icari had straight-up recruited the Ammei, Patth, and Kadolians to work on their portal system.

But what if that collaboration hadn't been voluntary? What if the three species had been coerced or outright forced into that service?

I looked over at the sleeping Bubloo. First of Three and the Nexus Six leadership were eager to pick things up where the Icari had left off. From my conversations with Nask I gathered the Patth were less than willing to play along, and of course the Kadolians had essentially vanished from the Spiral and any potential labor pools. Did Bubloo and his fellow Pakenrills have some kind of exotic skills or intuition that would enable them and the Ammei to bypass the Gold Ones' original triumvirate and complete the Nexus Six portal on their own?

If so, the next question was *which* Ammei.

First of Three and Nexus Six had their makeshift portal. But First Dominant Yiuliob had a strong political following, and a genuine full-range portal theoretically within his reach.

Which faction was trying to add Bubloo to a hoped-for winning hand?

"You said he'd gotten away from you a couple of times," I said. "Was he running from you, or from someone else?"

"Like who?" Robin asked, frowning.

"I don't know," I said, waving a hand vaguely. "Whoever brought him to Juniper, maybe?"

Robin shook his head. "If he came with anyone, they're being awfully quiet about it."

"No obvious names on the passenger lists?"

"No passenger lists at all," Robin said. "There's no record of him aboard a public transport, and no private ships on Juniper that are missing an owner." He snorted. "For all we know he could have arrived in a cargo box with breathing holes punched in the lid."

"Interesting," I commented. "The Commonwealth is usually more obsessive about travel records."

"As well I know." Robin scowled. "Let me clarify. There aren't any records that *I* know about. For all I know, the authorities could have a meter-high stack of information on Bubloo that they just don't want to share."

"Why in the world would they want to sit on something like that?"

"You must not have much experience with bureaucrats," Robin said with an edge of bitterness. "If Bubloo really is a Pakenrill somehow out of his zone, it's for sure some official has dropped the ball and is frantically trying to cover his butt. Double that if whoever brought him here is important enough to have people standing ready to cover his butt for him."

"Ah," I said. He was right on that score, anyway. And as far as importance went, right now the Patth hierarchy was pretty close to the top of the heap.

And just because Sub-Director Nask didn't want the Ammei to complete their portal didn't mean some other group of Patth might not have different views on the subject.

"What else do you know about Pakenrills in general?" Selene asked.

Robin shook his head. "Nothing, really. Interdiction status usually seals everything about the species in question. Even with a patient who might be one of them, I'm still locked out."

"Bubloo hasn't told you anything?"

"He's dropped a few comments here and there," Robin said. "But with his mental issues, I can't tell what's real and what isn't." He shook his head in frustration. "It's criminally absurd. How do they expect me to diagnose and treat with one hand tied behind my back?"

"How, indeed," I agreed. I looked at Selene, saw my own thought once again mirrored in her pupils.

Data seals might keep out most honest citizens. But most honest citizens didn't have Patth backdoor access codes.

"It's good of you to take him in," Selene said. "I can't imagine being alone on a strange world, especially for someone unfamiliar with the Spiral and its cultures."

"Like the ancient cultural custom of trading money for services," I said, eyeing Bubloo's nondescript clothing. "Comes in handy when it's time to eat."

"Which is the other strange thing," Robin said heavily. "Bubloo may be alone and lost, but he *does* have money."

I frowned. "Come again?"

"He has money," Robin repeated. "I don't know how much or where he keeps it. But every once in a while he pops up with a small certified bank check."

"What bank are they from?"

"Universal Trust."

"Which basically gives us nothing," I concluded. Universal Trust was one of seven or eight massive banking conglomerates with branches on practically every inhabited planet in the Spiral. The name of the issuing branch was encoded on their certified checks, but it wasn't information anyone else could access. "I see he's spending all that money on clothes, too."

"No, he mostly seems to spend it on drugs, medicinal and otherwise," Robin said grimly.

"Like the dysthersial?" I asked, deliberately mispronouncing the drug's name. If this doctor bit of his was just a role, he might miss the error.

"Dysthensial," he corrected absently. "Yes, like that. Though which category that one falls into is a bit unclear. It does seem to help with his arthritis, but at a horrible cost to his mental state." He shook his head. "Mostly, I live in fear that the next time he gets away from me and goes out to buy his drugs he'll be robbed. Or killed."

He sighed and got gingerly to his feet. "But that's my problem, not yours. Thank you for stepping up and helping me. Getting him back here would have been a monumental task without you."

"Glad to help," I said as Selene and I also stood up. "You need to get him to a bed or something?"

"No, he'll be fine right there," Robin said, offering me his hand. "Thank you again—"

"Who are you?" a weak voice came.

I looked over at the couch. Bubloo hadn't moved, but his eyes were now open. "Welcome back, Bubloo," I greeted him. "How do you feel?"

His eyes shifted to his right, as if he was pondering the question. Then they snapped back to me. "Who are you?" he repeated.

Out of the corner of my eye I saw Selene take a quiet step to her right, positioning herself downwind of Robin in the room's gentle airflow. "My name's Roarke," I said. "This is Selene. Do you need anything?"

Again, Bubloo seemed to ponder the question. Then, once again, he came back to attention.

But this time, his eyes shifted to Robin. "Who are *you*?"

"I'm Dr. Robin, Bubloo," the other said gently. "Dr. Christopher Robin. I've been treating you. Don't you remember?"

"Treating me," Bubloo repeated, sounding puzzled. "You're my doctor? Am I sick?"

"You've had some problems, yes," Robin said. "How are you feeling?"

"All right," Bubloo said, his voice sounding vague. Already starting to drift back to sleep, I guessed. "My doctor. Really?"

"Yes, really," Robin assured him. "Go back to sleep. We'll talk more in the morning."

"All right," Bubloo said. "My doctor." He shifted his gaze to me. "Roarke." To Selene. "Selene."

"That's right," Robin said. "Go to sleep, Bubloo."

Obediently, Bubloo closed his eyes. A moment later, his breath slowed into sleep.

Robin huffed out a sigh. "Did I mention that the drugs also play hob with both short-term and long-term memories?" he asked.

"You didn't, but that's not uncommon," I said. "And now, I believe we were on our way out?"

"Yes." Robin again offered his hand for our interrupted shake. "Nice meeting you both. If you need anything from me—anything at all—you can contact me through the Stylways Clinic. And again, thank you."

I'd been driving for about ten minutes before Selene finally looked up from her info pad. "Well?" I asked.

"I found the drug he gave Bubloo," she said, sliding the info pad back into its pouch. "It was seirplocor, a commonly prescribed sedative. It has a wide range of uses, one of which is as a site-blocker for a group of chemicals in dysthensial's class of meds."

"Sounds mostly legit, then."

"You were hoping it would be otherwise?"

"It might have given us more of a handle on Doc Robin," I said. "Right now, he's mostly a cipher."

"You just don't like do-gooders."

"I don't *trust* do-gooders," I corrected her. "The fact that Bubloo doesn't seem to remember him isn't exactly a vote in his favor, either."

"Robin was right about the effects of some drugs on memory."

"Which is why it isn't exactly a vote against him, either," I conceded. "Did he react at all to our names?"

"No."

"Mm." Unfortunately, all that meant was that either Robin already knew who we were or that our names didn't mean anything to him. Again, an indicator that could fall in either of two directions. "Anything about our general conversation seem odd?"

"Aside from the potentially interesting Belshaz connection?"

"Yeah, aside from that," I said. "I'm trying to remind myself that it might just be coincidence, but I'm having trouble hanging onto that thought. As my father used to say, *Nothing in this universe is completely pure, be it motives, coincidence, or luck.*"

"I agree," she said. "I *would* like to know how long Robin's been treating him, though. I'd also like to hear more of Bubloo's take on their relationship."

"You think it'll be different from Robin's?"

"I don't know," she said. "That's why I'd like to hear it." She paused. "One more interesting thing. On the way to Robin's apartment, I was close enough to Bubloo to smell something I remembered from when we were in the Juniper food prep area."

"During our brief jaunt from Nexus Six?"

"Yes," she said. "It was hard to tell for certain—all the food aromas were mixed together during that visit—but I think it might have been one of the Ammei root vegetables."

"Interesting," I said, trying to remember that section of our research on all things Ammei. "Do you remember how many of those plants could be grown in Juniper dirt?"

"I don't think any of them could. The ones they were growing here were in plots of imported soil."

"Courtesy of one of the other Nexus Six portals," I said, nodding. "I wonder if Bubloo's found a back door into the enclave."

"Or perhaps dysthensial isn't the only thing he spends his money on," she said. "It could be he just has a taste for Ammei vegetables."

I grimaced, my cautiously rising hope fading again. "True," I conceded. "Plus, if the Ammei are experimenting on him it would be entirely reasonable for them to occasionally feed him lunch."

"They're *experimenting* on him? When did Dr. Robin say *that*?"

"He didn't," I said. "That was *my* theory."

I spent the next two kilometers laying out my thoughts about Bubloo and the Pakenrills possibly taking the place of the Kadolians in the Ammei portal-building project. Selene spent the half kilometer after that pondering it in silence. "I suppose it's possible," she said at last. "But it would be an extraordinary coincidence."

"Would it?" I asked. "Remember, we're not just picking species out of a hat. The Kadolians have gone to ground, and suddenly a possible Pakenrill is kicked out of his mountains and into the spotlight? Incidentally, I don't suppose you have any idea what kind of terrain you lived in on the Kadolian homeworld, do you? Like in the mountains, maybe?"

"Now you're just being silly."

"I suppose."

"It's certainly an interesting theory," she continued. "But without knowing anything about Pakenrill physiology, there's no way to know whether they could play the role we used to for the Icari."

"Granted," I said. "Maybe we should help ourselves to those sealed species records and see what the Commonwealth has on them."

Selene was silent another moment. "You really think Bubloo can help us find the Juniper portal?"

"*Help* may be too strong a word," I said. "But if he's been inside the enclave, maybe we can figure out his route and use it ourselves."

"Unless, as you said, he was an invited guest."

"True," I said. "Still, if that *is* what's going on, we might be able to sift out some other useful information."

"Maybe."

I glanced at her, timing the look for when we were passing beneath a streetlight. Her pupils, I saw, held a troubled expression. "What is it?"

"I don't know," she said. "It's just... maybe it's just *too* convenient?"

"What, our running into Bubloo and Robin right at the moment when we're looking for a way into the Ammei enclave?" I shrugged. "I agree. But there's no law that says we can't take someone else's game and play it straight back at them."

"You think it's a game, then?"

"I don't know what it is," I said. "But if it *is* a scam, *why* is it a scam? What could Bubloo or Robin or anyone else be trying to accomplish with it? Bring us out into the open? We're already there. Grab us? In that case, they missed completely. Drug or otherwise incapacitate us? Robin didn't even offer us a drink. I just don't see any hooks in it. Do you?"

"Not yet," Selene said. "But that doesn't mean there aren't any. So we just watch and wait?"

"And we play it safe," I said. "Starting right now."

I pulled the runaround to the curb and turned off the engine. If my sense of direction was working tonight, we were now sitting half a kilometer downwind of the spaceport's west entrance, the closest one to the *Ruth*'s landing pad. "Anything interesting out there?"

Selene rolled down the window and leaned her head partially outside. I watched her nostrils flare and her eyelashes flutter for a moment, then started a proper surveillance scan of the area around us. It would be embarrassing to get ambushed just because I wasn't paying attention.

A minute later, she pulled her head back inside the vehicle. "Or it could be just be that the plan was for Robin and Bubloo to delay us," she said, her pupils gone ominous. "Mindi's somewhere near the spaceport entrance.

"So are two Patth."

CHAPTER FOUR

The barbeque place where we'd started the evening had cleared out somewhat in the hour we'd been away. I went to the take-out counter, accepted the proffered refund from the money I'd left for our earlier, non-eaten meal, and ordered a second meal to go. I added in two caff colas, and when the package was ready I made sure it included a pair of extra-long plastic drinking straws.

We headed back to the spaceport, again approaching from downwind. I expected Mindi and the Patth would have their attention directed outward into the city, watching for our return from wherever we'd spent the evening, and we got close enough for Selene to confirm they were still where we'd left them.

But instead of continuing on to the west entrance, I turned us around, circled south around the port, and came up to the east entrance. We paused there long enough for Selene to confirm there were no surprises nearby, then drove in and wove our way through the collection of landing pads toward the west entrance. I parked us a hundred meters from the *Ruth*, left Selene to watch the ship from concealment, and headed off on foot to deal with our uninvited company.

I was approaching from upwind, which meant that even if Selene had been with me her skills would have been of only limited use. Fortunately, her reading during our earlier recon had given me a good idea where my quarry was located.

As usual, she'd nailed it perfectly. The two Patth were fifty meters inside the west entrance, one lurking in the shadow of a light freight hauler's forward landing skid, the other five meters closer to the entrance behind a rolling diagnostic cart.

Mentally, I shook my head. The ideal setup for two sentries was for them to be more or less side by side, where each was in the other's peripheral vision. Having one of them significantly behind the other offered an enterprising lurker the chance to take out the backstop without alerting the front man. In this case, I was that lurker, and their casual sloppiness had set me up perfectly for the attack I had in mind.

I was running through the scenario one final time when a movement ten meters in front of the lead Patth caught my eye: a third watcher, hooded and muffled, in the shadow of the same freight hauler's aft-portside landing skid.

The two Patth reacted instantly to the movement, twitching from watchful patience to full alertness. The third figure, either sensing the fresh attention or more likely just giving the perimeter another check, half turned to the right, presenting me with a profile.

Even in the dim light I had no trouble recognizing Mindi.

She turned back, settling again into sentry mode. A few seconds later, the two Patth did likewise, and we were back to watchful silence.

I frowned into the night, trying to make sense of what I'd just seen. Clearly, the two Patth were watching Mindi. Had they tagged her as someone who might lead them to Selene and me?

Or were they watching her for some other reason entirely? I had no idea what that reason might be, but she'd been off my radar long enough to have found herself some mischief to get into.

Either way, my plan was now going to need a bit of tweaking.

Making sure not to make any noise, I pulled out my phone and keyed for messaging. *Mindi and two Patth at west entrance. Stop by Mindi and talk to her.*

Okay, Selene messaged back.

I put away my phone and pulled up my left sleeve far enough to get to the hidden compartment in the inside of the wrist. I popped it open, took out one of the knockout pills, then sealed it up again. I snagged one of the long drinking straws from my jacket pocket and slipped the pill into one end. As I'd anticipated, the fit was perfect, with the pill snugged in tightly enough to keep it from accidently falling out but loose enough for a little effort to easily dislodge it. I drew my plasmic and settled it into my right hand, adjusting my grip so that my thumb held the straw sticking out parallel to the barrel, the end holding the pill more or less even with the muzzle.

And with my preparations complete, I settled down to wait.

It wasn't a big spaceport, and the wait wasn't long. Fifteen minutes later, I spotted the glint of approaching headlights, and thirty seconds after that a runaround came into view. It slowed as it approached the gate, then rolled to a stop directly beside Mindi's hiding place.

Once again, the two Patth snapped to attention. The runaround's side window slid down, and I heard Selene's voice calling faintly. There was a moment of hesitation, and then Mindi reluctantly emerged from her shadows and walked to the vehicle. The Patth tensed up another couple of notches, hands now poised and ready to go for whatever weapons were hidden beneath their hooded cloaks.

Silently, I slipped out of concealment and headed up behind the rearmost Patth. With his full attention on the scenario playing out in front of him, he didn't have a hope of spotting my approach. I stopped a step behind him and touched my plasmic's muzzle lightly to the back of his hood.

Whatever he might have lacked in global awareness, he more than made up for in combat reflexes. Instantly, he spun around, his right arm snapping out at the shoulder, forearm angled upward with the fist pointing toward the sky, doing a horizontal sweep of the whole area above his shoulders in the classic technique for deflecting a weapon before its owner could fire.

Unfortunately for him, I knew the classics, too. Even before he started his turn I'd dropped my arm and plasmic to the level of his lower back, letting his forearm slash harmlessly through empty air. As the arm passed, I raised the weapon back to point at his face, leaning in close as if wanting him to see who it was who'd gotten the drop on him. His eyes widened with surprise and chagrin—

And as he reflexively opened his mouth to shout a warning to his partner, I blew into the back end of the straw and sent the knockout pill into his mouth.

The pills didn't act instantly, of course. But they were fast enough, especially since the sheer surprise of having something suddenly blown halfway down his throat froze his brain and his vocal cords for the necessary couple of seconds. I saw the flicker in his eyes as he broke free of the mental paralysis and took a quick breath.

And release it again in a huff as his eyes and mouth closed and he collapsed onto the ground.

Under other circumstances, I would have been charitable enough to catch his arm or collar on his way down and ease the impact of his fall. Here, with another armed Patth five meters away, he was on his own.

The muffled thud of his landing wasn't very loud. But it was loud enough. His partner spun around, whipping his weapon into view. He was halfway to bringing it to bear when his brain caught up with his eyes and he spotted me standing over his partner. For a second we held our positions, him with his weapon still angled to the side, me with mine pointed straight at his torso. Then, slowly, he lowered his gun to point at the ground.

I frowned. From this new angle I could see the weapon was a Babcor 17 4mm, a very high-end, *very* expensive rocket pistol. The weapon's range was definite overkill for the distance the Patth had set themselves up for with Mindi, and its penetration power was overkill for pretty much any non-armored personnel use at all.

The key and disturbing part of that being *kill.* My father had said the posts on Selene and me were both live-detain bounties. I'd suggested that whoever had put them out might simply want the fun of killing one or both of us personally, but I'd mostly meant that as a macabre joke.

So what was a Patth doing skulking around a spaceport with a weapon that every cash-strapped military in the Spiral wished they could buy in bulk for their armies?

Out of the corner of my eye I saw Selene get out of the runaround, her plasmic ready in her hand. "Selene?" I invited, nodding toward my standoff partner.

She nodded and moved cautiously toward him, her nostrils flaring rhythmically as she walked. If the Patth decided to try something stupid or desperate, the change in his scent ought to warn her before he could make his move.

Unfortunately, if my growing suspicion was right, this character had no need for either desperation or stupidity. Sure enough, he remained perfectly still as Selene relieved him of his Babcor and took a couple of steps back. With her now covering him from a safe distance, I knelt beside the Patth I'd drugged and ran a practiced hand quickly through all the usual places where weapons could be concealed. I found a matching Babcor 17, then kept going until I'd found his backup.

Which was, as I'd expected, a Jinxti plasmic.

I stared down at the Patth, the mahogany-skinned face looking cruel and nasty even in his sleep. Damn, and damn again. "Selene?" I called, shifting my attention and plasmic back to the Patth still standing. "Should we ask him nicely to drop his backup, or do you want to just shoot him now and save some time?"

The Patth's expression changed, just slightly. "There's no need for threats, Mr. Roarke," he said in an eerily cultured voice. He lifted his cloak with one hand, revealing the empty shoulder holster and the hip holster that was still occupied. He reached into the latter, drew out his own Jinxti with the first two fingers of his other hand, and set it gently on the ground in front of him. Then, just to show that he was also a professional, he backed up two steps. "If you wish to search further, you're welcome to do so," he added.

"That's all right," Selene said as I moved cautiously forward and retrieved the plasmic. "It's covered like a mother duck."

"Good," I said, nodding understanding. *Covered*—probably a sleeve weapon. *Duck*—two. The Patth on Alainn, I remembered, had also carried vertigo-dart weapons. That, plus the code phrase, probably meant he was carrying a twin-round sleeve vertigo airgun.

But even with two shots available, as long as Selene and I were spaced this far apart, he presumably wouldn't be stupid enough to try using it. "But we do appreciate the offer," I told him. "Are we seriously going to do this again?"

"Honor is everything, Mr. Roarke," he said calmly. "Even some of you humans recognize that."

"Yeah, but we don't usually kill for it," I pointed out. Mindi, I noted, had left the runaround and was walking over to join the party. I really wanted a good look at her expression, try to see how she was taking this, but I didn't dare take any of my attention away from the Patth.

"And no, don't bother to bring up Earth's past," I continued. "More to the immediate point, I thought the Purge laws had been revamped." I raised my eyebrows. "Or doesn't the family hold with these newfangled ideas? What was their name, again?"

The Patth looked over as Mindi came up beside Selene. "The family you refer to holds to the ancestral ways," he said. "And you did not forget their name, because Kiolven would never have spoken it to you."

"Fair enough," I said. I hadn't expected the question to shake anything loose, but it had been worth a shot. "So what are you doing here? I hope you're not going to try to tell me that Galfvi made it all the way to Juniper in his travels."

The Patth cocked his head slightly. "Who?"

A chill ran up my back. *Who?* Out of the corner of my eye I saw Selene's pupils register my same revulsion. Apparently, Galfvi's family had succeeded in their goal of wiping all memory of him and his dishonoring activities from the Spiral.

Unfortunately, that task had also included the elimination or attempted elimination of every non-family person he'd ever interacted with. Which even more unfortunately left only one reason I could think of why these two Patth were on Juniper.

I didn't want to ask the question. But I knew I had no choice. "So why are you here?"

"Come now, Mr. Roarke," he said. His cultured voice was unchanged, but something in his voice sent a fresh shiver through me. "Have you forgotten that you, too, have brought shame to the family?"

"Shall I?" Selene asked quietly.

For a long, agonizing moment I was sorely tempted. *Self-defense,* the legal justification whispered through my mind. He'd all but flat-out threatened to kill me, and Commonwealth law permitted the use of deadly force under those circumstances.

Or Selene and I could run. We had Nask's million commarks plus maybe three hundred thousand more in the silver-silk strands we'd picked up on Alainn. We had the *Ruth* and three more of Nask's false IDs, and I was pretty sure Nask wouldn't lift a finger to help that family work through their archaic vengeance protocols. We could hide out as long as we wanted to.

But I knew as well as anyone that violent lawbreakers were almost always eventually run to ground. And while *I* understood the underlying threat in the Patth's statement, a jury of my peers might not find it so conclusive.

More important, I'd never killed anyone who wasn't already waving a weapon in my direction, and this didn't seem the time to start. And if I wasn't willing to forever cripple my soul that way, I sure as hell wasn't going to let Selene do it to hers.

"We'll hold off on anything that drastic for now," I told her. "We can always kill him later if he becomes a nuisance." I shifted my plasmic's aim to the Patth sleeping at my feet. "Correction: we can always kill *them*."

"Are you sure?" Selene pressed.

I looked at Mindi. She was taking everything in, her expression carefully neutral, her hands hanging empty at her sides. "I'm sure," I said. "Doesn't mean I won't reconsider somewhere down the line."

"All right," Selene said, and I could visualize a mixture of regret and relief in her pupils. "What do we do with them?"

I gave the freight hauler looming above me a closer look. It was too dark to read the registry number, but the configuration was that of a perishable-goods transport. That kind of ship was fast, dedicated, and didn't stop for anything.

Even better, I could see that both outer cargo hatches were already sealed with customs tape. That meant that the crew was probably scheduled to lift soon, with only the final paperwork or one last drink on the town before they returned.

There was nothing I could do about the customs tape. But bypassing the hatch locks was another matter entirely. "We'll put them somewhere out of the way where they won't be found for a few hours," I told Selene. Holstering my plasmic, I squatted beside the sleeping Patth and took his arm as if preparing to lift him into a fireman's carry. Beneath the smooth cloth of his sleeve I found the hard cylinder of his sleeve gun. "Then we'll get the hell out of—"

Lifting up the limp arm and centering it on the other Patth, I squeezed the trigger.

There was the sharp *hiss* of released compressed air and the Patth jerked as the dart dug through his robe and pumped vertigo drug into his skin. He staggered, and for a second it looked like he was trying to line up his own two-shot right back at me.

But it was already too late. The drug was taking effect, sending him staggering with near-zero control over his limbs. He made one final effort to speak, his legs collapsed beneath him, and he toppled onto his side.

"Using the really potent stuff, I see," I commented, approaching him warily from his non-gun side as I pulled another knockout pill from my wrist stash. His face and mouth were both working in silent fury; picking my moment, I popped the pill into his mouth and held it closed. He got out one final glare, and then his eyes glazed over and he was out for the count.

"Freighter?" Selene asked, already working her info pad.

"Freighter," I confirmed, looking again at Mindi. "Hi, Mindi. Glad to see you've recovered from Vesperin."

"Mostly," Mindi said, her expression still strangely neutral. "Friends of yours?"

"Most of my friends aren't looking to kill me." I raised a questioning eyebrow. "Present company included, I hope."

Her lip quirked in a half smile. "Present company included. I see you've picked up a few new tricks."

"Tricks?"

Right on cue, the portside cargo hatch snicked open. "Like that one," Mindi said, looking up. "Nice. What are you going to do about the customs tape?"

"Push the edges together and hope no one notices," I said as Selene went to the hatch. She sliced carefully through the tape with her knife, then opened the hatch. "Plenty of room."

"You *do* know you're playing with fire, don't you?" Mindi asked as I got the first sleeping Patth into a fireman's carry and shuffled over to the hatch.

"Not to worry," I assured her. "These things are safe and fully climate-controlled. We'll truss them up to make sure they can't bang on the inner hatch until they've been on the road for a few hours, and that should be that."

"I mean disrespecting Patth that way," she said as I dumped the first Patth into the open space between the crash-webbed boxes. Selene was ready with a couple of plastic restraints and got busy while I went to retrieve the other one.

"Again, not to worry," I said, getting him up onto my shoulder. "They already want to kill me. Not much escalation possible from that point."

"How about in the lingering pain department?"

"There *is* that," I conceded, maneuvering the limp form inside and pulling out a couple of restraints of my own. "But I think the buyer at the other end of the post was already planning an extensive regimen, so again it doesn't much matter."

Selene and I finished tying them up in silence. When we were finished I closed the hatch and watched while Selene smoothed the edges of the tape together with the flat of her knife. "It's not perfect," she said, stepping back and studying her work. "But if they're in enough of a hurry to get off Juniper it should do."

"It's good enough," I told her. "All we really need is a few hours' head start."

"Yes," Selene said. She had turned enough into the light for me to read the quiet understanding in her pupils, that my talk about running was purely for Mindi's benefit.

Which turned out to be so much wasted effort. "What, you're leaving *now*?" Mindi asked. "After all the work you went through to throw the hunters off your scent?"

"What do you mean?" I asked cautiously. Her words and tone were light, almost joking. But her expression was intense and edging into suspicion.

"What I *mean*," she said, all hint of joking gone, "is that you illegitimately tapped into Burke's Spiral Patterns tipster board and left false data saying that you'd been seen on Xathru. What I also mean is that I came here to find out what the hell you think you're doing, *why* the hell you're doing it, and *how* the hell you're doing it."

Her quiet tirade was so unexpected that for a couple of seconds my brain totally disconnected from my voice. Selene's didn't. "You know that tipster boards don't come with any guarantees," she reminded Mindi calmly, her eyelashes fluttering hard as she tried to read the other woman's scent. "The data is only there to—"

"Only there to provide additional insight," Mindi cut her off. "Thank you—I know the marketing caveat by heart."

She turned her glare back to me. "So, do you give? Or do I call the badgemen about that?" She jerked a thumb toward the hauler's hold.

Abruptly, my brain caught up. "Wait a minute," I said, frowning. "If Burke's says we're on Xathru, why did you come to Juniper?"

"Because," she said stiffly, "the client's original post said you were heading here. I removed that tidbit, only to then see a mysterious Xathru tip suddenly pop up. When I dug deeper, I saw that while the system flagged the tipster as legit, there were no records of him anywhere else. That got me curious, so I decided to check it out in person."

I looked at Selene, saw in her pupils she'd caught the same anomaly that I had. "_You_ took down the Juniper tag?"

"Yes." She took a deep, slightly ragged breath. "Because as it happens, I work for Burke's these days. And if I want to _keep_ working for them, I need to find out what's going on with you and Juniper." She nodded again at the hauler. "And with _them_."

I sighed. General Kinneman would have my hide for even considering telling Mindi anything, if the general and I were still on speaking terms.

But as we'd already concluded, once Kinneman had me slated for lingering pain, there wasn't much else he could threaten me with.

"Tell you what," I said. "We have a couple meals' worth of Earth barbeque in the runaround. How about joining us aboard the _Ruth_ for some dinner and conversation?"

She looked at the hauler. "If it's all the same to you," she said, "I'd rather go someplace a little less likely to attract gunfire. How about _my_ ship?"

"Good enough," I said, starting toward the runaround. Not that her ship would be all that much safer than ours. Not for long. "Selene, you're driving."

CHAPTER FIVE

The Saffi who'd designed the spaceport had some unique ideas of how symmetry and visual balance should work. That made navigation through the aisles and workways challenging even at the best of times. Add in the twin facts that Mindi's ship was most of the way across the spaceport from the *Ruth* and that we'd just escaped from a pair of Patth who wanted to kill us, and I knew from the start that it was going to be a somewhat tense drive.

I didn't want to get into our side of the conversation until we reached more private environs, and so suggested that we pass the driving time with Mindi's recent history.

"Not really much to tell," she said as Selene wove our way through the sparse traffic. "I had a lot of time to think while I was in the hospital, and decided I might want to try something a little less dangerous than hunting for a while."

"I know that internal monologue," I said.

"I'll bet you do," Mindi said. "Anyway, Burke's was hiring, and I guess my résumé was impressive enough that they offered me an analyst's job."

"Nice," I said, and meant it. The various tipster boards hired a lot of former hunters, but most of them were sent out to wander the Spiral and keep their eyes and ears open. Functionally, it wasn't much of a step up from hunting, except that you got a steady income and you usually didn't get shot at. The relative handful of office-based analyst jobs were the most sought-after positions, and Mindi was much younger than usual for that post.

Of course, it might also have been that someone at Burke's wanted to hire her and felt she needed more time to recover from her injuries before booting her out onto the more rigorous side of the job. "Anyone of your colleagues I might know?"

"Probably," Mindi said. "Not supposed to get into names. Take a left past this yacht thing; I'm the Corsican light freighter to the right."

"All right," Selene said.

I frowned out the window at the ship Mindi had first pointed to. It was a yacht, all right, at least in the sense of being a good-sized private vehicle.

But it was a far cry from the usual flash-and-sparkle monstrosity favored by the rich and powerful who wanted to flaunt both attributes to the universe at large. This ship's exterior was quiet and subdued, with nothing to identify its owner or his or her corporate affiliation.

Could it be the ship the two Patth had arrived on? It would certainly fit with the low-profile nature of their mission. It might be worth a quick check to see if their scent was on the entryway. "Selene, pull over by the yacht, will you?"

"What are you doing?" Mindi asked.

"Minor detour," I told her, looking around as Selene brought us to a stop. There were several pedestrians and runarounds visible as the various ship crews finished their evening's activities and headed home. Unwelcome witnesses...but as long as we weren't too obvious about it we shouldn't attract any special attention.

Mindi was clearly thinking along similar lines, only in the opposite direction. "If you're planning to clobber someone else, you can let me out right here," she said. "I've had as much of that as I want for one night."

"No clobbering expected," I assured her as I got out. "This'll only take a second."

"Do you want me with you?" Selene asked.

"No, I've got it," I said. This was definitely a job for her, and normally we'd have gone up the yacht's zigzag ramp together.

But after our recent dustup I was feeling wary about letting her out in the open any more than I had to. It was just an assumption, after all, that Galfvi's family had sent only a single pair of Purge assassins to deal with me. "I'll take a quick swipe of the entryway pad and be right back—*Selene*," I protested as she got out of the driver's seat.

"A swipe may not be good enough," she said. "Besides, if we decide to go inside it'll look odd for you to have made two trips up and down."

I looked in at Mindi. She wasn't missing a word of this. "Fine," I growled. "We'll be right back, Mindi."

The yacht was somewhat flatter than the *Ruth,* with a correspondingly shorter climb up the zigzag to the entryway. "Okay," I said, ushering Selene to the hatch, my eyes starting a quick scan of the area, my hand resting on my plasmic's grip. If there was so much as the glint of a weapon, I was going to be damn sure I got in the first shot. "How many Patth are we talking about?"

"No Patth," Selene said, her face close to the entryway keypad. "Two Ammei." Out of the corner of my eye I saw her look up at me. "And—"

"Are the Ammei anyone we know?"

There was a half-second pause as she shifted gears from whatever she'd been about to say. "We know both of them," she said. "Rozhuhu and Fourth of Three."

I stared at her, my father's identification of Fourth of Three with Mycene's First Dominant Prucital flashing to mind. "Must be old home week," I muttered, feeling my eyes narrow. "Any idea how long ago they came through their respective portals?"

"I don't think they did," Selene said. "I'm not smelling any portal metal. I think it more likely they came to Juniper aboard this ship."

"Interesting," I said, eyeing the entryway thoughtfully. Mycene to Nexus Six to Juniper via portal was a half-hour trip at the most. Nexus Six to Juniper was even faster. But instead they'd taken the long road? "Also pretty inefficient."

"Maybe they didn't want Yiuliob to know they were coming."

"Okay, yes, that makes sense," I said. "Matter of fact, it's probably the *only* way it makes sense. So this is how Ammei travel when they're out in the real world?"

"I don't think so," Selene said, her pupils going dark. "I was starting to tell you that I also smell your father."

I felt my mouth drop open. "My *father*?"

"Yes."

I looked back at the area around us, my mind spinning. But if my father was still working for Kinneman and the Icarus Group, what was he doing on Juniper? And why was he in the company of representatives from both Nexus Six and Mycene?

He'd told us he was making the rounds of Ammei enclaves. Was Juniper just the next one on his list? But in that case, why bring Rozhuhu and Prucital with him? Were all of them negotiating with Yiuliob?

Was Kinneman trying to build a coalition against First of Three?

I looked at the hatchway. We could go inside. Right here, right now. We could get into the ship's onboard computer—the codes Nask had given us plus my own hacking skills would make that a reasonably trivial exercise—and try to figure out what he was up to. Two minutes to get in, ten to hack and download, one to get back out. He'd never even know we'd been here—

"Hey!" a distant voice came.

I looked over the zigzag railing. Mindi was outside the runaround and was peering up at us. "You going to be there all night? You promised me dinner, remember?"

"We should go," Selene murmured.

I took a deep breath. An opportunity that would likely never come again.

But as my father used to say, *Whenever you stick your neck out, be sure you've got enough room to pull it back in again.*

"We're coming," I called to Mindi, taking Selene's arm and easing her away from the entryway. "We should go before he gets back from wherever," I said in a quieter voice. "We'll sort it out later."

"Yes," Selene said as she started down the zigzag. "I'm sure we will."

Most people I'd met had trouble recognizing Kadolian sarcasm. I didn't.

In the end, I chickened out, backing off the full disclosure about Icarus that I'd intended to drop on Mindi. Instead, I just told her that there was a secret government-sponsored project searching for ancient alien artifacts, that Selene and I had recently been kicked out of it, and that the general in charge was on the hunt for us and might be the one who'd put up the posts.

My father had pointed out the financial dubiousness of that conclusion, but trying to give Mindi any more of the story would just end us up in weeds that weren't any of her concern.

I also skipped over the Patth backdoor codes, passing off our bogus tip as us knowing a really good hacker. Those details weren't her concern, either.

What *was* her concern was how she'd accidentally ended up in the middle of the Patth Purge laws that Galfvi's family refused to back down from.

"Because I *know* you?" she demanded when I'd finished. "That's it? They want to kill me just because I *know* you?"

"We've seen them do it," Selene said, her pupils dark with memory. "We've been told that the laws have been changed since then to only include Patth. This particular family doesn't seem to care."

Mindi picked up one of the rib bones, now picked clean, and turned it slowly between her fingers. "So how much territory does this vendetta cover?" she asked. "Juniper? This sector of the Spiral? The entire universe? My question is whether I can go back to my office at Burke's and forget about the whole thing."

"The individual they were hunting the last time had holed up on Alainn," I told her. "About as far on the back end of nowhere as you'd ever want to get. They found him in a few months, and killed four other people he'd worked with before they grabbed him."

"But *I* don't work with you."

"As far as I can tell, that doesn't make a difference," I said. "The only reason the first pair of Patth let us go was that we never even met their target. In this case, you were seen with me, and by their twisted logic you therefore know me. That's all that seems to matter to them."

"At least, that's what the Patth on Alainn said was important," Selene added.

"Whether you'll be safe at Burke's..." I shrugged. "No idea. I imagine security there is pretty solid, and that a couple of Patth showing up would at least raise some eyebrows."

"But sooner or later I'd have to go back to my apartment," Mindi said. "So why didn't they just kill me while I was waiting for you?"

"Probably because they didn't know who you were or what your relationship to me might be," I said. "As far as they could tell, you were just another hunter on our trail. Someone worth following, but until you actually made contact with us you weren't on their radar. You *have* kept your hunter credentials current, haven't you?"

"Yes, but I don't carry anymore." She made a face. "I should probably start again, shouldn't I?"

"Yeah, probably," I said heavily. "You need a gun?"

"Thanks, but I've got a couple stashed away in back."

"It might be better if you just left," Selene said. "They still don't know who you are, only that you made contact with us. If you leave Juniper right now, you'll probably be too much trouble for them to track down and find."

"Yes, I could do that," Mindi agreed thoughtfully.

Abruptly, she put down the bone she'd been fiddling with and looked me straight in the eye. "Which would be awfully convenient for you, wouldn't it? Me running away before I've finished my job. You logged an unauthorized tip, and I came to Juniper to find out how and why."

"I've already told you all that."

"Have you?" she countered. "You told me there's an alien artifact. What artifact? You said the Ammei enclave here is also looking for it. Why? You said you had a hacker who got you into the Burke's system. Who?"

"Mindi—"

"I'll tell you who," she cut me off. "Because there *wasn't* a who. You didn't hack, you backdoored. That means the Patth. Are you working for some group of them? Are they after this artifact, too?"

I sighed. I hated lying to her, and holding back important pieces of the truth qualified as lying. But for her safety, not to mention ours, I couldn't. "The whole thing is infinitely tangled, Mindi," I said with all the honest earnestness I could muster. "And a lot of the details aren't mine to give out."

"And would endanger you if you knew them," Selene added.

"Yeah," Mindi muttered. "Like I said: convenient."

"I wish we could tell you," I said. "Maybe someday we'll be able to."

"Sure." She picked up the bone again, eyed it, then set it firmly back onto the plate. "Well, I guess you'll want to get back to your ship now. Thanks for the barbeque."

"You're welcome," I said. "Thanks for not nailing us."

She shrugged. "I told you I'm not hunting anymore."

"No, but you're in the business of helping hunters." I cocked my head slightly. "So why?"

"Why did I erase the client's Juniper tip?" she asked. "Or why did I come here to warn you that I was onto your little scam?"

"Either. Both."

She held my gaze another moment, then lowered her eyes to her plate. "Vesperin," she said quietly. "I got shot on Vesperin." She looked up at me, her gaze suddenly blazing. "But I didn't *die* on Vesperin. Was that your doing?"

I frowned. "Excuse me?"

"That woman you'd met with," Mindi said. "The one you called Piper. She didn't shoot me. She didn't even draw on me. Was that because you'd waved her off?"

I looked at Selene. How was I supposed to answer that? "She and I have something of a relationship," I said, choosing my words carefully. "And yes, she *did* know not to draw on you." Or on anyone else who wasn't actively targeting her, I avoided adding. As my father used to say, *If you're going to get blamed for things you didn't do—and you will—don't be afraid to take credit you don't deserve, either.* "In case you're interested, after you and I spoke that day I finally found out her real name. Nicole Schlichting."

Mindi's eyes went wide, the blaze in her eyes faltering. "Nicole *Schlichting*? The *assassin*?"

"The one and only," I confirmed. "I *am* sorry you got hit by a wild shot."

"Me, too," Mindi said, her eyes taking on a reflective look. "It could have been worse. I don't know if she told you, but one of the other hunters also had his gun pointed in my direction. If she hadn't shot him first..."

I let her sift through her memories another moment. Then, with a small nod at Selene, I got to my feet. "And as you said, we need to get back to the *Ruth*," I said as Selene also stood up. "Thanks again for your hospitality and your assistance. I promise I'll tell you all about this as soon as I'm able to."

"I'd appreciate that," Mindi said, her eyes going distant again. "Thank *you* for calling Schlichting off me. You want me to keep up the deception that you're somewhere else when I get back to Burke's?"

"Thanks, yes, we'd appreciate that," I said. "But don't push it to the point of risking your job. We've dodged worse people than hunters."

"I'll bet you have." She frowned suddenly. "So if the post specified live-detain, why are the Patth trying to kill you?"

"They seem to be playing an entirely different game than everyone else," I said, feeling my stomach tighten.

"Fun times," Mindi said, standing up. "I'll see you out."

"Thanks," I said as we all headed to the entryway. "This might be a good night to use that deadbolt."

"Way ahead of you."

Selene was already perusing her info pad as I pulled the runaround away from the side of the lane and headed back toward the *Ruth*. We were halfway home when she straightened up and nodded. "That Bolfin freight hauler left on time," she announced.

"Good," I said. Odds were that if they'd discovered their unwilling stowaways, the resulting fracas would have delayed them out of their lift slot. "Where was it headed?"

"Randaire," she said. "An eight-day flight unless they kick up the speed."

"Any idea what a hauler like that is capable of?"

"I'd guess plus-twenty," she said. "Though as soon as they find the Patth..."

"They veer off to the nearest port and drop them," I said heavily. "Either with fistfuls of commarks or facefuls of bruises. In retrospect, it hardly seems to have been worth the effort."

"We bought ourselves at least a few extra days," Selene pointed out. "Especially since they'll still have to find a ship heading back here."

"True," I said. At this point, any slack we could work into our schedule could only help. "Okay. As I recall, our original plan was to take a day or two to watch the enclave entrance and take notes. The big question now is how our two new complications change that."

"*Two* complications?"

"Bubloo and my father."

"I assumed we'd just leave your father alone with his own plan."

"On a purely practical level, that's probably what it'll come down to," I conceded. "But I don't like him running his own game in our backyard. The chance of him running us into the fence is just too great."

"And vice versa?"

"Depends on whether his plan *needs* to be run into a fence."

We rode in silence another minute. "I assume we're going to sleep on the new plan?" Selene asked at last.

"Eventually," I said. "First, I need to send a couple of messages. Nearest StarrComm center is, where, Rosker?"

"Yes."

"Okay," I said, sifting through my options. Rosker was a solid eight hundred kilometers away—too far to drive, and I didn't want to lock us into a public transport schedule. "We'll take the *Ruth* there, send my messages, then come back."

"What if we can't get the same pad?"

"Then hooray for us, because we don't want it," I said. "I want something closer to Mindi's ship if we can."

Peripherally, I saw her turn her head to look at me. "She said she was going back to Burke's."

"She *implied* she was going back," I corrected. "But Mindi's too tenacious to just walk out on something she clearly finds interesting. Especially when it would look like she was running from deadly danger."

"She *is* running from deadly danger."

"I know," I said sourly. "Like I said, Mindi's stubborn. I suppose you noticed the triangle of little red lights just inside the entryway?"

"On the left at chest level?"

"That's them," I confirmed. "You'll note that it wasn't until we were on our way out that we could see them. The way they're placed, they're hidden from guests on the way in."

"Yes, I see," she said, her pupils going ominous. "What were they?"

"Pretty sure they were a phone scanner," I said. "She pulled our numbers and probably some of our calling history when we first walked in."

A quick kaleidoscope of thought and emotion swept across Selene's pupils as she ran a mental check of her phone's history and numbers. "She wouldn't have found anything incriminating," she concluded.

"Right," I said, nodding. I'd run a similar analysis on my own phone's potential vulnerabilities and come to the same conclusion. "And unless she has software that can punch through the guards Nask put on our phones, there's also no way she can track us. Still, there's no reason for her to have bothered with the scanner if she was heading home."

"Or the reader might have already been on."

"Unlikely," I said. "In a lot of places they're illegal to even own, let alone have running. The usual get-around technique is to have two entryway combinations, one that leaves it off, the other that turns it on. Guess which one she used."

"So she knew from the beginning that she was going to stay on top of us?"

"That's my guess," I said. "As I said: stubborn."

"Just like you?" Selene asked pointedly. "You *are* feeling obligated to protect her, aren't you?"

I felt my lip twitch. "She helped us out because she thinks I saved her from Nikki. The least I can do is not shatter that particular illusion."

"All right," she said, her pupils still a little wary. "Who are you going to call?"

"First will be Nask," I said. "He needs to know that Galfvi's family is again ignoring the rest of whatever passes for Patth civilized society. I'm also thinking that if I hint broadly enough he might send Huginn or Muninn to run interference for us."

"You think they could get here before Galfvi's hunters find their way back from Randaire?"

"Oh, I'm pretty sure Nask's minions are already here," I said. "He'll want to keep an eye on Yiuliob, plus there's a full-range portal lying around somewhere waiting to be claimed."

"In that case, Nask probably already knows we're here, too."

"Agreed," I said. "But even if he decides to play it cool and pretend he's halfway across the Spiral, he should at least know about our evening."

"It *would* be nice if he could do something," she said. "Who else are you going to call?"

"Next on the list is Tera," I said. "She's the only one we know who still has access to the Icarus Group database. I want to see if they have anything on our esteemed Dr. Christopher Robin."

"You could also ask Nask."

"I might," I said. "At the moment I'm inclined to keep the doc off Nask's personal radar, if he's not already there."

"Anyone else?"

"There might be," I hedged. "We'll see."

Actually, there was one more call I was definitely going to make, a call I doubted Selene would be happy about. But that conversation was a long flight and a runaround drive away. No point borrowing trouble before I needed to.

"Anyway, you should start checking in with Control for a lift slot," I said. "The night's going to be long enough as it is."

"Yes," Selene said, pulling out her phone. "I hope you're planning on at least *some* sleep tonight."

"I'm planning on getting as much as we can," I said darkly. "This may be our last chance at a decent night's worth."

CHAPTER SIX

There were some StarrComm centers I'd been to, mostly in larger cities, where they did a brisk business even in the dead of night.

The facility in Rosker was not one of them.

We arrived to find that, minus the three-person duty staff, we had the place largely to ourselves. We got a booth, I fed in the required number of commarks, and got busy punching in numbers.

I had no idea what the various local times were for the people I was trying to contact. But unless a specific time and date had been set up, the chances of actually finding someone available were miniscule. My conversations consisted of mail-drop messages, verbal or text, which would be answered in kind whenever the recipients happened to pick them up.

My requests were pretty straightforward, though the external trappings surrounding the calls were wildly different. The gatekeeper on Nask's drop kept a polite and rather detached demeanor throughout our brief interaction, though I was pretty sure he recognized me. Tera's drop didn't have a screener, and wasn't even in her own name, and I had to be extra circumspect with everything I said or implied.

And with those calls completed, I couldn't put off the final call any longer.

Selene wasn't as angry with me as I'd feared, though perhaps she was just hiding it well. What I saw in her pupils was more bemusement than resentment. She listened to my explanation, said she understood, and allowed me to continue without argument or even comment.

I did note, though, that our return flight was very quiet.

It was a couple of hours before local dawn when we got back to the Pikwik City spaceport. There was indeed an open slot near Mindi's ship, two pads down and around a slight curve, where we would be close but not immediately visible when she entered or left. I wouldn't be able to keep visual track of her movements, but that meant she also wouldn't spot us immediately.

It was a reasonable trade-off. I didn't know how she would react to my attempt at protective chivalry, but I wasn't in a hurry to find out.

Originally, I'd planned to get an early start on our stakeout of the Ammei enclave entrance. But with us having just spent most of the night traveling, I scrapped that thought in favor of letting us both get some much-needed sleep.

During our shipboard planning sessions I'd spotted a café with indoor seating that I'd decided would work well as our first observation post. I'd expected us to be there for breakfast; now we arrived just in time for lunch. But the lunch menu was good, too.

Our previous surveys of the various Ammei enclaves had shown that the aliens typically stayed close to home, and this one mostly followed the same pattern. A few non-Ammei, mainly Saffi but a couple of humans as well, went in and out the arched entrance, most of them with small trucks or autocarts. Probably buyers and distributors of the Ammei exotic foodstuffs, the role we'd pretended to play in that final probe into the Mycene enclave. During our surveillance three Ammei also emerged, grabbed individual runarounds, and headed into the city on unknown errands. One of them returned while we were on watch, while the other two remained elsewhere.

The main difference between this enclave and others we'd seen was the vegetable and fruit stand the Ammei had set up just outside the gateway arch where locals could buy their wares in non-bulk quantities. Even there, though, the Ammei maintained their traditional aloofness. The stand was manned, not by the Ammei themselves, but by a pair of young Saffi. The only Ammei presence I could see were four vaguely defined figures watching everything from the shadows inside the gate area. I couldn't see any weapons, but I had no doubt they were there.

There was no sign of either Rozhuhu or First Dominant Prucital. If my father had brought them here for talks with Yiuliob, they were either already inside the enclave or else still aboard the yacht.

It was late afternoon, and Selene and I had shifted observation posts three times, when my phone vibed with the call I'd known would eventually come.

Only it wasn't quite what I was expecting.

"Roarke?" Mindi's voice came. She didn't sound happy. "It's Mindi."

"Hi, Mindi," I said, mentally preparing for whatever she was going to unload on me about parking the *Ruth* two ships away from her. Misplaced gallantry—magnet for angry Patth killers—simple unwanted crowding—

"Don't *hi Mindi* me," she bit out. "You want to come get this idiot off my doorstep?"

I frowned. "What idiot?"

It was a legitimate question. Here on Juniper, there were a depressing number of people who could reasonably come under that heading.

The Patth family Purge assassins, for starters. They could have gotten back faster than I'd expected and be running on rage and injured pride. Or Nask could have gotten my message and sent Huginn to check up on me. Then there was First Dominant Yiuliob and any number of his Ammei thugs. Or Rozhuhu, or First Dominant Prucital.

Or my father.

I swallowed a curse. Of course it was my father. Who else? Sir Nicholas Roarke, negotiator to the stars, manipulator to the max, equally friendly to generals and the scum of the Spiral—

"He looks like a hobo," Mindi growled. "Some alien type I've never seen before. He's sniffing at my hatch and pounding on it and bellowing your name like a stray pet calling for his owner—"

"Wait a second," I cut her off, my brain skidding to a halt. *"Bubloo?"*

"Is *that* his name?" Mindi snorted. "Yeah, that's the kind of name I'd expect someone like that to have. Just get over here and throw a rope around him or something, will you? Free publicity isn't good for either of us."

"Yeah, we'll be right there," I promised, still feeling a little sandbagged. How had Bubloo even found Mindi's ship? "Oh, and you probably shouldn't let him in."

"Thanks, I already figured that one out," she said acidly. "Ten minutes, Roarke, or I maybe call in a post on him myself."

Selene was already collecting our binoculars and other surveillance equipment as I put away my phone. "Mindi's found Bubloo?" she asked as we both stood up.

"More like he found her," I said, taking one last look at the enclave entrance and heading toward the runaround stand. "She says he's calling for me—"

I broke off, my mind suddenly hitting a fresh wall. "He's at her hatch *calling for me*. The hatch you and I both touched last night."

For a second her pupils held only puzzlement. Then they turned disbelieving. "Are you saying he *smelled* you?"

"I think so," I said grimly. "Mindi even mentioned he was sniffing at the hatchway."

"Interesting," Selene said as she turned toward the runarounds.

But not before I got a glimpse of the fear in her pupils. "You okay?" I asked.

"I don't know," she said. "I think you were right, Gregory. He's like…"

"He's like you," I finished for her. "He's like the Kadolians."

I felt my stomach tighten. "First of Three's found the missing piece for his damn portal."

Mindi's ship was roughly equidistant from the spaceport's north and east entrances, and her entryway hatch faced east. I therefore took us in through the south entrance.

The port's daytime traffic wasn't much more impressive than its evening version, with maybe twice as many vehicles and people moving around or on the pads working on the various ships. But Bubloo's wailing had managed to draw a decent crowd from the overall sparseness. By the time we pulled up beside a short-range shuttle in view of Mindi's ship, I counted at least twenty Saffi and humans gathered at a deferential distance to gawk at the show.

"I'll bet his singing voice is just as bad," I said, craning my neck to look over the crowd. With me sitting and everyone else standing, my observation angle was terrible.

Fortunately, we had a better way to count noses.

"Okay, you're on," I said, rolling down Selene's side window. "How many are out there?"

Selene nodded and slipped off the wig she'd opted to wear today. The fake black synthetic was great for disguising her Kadolian hair, but it carried a slight aroma that interfered with her sense of smell the way a color filter would restrict someone's sight. She leaned slightly out the window and sniffed. I watched Bubloo's routine, mentally working out my plan...

"Four," Selene said, pulling her head back inside the runaround. "Maybe five."

I scowled. So the Ammei were already here. Not really surprising, given that it was Bubloo and he was shouting my name. Two for the price of one. "Any idea where?" I asked, craning my neck a little more. Wherever they were, they were being coy about it.

"In or near the crowd," Selene said. "It's hard to pin down other scents with all the Saffi in the area."

"Got it." Even with my limited human sense of smell I was aware that Saffi had a distinctive aroma. "Well, at least they can't just move in on him with all these witnesses hanging around."

"True," Selene said. "But neither can we."

"Wasn't planning to," I said, pulling out my phone. "Where did Doc Robin say he worked? Sty-something Clinic?"

"Stylways Clinic," Selene said, already busy with her phone. "Got it." She punched in the number and handed the phone to me.

The receptionist picked up on the fourth ring. "Stylways Clinic," a brisk Saffnic voice announced.

"Dr. Robin, please," I said.

There was a short pause. "There's no one on staff here by that name," the receptionist said.

I frowned at Selene. "Are you sure? Dr. *Christopher* Robin? He said we could contact him there."

"There's no one on staff here by that name," she repeated.

I clenched my teeth. Terrific. "Thank you," I said, and keyed off.

"Did I hear her correctly?" Selene asked, the surprise in her pupils shifting to suspicion. "She said they didn't know him?"

"Pretty much," I confirmed, looking back at the crowd as I

handed back her phone. "So much for Doc Robin being on the up-and-up. Looks like I get to walk across the shooting gallery after all."

"Maybe not," Selene said suddenly, pointing at a tall fueling pump about midway between us and Bubloo. "Between the dispenser and the flow readout. Is that what I think?"

I pulled out our binoculars and focused on the small lump on top of the pump housing. One look was all it took. "It is indeed," I said, handing her the binoculars. "Fur pattern's hard to see from this angle, but I'm pretty sure it's Pax."

And with that, our options had suddenly expanded. If Ixil and his outriders were on site, then McKell was surely also on the job. "Think I should give McKell a call?" I asked.

"I don't know," Selene said hesitantly. "It might draw unwanted attention to him."

"Yeah, good point," I conceded, running my fingers over the edge of my phone. "But if we don't—"

And right then, the runaround's back door popped open and someone slid into the seat behind Selene. I spun halfway around, grabbing for my plasmic—

"About time you two showed up," McKell said as he closed the door behind him. "Who's your loud friend?"

I huffed out a breath as the brief adrenaline rush drained out of my bloodstream. "What the hell are you doing here?" I bit out. "Never mind. Better question: How the hell did you find us?"

"This is where *I'd* be if I were here to watch your pickup street fair," McKell said calmly. "I assumed you'd read it the same way. So?"

"His name's Bubloo," Selene said, matching McKell's calm. Though to be fair, she'd had a fraction of a second's advance warning as his scent reached her through her open window. "He's an unknown species, but he may be of interest to the Ammei."

"I'd say he's of more than just interest," McKell said. "Ixil says there's a group of five of them watching from the west edge of the crowd."

"What are they doing?" I asked.

"Far as he can tell, just watching," McKell said. "Maybe waiting for the crowd to thin a little before they make their move."

"Afraid we can't let them do that," I said. "Selene says he's likely been to their enclave. She smelled one of their fancy veg on him." I gestured toward the distant ship. "There are also indications he may have a Kadolian-level sense of smell."

McKell gave a low whistle. "*That's* not good," he said. "You said First of Three needed a Kadolian and a Patth to make his jury-rigged portal work, right?"

"So it seems."

"So if they don't need the Kadolian part—"

"—and if they can beg, borrow, or steal a compliant Patth—" I added.

"—then we've got a problem," McKell concluded.

"Did you hear that?" Selene put in suddenly.

"Hear what?" I asked, frowning.

"Bubloo," she said, a sudden oddness in her pupils. "He called your name, then said *by the great twin globes, please let me in.*"

I stared at her, the back of my neck tingling. "By the great twin *globes*?"

"So he knows what portals look like," McKell said thoughtfully. "Interesting."

"But I didn't smell any portal metal on him last night," Selene said, her pupils showing some confusion. "Just Ammei and Ammei food."

"Maybe they told him about the portals," I suggested.

"And the *Gold Ones* reference?" she asked.

"He talked about the *Gold Ones*?" McKell asked.

"More like just dropped the name," I said. "Which we assume he also heard from the Ammei."

"Maybe," McKell said thoughtfully. "But here's the other question. Think back to the times you've been inside a portal. Is it obvious the things are made up of two spheres? As opposed to, say, two hollowed-out parts of a giant cube or a single giant sphere or something?"

I started to pop off with the obvious answer. Paused. Phrased that way, it really *wasn't* that obvious. "Okay, pointer for him to have maybe actually seen one of the things from the outside," I said. "Bear in mind that none of these dazzling mental gymnastics will mean anything if the Ammei grab him and squirrel him away somewhere. You and Ixil want to do the honors?"

"I'm thinking we should instead whistle up the badgemen," McKell said. "Let them hustle him out of here, then steal him back when they aren't looking."

"Not sure that's a good idea," I warned. "With bounty posts on both Selene and me, drawing badgeman attention might not be the best idea—hold it," I interrupted myself as a new figure appeared over the crowd as he made his way up the zigzag toward Bubloo. "Selene, is that who I think it is?"

"Yes," she said. "It's Dr. Robin."

"Who?" McKell asked.

"Dr. Christopher Robin," I said. "The guy who's supposedly treating Bubloo. I say *supposedly* because I talked to the clinic he claims to work for and they've never heard of him."

"Interesting," McKell said. "You think he's working with the Ammei?"

"If he is, he's doing a rotten job," I said. "Bubloo was in his apartment last night when we left. If he wanted to hand him over to Yiuliob, he could have done it right there and then."

"Unless Bubloo escaped," Selene pointed out. "Robin *did* say Bubloo had gotten away from him more than once."

"Even more interesting," McKell said. "Let's hang back and see what happens."

We watched as Robin made it to the top of the zigzag. Bubloo had either heard him coming or else smelled him, because he'd already stopped his pounding and calling and was waiting to face the newcomer with his back pressed hard against the entryway. Robin smiled and gave him a tentative hand wave, and started talking.

Unfortunately, way too softly for me to hear. "Selene?" I asked quietly.

"He's too far away," she said, her pupils showing frustration. "Maybe one of us should join them?"

"Better idea," I said, pulling out my phone and punching in a number.

Mindi answered on the first vibe. "This better be you saying you're about to throw a sack over this guy," she warned.

"Almost ready," I soothed. "Tell me you're listening to the conversation out there."

"Listening? Not really," she said. "Recording? Yes. I assume you want the feed?"

"Please," I said. "I owe you."

"I'll add it to your tab." There was a click—

"—worry when you disappear like this, Bubloo," Robin was

saying in a quiet, earnest voice. "Won't you please come back with me?"

"I need my friends," Bubloo said, his own voice anxious and confused. "Where are Friend Roarke and Friend Selene?"

I keyed my phone to speaker and held it between Selene and me. McKell leaned forward, holding his own phone over mine to feed the conversation to Ixil.

"I don't know where they are, Bubloo," Robin soothed. "But we'll find them. We'll find them together."

"But they were with us last night," Bubloo said. "How were they there if you don't know how to find them?"

"He can work basic logic, anyway," McKell muttered.

"They came with us from the taverno, remember?" Robin said. "You were ill, and they helped me get you to my apartment."

"*Your* apartment?" Bubloo repeated. "I don't live there?"

"You've stayed with me a few times in the past," Robin said. "When you were sick and needed me to take care of you. Don't you remember?"

"No," Bubloo said. "How many times?"

"A few," Robin said. "But you don't live there. You . . . actually, Bubloo, I don't know where you usually live. If you'll tell me I'll take you there."

There was a short silence. On the zigzag Bubloo had his head bowed, rubbing the fingertips of his two hands restlessly against each other. Indecision? Confusion?

Abruptly, the hand movements halted. "No," he said, a fresh firmness in his voice. "I will go with you to your apartment. Perhaps Friends Roarke and Selene will follow." He reached behind him to touch the entryway.

"They're not in there, Bubloo," Robin said. "But we can still go. Maybe they'll come see us."

Bubloo hesitated, then gave a single brisk nod. "All right." He peered over the rail at the onlookers. "They won't hurt me, will they?"

"No, because I won't let them," Robin assured him, holding out a hand. "Come on, let's go."

"That's our cue," McKell said, putting his phone to his ear. "Ixil? You get all that?"

I moved my phone back, gazing unseeingly at it as my brain suddenly went into an urgent spin. "McKell—"

"Okay," McKell said, putting away his phone. "Ixil and I will run interference for them. You two—"

"Just a minute," I said. "Something's wrong."

"What?" McKell asked.

"I don't know yet," I told him. "But something here isn't right."

"Roarke—"

"Give him a minute," Selene said. Her voice was soft, but there was firmness in her pupils.

McKell hissed between his teeth. "If we don't go now, we're going to lose them," he warned.

"That's all right," I said, fighting to chase down the elusive thought. "We know where they're going."

"And if the Ammei get there first?"

And then it clicked. "Robin told Bubloo we weren't aboard," I said. "How did he know that?"

"Probably because no one answered his knocking," McKell said.

"Yeah, maybe," I said. "But there's also the way he said he wouldn't let anyone hurt Bubloo. He was absolutely positive about it."

"He's a doctor, Roarke," McKell said, starting to sound impatient. "They're *supposed* to be soothing. We need to go."

I glared at the two figures working their way down the zigzag. On paper, I had to admit, McKell's explanation looked reasonable. It was indeed the sort of thing a doctor might tell a patient.

But I'd been a hunter once. I knew people, and I knew tones of voice. There was something here that just didn't track. "I don't know," I said. "He just sounds wrong."

"You're throwing a lot of weight on someone's tone," McKell warned. "But fine, let's assume you're right. How do we proceed?"

"Mostly the way we were already planning," I said. "Only now you and Ixil hang back and make sure Robin doesn't see you. You're our sleeve cards, and we don't want him knowing about you. We'll head to his apartment and meet up with him and Bubloo."

"All right," McKell said slowly. "You sure you don't just want to cut them loose?"

"Not yet," I said. "Whoever Bubloo is—*whatever* he is—I don't think they're working together. Whatever game Robin's playing, Bubloo's still a mystery we need to solve. Especially if he's the Ammei answer to their current shortage of Kadolians."

"Fine," McKell said. "We'll meet at Robin's apartment. What's the address?"

I gave it to him. "Just make sure Robin doesn't see you."

"Yeah—got that," he said. "*You* just make sure to remember everything you say so you can tell us later."

"No need for that," Selene said. "Pix and Pax should be able to scale the outside of the building—there's a network of vine tendrils along the walls they can climb. We'll make sure to open a window when we get there so they can listen in."

"There are vines on the walls?" I asked, frowning as I did a quick memory check. "I don't remember seeing them."

"I didn't see them, either," she said. "I smelled them."

"Got it," I said. "Clock's running, McKell. Selene, you're driving."

"Call if you need us," McKell said as all three of us popped our doors and got out. McKell disappeared around the nearby shuttle's stern, while Selene and I circled our runaround in opposite directions and got back into our new seats. "Where are we going?" she asked as she started the engine.

"That way," I said, pointing toward our right. "McKell said the Ammei were grouped on the west edge of the crowd. I want to see if we can get a look at them."

"*Just* a look?"

"And maybe get a game of follow-the-leader going," I said. "It occurred to me that we haven't established whether the Ammei are here because of Bubloo or because Bubloo's shouting my name. If it's the latter, they'll follow us and take some of the pressure off Robin and Bubloo. If it's the former, they'll ignore us and we can move in to backstop McKell and Ixil."

"Understood." She tapped the steering wheel in gentle emphasis of the fact that she was sitting behind it. "Either way, you anticipate having to jump out at some point?"

"Probably," I conceded. "And I know how much you hate me doing that when I'm driving."

CHAPTER SEVEN

The crowd was starting to dissipate as Selene wove us skillfully through the lanes between the ships and various islands of support equipment. Given that everyone else was heading away from Mindi's ship, the five Ammei still standing in a loose clump alongside a pair of runarounds were nicely conspicuous.

The fact that we were also heading inward made us likewise.

"They've spotted us," Selene said as we approached them.

"Good," I said. One of the five aliens had his scaly face turned toward us and I could see his mouth working. "It's always a bother to have to get their attention. Turn right past this next ship and see if you can pick up some speed."

"I probably can't," she warned as she made the turn. "Too many people around."

"That's okay," I said. "You just have to *look* like you're trying to get away."

"I can do that." She threw me a sideways look, and I saw a sort of black amusement in her pupils. "Any guesses?"

"Three on us, the other two on Bubloo," I said. "Convenient of them to have brought two runarounds. Could you tell if they're armed?"

She nodded, the amusement gone. "The same kind of hand weapons the Ammei in *Imistio* Tower were carrying."

I winced. Those sidearms were junior partners to the longer-range lightning guns we'd faced a few days ago on Mycene. I'd never seen one of the smaller versions fired, but I didn't expect the results to be any less horrible. "Better make sure they never get a clear shot, then."

"And hope they're working off the live-detain protocol on the bounty posts."

"Let's definitely hope that," I agreed. "Okay. Out the east entrance and turn north. Let's see if they were fast enough to get on our tail."

"Do you have a plan?"

"Of course," I assured her. "Remember that narrow alley you took us down on the way to Robin's place? Make our leisurely way that direction."

"All right," she said, a flicker of uncertainty crossing her pupils. "You *do* remember that was a trash lane, right?"

"And yesterday was pickup day in that part of the city," I said, nodding. "Yes, I remember the listings."

"I'm just pointing out the alley might not be as easy to navigate now as it was last night. Trash pickup vehicles are usually narrower than runarounds."

"Don't worry," I said. "It'll be perfect."

For the first two blocks I was afraid the Ammei had been too slow on the uptake to pick up our trail. But then I spotted them moving up behind us. Not as smoothly and invisibly as a hunter would, but they were nevertheless there.

What *was* surprising was that *both* runarounds were on the hunt.

"You see that?" I asked, nodding over my shoulder.

"Yes," Selene said. "So they aren't interested in Bubloo at all?"

"Not unless they had another squad outside your scent range and Ixil's eyelines that was tasked to get him," I said, trying to fit this new wrinkle into my theories. If the Ammei didn't want Bubloo, then what *was* he doing on Juniper?

"Maybe he's *too* secret?" Selene suggested. "If the Ammei following us were supposed to grab us and weren't told about Bubloo...?"

"Maybe," I said doubtfully. "But then how does all the rest fit together? The Ammei scent, the Ammei vegetables—"

"Maybe he just shops at their street stand."

"—*and* the Gold Ones and the great twin globes?"

"There's that," she conceded.

"Yeah." I shook my head. "We're missing something, Selene. There's something else at play here, and we don't have enough of the pieces."

"I agree," she said calmly. "I'm ready to start collecting them when you are."

"Just as soon as we lose our friends back there," I promised. "How much farther to the alley?"

"About two minutes."

"Good. Here's the plan..."

A minute and a half later she turned us onto a street I recognized from the night before. Twenty seconds after that, we reached our target alley and she took a hard right into it.

She was right about the alley being a trash storage area. She was also right about the dozen or so chest-high bins that now hugged the alley's right-hand side wall at both ends that left a passageway only a few centimeters wider than our runaround.

I was right about it being perfect.

She eased us at slightly lowered speed through the first part of the alley, skillfully negotiating the narrow space. Then, as our front doors passed the last of the bins at that end, she braked hard. I had my door open before she stopped, dropping out onto the pavement behind the bin. I barely got the door closed before she accelerated back to top speed, driving hard toward the far end. I crouched down out of sight behind my bin, drew my plasmic, and waited.

Selene was nearly to the other line of bins when I heard the slight squeal of tires on pavement as the Ammei vehicle blew into the alleyway behind her.

For a second I was afraid they would see the obstacles and abandon the chase. But then I heard the deeper rumble of the engine as they accelerated and roared after her. The runaround passed my position without stopping, clearly intent on taking advantage of the alley's wider central section to try to close the gap.

I was getting ready to stand up when the second Ammei vehicle shot past, riding the tail of the first.

I shook my head. *Amateurs.* Professional hunters would never commit their entire team to a location this ripe for evasion or ambush. As my father used to say, *Never want something so badly that you think the laws of physics and stupidity don't apply.*

Unless their entire team *wasn't* here.

I swore under my breath. If they'd figured out what we were doing—or worse, if they'd anticipated this exact maneuver—Selene was about to walk straight into a trap.

And I was out of position to back her up.

There was no time to come up with a new plan. Certainly no time to clue Selene in on the danger. I would just have to improvise as best I could and hope like hell I could pull this off.

Selene reached the line of bins at the far end and slammed on her brakes. For a moment she fishtailed with the sudden deceleration, then straightened out and came to a halt with the front end of the runaround now poking out of the alley, just far enough to get the driver's-side door clear of the wall while blocking everything behind her. Even as the two Ammei runarounds slammed to slightly wild stops of their own to keep from ramming into her, Selene popped her door and hurried to her left across the alley mouth and out of sight.

The rear Ammei vehicle was starting to back up, presumably hoping to get out from behind the roadblock before Selene disappeared entirely, when I fired a plasmic shot into each of its rear tires. The runaround twitched once and stopped dead.

My original plan had been to now do a quick escape of my own, backing out the alley's entrance and meeting up with Selene halfway around the block. But with my fresh concern for her safety and whatever might be lurking out there, I didn't have the luxury of spare time.

So instead of retreating, I charged.

The doors of both runarounds were starting to open as I reached them. A quick plasmic shot into both alley walls to warn back the passengers, and I leaped up onto the trunk of the rear vehicle, sprinted up onto the roof and down onto the hood, then jumped across to the lead vehicle and repeated the maneuver, ending with one final run across Selene's abandoned runaround. Jumping back onto the walkway, I headed after Selene, hoping I wasn't too late.

I nearly was. Just as I'd had to improvise, so had she. Instead of walking down our side of the street, as she'd planned, she was weaving her way quickly through the traffic, her white hair glinting as she dodged between and around vehicles, creating a pocket of chaos that threatened to snarl everything around her.

Halfway down the block, an Amme was standing on the street side of a parked van, watching the oncoming traffic as he waited for an opening to head off after her. As I started toward him, he half drew a weapon from under his tunic.

There was a lot to be said for slug guns, with their decent range, excellent stopping power, and the inherent difficulty involved in pinpointing the shooter. But for sheer shock and awe, there was nothing like the sudden flash of heat across your face from a plasmic blast exploding onto the ground a meter in front of you.

Evidently, the Amme thought likewise. He jerked back from my warning shot, snapping his arm up in front of his face to block the heat and twisting his head around trying to locate me. He spotted me and drew his weapon a little farther from beneath his tunic. I lifted my aim warningly in response and waited.

Some of the people I'd dealt with over the years were amazingly slow to take that kind of hint. This one, fortunately, wasn't. Tucking his weapon back into concealment, he popped the van's door and disappeared back into it. Two seconds later, he pulled away from the walkway and into a U-turn that did its bit to further disrupt the traffic flow.

Unfortunately for the harried locals, it wasn't over yet. I still had five annoyed Ammei somewhere behind me, and I no intention of sticking around long enough to find out just how angry they were. Bracing myself, I waded into the street.

Saffi tended to be chivalrous toward their females, and I assumed that aspect of their culture had come into play during Selene's mad dash through traffic. Me, not so much. Running the gauntlet was like something out of a frenzied nightmare, and I suspected that the main reason I wasn't seriously hurt was because none of the frustrated drivers felt like sitting under a badgeman's stare while they filled out the necessary accident paperwork.

A long minute later, I made it to the walkway on the far side. Selene was nowhere to be seen, but even as I ducked out of sight into a nearby restaurant she messaged that she'd passed through to the next street and was waiting with a new runaround. My restaurant turned out to have a central open-air dining area with another entrance on the far side, and a minute later I'd also made it through.

Selene was standing beside a runaround, her right hand out of sight inside her jacket, presumably with a ready grip on her plasmic. She spotted me, and I saw the relief in her pupils as she opened the driver's door and got in. I climbed in the other side and we were off.

"Are you all right?" I asked as she eased us into the traffic flow. This time, at least, we were going the right direction and staying in the approved lanes.

"I'm fine," she said, tension visible in her pupils. "You?"

"No problems," I said. "Though I'm guessing a voting majority of Pikwik City's populace is mad at us right now."

"Probably," she said. "What happened back there?"

"Nothing exciting," I said. "I ran over the tops of the cars and spotted an Amme who looked like he was about to come after you. I brushed him back, and he thought better of it and took off."

"That was the enclosed van, right?"

"Yes."

"Did you see if anyone else was in there with him?"

"No," I said. "Like you said: enclosed."

"What about the Amme's face? Did you get a clear look at him?"

"Not really," I said, feeling my eyes narrow. She was being awfully persistent with this line of questioning. "I was mostly focused on his weapon. Why, was it someone we know?"

"I think so," she said, her pupils going grim. "It was hard to tell in the open air, but I think it was Rozhuhu."

Something cold ran up my back. "You're sure?"

"Pretty sure," she said. "I only got a whiff as he opened his door." She hesitated. "And I think your father may have been with him."

I took a careful breath. "I see," I said. As a rejoinder, it was pretty bland, but only because the other possibilities that sprang to mind were words I tried not to use in Selene's presence. "Well, they do say everyone has his price. Nice to see that my father's is at least a hefty one."

"You think he's after the bounty?"

"Don't you?"

"I don't know," she said, and I saw puzzlement in her pupils. "If that's what he's after, why didn't he turn us in on Mycene?

For that matter, why did he tell us about the bounties in the first place?"

"Sometimes it takes time for a wad of money that big to work its way through a person's conscience."

"You know that doesn't make any sense," she said with mild reproach. "Not with your father."

I glowered at the late afternoon traffic making its way along the street in front of us. But she was right. My father was quick to make up his mind on things like this, and was always driven more by logic and balance than by emotion or desire.

After all, as he used to say, *Ego, greed, and stubbornness are ninety percent of the levers you'll ever need.* And he never liked having levers other people could use on him.

"What I don't understand is how he anticipated we'd be there," Selene continued.

"He knows me pretty well," I said. "On top of that, he's probably got access to everything Kinneman and the Icarus Group have compiled on our activities and techniques. He's always been good at finding dots and connecting them." I took a deep breath. "Okay, fine. If he's not after the bounty, why come after you? Or after me, or after both of us?"

"*And* why here?" Selene added.

I frowned. "What?"

"We just decided he could have handed us to the Ammei on Mycene," she reminded me. "If not there, why here?"

There were several pointed answers I could give to that question. But beneath my emotional swirl, I knew it was a good question. "Okay," I said slowly, forcing myself to think it through. "As far as we can tell, there are two main Ammei factions: one led by First of Three on Nexus Six, the other by First Dominant Yiuliob here on Juniper. We also saw that the Ammei leadership on Mycene was split. If he'd turned us over to them, it would have been a toss-up as to which side got us."

"Yes, that makes sense," Selene agreed. "Do we know which side your father's on?"

"If he's still working for Kinneman, then presumably whichever side Kinneman thinks will get him what he wants," I said. "If he's *not* with Kinneman, I have no idea." I considered. "Actually, come to think of it, I guess I have no idea either way."

"Well, First of Three brought in Rozhuhu and First Dominant

Prucital to meet with us," Selene reminded me. "If they're both here with your father, maybe that means he's on First's side?"

"Or else First brought them in to impress them with his power," I said. "They may only be potential allies. Or it could be that they actually support Yiuliob and First was pressuring them to switch sides. Or Kinneman is trying to play the sides against each other in hopes of sparking a civil war he can clean up after."

"That's a horrible thought," Selene murmured. "Would your father really go along with something like that?"

"I don't know," I admitted. "Six months ago I'd have said not a chance. But with First of Three threatening the Commonwealth *and* the Patth *and* the Kadolians..." I huffed out a breath. "You know my philosophy on this sort of decision: I start with whatever benefits you and me. If that's a wash, I do what I think is best for the universe at large. I don't know if my father thinks that way, but I can see situations where letting two dangerous sides take each other out would seem to be the best thing for everyone else."

"And you'd support that?"

"In general, I don't know. In this case...I still don't know."

She drove in silence another two blocks. "So where do we go from here?" she asked at last.

"We start by finding out who exactly Christopher Robin is," I said, relieved to be back on a topic that didn't involve civil war or genocide. "After that, I want some answers from Bubloo."

"*Sensible* answers?"

"Yeah, good point," I said. "I suppose we can always hope."

"Yes." Another pause. "What kind of weapon was it?"

"A Villiwink net gun," I told her.

"At least they still want us alive."

"Yes," I agreed, my comment to my father back on Mycene sending a fresh shiver up my back. *Or else,* I'd suggested, *the client wants the privilege of killing us himself.*

The sky to the west was darkening by the time we reached Robin's neighborhood. I had Selene park the car three blocks from his building, just in case someone had grabbed our plate number, and we walked the rest of the way.

This time, as we went along the walkway to the entrance, I spotted the ivy-like plants crisscrossing the building's outer walls.

I expected Robin to be surprised by our arrival. But the only emotion I saw on his face as he opened the apartment door was relief. "*There* you are," he said, stepping back and beckoning us inside. "I was worried about you."

"Really?" I asked, throwing a quick look around the common room as we walked in. Bubloo was sitting on the conversation circle couch, an intense look on his face as he peered down at an info pad on his lap. Aside from him and Robin, there was no one else in sight. If my father had anticipated this one, he was apparently running late. "Why?"

"I heard there was an incident at Twenty-fifth Road and Brostle Thoroughfare involving a human couple." His face puckered a little as he looked at Selene. "Or a couple who appeared to be human, at any rate," he amended. "I daresay eyewitness reports on Juniper aren't any better than those anywhere else."

"But probably no worse, either," I said. "What kind of incident?"

"The details were fuzzy," Robin said. "But it sounded like a couple of wrecked vehicles were involved, plus some dangerous running through traffic. There may have been a few shots fired, too."

"Sounds messy," I said. "Glad we took a different route. Was anyone hurt?"

"Not from what I've read," he said. "But as I said, fuzzy. Please; sit down. Can I get you anything?"

"No, thanks," I said, beckoning to Selene and taking the opportunity for a close look at her pupils. No additional concerns or cautions. Apparently, things in here were as nonthreatening as they looked. "Hello, Bubloo. How are you feeling today?"

"No," he said, tapping the info pad impatiently. "No no no no. This is *not* the right way to cook a radixiam mix."

"Isn't it?" I asked politely, walking over to one of the chairs near him. I looked at Selene, and as I motioned her to join me I saw by the sudden alertness in her pupils that she'd also caught the key word. Radixiam, if I remembered correctly, was one of the more popular and accessible blends of Ammei exotic vegetables. Was the root vegetable she'd smelled on Bubloo the night we first met a part of that mix? "What exactly is radixiam?"

"Only a blend of the most succulent vegetables in the universe," Bubloo said, looking up at me. "Oh—Friend Roarke. You *did* find us. Friend Christopher said you would. I'm happy to see you."

"Friend Christopher was right," I said, "and I'm happy to see you, too. How are you feeling?"

"I'm fine." Abruptly, he stood up. "I must now go and cook. Friend Christopher, may I use your kitchen to cook in?"

"Yes, of course," Robin said. "But if you're looking for radixiam mix, I'm afraid I'm fresh out."

"I know," Bubloo said. "I can smell which foods and spices you have. No drama—I will cook radixiam another time. For all of you," he added, giving Selene and me a disturbingly human smile before turning toward the kitchen door. "No matter. This will also be delicious."

"Bubloo—" Robin said, starting to follow.

"He'll be fine," I assured him as Bubloo disappeared through the doorway. "Anyway, we need to talk."

"About what?" Robin asked, sending a lingering look at the kitchen door before turning back to me.

"I have a couple of questions," I said, shifting my attention to Selene. "Selene? You all right?"

"Yes, I'll be fine," she said. Instead of joining us in the conversation circle she'd moved over to the wall beside one of the windows. "The spice mix in the kitchen is somewhat... intense. May I open this window, Dr. Robin?"

"Of course," Robin said, taking a step toward her. "I'm sorry. Bubloo wanted to see my herbal selection—I wasn't aware he'd opened any of them. Do you need to step outside?"

"No, that's all right," Selene assured him, unlocking the window. "I just need a little fresh air in here."

"Certainly," Robin said, scooping up a chair from the circle and carrying it over to her. "Here," he said, setting it down. "Feel free to open it all the way if you need to."

"Thank you," she said, sitting down. She looked at me, her pupils showing quiet satisfaction.

"Yes, thank you," I added to Robin, smiling some satisfaction right back at her. I'd almost forgotten her promise to open a window so Pix and Pax could eavesdrop. "Come over here, Doc, will you? We need to talk."

"In a minute," Robin said, starting toward the kitchen. "I should check on Bubloo."

"I insist," I said.

"But—" Robin broke off, his face going rigid as he saw the plasmic pointed at him. "Roarke? What's going on?"

"That was *my* question," I said. "Sit down, please. Keep your hands visible."

"Of course." Robin walked back to the circle and sank into the chair across from me. He started to fold his arms across his chest, apparently thought better of it, and instead laid his forearms out along the chair arms, leaving his hands to dangle off the ends. "What can I do for you?"

"You can start by telling us who you are," I said. "And don't bother with the *Dr. Christopher Robin* bit. We talked to the Stylways Clinic, and they say they've never heard of you."

I raised my eyebrows. "So who the hell *are* you?"

CHAPTER EIGHT

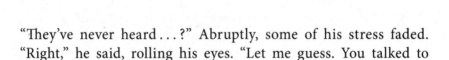

"They've never heard...?" Abruptly, some of his stress faded. "Right," he said, rolling his eyes. "Let me guess. You talked to Frufrei, the receptionist."

"We talked to *a* receptionist," I said, frowning at him. "I didn't get her name."

"No need," he said. "That'll be Frufrei. And she said—let me guess—she said I wasn't on staff there. Right?"

I flicked a glance at Selene. Her pupils still showed caution, but there was nothing there to suggest this was just an act. "Right," I said.

"That's because I'm *not* on staff," Robin said. "I'm an outside consultant, brought in three weeks ago to handle some of Dr. Abrams's caseload while he's at a conference on Randaire."

"And the clinic somehow forgot that?"

"You never *asked* the clinic," Robin said acidly. "You only asked Frufrei. She has a...shall we say *unique* view of who should be allowed to receive calls in her facility and who shouldn't."

"Sounds like someone in need of firing," I said, eyeing him closely. The explanation made a certain amount of lopsided sense, I had to admit. And Frufrei *had* used the magic words *on staff* when she denied knowing any Dr. Christopher Robin.

But there was still Robin's absolute certainty that he could protect

Bubloo from the crowd. "We'll pass on that for the moment," I said. "Tell me about your life before you were a doctor."

His forehead creased. "You mean like what other jobs have I held?"

"Jobs, professions, background," I said. "I'll take whichever's most interesting."

"Yes, I imagine you will." He glowered at the floor a moment, then huffed out a heavy sigh. "Fine. It can't make much difference anymore. I began life as a criminal." He raised his eyebrows. "Shocked?"

"Not especially," I said, flicking a look at Selene. She'd left her window seat and moved around behind Robin where she could get a better reading on him. "What flavor criminal are we talking about?"

"Whatever flavor our neighborhood gang needed at any given moment," he said. "They started me as a runner and lookout, then moved me into driving, background muscle, and general job support."

"Did you ever kill anyone?" Selene asked.

Robin's lip twitched. "No, but I had to stand by and watch a couple of sanctions. I'd gotten pretty good at the background muscle stuff, and the boss wanted me to move up to enforcer. Thought I should see what the job entailed."

I thought about our occasional traveling companion Floyd, who'd started in a similar position for Luko Varsi and managed to stay alive long enough to get into an overseer position. "Not a lot of job security in that branch of the business," I pointed out.

"Not to mention life security," Robin agreed. "I also didn't like the idea of killing someone just because he was a rival. Especially when he hadn't done anything to me personally."

"I'll bet the boss was thrilled with that attitude."

"Luckily, I never had to express it to him," Robin said. "It was about that time that I pulled my head out of the sand long enough to notice that my father, the local doctor, was effectively immune from all the chaos and urban warfare around us. Everyone needed his services, and he was willing to treat anyone, so no one wanted him hurt."

"Understandable," I agreed. "So you suddenly discovered a lifelong desire to be a doctor?"

"Something like that," he said. "I had the genetic aptitude for the job, and I'd watched my father enough to know I could handle the blood-and-guts parts. The boss knew my father wouldn't be able to do the job forever, so he found me a school and financed me through. I worked for him—and the rest of the neighborhood—for eight years, after which I moved on, switched specialties"—he waved a hand around the room—"and ended up here."

"Very nice," I complimented. "Very storybook. And the boss didn't mind you running out on him?"

"Someone else had taken over my job by then," Robin said. "Someone with, shall we say, more enthusiasm for the overall profession."

"Mm." Actually, to be fair, it wasn't any more preposterous than my father's own path from criminal fixer to respectable negotiator. "How did you know we weren't aboard that ship?"

"You didn't answer Bubloo's knock," Robin said, sounding puzzled by the question. "A man who'd risked his own safety to help a stranger would hardly ignore an urgent call from that same person."

"No, of course not," I said. Again, a nice, reasonable, pat answer.

And yet, there was something about it that bothered me. Maybe it was a little *too* reasonable and a little *too* pat. I looked at Selene and raised my eyebrows.

But she merely shook her head and began a casual drift back to her window seat. If Robin's scent had shown any change during his story, she hadn't picked up on it.

"Anything else you want to know?" Robin asked.

"Not right now," I said. "I'd like a quick look in your wallet, if I may."

For a second his expression started changing to a glower. Then it cleared. "Fine," he said, and reached inside his jacket. I tensed; but the hand reappeared with only the requested wallet. He lobbed it to me, then leaned back in his chair, his body language one of silent protest. I set my plasmic on my lap, noting as I did so that Selene now had her hand on her own weapon, just in case we'd been wrong about Robin. I opened the wallet and started a methodical search.

Working for the Icarus Group, and for Varsi's organization before that, I'd seen and handled some of the best forged documents the Spiral had to offer. Robin's were either genuine or in the same rarefied class as those which Admiral Sir Graym-Barker's people had provided for Selene and me. There was a regular Commonwealth ID, a medical practitioner's license, a couple of membership cards for professional associations, two bank credit cards, a medical emergency card embedded with Robin's physiological profile and data, and two hundred commarks in cash and another three hundred in certified bank checks.

"Thanks," I said, closing the wallet and lobbing it back to him. "So you promising Bubloo protection wasn't just your bedside manner?"

"No, there was experience behind it," Robin said, his tone briefly going a little dark. He thumbed quickly through the wallet, as if making sure I hadn't sleight-of-handed any of the cash or checks away, then returned it to his jacket. "I *am* surprised you picked up on that."

"It was mostly your air of confidence," I said. "That, and the way you move. Catlike, I think they call it. One of the marks of a professional."

"And you should know," Robin said, nodding over his shoulder at Selene. "The way she picked up guard duty right as you set down your weapon shows a pretty fair degree of professionalism on your part, too."

I frowned. "Sorry?"

He smiled faintly and nodded again, this time over my shoulder. "That etchwork platter in the display cabinet provides very nice reflections."

"Ah," I said. "And there are little things like that."

He shrugged. "Former criminal. What about you?"

"Former hunters," I said.

"Friend Roarke?" Bubloo's voice came from the kitchen. "Are you hungry for deliciousness?"

"Are we finished?" Robin asked softly. "I'd just as soon Bubloo not know anything about this. He has enough stress in his life just from the chaos he himself brings to the table."

"I noticed," I said, slipping my plasmic back into its holster. "Yes, I think we're done." I raised my voice. "Yes, Bubloo, I'm hungry. What have you got?"

"Deliciousness." The kitchen door opened and Bubloo backed through the doorway into the common room. He turned to face us, and I saw he was carrying a large platter in front of him, loaded like a caterer's tray with a variety of appetizer-sized items in the shapes of puffs, squares, and squiggle crackers. "It's not radixiam," he said apologetically. "But they are all still delicious. And I *shall* make radixiam for you soon."

"Maybe at your home?" Robin suggested, beckoning Selene to come join us in the conversation circle. "I'd guess you have the finest radixiam mix there."

"My home?" Bubloo asked, sounding puzzled as he set the platter down on the rolling drinks tray that Robin had used the previous night to hold his syringe and meds. "You wish to come to my *home*?"

"Yes, of course," Robin said, picking one of the squares and taking a cautious bite. "We've talked about that, how letting me see how you live can uncover aspects of your personality that will help in your treatment. Don't you remember?"

"No," Bubloo said, peering closely at him as Selene sat down beside me. "Have we spoken before?"

Robin's eyes flicked to me, and I saw a brief tightness around his mouth. "Yes, Bubloo, many times," he said gently. "Do you remember last night? Do you remember Roarke and Selene helping us get back here?"

Bubloo looked at me, then at Selene. "I remember what they smell like," he said uncertainly. "Are those the same faces they were wearing?"

"Yes, they are," Robin said. "Humans only have one face—"

"Yes!" Bubloo said suddenly, pointing the half-eaten squiggle he was holding toward Selene. "I remember you. You're the Kadolian!"

"That's right," Robin said, giving Selene an odd look. "You've spoken to me about them."

"I've spoken to *you*?" Bubloo asked, his momentary excitement fading again into confusion. "I don't remember." He gave a sort of sibilant sigh. "I am so weary of this, Friend Christopher. I speak to you of Kadolians, yet do not remember. The Gold Ones speak to me of the one Kadolian, yet their purpose isn't clear—"

"The Gold Ones talked to you about Kadolians?" I interrupted.

"Of course, Friend Roarke," Bubloo said. "But not *all* the Kadolians. Only the chosen one. The one destined to free the rest of her people."

"*Her* people?" Robin pounced on the word. "The Gold Ones specifically said the one Kadolian would be female?"

"I think so," Bubloo said. He looked closely at the squiggle in his hand as if wondering how it got there, then took another bite. "But would they really have been so precise?"

"You tell us," Robin said, some impatience creeping into his tone. "You're the one who was there."

"Can we back up a little?" I asked. Out of the corner of my eye I saw Selene's eyelashes suddenly fluttering. Something from Bubloo? From Robin? From both? "I want to know a little more about these Gold Ones. Who are they? What do they look like?"

"They are gold," Bubloo said, as if that part should be obvious. "They look like—"

"Are you all right?" Robin cut him off, his eyes on Selene.

"Yes, I think so," she said, getting a little unsteadily to her feet. "I just need a little air."

I felt a tingle between my shoulder blades. The sky outside the open window was to full darkness now, and a light breeze was ruffling at the edges of the curtains.

But I knew none of that was what had caught Selene's attention. Some new scent was on the wind, something that required a closer look.

And if there was new information out there, I needed to be in on it.

"Let me help you," I said, standing up and catching up with her. I took her arm and walked the two of us carefully toward the window. "What is it?" I asked softly.

"Someone crushed one of the vine berries," she whispered back. "Probably Pax. I think Ixil wanted him to get my attention."

I nodded and we continued the rest of the way to the window. There, as expected, we found Pax crouching on one of the vines looking up at us, a folded piece of paper tucked under his front leg.

I took the paper as Selene set her hands on the sill and leaned partially outside, her nostrils and eyelashes working the air. Keeping my own hands below the level of the sill out of Robin's sight, I unfolded the paper.

The message, in McKell's handwriting, was very brief.

Badgemen approaching. Hunters gathering. Unknown woman watching from rear.

"Terrific," I growled, showing Selene the note. "At least our Patth stalkers aren't here." I frowned out into the night, at the dark skies above and the streetlamp-lit ground below. "They *aren't* here, are they?"

Because if they were, and if the woman McKell had tagged was Mindi, we couldn't just cut and run and leave her out there alone.

"I don't smell any Patth," Selene assured me, her pupils in the faint light showing puzzlement. "But the woman he mentions isn't Mindi. It's . . . I've smelled her before, I think, but the scent is too faint for me to get any more."

"Well, we can leave that mystery for later," I said. "Or until she starts shooting at us, whichever comes first. Any idea how many hunters we're talking about?"

"Unfortunately, hunters smell just like ordinary citizens."

"Yes, we should get someone to fix that," I said, looking around. But there were too many corners, bushes, trees, and shadows. A whole army could be down there looking up at us and I'd never spot them. "Maybe put something in the license. What about weapons?"

"I can't smell anything," she said. "There's too much wind and distance."

"Understood," I said, tucking McKell's note out of sight in my sleeve. "I just hope everyone remembers the live-detain part of the post. Come on—we need to move."

We headed back to the others. In our absence Robin and Bubloo had made a significant dent in the appetizers, and Robin was talking Bubloo's leg off about all the information a xenopsychiatrist could glean from a home visit. Both of them looked up as we joined them. "Everything all right?" Robin asked.

"She's fine," I said. "But we need to get back to our ship. Thank you for your hospitality, Doctor, and for your deliciousnesses, Bubloo—"

"But you can't leave," Bubloo said scrambling to his feet, an agitated look on his face. "Not now. I'm going to make you radixiam, remember?"

"Another time," I said, easing Selene toward the door. "Besides, you don't have the ingredients, remember?"

"Of course I do," he said. "I have them at my home. We can go there together."

Robin stiffened. "You have—? Yes, by all means," he said, standing up. "Let me get our jackets and we'll go."

"Wait a minute," I protested as Robin hurried to a chair with a pair of jackets draped over its back. "It's getting late, and you must both be tired—"

"My home has resting places," Bubloo said eagerly. He took one of the jackets from Robin, raised it above his head with both hands, and let go, letting it slide down his arms and into place.

"No," I said firmly. "I appreciate the offer, but no."

"Why not?" Robin asked, a sudden wary look in his eye. "Company?"

"Badgemen," I said, choosing the simplest of all the possible answers.

"Badgemen? Pfft," Bubloo said disdainfully. "Those who commit no crimes have no fear of enforcers of the law."

"Sometimes things get complicated," Robin said. "I know how badgemen operate. The rest of you stay here and I'll get rid of them."

"That's not necessary," I insisted. We didn't have time for this. "This is something—"

And right then, just as I caught the sudden flare of Selene's nostrils, there was a knock at the door.

"Wait here," Robin ordered, striding across the room with a very undoctorlike set to his jaw.

Bubloo was quicker. He scuttled ahead of Robin, reached the door a good two steps ahead of him, and pulled it partway open. "Good evening, Friend Badgemen," he said cheerfully, leaning his head out into the hallway. "I am Bubloo. How may I assist?"

"Stand aside," a stiff voice came from outside. A Saffi hand appeared over Bubloo's shoulder and shoved the door fully open, revealing two Saffi badgemen, a sergeant and an officer. "We seek a human named Gregory Roarke," the sergeant continued, his eyes sweeping the room and landing on me. "Are you Gregory Roarke?"

"I'm Dr. Christopher Robin," Robin put in before I could answer. "This is my apartment. May I ask why you're here?"

A sudden shiver ran up my back. Come to think of it, why *were* they here?

This wasn't my place. We'd met Robin and Bubloo barely a day ago, with no history before that, and precious little communication since then.

So how had the badgemen known to look for us *here*?

I felt my lip twist. McKell, of course. He'd seen the hunters gathering in the neighborhood—how *they'd* found us was another good question—and had decided to pull the trick he'd suggested for Bubloo. He'd called the badgemen down on us, planning to spring us when the opportunity presented itself.

Under some circumstances that would have been a decent enough plan. But not this time. We had Bubloo right here, with whatever he knew about the Gold Ones still locked in his addled brain. If Robin was able to talk him into taking the two of them to Bubloo's home while we were gone we might lose track of both of them.

Which just left the question of how to get out of here without having to assault a pair of badgemen.

"A runaround rented to Gregory Roarke was abandoned in an alley off Twenty-fifth Road," the sergeant said. He was talking to Robin, but his eyes were fixed on me. "That is a violation of the vehicle rental agreement."

"And for *that* Pikwik City sends badgemen to harass honest visitors?" Robin asked disdainfully. "Are there no other more serious crimes to be dealt with?"

"It's also not a violation," I added. "The front of the car was sticking out of the alley, visible and easily accessible from the street."

"You *are* Gregory Roarke, then?" the sergeant said, his hand dropping to his holstered sidearm.

I felt my muscles tense. Or it could also be that these two weren't badgemen at all, but masquerading hunters who'd been lured by the promise of big money to take the huge risk of impersonating law-enforcement officials.

In which case, I had about two seconds to do something about it. I half turned my left side toward them, putting my right hand into partial concealment. If I was wrong—if they were indeed badgemen—firing a plasmic at them would be a guaranteed death sentence. But getting taken to someone who was willing to pay two million commarks for me wouldn't be a hell of a lot better. I got a grip on my plasmic, hoping I could get the drop on them and not have to actually fire.

I never got to find out how it would have ended. Once again, Bubloo managed to get ahead of the curve. "Please," he pleaded, moving between me and the Saffi. "You mustn't take my friend away."

"Out of the way, alien," the sergeant bit out. His weapon was nearly clear of its holster now—too late for me to get there first—

And as he started to raise the weapon to firing position, Bubloo took a final step toward him, rested his hand on the Saffi's chest for balance, and blew a stream of breath into the other's face.

My knockout pills worked pretty fast. A well-tuned badgeman stunner worked even faster.

Bubloo's breath beat out both of them. Before the Saffi even had time to twitch back, his eyes rolled sideways and he collapsed onto the hallway floor. His partner hadn't even begun to gape when Bubloo repeated the lean-and-puff, and sent him to join his buddy.

For a moment no one moved or spoke, the sheer unexpectedness of it freezing muscles and voices. Bubloo turned back to face us, an uncertain look on his face. "Did I do wrong?" he asked, his voice trembling.

"No," Selene said, her own voice sounding a little odd. I focused on her pupils, saw confusion there. "No, not at all. They were going to—" She broke off, looking helplessly at me.

"They were imposters," I said, my earlier suspicion turned to dark certainty. "Badgemen on Juniper are issued Rakkre six-mil slug guns." I pointed to the weapon partially resting in the Saffi's limp hand. "That's a Bloove dart gun, with an option of curare or vertigo loads. Favored by bounty hunters who plan to get up close and personal to their target."

"He's right, Bubloo," Robin seconded, squatting and scooping up the weapon. "They're hunters who came here to grab Roarke and Selene."

"To *grab* them?" Bubloo breathed. "But why?"

"Later," I said. "These are just the first two in a long line of trouble. Unless we want to find ourselves in the middle of a full-blown war, we need to get out of here."

"Out of here, and into a safe place," Robin added. "We can't go to Roarke's ship, Bubloo, or anywhere else the hunters might know to look for them. Your home is the only safe place we can go. We need you to tell us where it is, and we need you to tell us now."

Bubloo hesitated, then drew himself up. "Yes. Agreed. We shall go to my home. No hunters will reach us there."

"Sounds good to me," I said. I held out a hand to Selene,

using the movement to confirm visually that the window was still open. If Pax was still lurking out there... "What's the address, in case we get separated?"

"Never mind that," Robin said. "We need to stick together."

"That's the plan, yes," I said. "But as my father used to say, *When you're on the run, don't expect you'll get to choose your companions or your route.*"

"Friend Roarke is right," Bubloo said. "Come to the gate at 42668 Eastern Blackcreek Street. My home is inside the gate, at 72 Harbin Way."

"Got it," I said. "We left our runaround three blocks away. We'll try there first."

"Better idea." Robin poked one of the Saffi with the toe of his shoe. "How about we take *their* vehicle? It's bound to be closer."

"Good idea," I agreed. "Check their pockets for the keys. I'll scout the stairway, see if anyone down there looks like they want to start Act Two. Selene, you're with me."

"I'll go with you, too," Bubloo said eagerly.

"No, you'd better stay with me," Robin said. "Like Roarke said, it's not safe out there."

"But I can help." Bubloo touched his lower lip, an almost mischievous look on his tattooed face. "You have seen already that Saffi do poorly with etquis spice."

"But—" Robin began.

"Just find the damn keys," I cut him off. "We'll find the damn vehicle. Come on, Bubloo."

Robin was right about the fake badgemen not wanting to herd their captives any farther than they had to. Still, I had to admire the sheer chutzpah involved in parking their van on the walkway right outside the building entrance. With speed and convenience at the top of their minds, they'd left it unlocked, and I had Bubloo and Selene inside and belted in when Robin arrived with the keys. I offered to drive, accepted his blunt refusal without argument, and half a minute later he'd backed us along the grass and onto the street and we were off.

Which left just one final, nagging mystery.

Robin gave voice to it first. "So where's this line of trouble you said was waiting?" he asked.

"Good question," I said, studying the view in the side mirror. The van had been an obvious target, parked by the building entrance the way it was. *Someone* out there should have had time to at least try to disable it. "I had it on good authority that they were there. Apparently, my source was wrong."

"This source being . . . ?"

"It was me," Selene spoke up from the back seat beside Bubloo. "I thought I smelled hunters."

Robin gave a little snort. "Really. So what exactly do hunters smell like? As opposed to random citizens?"

"Well, you can start with weapons," I said. "Most ordinary citizens don't carry them."

"Right." Robin took his eyes off the road long enough to throw me a suspicious sideways glance. "Just because I'm a doctor doesn't mean I'm stupid. You two weren't taking in the night air over by the window. Who were you talking to?"

I clenched my teeth. McKell and Ixil were still the best sleeve cards we had, and I had no intention of giving them up without a seriously good reason. "I don't know what you're talking about—"

"It's all right, Gregory," Selene said. "We were talking to a hunter we know. She warned us that others were gathering."

"Of course she did," Robin said with a scowl. "Let me guess. She urged you to get out right now before all was lost?"

I suppressed a smile. As my father used to say, *Sometimes, if you're extremely lucky, your opponent will hand you the alibi you've been hunting for.* "I think you're right," I conceded. "She wanted us clear before the fake badgemen showed up and undercut her."

"Exactly." Robin shook his head. "A word of advice, Roarke: Don't hand out trust to just anyone."

"I warned you about that," Selene added. "I know I said she was all right. But sometimes faint or distant clues take time to register."

I looked over my shoulder at her. She was sitting quietly, staring straight ahead . . . and as we passed beneath a streetlight I saw the fresh tension in her pupils.

Had she chased down the elusive scent she'd picked up outside Robin's building?

"I understand," I said, searching for an innocent-sounding way to draw her out without Robin or Bubloo picking up on what we were doing. Hopefully, she was working on a similar strategy from her end. "And no, I don't blame you. Just one of those things."

"Thank you," Selene said.

"Out of curiosity, what did you smell that put you onto her?"

"Fear."

I frowned. "Fear?"

"Yes," she said. "But don't worry, Gregory. Others may fear the events of the night. We do not."

"I sometimes fear the night," Bubloo said quietly. "The night is darkness and mystery."

"It can be, yes," I said, frowning as I ran Selene's words through my mind. *Don't worry, Gregory. Others may fear the events of the night. We do not.*

It was a clue, of course. The sentences were reasonable constructions within the rules of the English language, but there was a definite non-sequitur feel to them. Clearly, Selene wanted me to dig beneath the surface to figure out what she was trying to say. *Others may fear the events of the night. We do not.*

I felt the breath freeze in my throat, a scene abruptly flooding back to mind. She and I standing in *Imistio* Tower on Nexus Six, listening as First of Three told us his plans for returning the Ammei to their glory days. Selene, using those same words as I was taken away, in order to clue me in that Huginn, Sub-Director Nask's chief Expediter, was ready to work with us against First's plans.

Only Huginn was a man. Selene had just said *she* warned us. And the only human female who'd been in that room...

"A lot of people don't like the night, Bubloo," I said. "I feel that way, too, sometimes. Sometimes, when you're afraid, you just have to circle the wagons and hope."

"Circling is good," Selene agreed soberly.

"That sounds lovely," Bubloo said.

I nodded, my stomach forming itself into a hard knot. *Circle the wagons.*

Huginn hadn't been the only Patth Expediter in that room. There had also been a woman who'd introduced herself as Circe.

A day ago, I'd messaged Nask in hopes that he would send Huginn to run interference for us against the gathering hunters and the Patth Purge agents. He'd sent help, all right.

But not Huginn. Instead, he'd sent Circe.

A woman who, back on Nexus Six, had been ordered to kill me.

CHAPTER NINE

Eastern Blackcreek Street, not surprisingly, ran along Black Creek, a slender, fast-moving ribbon of water that formed part of Pikwik City's southeast border. For part of that length it also formed the boundary between that section of the city and the Ammei enclave, a fact that raised several intriguing possibilities. I was working through some of them when we reached the part of the street Bubloo had specified.

To find a gate and a fence, and what appeared to be a slum behind them.

"This can't be right, Bubloo," Robin said, fingering the steering wheel uneasily as he rolled us to a halt a cautious distance from the gate and the three large and unfriendly looking Saffi loitering beside it. Possibly a normal slum; more likely, given the look of the gate guards, a criminal slum. "This can't be where you live."

"But it is," Bubloo insisted. "Seventy-two Harbin Way, just as I said. Through the gate and a turn to the left." His hand came up and made a swooping gesture to the left, like a child flying an imaginary spaceship. "Four streets to the left beside the creek. Come—I'll show you."

"Selene—grab him," I snapped.

Too late. Before she could get a grip on his arm, Bubloo had popped the van door and hopped outside. Before I could open my door for my own shot at stopping him, he was already past and trotting toward the gate.

"Damn," Robin bit out as he grabbed for his own door release. "Roarke?"

"On it," I said, popping my door. "I hope you kept that Bloove."

"Yeah, got it right here," he said. He pulled the dart gun from his jacket pocket.

And to my dismay he tossed it across the seat to me.

"Wait!" I protested, bobbling the weapon a moment before getting a grip on it. "You keep it. I've got my own gun."

"You really want to go full-lethal out there?" Robin shot back. "Anyway, you're the former hunter who's been trained in this sort of thing."

I hissed out a breath. But he was right. "Selene?" I asked as she got out of the van behind me.

"They're not happy," she warned. "And I don't think the hostility is directed at Bubloo."

Which, by quick process of elimination, left us. "Great," I muttered. "Well, we can't hang out here forever. Come on."

I headed toward the group at the gate, Selene at my side, Robin hanging back a couple of paces. Ahead of us, Bubloo reached the Saffi and waved cheerily at them. "Greetings, friends," he said. "I am Bubloo."

"Be silent, alien," the Saffi in the middle bit out. He wasn't looking at Bubloo, but at us. "You—human!" he called, fingering what appeared to be a three-section nunchaku slid into his waist sash. "Why do you drive a vehicle not your own?"

"Oh, crap," Robin muttered from behind me. "I'm guessing they know the lads who tried to jump us."

"Or at least recognize their van," I said, freshly aware of the Bloove half concealed in my hand. Airguns were generally close-in weapons, but it ought to have better range than his nunchaku. If the Bloove was loaded with vertigo darts, I should be able to incapacitate the whole group before they could damage any of us, Bubloo included.

If it was loaded with vertigos. If the fake badgeman had instead decided to ignore the live part of the bounty post and opted for curare darts, I was teetering on the edge of a triple murder charge. "Doc?" I murmured over my shoulder. "Did you check the loads?"

"I—no," he said. "No, I was driving and..." He trailed off.

"Yeah," I muttered. So much for the Bloove. "All right, we play this by ear. Everyone be ready to move."

"Did you hear me, human?" the Saffi called. He had a grip on the three-section now, but hadn't yet drawn it free. "Why do you drive that vehicle?"

"It was necessary," Bubloo said. "If he had not done so, the badgemen would have confiscated it." He stepped up to the Saffi and lowered his voice. "The *true* badgemen."

The Saffi looked down at him, putting his face in perfect position. Bubloo put his hand on the other's chest, and I braced myself for a repeat performance of the scene at Robin's apartment.

But Bubloo didn't blow into the Saffi's face. He looked up at him, and for a long moment they held that pose. "You understand, don't you?" Bubloo asked, taking a step back and moving to the Saffi on the right. Once again he leaned in, and once again I prepared myself.

Once again, the drama didn't happen. Bubloo held the Saffi's gaze a moment, then crossed in front of the first Saffi to the third of the trio and repeated his plea for understanding. I kept walking, wondering if maybe whatever residual etquis spice was still on Bubloo's breath wasn't enough to drop its victims but could still temporarily incapacitate them. The big question then would be how long the effect would last.

Bubloo finished his final soul-gazing session and turned back toward us. "It's all right, friends," he called. "You're welcome here. Please; come with me."

The Saffi in the middle of the group stirred. I braced myself, deciding that if this went sideways my best shot would be to hurl the Bloove at the face of whichever alien made the first move—

"Yes," the Saffi said in a subdued voice. "You are welcome here."

Beside me, Selene made an odd sound in her throat. "Gregory?"

"No idea," I said. "You get anything?"

"Their moods have shifted," she said. "I don't know from what to what. But they've shifted."

"All three of them?"

"Yes."

"The same way?"

"I think so."

I eyed the newly docile guards as one of them swung the

gate open for Bubloo. Whatever this etquis spice was, it was pretty potent stuff, at least against Saffi. "Let's hope it lasts long enough for us to make ourselves scarce," I said. "Bubloo, how far is your home?"

"Not far," he said cheerfully, beckoning to us. "Come. I have promised you radixiam. Come and taste the deliciousness."

On the ride across Pikwik City, I'd formed a mental image of Bubloo's home as a small, dilapidated shack that no one else wanted. His interaction with the Saffi guards and their obvious disdain for anything non-Saffi had added the likelihood that the shack was set apart from the neighboring houses, where Bubloo would have privacy and no one else would have to interact with him.

Usually, the ideas I came up with in those mental exercises were fifty percent accurate at best. In this case, I'd hit the nail squarely on the head.

"I was fortunate indeed to find such a home," Bubloo said as we walked past the last of the Saffi houses and continued on toward a lone structure sitting a few meters this side of the rippling creek I could see glinting in the moonlight. "I was told that there was a risk of springtime flooding, but here in late summer there is no such danger."

"I'm still surprised they let you move in," Robin commented. "This community seems to be exclusively Saffi."

"They are all Saffi here, yes," Bubloo confirmed. "But they are also not wealthy. The owner was happy to accept payment for the home."

"I imagine he was," Robin said. "What about the others in the community who aren't the owner?"

"What about them?" Bubloo asked. "All have welcomed me with cheerfulness."

Robin threw me a skeptical look. "I'll take your word for it," he said. "But in my experience, strangers and money are a bad combination. It often leads to theft or straight-up robbery."

"Unless," Selene put in quietly, "everyone here is aware of your proficiency with etquis spice."

Bubloo hunched his shoulders. "I don't like doing that, Friend Selene," he said in a low voice. "It's not fair to them."

"I wouldn't worry about it," I said. "It's hardly your fault if Saffi have a low tolerance for the stuff."

"But they don't," Bubloo said. "Not all Saffi. That's what's unfair. I told you the Saffi here aren't wealthy. The result is that their diet is low in certain important nutritionals. There is also—" He broke off.

"The drugs you've been taking?" Robin asked gently.

Bubloo gave a sort of burbling sigh, like he was exhaling under water. "I need them, Friend Christopher," he said, and I could hear the guilt in his voice. "You don't understand. I need them to help me breathe."

"You talking about the dysthensial?" I asked.

"You know about the dysthensial?" Bubloo asked. He shot a look at Selene. "Ah. Yes. You smelled it when we first met, didn't you? Remarkable people, the Kadolians. Yes, dysthensial is especially important. The air here . . . I don't know how to describe it. There are things in it. Before, they weren't a problem. Now, they are."

I looked at Selene, saw the growing thoughtfulness in her pupils. "What kind of things?" I asked. "Allergens? Insufficient oxygen?"

"Something that blooms in late summer?" Robin suggested. "That might explain why it's happening now."

"That could be," Bubloo said. "At first they gave me other drugs. But then I left, and I couldn't get them."

"Who gave you the drugs?" I asked. "The people who brought you here from Belshaz?"

Bubloo turned his head sharply to stare at me. *"Belshaz?"* he echoed. "There *is* a Belshaz, then?"

"We think it's where you come from," Robin said. "Who brought you here, Bubloo? Was it the Ammei?"

"Yes," Bubloo said uncertainly. "Maybe. The Gold Ones were there. I remember that."

I felt my pulse pick up. Finally, we'd made it back to the Gold Ones. "Who are the Gold Ones, Bubloo?" I asked. "What are they like?"

"We're here," Bubloo said, stopping at the front door of his house. "Do you have the key, Friend Roarke?"

"Sorry, no," I said, eyeing the lock. It was a plain tumbler type, and one of the simpler versions. With the right tools it should be easy enough to pick. Without them, it would still be possible, just a little slower. "But I can probably get us in," I continued. "Let me take a look."

"Oh, no—wait. I remember!" Squatting, Bubloo dug his fingers into a clump of smooth rocks filling the gap between the ground and the top of the house's cracked foundation. For a moment he felt around, muttering alien words under his breath. Then, with a triumphal flourish, he pulled out a key. "Here," he said, offering it to me. "Here, Friend Roarke. Would you open it, please?" He smiled. "I was unable to prepare a full meal at Friend Christopher's home. Now, I will cook you radixiam."

"Sure," I said, filtering the frustration out of my voice as I took the key. So much for the Gold Ones, at least on this pass. With the prospect of food on the horizon, it could be a long time before Bubloo circled back to that particular topic.

And I didn't dare push the subject. So far Robin hadn't shown any particular interest in the name, and I didn't want to raise it any higher on his personal radar.

I took a deep breath and fit the key into the lock. As my father used to say, *Patience is a virtue that no one wants to cultivate, but everyone wants the other guy to have more of.*

I'd spent a lifetime cultivating my patience. I was still cultivating it.

I could only hope that Bubloo gave us what we needed before all that patience ran out, and I strangled him.

The house's interior was a depressingly good match for the ramshackle exterior, consisting of a small living/cooking area, a small bedroom, and an extremely small bathroom. The furnishings were minimal—compact couch and two plastic chairs in the living area, a cooker and refrigerator in the kitchen nook, and a narrow bed and nightstand in the bedroom. A couple of large covered storage bins flanked the door to the bedroom, with another bin beside the outside door. The walls and ceiling were old and stained, with random sections of the inner walls either broken apart or looking like they wanted to be. It was the sort of place where the owner not only wouldn't charge much rent, but might actually pay someone to take it off his hands.

But at least Bubloo had been able to assemble enough kitchenware to put together a reasonable meal. The pantry was surprisingly well stocked, including various spices and sauces, plus a bag of the radixiam mix Bubloo had promised to feed us. Before we'd even finished looking around he was at the prep counter, pulling out spoons and bowls and getting to work.

I'd hoped to take a quick look outside while he cooked, but

along with the rattling of cookware he ran a rambling monologue about cooking, the local weather, and the challenges of living beside a creek whose resident frog population could keep a person awake at night. I didn't want to be elsewhere if he happened to sideswipe a mention of the Gold Ones.

Unfortunately, that topic never came up. He finished his prep, and while he scooped his creation onto four plates Robin and I pulled the two chairs over to the couch. There, with Bubloo and Selene taking over the couch, we ate with our plates on our laps like it was an indoor picnic. Between bites, Bubloo entertained us with some more talk about cooking.

Still, the meal was pretty good.

"I know it's getting late," Bubloo apologized when we'd finished and stacked the plates in the sink. "Thank you for your company. It has been long since I've been able to talk with friends."

"We were glad we could be here for you," Robin assured him, looking pointedly around the room. "But I thought you said there would be places to sleep."

"Yes, indeed," Bubloo said. "In that chest, the one by the bedroom."

"In the *chest*?" Robin asked, eyeing the storage bin.

"I'll look," Selene volunteered. She went to the indicated bin, opened it, and looked inside.

And turned back to Robin and me, her pupils showing amusement. "Here," she said, pulling out three wadded sets of mesh, one each green, blue, and red. "Where are the hooks, Bubloo?"

"There are two sets beside the creek, two more beside the walkway," he said, his voice suddenly worried. "Humans *can* sleep in hammocks, can you not?"

I let out a quiet breath. So the wadded mesh were hammocks. Terrific.

"Of course we can," Robin assured him. "I'm told that in Earth ships of old, that was how most of the crew slept for months on end. We can certainly make do for one night. Roarke?"

"Sure," I said trying to sound at least neutral about the whole idea. Hammocks were places to rest, after all, and that was all Bubloo had promised. "I guess—"

"We'll take the ones by the creek," Selene jumped in, the amusement suddenly gone from her pupils. "If that's all right with you, Dr. Robin?"

"Sure," Robin said. "I'd just as soon be close to the door in case Bubloo needs me."

"Oh, you don't have to be outside, Friend Christopher," Bubloo said. "You can sleep there, on the couch. Though it might be less comfortable than the hammock," he added doubtfully.

"The couch sounds great," Robin assured him. "Thank you."

"Yes," Bubloo said, his voice distant as he gazed at the couch. "The Gold Ones sometimes slept on couches like that. Though they called them beds. But they had the same high sides, one on each, and the same at head and foot. Perhaps they *were* merely couches."

"Yes—the Gold Ones," I jumped in. "You were starting to tell us about them. Who they were, what they looked like—that sort of thing."

"What they looked like?" Bubloo repeated, frowning. "Why, like all other Ammei except for the gold scales."

I felt my mental floor slip a few degrees sideways. "Excuse me?"

"The Ammei have scales instead of skin," Bubloo said. "In that way they are like snakes or fish."

"More like pangolins, I've always thought," Robin offered.

"Yes, yes, we agree they have scales," I said. "You said the Gold Ones' scales are *gold*?"

"Why, yes," Bubloo said, sounding surprised at my surprise. "Though I'm sure it's only paint. Surely they aren't born in such a way."

He brightened. "But that's them, not us. Friend Selene, my bathroom facilities are very limited. Would you care to use them first?"

The hooks Bubloo had described were set into the roof beneath the eaves, reasonably well protected from the rain, assuming it came straight down. Untangling the hammocks took a little effort, and getting into them was even more problematic.

The task was made all the harder by the lingering flavor of radixiam in my mouth mixed with the more bitter taste of disappointment.

"All you all right?" Selene asked quietly when we were finally lying head-to-head in our respective bed slings.

"Is it that obvious?" I asked, trying hard not to be nasty. My grand expectations were my fault, not hers.

"It is to me," she said. "The Gold Ones?"

I sighed. What could I say?

We'd already deduced that the portal system had been created and run by a triumvirate of Ammei, Patth, and Kadolians. But during our time on Nexus Six there'd been hints that some other shadowy species was above them, a group of overseers who held ultimate control over the whole thing. The Icari.

Only apparently they weren't real, or at least they weren't their own species. If Bubloo was to be believed, our mystery players were nothing more than an elite stratum of Ammei who liked to impress their minions by slathering gold paint over their scales.

Selene was still waiting for an answer. I supposed I owed her one. "When I was a kid, my dad really liked an old Earth playwright named William Shakespeare," I said. "Used to quote him all the time, at least until he started working on his own sayings. The prose was pretty dense, and most of it went over my head. But one of the lines stuck with me: *There are more things in heaven and earth, Horatio, than are dreamt of in your philosophy.*"

"So there are," Selene said. "I would guess that neither Shakespeare nor Horatio ever expected Kadolians."

"Or Patth, or starships, or portals," I said. "No argument there. The point is that I took that line as sort of a challenge. I wanted to find things that even your modern-day Horatio had never dreamt of. I wanted to push against the boundaries and find brand-new surprises."

"I would say you've succeeded." She twisted her head around to look at me, and I saw sudden understanding in her pupils. "Is *that* why you wanted us to become trailblazers?"

"Well, mostly it was because I was tired of being shot at," I said, running the fingers of my artificial left arm along the hammock's smooth mesh. "But I'll admit there was an echo of old Horatio in there somewhere."

Selene was silent for a few seconds. "Bubloo could be wrong, you know," she said. "The Icari could still be out there. Maybe Bubloo's one of them."

I snorted. "You see anything gold about him?"

"Maybe he's the one who uses gold paint."

"You *smell* anything like paint on him?"

"Well . . . no," she conceded. "But he might not have played that role recently."

"Not with his mind messed up the way it is." I shook my head. "Unfortunately, I have to admit it makes more sense this way. That it was just a cadre of Ammei running the show all along. We humans didn't need outside help to create dictators and oppressive organizations. Why should the Ammei?"

"I still think the Icari are out there." Selene lifted a hand and pointed to a random section of sky. "Somewhere right up there. Watching us and waiting for the right moment to come swooping in."

"You've been reading way too many star-thrillers," I said. "Heroes don't swoop anymore."

Still, just talking with her about it had raised my spirits a little. "Thanks, Selene. You're a good friend. Plus apparently being the Kadolians' only hope."

"At least according to Bubloo," Selene said, and I could imagine the amusement in her pupils. "I don't think Kadolians swoop, either."

"I seem to remember you swooping in once or twice when the occasion called for it," I reminded her. "Speaking of occasions, I assume you had a reason for wanting this side of the house instead of the other? Ixil and McKell, maybe?"

"I *did* smell Pax once during dinner," Selene said. "But he's not here now, so I assume he was just scouting. More important..." She hesitated. "I think one of the Saffi from the van we borrowed passed near Bubloo's house while we were organizing the hammocks."

I winced. A lot of people enjoyed lounging in hammocks, but from a purely tactical standpoint they were about the worst place a person could find themselves in a gunfight. Not only were we hemmed into very restrictive spaces that were impossible to get out of quickly, but our lines of fire were basically limited to a cone directly in front of us. The fact that Selene had set us up to be facing opposite directions didn't do a lot to alleviate that shortcoming. "I trust you're not smelling him now?"

"No, I think he just walked past earlier without stopping," she said. "But if he recognized Bubloo at Robin's apartment and knows he lives here, he might be back."

"No doubt with a few friends to keep him company," I said sourly. "I was just noticing how comfy that ground down there looks. Or maybe I could sneak into the house and take one of those marvelous plastic chairs."

"I don't think that's necessary," Selene said. "I'll smell him before he gets in shooting range."

"It had better be *way* before he gets in range," I warned, wiggling my elbows as a reminder of just how trapped we were. "I'm fresh out of etquis spice to breathe at him."

"Yes," Selene murmured. "What do you think about that explanation?"

I shrugged. "My first inclination was to call bull on it. I mean, a way to incapacitate a whole planet's worth of Saffi that's that easy to use? Pretty sure we'd have heard of it by now."

"Plus, there isn't anything called etquis spice in the records," she said. "I looked during the drive from Robin's apartment."

I nodded; I'd noted the faint glint of reflected light on the van's ceiling while she worked her info pad. "So, something he made up completely."

"Or a local name," Selene said. "*Or* something new to Juniper."

"Oh, *that's* an interesting thought," I said, frowning into the night. "We already know he's been getting into Ammei exotics."

"That's what I was thinking," Selene agreed. "And as far as the whole planet is concerned, he *did* say it only worked on malnourished Saffi."

"And only when you add dysthensial and maybe other drugs into the mix," I said. "So, maybe it's not so much bull as an exotic, one-in-a-million chemical mixture that does the trick."

"Though that then raises the question of how he discovered its effects."

"Maybe he saw the Ammei use it on the Saffi?" I suggested doubtfully.

"Or maybe there's more to it," she said. "Did you notice his ring?"

"That thick black thing? What about it?"

"I don't know," she said. "But there's something strange about it. Did you notice that he moves it from one finger to another?"

I frowned. "Say again?"

"He moves it from one finger to another," she repeated. "When he was cooking he had it on the ring finger of his left hand. But earlier, when he was talking to the gate guards, it was on the first finger of his right hand."

I pulled up my mental images of those scenes. But for once, my carefully cultivated global awareness failed me. "Sorry, I don't remember either of those details. I'm impressed."

"Don't be," she said. "I had more reason to keep track of it than you did. It's Icari metal."

I felt my eyes widen. "Really. Why didn't you say anything about this earlier?"

"Because I wasn't sure," she said. "The night we met Bubloo his scent was heavy with Ammei food smells and dysthensial, which masked the ring-metal smell. It was only this evening, back in Robin's apartment, that those scents had faded enough for me to be sure."

And from that point until now she and I hadn't been alone long enough for her to clue me in. "So what are you suggesting? That Icari metal is somehow part of the magic formula?"

"I don't know what I'm suggesting," she admitted. "I'm just pointing it out and wondering what it means." She paused, and I heard her sniffing the air. "You have a thought."

"Half a thought, maybe," I said reluctantly. "I probably shouldn't mention it until I have a chance to think about it."

"Or we could think about it together."

I sighed. But she was right. "Okay. We've been assuming that the Ammei brought Bubloo to Juniper as a possible replacement for Kadolians. But what if they tested him and realized he wasn't good enough to help them with First of Three's homemade portal?"

"Then shouldn't they have sent him back?"

"That would have been the simplest response," I agreed. "*Or* they could have found another use for him." I braced myself. "Such as trying to get us to link up with him so that when they're tracking him they're also tracking us. Or, rather, tracking you."

"With the ring being the bait?"

"Basically."

She took a moment to digest that. "Two questions," she said. "One, in that case why haven't they already moved in? Their enclave is right across the creek."

"The maps show a thick hedge along the water as part of the barrier," I pointed out. "I didn't see any gates marked."

"But they could still go around or over," she said. "More importantly, why does Bubloo keep moving the ring to different fingers?"

"Maybe it's heavy and uncomfortable and he shifts it around to spread the misery?"

"Why not just put it in his pocket?"

"I don't know," I said. "People with mental issues often have physical tics that can manifest like that. Maybe the ring's his version of a security blanket. As to why the Ammei haven't moved in, maybe they don't want to grab you with witnesses around."

"Which suggests we should stay close to Dr. Robin."

"Maybe," I said. "Personally, if we're going to keep an inconvenient witness around, I'd rather it be someone who's better armed."

"Like McKell or Ixil?"

"I could live with that." I frowned as my phone vibed. "Interesting timing," I commented as I dug into my jacket pocket. With the hammock's constraints, it wasn't easy. "I wonder if they're eavesdropping from the other side of the creek."

"No, they're not nearby." Selene paused. "Pax is back, though."

"Good," I said, frowning at the unfamiliar number on the phone's display. I keyed it on and held it to my ear. "Yes?"

"Hello, Roarke," a woman's calm voice came. "Time to come out and play."

I squeezed the phone hard. The voice, unlike the number, *was* familiar. "Hello, Circe," I said, keying for speaker and holding it where Selene could also listen. "We were just talking about you."

"I'm flattered," she said. "Where are you?"

"Safe, sound, and settled in for the night," I said. "Why?"

"Well, get unsettled," she said. "We have work to do."

"Such as?"

"Your two Patth friends are back."

The cool nighttime air suddenly felt colder. The Purge assassins were back *already*? "Really," I said.

"Really," she assured me. "You interested in seeing what they're up to?"

I looked at Selene, saw the worry in her pupils. "Where are you?" I asked.

"Spaceport, one pad east of your friend Mindi's ship," Circe said. "Got one of them in view. You need a ride?"

"No, you'd better keep an eye on him," I said, getting a hand on the edge of my hammock and trying to ease my way out. "I'll find my own way in."

"Make it quick." The phone went dead.

"What are you going to do?" Selene asked as I finally got my feet on the ground.

"I just want to see what she's found," I said, slipping my shoes on.

"*Just* what she's found?"

"I'm not going to kill anyone in cold blood, if that's what you're asking," I said, looking around. "Pax? Come on, buddy, shake a paw."

"He's over there," Selene said, pointing to a clump of reedy plants beside the creek as she eased her legs over the side of her hammock. "Come here, Pax."

"Whoa," I said, putting a hand on Selene's shoulder. "Where do you think *you're* going?"

"With you, of course," she said as Pax emerged from the bushes and trotted toward us. "You might need me."

"What I need is for you to be safe," I said firmly. "That means you stay here."

"With Dr. Robin and Bubloo?"

"And behind a locked gate with a bunch of Saffi who don't like strangers," I said. "And if we're lucky, maybe we can whistle up some proper backup. Come here, Pax."

The outrider came to a stop and looked up at me expectantly. "Ixil, I need to go out," I said. "Can you and McKell keep an eye on Selene? I think she'll be safe here for tonight, but she may have to leave at a moment's notice. I'll be back as soon as I can." I nodded. "Okay, scoot."

Obediently, Pax turned and scampered back the way he'd come. "I'm off," I said to Selene as we watched him go. "Be safe."

"You, too," Selene said. I could see the unhappiness in her pupils, but I could also see that she'd tracked the same logic I had.

If Bubloo was working for the Ammei, and Selene was their target, letting herself be lured out of relative safety into the solitude of the night would be a bad idea. If, on the other hand, Bubloo was the target, one of us needed to stay here and watch over him.

And if *I* was the target, we might as well have it out now.

CHAPTER TEN

The borrowed van we'd arrived in was gone when I reached the street, no doubt reclaimed by its owner before he walked or drove past Bubloo's house. The city maps showed the nearest runaround stand was five blocks away, but I'd only gone a block before I found one parked beside the walkway. Feeding commarks into the slot, I headed for the spaceport.

I spent the entire drive watching and waiting for the ambush I was ninety percent certain was poised to spring on me. It was a welcome relief when I arrived at the landing pad Circe had specified without so much as any of Pikwik City's late-evening motorists running a stoplight.

Circe herself was waiting beside the parked freighter. She'd opened the starboard-bow access panel and was elbow-deep in the electronics inside. Back on Nexus Six I'd noted how strikingly attractive she was; here, dressed in mechanics' coveralls with her hair pulled back in a ponytail, that was still the case.

Though the fact that she was a cold-blooded operative for the Patth did a lot to modify the impact of those physical attributes. "Am I that late?" I asked as I came up to her. "Or did you just get bored?"

"Idle hands are the devil's playground," she said, reseating a final component and closing and sealing the panel. "Most people don't ask questions if you look like you're supposed to be there."

"The ship's actual owners being a notable exception," I said, looking around. "Especially when you look more like a fashion model than a mechanic. Where is he?"

"He just went inside," Circe said, nodding toward Mindi's freighter. "The other one hasn't shown his face."

"Wait a minute," I said, frowning. "Mindi just let him in?"

"Hardly," Circe said. "He popped the lock—Patth electronic magic that he's probably not supposed to have—and went in on his own."

"Did he, now," I said, frowning a little harder. Mindi knew that sooner or later the two Patth would be back, and that they'd be loaded for Kodiak. She wouldn't be in there without making sure the mechanical deadbolt was solidly engaged. Ergo, she wasn't at home.

And when she came back, she would walk in on a Patth killer.

"Did you see where Mindi went?" I asked, pulling out my phone.

"Somewhere east," Circe said. "If you'd wanted me to stop her you should have said something."

"That's all right," I said, punching in Mindi's number. It rang twice—

"This better be important, Roarke," Mindi's warning came in my ear.

"Trust me," I assured her. "Where are you?"

"Why?"

"Remember the two Patth from the port's west entrance?" I said. "They're back."

There was a short pause. "Okay," she said. "I'll keep an eye on my backtrail."

"You'll need to do more than that," I said. "One of them is currently inside your ship."

"Damn," she muttered. "What about the other one?"

"Current location unknown. Where are you?"

"Traveler's Edge," she said. "It's a taverno just outside the port. About three minutes from my ship as the runaround curves."

"I know where it is," I said. "Any good reflective surfaces in there with you?"

"Yeah, yeah, working on it," she said. "Nothing...nothing... damn. There's a Patth here, all right. I think it's one of them."

"What's he doing?"

"Sitting at a table by himself nursing a mug of something," she said. "Trying really hard to look like he's not watching me."

"You're sure he is?"

"Like you said: reflective surfaces."

I grimaced, thinking back to the Babcor 17s we'd taken off the two Patth. "I don't suppose you're wearing body armor?"

"Haven't for years," she said. "There are enough armored hunters walking around out there that I figured the Trollwear company didn't need me to boost their profit margin. I may need to rethink that. You got a plan?"

"Hang on," I said, sifting rapidly through my options.

And not just through my options, but through the whole scenario. Something here wasn't quite right. In fact...

I looked at Circe. She was just watching me, her expression studiously neutral. If she knew or suspected anything, she was keeping it to herself.

So why would a pair of killers break into the ship of one of their targets?

I took a deep breath. This was only a hunch, but right now it was all I had. At least there was a way to test this one. "You have a back door into your ship?" I asked.

"Of course," Mindi said cautiously. "Starboard external cargo hold, forward end. Fake bolt at eleven o'clock; turn clockwise to release. Is that how I'm getting in?"

"That's how *I'm* getting in," I said. "But first I want to make sure you're free and clear. Three-minute travel time, you said?"

"Yeah, but don't worry about it. I can take care of myself."

"I'm sure you can," I said. Which was only partly a lie. She certainly *thought* she could deal with him, but she hadn't seen one of these Purge squads in action. "It's really just a bit of recon I need to do for my own benefit."

"Call it whatever you want," Mindi said. "Just don't get in my line of fire."

"Absolutely," I promised. That one, at least, was one hundred percent truth. "I'll be there in a couple of minutes. Sit tight."

Traveler's Edge was mostly how I remembered it looking on the map. It was decently large, especially for a place right beside even a minor spaceport where real estate was pricey, with an exterior that was distinctive if a little bland. Through the large windows that lined the dining room walls I could see an interior that was trying equally hard not to offend any species' sensibilities.

But since the picture I'd seen had been taken, the building's owners had added something new. Looping around part of the western side was a fenced-in outdoor dining area consisting of ten tables and its own bar, featuring a décor that included wood carvings and real-live flaming tiki torches. Three of the tables were occupied by Saffi, while a fourth hosted a pair of k'Tra.

Unfortunately for my recon plan, the patio and its occupants blocked a couple of the inside dining area's windows. Keeping well back from the place, I walked around the building's perimeter, taking advantage of as much shadow as I could, hunting for a better view. Twenty meters to the south I found a good spot, pulled out my binoculars, and began my survey.

The inside dining room was busier than the patio, but it was hardly overcrowded, and it took only a minute for me to locate Mindi and the Patth. The former was seated midway between the bar and the western wall of windows, while the latter was holding down a table along the room's northern edge. Their relative positions put the Patth at about Mindi's four o'clock, where he technically couldn't see her without turning his head far enough for his sight lines to clear the edge of his hood.

But as she'd already pointed out, the taverno had a lot of reflective surfaces.

For a moment I studied their positions, mentally working out the details of my idea. Mindi had a drink and a small plate in front of her, probably either bread or an appetizer, but it didn't look like her main course had arrived yet. Her phone was close at hand, on the table beside the plate. The Patth had only the mug, but as I watched a server came up and delivered a bowl about the size of Mindi's appetizer plate. The Patth said something, the server responded, and as the server headed back to the bar the Patth picked up a spoon and dipped it into the bowl. Tentative conclusion: neither of them had plans to leave any time soon.

I could work with that. Taking one last look, I pulled out my phone and punched in Mindi's number.

Through the window I watched her retrieve the phone and key it on. "You call me away before my steak gets here, and you're *really* going to owe me," she warned.

"Wouldn't dream of it," I assured her. "Feel like a little talk and tell?"

"Sure."

"Great," I said. "I want you to say *Where are you?* into the phone, just loud enough for your dining companion to hear. Then look to your nine and say *Okay—I see you.* Turn back forward and say *Okay, but I'll be another hour.* After that hang up or improvise, your choice."

"Got it. When?"

I focused my binoculars on the Patth. "Whenever you're ready."

She launched into the exact sort of low-key, one-sided conversation that I'd hoped for. A couple of exchanges, and then she said the magic words. "So where exactly are you?" She paused half a second, then turned to her left and craned her neck. "Yeah. Okay—I got you."

And just as I'd hoped, the Patth turned a little to his left, just far enough to look along Mindi's sight line at her supposed conversational partner. He held the pose two seconds, then returned to his mug and bowl.

Mindi spouted off a couple more lines, just to make it sound good, then dropped the script. "Well?" she asked.

"He looked, all right," I confirmed. "I'm pretty sure that means he's not so much looking to kill you as he is watching you. Probably hoping you'll lead him to either Selene or me."

"Yeah, I'm okay with that," she said.

"Glad to hear it," I said. "Go ahead and finish your dinner. When you leave, make your approach to your ship from the south instead of the east. Hopefully, I'll have it cleared by then. If not, I'll meet you two pads south and we'll discuss strategy. Okay?"

"If you think you have to," she said. "But if you're not here by the time I finish dessert, that's it. Got it?"

I smiled at the new bit of script. "Nice touch," I complimented her. "Pins him down until you leave. Enjoy your steak."

"I intend to."

I hung up and punched Circe's number. "Any movement from our impulse shopper?" I asked when she picked up.

"No, he's still inside," she said, and I could hear the frown in her voice. "So he's an impulse shopper now? Your message to Sub-Director Nask said he was an Uroemm family Purge assassin."

"I'm not so sure anymore," I said, heading back to my run-around. So it was a family named Uroemm who'd caused so much grief on Alainn and was hoping to do likewise here? Names were always nice things to have. "Or maybe killing us has just taken second place to something else. His partner is currently sitting in a local taverno watching Mindi, by the way."

"Hoping you or Selene will show up?"

"That's my guess," I said. "The point is, if he's only watching and not shooting she should be safe, at least for now. Especially if you're willing to run interference for her."

"I think not," Circe said a little stiffly. "Sub-Director Nask sent me to watch over *you*, not some random friend."

"Understood," I said. Actually, if I was being totally honest, Mindi was more a random acquaintance than a random friend. But friend or not, random or not, I'd unintentionally put her in the Uroemm family's line of fire. I had to do whatever I could to keep her from getting killed. "Luckily for you, there are more people out there who want me alive than who want me dead. That should ease your burden a little."

"One can hope. Still doesn't mean I take orders from you."

"I just want you to make sure Mindi gets back to her ship okay. Can you do that without straining your orders?"

There was an audible, definitely overly dramatic sigh. "Fine. But just this once."

"Thank you," I said. "She'll be coming in from the south after she finishes dinner. Make sure she gets in safely."

"Your wish is my command," Circe said, adding an edge of sarcasm to her tone.

"Thank you again," I said. "If you'd prefer, you could go to the Traveler's Edge taverno right now and walk her home."

"Don't push it, Roarke. I trust you're not just going to charge in on him."

"Of course not," I assured her. *Whatever I could to keep her from getting killed.* "Hunter ships always have back doors."

The starboard cargo hold's outer hatch was unlocked, and the hold itself was empty. The bolt Mindi had specified worked perfectly, opening up part of a sectional metal wall and letting me through the aft bulkhead of the ship's engine room.

For a long minute after closing the hidden door I stood

silently, all my senses straining. Wherever the Patth had settled down, he was being very quiet about it.

But there were tricks a clever hunter could use. Still watching the hatchway that led from the engine room to the rest of the ship, I crossed to the functions monitor station.

I'd noticed on our last visit that while Mindi's ship was quite a bit bigger than the *Ruth*, that extra floorspace translated into only three additional rooms. Two of those were extra passenger cabins, the four of them clustered together aft of the main entryway and forward of the storage compartments and the engine room.

The logical place for an ambush was one of those sleeping rooms, the part of the ship where Mindi would inevitably end up. But after my observations and tentative conclusions from the Traveler's Edge I no longer thought that was how our Patth expected to close out their day.

As I'd expected, none of the four cabins showed any power usage or oxygen consumption. Mindi's office, though, a small room across the main corridor from the dayroom, showed significant readings of both.

Of course, the Patth could be playing it coy, sitting in a darkened compartment with his own oxygen supply, waiting for someone to make that exact rookie mistake. As my father used to say, *No matter how smart or devious you are, you'll eventually come up against someone who's smarter and more devious. You should have an especially good cover story ready for that occasion.*

In my experience, though, I'd found that cover stories worked best if you were also armed. I drew my borrowed Bloove airgun—I'd confirmed back at Bubloo's house that it was loaded with vertigo darts—and headed forward.

As was typical in ships this size, the central corridor was long and straight. Mindi had left the ceiling nightlights on, which let me navigate without the fear of bumping into something or someone. But her office light was also running on low, and it wasn't until I was halfway there that I could positively confirm there was indeed an extra bit of glow spilling out through the open hatchway. Alert for a startled face or the muzzle of a weapon to make a sudden appearance, I kept going.

Whatever the Patth was doing in there, he apparently wasn't interested in peeking around corners. I made it to within a couple of meters of the hatchway and stopped. I returned the Bloove to my belt, stroked the thumbnail of my artificial left hand to turn it into its mirror mode, and silently covered the rest of the distance to the hatchway. I listened for a moment without hearing anything, then eased my thumbnail around the edge.

The Patth was there, all right. He was sitting at Mindi's desk, her computer open in front of him, his eyes focused on the display. His fingers were moving slowly, scrolling across whatever file he was on, possibly pulling up a new one. There was a scowl on his face, and I could see his mouth moving as if he was talking silently to himself.

I watched for another moment. Then, as carefully as I'd eased my thumb around the corner, I eased it back. For a moment I continued to stand there, listening to the soft sounds of fingers on keys, wondering if I should step into view and confront him.

But that would eliminate any advantage I might be able to glean from my private knowledge that he'd been in there. More important, I couldn't think of any questions I could ask that wouldn't be met by one or more bald-faced lies.

Plus the fact that if his reflexes were fast enough, I might end up getting shot.

So instead I began retracing my steps along the corridor, walking backward so I could keep the office hatchway in sight. I made it to the engine room without incident, and three minutes later I was again out in the night air with the cargo hatch closed behind me.

I was sitting quietly behind the forward landing skid of the next ship over when the entryway opened and the Patth emerged. Sealing the hatch, he walked down the zigzag and headed away at a brisk walk.

I was still there when, half an hour later, Mindi finally returned. She parked her runaround at the side of the road, gave the area a quick but careful look as she got out, then headed toward her ship.

I saw no sign of Circe. But then, I hadn't expected to.

"How was dinner?" I asked as I left my pool of shadow and walked toward her.

She jerked and spun toward me, her plasmic making it halfway out of its holster before her brain caught up with her eyes and she recognized me. "Bad idea, Roarke," she growled, giving the area another quick scan. "You alone?"

"My Patth is gone, if that's what you mean," I said. "Sorry about the shock. It wasn't intentional."

"Yeah, that would have made for a lousy gravestone quote," she said, giving me a speculative look. "My Patth left the taverno the same time I did. Haven't seen him since. So you really think they've changed their minds about killing us?"

"More like they've temporarily put it aside in favor of surveillance and intel," I said. "On a totally unrelated subject, can you backtrack activity on your ship's computer?"

Her mouth compressed into a thin line. "He shouldn't have been able to get in at all."

"The Patth have never been good with boundaries." I gestured toward the hatch. "Shall we?"

For the first ten minutes Mindi didn't say anything, but punched at the keyboard in taut silence. For my part, I didn't dare move, hardly even dared to breathe, as I watched her face go from disbelieving to insulted to angry to furious. "Well?" I asked when her fingers finally paused.

"He got into my files," she said. "My *Burke's* files. The security barriers in that section are supposed to be unbreakable."

"Like I said: Patth and boundaries," I reminded her. "Was it just general snooping, or was he after something specific?"

"Oh, it was specific enough," she said, swiveling the display around to face me. "Recognize him?"

I winced. It was my face, surrounded by a whole lot of my public and private information.

My hunch had been right. Instead of just flailing around looking for my known associates, this pair had decided to let someone else do all that legwork. "I usually take better pictures than that," I said. "Is that my Burke's file?"

"Yes," she said. "Which means it's pretty much everything anyone's got on you."

"You work for such wonderful people," I said, running my eyes down the data lists. "It doesn't happen to mention who put out the post on me, does it?"

"That's the strange part," she said, swiveling the display back around. "It doesn't."

"I'd think that would be near the top of any Burke's listing."

"You would, wouldn't you?" she agreed. "But it's not." She

tapped a spot on the display. "What *is* here is your current location, courtesy—at least officially—of me."

"Let me guess. I'm on Juniper?"

"Nope," she said. "Which is yet another weird bit. After all the
work you did to tag Xathru, you'd think the Path would want to
point hunters back here. But he didn't. He pointed them to Niskea."

I felt my eyes widen. *"Niskea?"*

"Specifically, the Yellowdune ruins." Her eyebrows went up a
millimeter. "I gather from your reaction you know the place?"

"A little," I said, feeling the ground once again shifting under my
feet. Niskea was where Nicole Schlichting and I had had a run-in
with another set of bounty hunters. "Remember the government
project I told you Selene and I used to work for?"

"The one hunting alien artifacts? Sure. Is Yellowdune where
you found some of them?"

"We didn't, no," I said. "But someone else might have. The
last time we were there the Path were poking around the area." I
shrugged. "But then, they were poking around a lot of places, so
who knows?"

"Not me, anyway," Mindi said. "What I don't get is the *why.* This
can't possibly affect you, not with Niskea a solid twelve-day flight
away. No one who's already here is going to bother with it." Her
face seemed to harden a little more. "Unless they're trying to make
me look bad. Deliberately posting a false tip is a serious charge."

"I doubt that's their plan," I assured her. "But maybe it's not as
pointless as it looks. On paper, no one who's already focused on
Xathru is going to bother with Juniper, either. Yet I have it on good
authority that we had to drive through a pack of hunters earlier today."

"Really. How many hunters, exactly, to a pack?"

"Don't be snide," I chided mildly. "And I don't know how many
were there. I never actually saw—oh. Of course."

"Of course what?"

"Circe," I said, the name tasting a little sour on my tongue as
the pieces fell together. "She was right there."

"Who's Circe?"

"Our guardian angel du jour," I told her. "Commas to commarks
she's the one who cleared out our backtrail for us. Impressive."

"Only if they were actually hunters," Mindi said. "I checked
the planetary control entrance records earlier, and there aren't a
lot of them on Juniper at the moment."

"Really," I said, frowning. "If they weren't hunters, who *were* they?"

"Probably local thugs," she said. "You run a bounty high enough and they come oozing out of the baseboards, figuring they can pay the dues and get official once they've got the target in hand."

I shook my head. "That wasn't how things worked in my day."

"In *your* day?" she echoed mockingly. "That was all of, what, seven years ago?"

"Closer to seven and a half."

"Whatever," she said. "I hate to break it to you, but the field was just as crowded with amateurs then as it is now. It's just that most of them were so incompetent that you usually finished your hunt and were gone before they even made it onto the scene. But trust me, they were there."

"I'll take your word for it," I said, eyeing her closely as a new thought suddenly occurred to me. "You *did* say you had your license, right?"

Her eyes narrowed. "Yes. I should also mention that Burke's takes a dim view of their employees hunting while on the payroll."

"Probably something most people aren't aware of. Good to know." I stood up. "Well, it's late. You should get to bed, and I should get back to Selene." I paused, something cold suddenly running up my spine. "You said my file had everything about me?"

"Pretty much," she said. "Anything in particular you're ashamed of?"

"Several things," I said. "Did it list my past associates and contacts?"

"It did," she said, eyeing me closely. "And yes, my name is in there."

I braced myself. "Is my father's?"

"Sir Nicholas Roarke?" she asked, her eyes narrowing a little more. "Yes."

I nodded, trying to work moisture into a suddenly dry mouth. "Thanks," I said. "And thanks for an interesting evening."

"Any time," she said, still gazing hard at me as she also stood. "Come on, I'll walk you out."

"Very chivalrous of you," I said as we headed aft.

"Chivalrous, hell," she retorted. "I just want to lock the deadbolt behind you."

❖   ❖   ❖

Selene was awake when I returned to Bubloo's house, lying in her hammock and breathing with a slow, rhythmic sampling of the air. Crouching a few meters away were Pix and Pax, one at each end of the house, clearly on sentry duty. I greeted the outriders quietly, told them they could leave, and added a message to Ixil thanking him for watching over Selene. They gave acknowledging squeaks and scampered away toward the creek as I once again navigated my way into my hammock.

"Did you find Circe?" Selene asked quietly when I was finally settled.

"Circe, Mindi, and a whole lot of interesting stuff," I told her. "Settle in—you're going to love this."

She lay silently while I ran her through the evening's activities. "So you don't think the two Patth were sent here to kill us?" she asked when I'd finished.

"If the Uroemm family are the ones who went after Galfvi on Alainn, they may very well have been," I said. "But it certainly reads like they've had second thoughts. You have to admit that two million commarks—double that if they can grab both of us—is a pretty tempting number."

"The question is whether it's tempting enough to defy their family for," Selene said. "Did Circe give you any more details?"

"About the family?" I shook my head. "No. I'm actually kind of surprised she opened up far enough to drop their name. But then, I get the sense that Nask doesn't much care for the family and that the feeling is mutual. Pointing hunters to the Yellowdune ruins Nask's people were working, for starters, is just plain petty."

"*If* they're the ones who posted that," she cautioned. "We don't know that for sure. What's our next move?"

"Good question," I admitted. "First priority is still to find out what Yiuliob knows about Juniper's alleged full-range portal and hopefully use that data to find the thing ourselves. That means getting into the Ammei enclave and sifting through their records, which probably means hitting up Bubloo for his private route into the place."

"Though he may only be going to whatever fields or greenhouses they have," Selene pointed out. "The records we're looking for will be someplace more secure."

"I know," I said. "But the first step is still to get past the hedges and fences and all the rest of their first-line security."

"True." Selene paused. "What do you think about contacting your father? If he's here with Prucital and Rozhuhu, he may be negotiating with Yiuliob. If he is, they presumably will be letting him into the enclave."

"And you think we might be able to piggyback on his route?"

"Or at least see if there are any gaps in their security we can exploit."

I chewed at my lip. "I don't know, Selene. He may be negotiating, but he may be here for some other reason entirely. We don't know what that is, and we don't know whose side he's on. We pop our heads up, we might get them taken off at the collarbone."

"I can't see your father putting us in danger, no matter which side he's on."

"It wouldn't necessarily be his choice." I held up a hand. "Okay, look," I added quickly to forestall further argument. "It's been a very busy day, we're both tired, and things always look different after you've had some sleep. At the very least, we're going to want to spend a few days poking around the enclave and looking for our best way in. Once we've done all that, we can think about whether or not to bring in my father."

"What if he finishes his job earlier?"

"I don't think he will," I said. "He's the slow and steady type, and Ammei politics are a Gordian-class mess. We can keep an eye on his yacht, too, see if it looks like it's getting fueled or otherwise prepping to leave." I considered. "Actually, I'll bet it's in view of Mindi's security cameras. I can ask her to watch it for us."

"I'm sure she'll be happy to do us another favor," Selene murmured.

"Well, we may have to actually buy this one," I conceded. "Again, let's table this and revisit in the morning. Okay?"

"All right," Selene said, and I could visualize the tension fading from her pupils. She didn't like us arguing any better than I did. "Sleep well, Gregory."

"I will," I said, shifting my shoulders and hoping I wasn't lying to her. I hadn't slept in a hammock since my father took me camping that one and only time, and those memories were definitely not among my most cherished. "You, too."

❖   ❖   ❖

Still, as my father used to say, *If you're tired enough, you can sleep across the top of a chain-link fence.* I was definitely tired enough, and to my relief I dropped off almost instantly.

I'd hoped to get in six or seven hours of sleep. Instead, I got just over five.

"Roarke!" Robin's voice hammered into my ears, his hand squeezing and shaking my upper left arm. "Roarke, wake up."

"Yeah, I'm awake," I answered in a slightly slurred voice, wondering if he realized just how close he'd gotten to getting shot. I'd tucked the Bloove under my left forearm before falling asleep, and my right hand was already closed around the grip when I made it back to full consciousness. To my right, dawn was well on its way to coloring the Juniper sky. "What is it?"

"It's Bubloo," Robin said, his tone a mix of anger and guilt. "He's gone."

CHAPTER ELEVEN

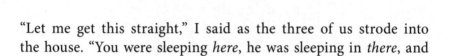

"Let me get this straight," I said as the three of us strode into the house. "You were sleeping *here*, he was sleeping in *there*, and somehow he waltzed past you without you even noticing?"

"Who says he waltzed past *me*?" Robin bit back as he and I stopped in the middle of the common room. Selene, for her part, continued on to the bedroom. "The bedroom's got a window, you know. Who says he didn't climb out that way and waltz past *you*?"

I took a deep breath, forcing away the sleep-fogged anger and trying for calm and understanding. It wasn't like Robin was the only one who knew of Bubloo's fondness for disappearing acts. "Selene?" I called.

"There's no sign of anyone else having been here," she said as she returned to the common room. "I think he left of his own volition."

"At least he wasn't kidnapped from under our collective nose," I said. "So where would he go in the middle of the night?"

Robin snorted. "Where else? To buy more of his drugs."

"Or perhaps to get food," Selene said. "The Ammei street stand won't be open yet, but we think he's got a private way inside the enclave. Predawn darkness would be an optimum time for that."

I felt a stirring of hope. And if that was where he'd gone, his scent should be fresh enough for Selene to follow. To find him *and* his secret entrance. "The point is that we need to find him," I said, heading back toward the door. "Let's go."

"And let's make it fast," Robin added, falling into step beside me. "As soon as the Ammei wake up, the secrecy part goes away." He threw an odd look over his shoulder at Selene. "I guess we'll see if Bubloo's stories about Kadolians are true."

"I guess we will," I said, stepping out onto the street. This neighborhood, at least, was already awake, with quite a few Saffi out and about. Briefly, I wondered if we might run into the fake badgemen from Robin's apartment, then put it out of my mind. I had their airgun, and if they got in my way I was more than willing to empty the whole magazine into them. "Which way, Selene?"

I didn't know what vague and probably half-fictional stories Bubloo had told Robin about Kadolians, but it was quickly clear that the good doctor hadn't really believed any of them. I could see the growing disbelief in his expression as Selene led the way down the street, occasionally pausing to sniff the top of a fence or crouching to sample one of the walkway's uneven concrete slabs. Mostly, though, she just strode along as if this was something she did every day.

Depending on which specific day you were talking about, it was.

We'd taken a zigzag path through the neighborhood to a point four blocks from Bubloo's house when Selene finally came to a halt. "There," she said, pointing to a squat building that was larger than Bubloo's but if anything looked even more ramshackle. "That's where he went."

Robin made a rumbling sound in his throat. "If that's where he's been getting his drugs—"

"Then we pay the nice gentlemen for their product and take Bubloo home," I said firmly. "Or were you thinking I should start a gunfight with all of us in the middle?"

"No, you're right," Robin said reluctantly. "I'm sorry. It's just... I'm getting so tired of this."

"No argument here," I assured him. "But charging in on criminal activity with weapons hot is generally considered stupid unless there are no other options."

"Which might turn out to be the case here," Selene warned,

still sniffing. "The false badgemen from your apartment have also been here."

I sighed. As my father used to say, *The real world is where plans and options go to die.* "Okay," I said, getting a firm grip on the Bloove currently tucked out of sight inside my jacket. "Let's go."

It took thirty seconds and three firm sets of knocks before the door finally swung open to reveal a tired-looking Saffi female. "Yes, it is you," she said before any of us could speak. "I knew it would be. They are gone."

"Who are?" I asked, looking past her shoulder. The visible parts of the room behind her seemed unoccupied.

"My sons." She paused. "And your friend."

"You mean Bubloo?" Robin asked.

"The alien came to them earlier," the Saffi said. "He offered to return their weapon. But they had already seen the post. They put him in a vehicle and took him away."

"Wait a minute," Robin said, sounding confused. "What post? Are you saying there's a *bounty* on him?"

"Not a bounty." She closed her eyes, which I'd heard was typical of Saffi trying to recall memories. "He is a *person of interest.*"

"*Damn,*" Robin bit out. "What the hell—?"

"Yeah, hold that thought," I said, pulling out my phone and punching in Mindi's number. If she'd delayed her bedtime much past my departure, I knew, she wasn't going to be happy about being dragged out of bed at this hour. But there was nothing I could do about that.

Sure enough. "Roarke?" she demanded when she finally came on. "You have any idea what time it is?"

"Yes, and I haven't had enough sleep, either," I said. "Sorry, but this is important. An alien named Bubloo, possibly a Pakenrill. What kind of post is out on him?"

"You can't check this stuff yourself?"

"I don't have the real-time access you do," I said. "I'm told he's listed as a person of interest. I need to confirm, and also a quick refresher on the rules for that classification."

"Good luck on that one," she said. "POI's always been a pretty vague category...okay, here he is. I'll be damned. You're right: Bubloo, Pikwik City, Juniper, person of interest. Posted three hours ago. Live-detain, one hundred thousand on delivery...well, well."

"Well, well what?" I asked, nodding confirmation to Selene.

"The name on the post." She read it off. "Sound familiar?"

I took a deep breath. "Thanks," I said. "I owe you."

I keyed off without waiting for her reply and turned to Robin. "We should get this out of the public eye," I told him. "Take the lady inside and get everything you can about her sons and Bubloo. What time they left, what kind of vehicle they were in, where they said they were taking him—everything."

Robin started to object, took another look at my face, and changed his mind. "Sure," he said. "Ma'am?"

The Saffi was probably not as good at reading human expressions as Robin was. But she also got the message. Without a word, she backed into the house. Robin walked in and closed the door behind him.

"What is it?" Selene asked, her pupils tense.

I just gave her a silent look and punched in another number. Two rings...

"I was just about to call you," my father said.

"I'll bet you were," I ground out. "Where is he?"

"Don't worry, he's safe," he said. "Who is he?"

"What do you mean, who is he?" I demanded. "*You're* the one who put out the post on him."

"Actually, I didn't," he said. "In fact, I just got wind of it about an hour ago."

"Of course you did," I snarled. "Did you think I wouldn't find out your name is on it?"

"*Yes,* my name is on the post," my father said with strained patience. "But I didn't put it there. Nor did I put out the post."

"Then who did?"

"I don't know," he said. "As I said, I only found out about it an hour ago. I was still trying to backtrack it when I got a call from a couple of Saffi telling me they had my quarry and told me where I could pick him up."

"And of course you went."

"I know it's early, Gregory, but kindly kick your brain into gear," he said, some frost forming on his words. "Someone went to a lot of trouble to get Bubloo handed to me. Don't you want to know who and why? *I* certainly do. So: back to the top. Who is he?"

I squeezed the phone hard. I knew how glib my father could

be and how earnestly he could lay out a lie like it was truth carved in the original stone.

But for once his words and his logic rang true. It was already clear that Bubloo and his abilities were something both Ammei factions would fight for. If some third party had suddenly joined the game, we needed to dig out every bit of information we could about them. "Like the post says, he's a person of interest," I said. "He might be a Pakenrill from the Belshaz mountains. That name ring any bells?"

"Pakenrill or Belshaz?"

"Either."

"Never heard of Pakenrills," he said thoughtfully. "But Belshaz is the planet that hosts one of the Ammei enclaves. Could just be coincidence, of course."

"Sure," I said tartly. "Do I need to remind you of your opinions on coincidence? I can dredge up at least three quotes on the subject."

"Thanks, I remember them," he said. "What's your reading?"

"I don't know about Pakenrills in general, but Bubloo's something of a mess," I said. "Doped up with various drugs, possibly a collection of legit meds and street offerings. He also has a sense of smell that rivals Selene's."

My father gave a low whistle. "Well, *that* could definitely be a game-changer. You think First of Three is hoping to use him to finish fine-tuning his portal?"

"That's my current working theory," I said. "The question is why *you*?"

"What other options are there?" he countered. "The only other path back to Nexus Six runs through the Juniper enclave."

"Which effectively means it *doesn't* lead to Nexus Six," I agreed reluctantly. "It mostly leads to First Dominant Yiuliob."

"Exactly," my father said. "The same reason First Dominant Prucital and Rozhuhu preferred to travel incognito with me aboard the *Median*."

"The *Median*'s your fancy yacht, I assume?"

"Yes," he said. "The name doesn't reference the mathematical term, by the way. It's a truncated version of *mediator*."

"I wasn't wondering," I assured him, rolling my eyes. He could get pedantic at the most ridiculous times. "So what are you going to do with him?"

"For now, just put him aboard the ship," he said. "I told the two Saffi to keep quiet about handing him off to me. If they comply, Yiuliob and any hunters currently on the job will hopefully keep beating the bushes while I try to figure out the next step."

"Bubloo may have some suggestions along that line."

"I have no doubt," my father said sourly. "Though I'll probably have to wait for him to sleep off whatever he's got in his system."

I frowned. "You say he's *sleeping*?"

"Like the proverbial log," he said. "I'd barely gotten him into the runaround's back seat when he settled in and dropped off."

"Interesting," I said. Especially since the way the fake badge-men's mother had described the scene had suggested Bubloo was perfectly awake and coherent.

Had he taken something that had a delayed reaction? Or had she simply lied about that?

Or...

"You've checked to make sure he's still back there?" I asked, trying to sound casual.

"Please, Gregory," my father said. "I *do* still know how this works. The doors are solidly locked, I can see him in the mirror—uh-oh."

"He's gone?"

"Worse," my father said. "A pair of vans loaded with Ammei just crossed the intersection in front of me."

"Headed where?"

"Toward the spaceport," he said. "And I'm pretty sure Yiuliob was one of the passengers."

I hissed out a breath. "Where are Rozhuhu and Prucital?"

"Don't worry, they're inside the *Median*," he said. "Yiuliob won't know they're there."

"Unless he already knows they're on Juniper."

"I don't know how he could—wait! No, no—*don't*!"

"What is it?" I snapped. "Dad?"

"He's gone," my father snarled, his voice disbelieving. "He just—"

"Who?" I cut him off. "Yiuliob?"

"Bubloo," he bit back. "He opened the door—he shouldn't be able to—"

"Never mind that," I interrupted. "Where is he?"

"Out there," my father said. "He just jumped out into the street and ran."

"So go get him."

"I can't," he said. The moment of shock had passed, and he was back on balance. "I can't turn around or get to a side street—traffic's blocking me. Anyway, he's already out of sight."

"Okay, we're coming," I said, grabbing Selene's arm and hurrying us back down the street toward the main gate. "Where are you?"

"Eighteenth Road and Pakli Arch Street," he said. "You know where that is?"

"We can find it," I said. "We'll be there as soon as we can grab a runaround."

"I'll start cruising the area," he said. "If I see him, I'll call you."

"You do that," I said. "See you soon."

I keyed off. "Bubloo's gone walkabout," I told Selene.

"So I gathered," she said. "But we can't—"

"Hold it," Robin called from behind me. "What's this about Bubloo? He's gone *what*?"

I clenched my teeth. I hadn't heard the doctor come out of the house and assumed he was still inside and out of earshot. "He got away from the person the Saffi sold him to," I said. "We've got a handle on where he is, but we have to get moving."

"We can't go," Selene insisted, pulling back unexpectedly against my grip. "We have other duties today. Remember?"

I grimaced. Duties such as finding a way into the Ammei enclave and digging into Yiuliob's records on their portal search. "That can wait," I said.

"I don't think so," she said, lowering her voice. "The radixiam mix he served us for dinner was fresh enough that I might still be able to pick up his residual scent from that trip. If I delay too long, we may lose that chance."

I squeezed my free hand into a frustrated fist. She could pick up scents as much as a week after the person had passed by, but that assumed something didn't come along to wipe away those complex chemicals. Depending on how deep the stream was and whether Bubloo had had to wade through the water to get to the enclave, Selene's window of opportunity could be severely truncated. "Or we could find him and have him show us the back door himself," I countered.

"*If* we can find him," she countered. "And if we can find him before...you understand."

My fist tightened a little harder. Before whoever put my father's name on that post in order to lure Bubloo to a known location showed up to grab him.

"Look, I don't know what's going on," Robin said into my hesitations. "But maybe we can have this both ways. How about if you and I, Roarke, go look for Bubloo while Selene does whatever the scent thing is you're talking about?"

"Not an option," I told him. "Where we're going it's not safe for Selene to go alone."

"So you go with her and I'll help your other friend find Bubloo," Robin offered. "Just tell me where I'm going and who I'm connecting with."

"That might work," I said cautiously, trying to think. Unfortunately, that would put my father alone with a man I still had reservations about. Not something I was comfortable with. "Try this," I offered. "You two head into the city and help Sir Nicholas with his search for Bubloo. I'll go work on this other thing." I looked at Selene, saw the sudden confusion in her pupils. She knew full well that I didn't have a hope of finding Bubloo's scent on the enclave hedge or anywhere else.

But I didn't have to. If I could find a gap in the hedge that showed someone had gone over or through, that would be enough to at least get me started.

And as it happened, I knew someone who'd been in the hedge area just last night. "I'm thinking the huntsman and his sidekicks would be available to lend me a hand."

Some of the confusion in Selene's pupils cleared. But just some of it. "I should still go with you," she said. "Maybe the huntsman could join Sir Nicholas instead."

I shook my head. "You know how shy Sir Nicholas is with people. It'll be pushing it enough with you and Dr. Robin."

Her pupils gave a little wince, and I knew she'd caught my concern. Bad enough for any Amme who happened along to see Selene and me with my father. It would be far worse if they connected him to McKell and Ixil. "I suppose," she said reluctantly.

"And speaking of shyness," Robin put in, "Bubloo is out there alone and we're wasting time. Are we going, or aren't we?"

"We're going," I said. "You and Selene find a runaround and head to Eighteenth Road and Pakli Arch Street. Along the way, Selene, you can call Sir Nicholas for any updates. I'll head back to Bubloo's place, grab a couple of things, and go do this other thing."

"Sounds like a plan," Robin said. "Come on, Selene. Time to give that Kadolian nose and eyelashes of yours a workout."

Selene nodded acknowledgment, her eyes solidly on me, her pupils troubled. "Be careful, Gregory."

"I will," I promised. "Just find Bubloo and bring him home."

I said my final good-byes as we reached Bubloo's house, then headed inside while the two of them continued on toward the gate. I stood beside one of the front windows, watching their progress; and when they turned the last corner and were finally out of sight I headed out back to the creek. "Pix?" I called softly. "Pax? Anyone there?"

From a clump of reeds came a soft squeak, and Pax bounded into view. On his back, I saw, was a custom-made harness with a phone and data stick tucked into it. He stopped at my feet and gave another squeak. "Right," I said. I crouched beside him, freed the phone, and keyed it on. "I'm here."

"Are you two all right?" McKell's voice came.

"Selene and I are fine," I said. "Bubloo, not so much. He's had a person-of-interest post put out on him, which led to my father, who promised he had nothing to do with the post and then promptly lost him in Pikwik City. I sent Selene and Doc Robin to help with the search. My question for you is whether Ixil's scouting expeditions last night turned up any spots along the Ammei hedge that looked as if someone Bubloo's size might have made a habit of going in and out." I ran out of breath and stopped.

"And if so, you plan to try the back door yourself?"

"I at least plan to take a look. So?"

"Hang on."

The phone went silent, and I turned my attention to the hedge. It was the first time I'd seen it in full daylight, and I was struck by its rich texture. The only color I could see was green, but there were at least a dozen shades represented, all woven together as if eleven different plants had been grafted onto some hardy and forgiving base plant. Near the top, through small gaps in the leaves and vines, I could see some faint metallic glints. Apparently the Ammei had installed a backstop wall behind or down the middle of the greenery.

"Roarke?"

"I'm here," I said.

"Okay," McKell said. "Bear in mind that the hedge is about two kilometers long and the outriders only covered about a quarter klick of it. That said, Ixil did identify three possible gaps, the most intriguing being right across the creek from Bubloo's house."

"Sounds good," I said. "I'll start with that one."

"Hang on—we're not done," McKell said. "See that data stick? It's preloaded with a program that should theoretically grab the relevant portal information out of any Ammei computer you can get to."

"Impressive," I said, pulling out the data stick and eyeing it. There was nothing on the casing that would mark it as suspicious if some Amme caught me with it. "Of course, that assumes they're using standard computer systems."

"I think that's a fair assumption," McKell said. "After all, they sell exotic veggies to the rest of the Spiral."

"Which just means their commerce computers will be industry-standard," I pointed out. "Their private systems may be something entirely different."

"Could be," McKell agreed calmly. "If you don't want our help, you're welcome to leave the data stick and root around in there on your own. Leave Pax there, too, if you don't want the company."

"No, at this point I'll take all the help I can get," I said. "Speaking of company, I don't suppose either of you would like to come along? I'll buy lunch."

"Tempting," McKell said. "But Ixil needs to set up a diversion at the main gate in case you need to run that direction, and I need to go find Selene."

"And Bubloo?"

"Right now, just Selene," he said. "Whatever you bring back, it'll probably be in Ammei language and script. We're hoping it's close enough to Kadolian for Selene to at least start a translation for us."

"She may be able to decipher the script," I agreed. "No promises on the text itself."

"No, but right now it's as good as we're going to get," he said. "If we get desperate, we can always give it to your father to pass on to General Kinneman and his translators."

"Personally, I'd have to be a considerable distance past desperate," I said. "Anything else?"

"Just good luck and good hunting," McKell said. "Remember that the enclave has full track-and-scramble, so even if you find a spot where the phone works, don't try it."

"Understood," I said. "Good luck to you, too."

I slipped the phone and data stick into my pockets, scowling. Between the walls and hedges, the gate guards, the gossamers on top, and the signal jamming below, Yiuliob's little realm was about as secure as was possible in the modern world.

Time to see if maybe he'd missed a bet.

Pax was looking up at me expectantly. "Ready," I said, waving toward the hedge. "Lead the way."

He gave a squeak and ran over to the creek. There he stopped, looking expectantly back at me.

"Right," I said, walking over to join him. The creek wasn't all that wide, but it was fast-moving and I knew enough about nature to know that stepping into a body of water you couldn't see the bottom of was generally a poor idea. I reached him and peered into the creek.

And smiled. Up close, I could now see the line of barely submerged stepping stones that Pax had stopped beside. "Got it," I said, squatting beside him. "You want a ride?"

In answer, he leaped into my open arms. Tucking him securely into the crook of my left arm, I started across.

As my father used to say, *Someday you'll find yourself walking alone into the unknown. When that happens, be alert, be calm, and be resourceful. And don't expect it to be fun, because it never is.*

CHAPTER TWELVE

———— ❖ ————

The current was every bit as impressive as it looked, and even with only a couple of centimeters of water pushing against my shoes I had to step carefully to maintain my equilibrium against the flow. But I made it across without losing either my balance or my dignity.

"Okay," I said as I set Pax down on the narrow strip of dirt between the creek and the hedge. "Let's see what McKell considers intriguing."

Pax squeaked and headed downstream. Five meters later he stopped, turned to face the hedge, and squeaked again.

"Really *was* right across the creek," I murmured, again moving to his side and studying the greenery. At first glance, this part of the hedge didn't look any different from any other part.

But as my father used to say, *Never take anything at face value, especially if you got to watch them slather on the makeup.* The makeup in this case was the fact that one section of branches overlapped the next one over, but with a thirty-centimeter gap between them, front to back, that wasn't visible except from my current vantage point. A little experimentation showed that the next section of greenery inward was only loosely connected to the branches around it, mostly attached to the rest of the hedge only by interwoven vines.

I took a quick look around, confirmed that no one was in sight. Then, setting Pax on the ground behind me, I eased myself into the gap. I sidled to the end of the inner greenery and pushed it farther aside. The next layer of branches was also only attached by vines, and I moved past them. I took another step inward to the next layer and got a grip on the branches.

And froze. Hanging down directly in front of me between my current layer of branches and leaves and the next group inward was what looked like a three-centimeter-thick vine.

Only it wasn't a natural vine. It was an artificial cable, hanging loosely from some tethering point high above it, colored and textured to match the rest of the greenery.

It also wasn't alone. Now that I knew what to look for, I could see more of them, running parallel to each other about a meter apart, hanging in a neat row like the bars of a fence.

They weren't bars. They were sensor cables.

And it wasn't a fence. It was a mousetrap.

I mouthed a useless curse, my mind flashing back to the metallic glints I'd seen from outside the hedge. That observation had naturally led me to the assumption that the Ammei had put an additional barrier inside the hedge to keep out intruders. I'd been keeping an eye out for that metal, as the designers had no doubt anticipated I would. It was only by sheer luck that I'd spotted the more subtle sensor system before I walked straight into it.

Unfortunately, that revelation had come too late. If someone was monitoring the sensors in real time, Yiuliob's soldiers could probably be on me even before I made it back across the creek and out of sight in Bubloo's house. I had my plasmic and the Bloove, but even if I was willing to take things to that level I had zero justification to start shooting. Bad odds or not, my best bet was still to run for it and hope the sensors were simply being recorded for later viewing.

I frowned, leaning a cautious couple of centimeters toward the cable directly in front of me. Was that a thin, nearly invisible line running vertically along its entire length? I took a closer look, this time focusing on the cable's exterior. The entire surface wasn't layered with sensors, I saw now, but only the side edges. Apparently, the idea was to catch a potential intruder as he walked between two of the cables, simultaneously triggering the sensors on each one. Not only would that instantly mark his position, but having no sensors on the front and back would limit the false alarms that might otherwise be caused by birds or small animals moving parallel to the sensor line.

So what was the thin line I was seeing in this particular cable?

Easing my right hand toward it, being careful to stay clear of the side sensors, I touched the line with my forefinger.

It wasn't a line. It was a crack. And not just in the surface, but all the way through the cable.

For a long moment I stared at it. It couldn't really be this easy, could it?

Only one way to find out. Withdrawing my hand, I drew my knife, eased the point into the crack at about eye level, and gently turned the blade.

Without even a token attempt to hold together, the two halves of the cable separated, not just around the knife but all the way from that point downward. I waited a moment, then reached my other hand into the gap and pushed the two halves farther apart. I moved them farther and farther until the opening was large enough for me to fit through. The cables on either side presumably recognized that the individual halves of my cable had moved closer, but apparently the system wasn't programmed to worry about that.

And with no sensors directly to either side of me, the alarm protocols weren't activated. Gingerly, I slipped through the opening I'd made and got to the other side. I paused, holding them apart while Pax came through behind me, then eased the two halves of the cable back together. The gap closed, leaving a supposedly secure and impenetrable barrier behind me.

Sometimes, it really *was* that easy.

The central fence I'd expected never materialized, but I did encounter a second sensor line two meters short of the hedge's far side. This time, the overhead foliage along my route had enough of a gap that I could see that the sensor cables were attached to a shiny metal cylinder running horizontally near the top of the hedge. That cylinder, or rather the one handling the first set of sensors, must have been the source of the glints I'd seen, which had prompted my false assumptions about a fence. Again, no doubt by deliberate design.

I knew from our time on Nexus Six that the Ammei were clever and devious. I hadn't realized they could also be subtle.

Pax and I reached the far side of the hedge, once again emerging through the same kind of disguised gap setup as on the other side. Beyond it was a small field about two hundred meters wide and a hundred meters long, plowed into neat furrows that hosted a wide array of different plants. The field was bordered by a ring of short, three-meter-tall trees, with a narrow vehicle road running between the trees and the cropland. Other, narrower lanes crisscrossed the field itself, allowing access or perhaps marking the edges of various crop divisions. At the far end, the road passed between a pair of large sheds, went through a gap in the trees, then turned left toward the north, where the enclave's residential areas and main gate were located. There were no Ammei in sight, either in the field or on the road. Apparently, the working day hadn't yet begun for them.

Ten meters to my left, half hidden in a barely adequate space between two of the trees, was a small, one-person car.

I frowned. An empty vehicle, in a vacant field, all the way across that field from the exit. Something Bubloo had arranged when he sneaked in to steal his precious radixiam plants? Or had it been left here by some other person for some other reason?

Either way, its presence had now expanded my options from two to three: I could take a partial win and back out of the enclave in hopes of coming back later; I could set off on foot and hope to find computer access before someone spotted me; or I could take the car and hunt down a computer in comfort.

As a practical matter, it really boiled down to the third choice. There was no way I would get very far on foot, and we didn't have time for partial wins.

"Come on, Pax," I said, beckoning. "Let's get this thing on the road."

Which might prove easier said than done, I realized as we neared it and I got a better look. Along with being small, it was also old, its seats torn and several of its windows cracked. There were dents and a fair amount of rust on the body, and a peek at the control board showed a critically low power level. It was possible, maybe even likely, that the thing was sitting here because no one wanted it.

Still, even if it conked out somewhere along the way, it would take me farther than I could get on foot. I climbed in, settled Pax onto my lap, and after a couple of tries nursed the engine to life. We headed along the outer road, passed between the sheds, and followed the road as it turned north. We passed through another stand of small trees, which opened into two more fields, one on each side of the road, each of them about the size of the one we'd just left. Unlike that one, each of these fields was populated by about a dozen workers. I hunched down as far as I could in my seat, but none of the Ammei seemed to notice me. We passed through the fields and another stand of trees and entered another open area, this one with a long forested zone to our right and a line of small buildings and parked vehicles of various sizes to our left. A couple of hundred meters ahead, the road I was on split in two, one branch curving around the buildings to the left, the other disappearing around the forest to my right. Fifty meters past the split were more buildings and roads, apparently the southern edge of one of the enclave's business or residential areas.

But at the moment, all of that was of only secondary importance. Midway down the forest I could see a wide opening in the trees that was flanked by four armed Ammei...an opening I had a sudden sense of having seen before, only from the other side. I hunched down a little further as I drove past, my full attention on my brief glimpse into the area beyond the gap.

Beneath a massive tent canopy, a few meters behind the guards, were two rows of small computer-equipped desks, though only two of the desks were currently occupied. A few meters farther in were six longer tables, this group with not just computers, but also multi-scan sensors, stacks of packaging materials, and neat collections of vegetables and fruits. A few more Ammei were at work in that area, sorting through the array or boxing them up.

And beyond all the tables, I could see a metal dome rising from the ground.

I swallowed through a suddenly tense throat. I'd found the Gemini portal that linked Juniper to Nexus Six.

I drove past without slowing, taking the branch of the road that went around the forest to the right. I continued for twenty meters, then rolled to a casual stop beside the trees. Ahead, beyond the forest, were more of the business and residential areas, with several more roads and a quite a few vehicles in view. I waited a few seconds, reluctantly concluded there was no chance that I would ever be completely out of sight, and hopped out of the car. With Pax at my heels, I ducked into the partial concealment of the trees and headed inward.

The trees were spaced just far enough apart to offer decent visual cover without being a serious obstacle to progress. But here, unlike back at the hedge, the Ammei had installed an actual fence that snaked through the trees and blocked access.

Unfortunately for the designers, they hadn't taken intruders the size of Kalixiri outriders into account.

"I hope Ixil was clear on what you need to do," I muttered as I tucked McKell's data stick gingerly between Pax's teeth. "That one over there is probably your best bet," I continued, pointing at the closest computer desk, currently unoccupied. I waited for all the workers to be looking somewhere else... *"Go."*

Pax gave a soft squeak around the data stick and slipped through one of the gaps in the fence. He scampered across the open ground, keeping low. I watched tensely, waiting for the inevitable shout of discovery.

But the area remained quiet. My guess was that there were enough small animals in here that everyone was used to seeing them, and that no one was looking closely enough to realize that Pax was something new. He reached the target desk, hopped up onto it, and carefully plugged the data stick into the computer.

I huffed out a silent breath. The first hurdle, the question of whether or not the Ammei were using standard computers with standard receptacles, had been passed. The next hurdle was whether or not the program McKell and Ixil had crafted would work with the local software.

For maybe half a minute Pax crouched beside the computer. Then, perhaps responding to an indicator sound I couldn't hear, he pulled the data stick out with his teeth, turned around, and headed back to me.

I watched him out of the corner of my eye, my main attention on the workers. Again, they didn't seem to notice what was happening. Pax reached the trees, slipped through the fence, and stopped in front of me.

"Good job," I said, taking the data stick from his mouth and returning it to its slot on his harness. Scooping him up into my arms, I headed back toward our car.

We were one line of trees away from the street when everything fell apart.

Two of the guards I'd seen at the entrance to the portal clearing were standing by the vehicle, their eyes methodically scanning the area. I managed to duck behind a tree as one of them turned in our direction. Shifting Pax to my right arm, I turned my left thumbnail into a mirror and peeked out.

Apparently, I'd gotten under cover in time. The two guards were still looking back and forth, with no indication that they'd spotted me.

But that grace period wouldn't last long. My best bet would be to hit them each with a vertigo dart and try to get to the car while they were incapacitated. But the alert had surely already been sounded, which would make a run back to the hedge problematic at best.

Still, with at least a kilometer or two of populated enclave lying between me and the front gate, the hedge was my best bet. McKell had said Ixil would set up a diversion at the gate, but unless he was planning a full-on mortar attack it wasn't likely to be good enough to get me out.

So; the hedge it was. Shifting Pax back to my left arm, I drew the Bloove and flicked off the safety.

But it was too late. Even as I pressed the airgun and my hand against the tree trunk and lined it up on the first guard, another car raced up beside them. It slammed to a halt and two Ammei wearing upper-class hats hopped out. They hurried over to the guards, all of them jabbering as the newcomers did their own quick visual sweep of the area. Their heads moved into line with my mirror, and I got a quick but clear look at their faces.

The one in the more elaborate hat was Overseer Quodli, one of First Dominant Yiuliob's top people. The last time I'd seen him he'd been working the portal receiving area, which made it reasonable that he would be the first official on the scene of an alien intrusion. The second Amme...

I felt my mouth drop open. The second Amme was Rozhuhu, my former translator, ally of First of Three and the Nexus Six hierarchy, currently a passenger on my father's yacht.

And it made no sense whatsoever for him to be here.

Maybe I made a startled sound without realizing it. Maybe Pax twitched part of his body that wasn't quite hidden by the tree. Whatever it was that caught their attention, suddenly all four Ammei spun to stare straight at me. "Alien!" Quodli shouted as the two guards raised their weapons into firing position. "Show yourself or die."

I sighed. So much for any escape plan. "Don't shoot!" I called, flicking the Bloove away in a spinning arc that dropped it a couple of meters away from me. With their attention hopefully distracted for a couple of seconds, I pulled the data stick and phone from Pax's harness and slipped them into my pockets. Then, with both hands held wide open, I stepped out of concealment. I caught a look of recognition on Rozhuhu's face . . .

An instant later, he twisted his head away from me and snapped out something in the Ammei language. The two guards raised their weapons a little higher, lowering them only at an even sharper order from Quodli. A second command, and one of the guards handed his weapon to the other and strode toward me. "Stand motionless," Quodli ordered. "Set the animal down."

For a moment I was tempted to point out that I couldn't put the outrider down and stand motionless at the same time. But Quodli didn't look like he was in the mood. So I merely nodded, gave Pax's back a gentle stroke that was supposed to look soothing but was actually me making sure his harness's pockets were fully sealed down, and lowered him to the ground.

The guard reached me and did a quick weapons frisk, relieving me of my plasmic and lobbing it back to his partner. Another pass lost me my knife, multitool, info pad, both phones, and the data stick. He passed those to the other guard, as well, then produced a set of plastic restraints and secured them around my wrists. "Come," Quodli ordered.

"What about him?" I asked, nodding down at Pax.

"Leave it," Quodli said shortly. "Come."

"I can't just leave him," I said, holding my ground. "He's not mine. I can't let him die out here alone."

Rozhuhu muttered something. Quodli ignored him, and for a moment he studied me. "Pick it up," he said at last. "You are responsible for its actions. If it harms anyone, you will answer for it."

"Understood." Stooping down, I offered Pax my bound arms. He leaped up, maneuvering himself into a more or less comfortable position. "He won't hurt anyone," I added as I straightened up.

"We shall see." Quodli gestured to his car. "Come."

CHAPTER THIRTEEN

— ❖ —

I'd thought Quodli might take us back the way Pax and I had come, following the depressing logic that a lonely field would be a nice quiet place for an interrogation and would offer the added bonus of an easy burial afterward. But instead, he headed north toward the main part of the enclave.

There was no way of knowing where we were going or how long it would take. But with Quodli and Rozhuhu in the front seat, the two guards squeezed in on either side of me, and Pax curled up on my lap with his head resting on my bound hands, I was pretty sure the overall hope was that the trip would be quick.

Quodli, at least, had plenty to keep him from getting bored. He spent a lot of the drive talking on his phone, and while I couldn't understand the conversations I could tell from his tone which of them were orders to subordinates and which were reports to superiors.

Between calls he spent a lot of time talking to Rozhuhu. The tones of those discussions did not always sound friendly.

The talking was over, and the front seat had settled into a sort of stony silence, when Quodli pulled us to a halt in front of a three-story building that featured the same kind of sweeping swatches of color that decorated *Imistio* Tower on Nexus Six. I scooped up Pax as the guards moved aside, and was escorted into a small room with a plain desk and straight-backed chair in one of the rear corners. Two additional chairs had been set up, one on either side of the desk, with a third chair in front of the desk and facing the others.

It was pretty obvious the latter seat was mine, but Quodli made sure there was no confusion by personally marching me to it. He gave me a final, hostile look, then he and Rozhuhu strode out. A quick look back over my shoulder confirmed that the two guards were still with me, watching alertly from either side of the door.

I helped Pax arrange himself more or less comfortably in my lap and settled in to wait.

The car trip had been relatively short. The waiting time more than made up for it. I'd been sitting there for nearly two hours, idly looking for a pattern in the desk's wood grain, when the door finally opened. Craning my neck, I turned my head to look.

Leading the procession were two more armed guards, this pair far more lavishly dressed than the ones from the portal area. Some kind of ceremonial garb, I assumed, more fitting for government work than for standing under a tent in the middle of a forest. Fancy or not, though, they hadn't forgotten to bring their sidearms. They stepped to either side of the doorway as they entered, revealing Quodli, now arrayed in some fancy garb of his own. Following him was First Dominant Yiuliob himself, in an even fancier outfit and a hat that was nearly as elaborate as the one I'd seen First of Three wearing on Nexus Six.

Striding in behind them, his plain dark robe in sharp contrast to all the Ammei finery, was one of the Patth Purge assassins.

The latter three strode silently past me toward the desk as the two portal guards who'd been standing watch exited the room, their door-warder duties now assumed by the fancy-pants pair. One of the latter closed the door, and I turned back to the others as Yiuliob settled into the desk chair, Quodli seating himself on Yiuliob's right and the Patth on his left.

As my father used to say, *Always get in the first word when you can, even if that word is just hello.* "Good morning, First Dominant Yiuliob," I said politely. "My apologies for disrupting your day's schedule this way."

The Patth stirred and made as if to speak— "Good morning, Roarke of the humans," Yiuliob replied calmly. Reaching into an inside pocket, he pulled out my two phones, my info pad, and the data stick carrying Pax's stolen computer files. Making something of a show of it, he carefully arranged the items in a neat row on the desktop in front of him. "Your manner suggests you don't recognize the depth of danger in which you currently stand."

"I am, in fact, fully aware of it," I assured him, "and I'm sorry if my words gave you that impression. I was merely hoping to set the mood for a reasonable and cordial conversation."

"Do you truly believe you deserve such civility?" the Patth put in harshly.

"In my experience, reason and courtesy are usually related to how much each party thinks they can obtain from the other," I said. "But you have me at a disadvantage. You know my name, but I don't know yours."

"Nor shall you," he said. "The nagging of that unanswered question will be one additional part of the pain you will feel in death."

"Suit yourself," I said with a shrug. "But since we're all about to have a conversation, I really need to call you *something*. I guess we can go with *Uroemm Family Lackey Number One*."

He gave a small twitch. "What did you say?" he demanded.

"I'm sorry," I said with feigned concern. "Was I not supposed to know it's the Uroemm family that's running roughshod over Patth Purge laws?"

For a long moment he stared arrows at me, his right hand making small twitches toward the opening of his robe. Selene and I had relieved him of his weapons before stuffing him into the freight hauler's hold, but his body language strongly suggested he'd rearmed himself since his return. "Daxtro," he said quietly.

"Excuse me?" I asked, leaning a little closer.

"Daxtro," he repeated in a voice like he was chewing on gravel.

"Nice to meet you, Daxtro of the Patth." I looked back at Yiuliob, who was watching our interaction closely. "My apologies for the delay, First Dominant, but I thought we should clear that up."

"And that you should remind me that the arm of the Patthaaunutth Director General is long?" he asked pointedly. "You are perhaps not as subtle or clever as you think."

"Yes, others have made that same observation," I agreed. "The point still needed to be made."

"Consider it so," Yiuliob said. "Also consider that I have no need to fear the Patthaaunutth, Roarke of the humans. Once I have Nexus One and all our goals have been achieved, even they will cower in fear before me."

"I'm sure they will," I assured him. This was the first I'd heard about anything called Nexus One. Still, in retrospect, I should have realized that if there was a Nexus Six the integer count was likely to continue in both directions. "When will that be, again?"

"When I have Selene of the Kadolians," he said. "Where is she?"

I'd known that question would be coming my way sooner or later. Even so, there was a deeper and darker anticipation in Yiuliob's manner than I was prepared for. "No idea," I told him. "Off somewhere."

"You lie," Daxtro accused. "She is with you. She is always with you."

"Except when she's doing something else," I said. "I like your soldiers' armbands, by the way, First Dominant. I believe I've seen them before."

"On Popanilla, I presume," Yiuliob said.

"Yes, I think that's right," I agreed. "I have to say that, as prisons go, Shiroyama Island didn't seem too bad."

"Then you have never suffered the shame of defeat," Yiuliob bit out. "Nor have your—" He broke off, visibly pulling himself back together. "That is the past," he said more calmly. "Who is Bubloo?"

I frowned. *That* one I hadn't anticipated. "What are you asking *me* for?" I countered. "*You're* the one who brought him to Juniper."

"Why do you say that?" Yiuliob asked.

Cat toying with mouse? Or a legitimate question? I looked at Quodli and Daxtro, but neither of them was giving anything away. "I'm told there's no record of his arrival on Juniper via regular transport," I said. "That leaves either a private ship or your portal."

"*Our* portal?" Yiuliob asked.

I felt my stomach tighten as I belatedly saw the full implications of both his question and Bubloo's unexplained appearance on Juniper. "The Gemini portal here in your enclave, yes," I said, trying to sound like I hadn't caught anything else from his question.

Because if Bubloo had actually come in via the suspected full-range portal, he had suddenly become a far more important target than even Selene.

Which raised the question of why the post Mindi had told

me about was only offering a hundred thousand commarks. Did whoever was behind it not realize Bubloo's true value?

"I really don't know much about him," I continued. "He uses or abuses several drugs, his attention span is iffy at best, and he drives his xenopsychiatrist crazy. Species-wise, he may be a Pakenrill, but that hasn't been officially established."

Yiuliob looked at Quodli. "Overseer?"

"Searching, First Dominant," Quodli said, pulling out his info pad and working the keypad. He peered at the display, then handed the device to Yiuliob. "A Pakenrill," he said.

For a few seconds Yiuliob gazed at the info pad. He asked Quodli a question, got what sounded like a negative in reply. "Perhaps we can find a better picture," he said, switching back to English as he handed Quodli back the info pad. "Where is Selene of the Kadolians?"

"I already told you I don't know." I nodded to the phone beside him. "If you'd like, I can call and ask her."

Daxtro stirred. "We waste time, First Dominant," he muttered.

"I also suggest that if you want Selene of the Kadolians alive, we continue this conversation without Daxtro of the Patth," I added. "The Uroemm family wants her dead, and Daxtro's here to carry out that wish."

"He also wishes *you* dead, Roarke of the humans," Yiuliob said calmly. "Yet he has agreed to refrain from his mandate until Juniper Glory has achieved our purpose."

"Really," I said. "He told you that, did he?"

"You doubt the word of a Patthaaunutth?" Daxtro demanded.

"I doubt *your* word, anyway," I told him. "I've seen the Uroemm family in action—"

I broke off as Yiuliob suddenly raised his hand for silence. In the new stillness I heard the faint hum as my phone vibrated against the desktop. Yiuliob let it vibe one more time, then looked past my shoulder and motioned the two guards forward.

"It's probably a junk call," I warned. "I get people all the time trying to sell me insurance."

"Come," Yiuliob ordered, beckoning me forward as the two Ammei guards stopped beside my chair. I stood up and walked to the desk, Pax nestled in my arms, the guards close on either side of me. "You will tell her where you are," Yiuliob said, his voice dark. "You will tell her your life depends on her cooperation. If she surrenders, you both live." Daxtro stirred, but didn't speak. "If she doesn't," Yiuliob continued, "you both die."

"Understood," I said, my heart picking up its pace. This was it. "That button—right there—is for speaker."

He eyed me closely for one more vibe, then keyed on the phone. "Selene?" I called toward it. "Everything all right?"

"Afraid Selene's not taking calls at the moment," Mindi's voice came. "Where are you, Roarke?"

It took me a moment to find my voice. *Mindi?* "In a small room with four Ammei and a Patth," I said carefully. Because according to the display I was reading upside down, this call was coming from Selene's phone. "Has something happened to Selene?"

"No, no, Selene's fine," Mindi assured me. "She's right here with me, in fact."

"Great," I said. "Can I talk to her?"

"In a minute," Mindi said. "You see, Roarke, I had a long think last night and decided life's too short to pass up a two-mil bounty when it's just sitting there looking at you."

I felt a chill run up my back. "Meaning?"

"Meaning I decided today would be Christmas," she said. "You said you were with some Ammei and a Patth? Any of them in a position to make a deal?"

"I am First Dominant Yiuliob of the Juniper Ammei," Yiuliob spoke up. "Identify yourself."

"My name's Mindi," she said. "I assume you're holding Mr. Roarke?"

"I am."

"Good," Mindi said. "Here's my offer. As I'm sure you know by now, there's a two-million-commark live-detain bounty on him. I'm willing to take him off your hands for two point five."

"No," Daxtro said before Yiuliob could answer.

"Who's that, the Patth?" Mindi asked. "Hello, Patth. Are you in charge, or is the Amme?"

"I am in charge," Yiuliob said firmly. "I make you a counteroffer. I will keep Roarke of the humans and you will give me Selene of the Kadolians for two million commarks."

"What, two mil even?" Mindi snorted. "You're kidding. Why should I deal with you when I can get the same price from the buyer?"

"The buyer may be distant," Yiuliob pointed out. "I am here."

"That's okay—I like to travel. Besides, I want to see who exactly this mysterious buyer is."

"Here's an idea," I spoke up. "While you two haggle, let me talk to Selene."

"*After* we make the deal," Mindi said. "Not before. Well?"

"You offer a larger sum for Roarke of the humans than the buyer will pay," Yiuliob pointed out. "How does this gain you?"

"If you played Earth poker, you'd know that two of a kind beats a high card," Mindi said. "If I can offer the buyer a matched set, I should be able to talk the total price up considerably."

"A moment," Yiuliob said. "I must consult." He peered at the phone, found the mute button and punched it. "Overseer Quodli?"

Quodli said something in the Ammei language. "If you're wondering if the phone can be traced," I offered helpfully, "no, it can't. Sorry."

"I did not ask you," Quodli snapped, glaring at me.

"Just saying," I muttered.

"No matter," Daxtro said, standing up. "I know which ship is hers. Keep her talking and my partner and I will take them both."

"Sit down," Yiuliob ordered.

"We shall return with her in less than—"

"Sit *down*."

The room went deathly quiet. The two of them locked eyes, Daxtro standing over Yiuliob, Yiuliob sitting but nevertheless clearly the stronger one. Daxtro's eyes flicked from the First Dominant to the guards flanking me, probably wondering if he could take both of them before they could return fire. I saw his gaze drop to their belt-holstered weapons, doing the math on whether they could get to them faster than he could get to the weapon he had tucked away inside his robe. His shoulders sagged a millimeter, and he silently resumed his seat.

Yiuliob eyed him another couple of seconds, then turned to me and did likewise. Then, he reached over and unmuted the phone. "If Selene of the Kadolians is truly with you, she must speak," he said firmly. "Until then there will be no further talk."

I heard Mindi sigh. "Fine," she said. "Hold on." There was a pause...

"Gregory?" Selene said tentatively. "Are you there?"

I felt a hard knot form in my stomach. So Mindi did indeed have her. "I'm here, Selene," I said. "What's going on?"

"I'm sorry, Gregory," Selene said. "She came up behind me and I...I just didn't see her in time, that's all."

"It's all right," I said, keeping my voice low and soothing. So Mindi had sneaked up behind her, had she? As a story and an excuse it sounded reasonable enough.

Except that it wasn't even close. Selene didn't depend on sight for detection and evasion. With her sense of smell, even facing into the wind she'd have known Mindi was coming up on her.

What the hell was going on?

"She says she's trying to buy you back from the Ammei," Selene continued. "Is that true?"

"It is," I said. "And if you ask me, it's a pretty fair deal. First Dominant Yiuliob knows from our visit to Nexus Six just how hard it is to hang onto the two of us. Even without the bonus money Mindi's offering, the offer would be worth it just to let her handle that headache."

"I make a better offer, Selene of the Kadolians," Yiuliob said. "You join Roarke of the humans with me and you retain your life. Or you stay with your current captor and die." He paused. "As does she." He jabbed a finger on the phone, cutting off the connection.

"What do you mean, as does she?" I asked carefully as the guards each caught one of my upper arms and started me walking backward toward my chair. "What have you done?"

"My soldiers are on their way to her ship," Yiuliob said with dark satisfaction. "When they find her—"

I didn't wait to hear any more. Straightening my arms, I tossed Pax in a flat arc directly toward Daxtro's face. The two Ammei guards tightened their grips—

And as Daxtro reflexively flung his hands up to intercept the creature arcing toward him, I snapped the last thread of plastic that Pax had left intact when he chewed through my wrist restraints during the car ride.

The Ammei research that Selene and I had done during the past three months had included a lot about their physiology, including weaknesses that could be exploited in either negotiations or a fight. With the guard on my left still hanging uselessly onto my upper arm, I swung my left hand in a karate knife-edge to his throat, staggering him back and loosening his grip as his lower nervous system twitched in reaction to the blow. The guard to my right twisted around toward me, trying to bring his other hand into play, and was likewise thrown off-balance as my right foot snapped against his right knee and then across into his left. I twisted free from the now faltering grips on my upper arms, snatched the weapon from my left-hand guard's holster, and charged toward Daxtro.

The Patth saw me coming, but with both hands fully occupied keeping Pax's claws away from his face there was nothing he could do to stop me. I slapped the Ammei weapon against his forehead—I'd studied some Patth physiology, too—then tossed the weapon across the room and grabbed Daxtro's right forearm. Swiveling around on my left foot, I pulled his right arm straight, pointed it back at the two guards, and sent a dart from the hidden sleeve gun into each of them. Still holding the arm, I dug under his robe with my right hand and yanked out his shiny new Babcor 17. I straightened, backed away, and shifted my attention to Yiuliob and Quodli. "Don't," I warned.

The two of them were sitting like living statues, clearly stunned by what had just happened. Yiuliob's hand was on my phone, Quodli's on the grip of his holstered weapon. I twitched the Babcor in silent emphasis, and both slowly moved their hands away from their targets. "I *did* warn you, First Dominant, about trying to hold onto me," I reminded him, throwing a quick look at the guards I'd shot. To my relief, they were twitching with the effects of vertigo drug. I'd banked on Daxtro still using nonlethal loads in his sleeve gun, but there hadn't been any way to confirm that before I had to open fire. "Just stay calm," I added, stepping to the desk and picking up my phone. Holding it in my left hand, I keyed it on.

Nothing. "First Dominant?" I prompted, twitching the Babcor again.

"I allowed the phone scramble system to be opened only for one call," he said. "It has since closed."

"Open it."

"No." He inclined his head thoughtfully to the side. "Do you kill me for this, Roarke of the humans?"

I clenched my teeth. But even if shooting him would get my phone working again—and it probably wouldn't—there was still no way I could justify such a thing. "No, of course not," I conceded. "On your feet. You, too, Overseer. We're all going for a ride. Just leave your gun on the desk, Overseer."

"Do you truly believe you can escape from here?" Yiuliob asked as he and Quodli stood up. The latter, under my watchful gaze, pulled his sidearm from its holster and laid it on the desk.

"I think so, yes," I said. Stepping back over to a glowering Daxtro, I did a quick check for other weapons. I found one—the Jinxti plasmic I was expecting—and sent it skittering across the room. "Because just as I won't kill you for blocking my calls, you won't allow innocent Ammei civilians to die just to keep me here. Especially when you'll presumably have lots of chances down the road to reel me in again."

"Do you threaten my people now?" Yiuliob demanded.

"*I* don't, no," I said. "But there are those who'll get caught in the crossfire if your soldiers refuse to let me leave. There will be others who might be trampled in the panic that could ensue during whatever diversionary action my allies deem necessary to assist in my exit." I raised my aim a couple of centimeters. "And then there's you and Overseer Quodli," I added quietly. "You'll be right in the middle of it. And in my experience, the level of soldiers' enthusiasm is too often greater than the level of their marksmanship."

Quodli gave Yiuliob a sort of furtive look. "First Dominant?" he murmured.

Yiuliob didn't answer, but kept his gaze on me. "What do you want?"

"Safe passage out of the Ammei enclave," I said. "A recall of the soldiers you have heading for the spaceport. That's all."

"If I refuse?"

"Then I'll probably die today," I admitted. "You might, too. Certainly most or all of the soldiers you sent will. Worst of all, Juniper Glory will never get Selene, because in all the chaos Daxtro of the Uroemm family will find a way to kill her."

Yiuliob considered. Then, he gave a slow shake of his head. "I cannot make decisions on the basis of terrible consequences that may or may not occur. Do what you must, Roarke of the humans. I will do the same."

I sighed. I'd hoped that the worst-case scenario I'd painted would be enough. Clearly, I needed a list of even more drastic consequences.

Only I didn't have anything more drastic to offer. If Yiuliob's own potential death wasn't enough to unstick him from his stubbornness, nothing else was likely to do so.

But as my father used to say, *Ego, greed, and stubbornness are ninety percent of the levers you'll ever need.* I'd tried ego, and I'd run full-tilt into stubbornness.

Time to try greed.

"Let me sweeten the pot, then," I said. "Selene and I are going to find the full-range portal that's hidden somewhere on Juniper. When we do, I'll give you its location."

Daxtro spat something. "He bluffs."

"No, he absolutely doesn't," I said, watching Yiuliob. "You may not know our record, First Dominant, but Selene and I have either located or assisted in the location of no less than five Icari portals. Let me go, and we'll find this one, too."

"First Dominant—"

"Silence, Daxtro of the Patthaaunutth," Yiuliob said. "How do you think to find this portal?"

"The same way we found all the others," I said, feeling sweat breaking out on my forehead. Every minute I was stuck here was another minute for Yiuliob's soldiers to get in position around Mindi's ship.

And it wasn't just the Ammei who posed a threat. The minute Mindi registered Selene's capture, assuming that was part of her plan, the post would go out marked as fulfilled, which under normal circumstances would take the heat off. But with two million commarks on the line there would be a few hunters who would hesitate only a minute before deciding to ignore professional ethics and try for a poach. Local thugs who got word of the bounty wouldn't be slowed down even that much.

"You could ask anyone who's worked with Sub-Director Nask about my record of keeping my word," I added. Out of the corner of my eye, I saw Daxtro's flash of anger at the mention of Nask's name.

So whatever history lay between Nask and the Uroemm family, it was still fresh enough for a solid simmer. A little something to tuck away for the future.

Yiuliob stirred. "I will hold you to that promise," he said. "And know this, Roarke of the humans: Whether or not you deliver the portal, Juniper Glory *will* one day rule the Spiral. If you have lied to me, there will be punishment such as you cannot imagine."

"Understood," I said, beckoning to Pax. "You and the Uroemm family can compare torture techniques later. Do we go?"

"We go," Yiuliob said. "Overseer Quodli, you will remain and restrain Daxtro of the Patthaaunutth from communicating with his colleague."

"Thank you, First Dominant," I said. "You won't regret this." I nodded toward my phones and info pad. "May I?"

"Your devices remain here," Yiuliob said, watching Pax climb my clothing and settle onto my shoulder. "I will follow you, Roarke of the humans," he added, gesturing to the door.

I smiled and gestured in return. "With all due respect, First Dominant Yiuliob," I said, "I'd prefer to follow *you*."

CHAPTER FOURTEEN

After all the drama of the interrogation room, I fully expected Yiuliob to pull some last-minute trick before we were out of the enclave.

To my surprise, he didn't. He drove us to the archway leading into Pikwik City proper, watched me get out, and waited there until I was outside the enclave.

Of course, as I'd pointed out, he would have other opportunities to track me down. It was also clear that he genuinely believed he and Juniper Glory would end up as masters of the Spiral. I still didn't know exactly how he intended to achieve that goal, but his confidence was more than a little unnerving.

My original plan, before I'd been hauled into Yiuliob's office, had been to call McKell as soon as I was out from under the Ammei track-and-scramble and arrange for him to pick up Pax and the data stick. But that opportunity had long since vanished. Worse, with both phones gone, my two communication options seemed to be snatching one from some passerby and hoping I could send a warning about Mindi and Selene before the badgemen jumped me, or grabbing a runaround and hoping I could get to Mindi's ship before Yiuliob broke his promise and deployed his forces to the area. Or Daxtro broke something else and did likewise.

Having tried out the Ammei version of a prison cell, I wasn't really interested in seeing the kind of accommodations the Saffi badgemen could offer. Luckily, there was a runaround stand only a hundred meters from the enclave gate. Hurrying down the walkway as fast as I could without drawing too much attention, I reached the stand, pulled open the driver's door on the nearest one, and started to get in.

And jerked to a halt as Pax's claws dug briefly into my shoulder. "Pax!" I snapped, glaring up at him as he sent a loud squeak directly into my ear. "What the *hell*—?"

I broke off as an answering squeak came from somewhere nearby. I looked that direction, to find Pix crouched on top of a decorative stone fence that marked the edge of a small park. "Right," I muttered, closing the runaround door and heading instead for the park. Pix waited until we were within a few meters, then took off, running along the fence and heading for the far end of the park. I picked up my pace and followed.

I was passing a line of parked vehicles when the passenger door of one of them abruptly popped open and a hand waved toward me. "Get in," McKell's muffled order came from inside.

I skidded to a halt by the door, nearly losing my balance as Pax shoved off my shoulder and took off after Pix. "I said *get in*," McKell repeated.

"Heard you the first time," I snapped as I threw myself onto the seat. I still didn't quite have the door closed when McKell peeled away from the curb and sent us racing down the street.

"You all right?" he asked, throwing a sideways glance at me. "We were starting to think we'd lost you."

"You almost did," I told him. "And if we don't hurry, we might still lose Selene."

"So I heard," he said grimly. "Ixil said there's a report out that your friend Mindi's called the bounty post on her."

"Mindi's doing *something*, anyway," I said. "Whether it's calling the bounty or something else, I don't know."

"Well, get busy and figure it out," McKell said. "The badgemen channel reports there are a bunch of undesirables gathering at the northeastern end of the spaceport."

I hissed out a tense breath. The section where Mindi's ship was parked. "This the best speed you can make?"

"In city traffic, yes." McKell gave me another look. "You armed?"

"Armed and a half," I assured him, easing the Babcor partially out of concealment beneath my jacket for his inspection. "A part-ing gift from a Patth admirer."

McKell gave a low whistle. "Nice. That a Babcor?"

"Four-mil rocket pistol," I confirmed, sliding it back out of sight. The last thing I needed was for a passing badgeman to catch a glimpse of the weapon and pull us over. "What's the plan?"

"We head to Mindi's ship and assess the situation," he said. "If we can handle it ourselves, fine. If not...let's just say Ixil is planning to be ready with some heavier firepower."

I frowned. "Since when do you carry artillery aboard the *Stormy Banks*?"

"You do what you have to in this business," McKell said. "And for the record, we're not the ones carrying it."

"Oh, well, *that's* clear," I muttered, a sudden unpleasant premo-nition hitting me. McKell and Ixil didn't have access to advanced weaponry, not after getting booted from the Icarus Group.

But my father *was* still working for General Kinneman. And I'd seen his powers of persuasion.

"Let's just hope we don't have to use it," McKell said. "One hates to draw more attention than one needs to."

"True," I said. "But one also hates to see one's friends get killed or kidnapped."

"One does, indeed," McKell said, easing down a little harder on the accelerator. "Ixil should have collected his outriders by now and be on his way. Let's see which of us gets there first."

McKell had said the badgemen were warning of undesirables gathering at the spaceport. For once, the badgemen had under-estimated the situation.

They weren't just undesirables, they were clearly the scum of Pikwik City. And they weren't just gathering, they were launching an unhurried, almost casual assault on Mindi's ship.

"I make it sixteen," McKell said as we sat in our parked runaround on the far side of a heavy cargo hauler one pad over. "Maybe seventeen."

"I see eighteen," I told him, pointing to a Saffi off to the side.

"I think that one's just watching the show," McKell said. "Either way, even considering the low-grade weapons they're likely to have, we're still seriously numbered and outgunned. You notice where they're all looking?"

I nodded. From our current position, watching the assembled thugs beneath the cargo hauler's underside, we couldn't see anything more than a couple of meters above the ground. "They're looking up," I said. "Probably at the zigzag and entryway."

"Yeah." McKell popped his door. "Let's get a closer look."

We got a couple of hard stares from some of the loitering criminals as we headed around the hauler's stern. But so far no one seemed inclined to challenge us. We emerged on the other side into full view of Mindi's ship.

And found out why everyone was looking up. There were three figures at the top of the zigzag. Two were Saffi, undoubtedly locals, busily stuffing what looked like pasty-white bread dough into the crack around the entryway hatch. The third figure, a pace behind them where he could supervise the operation, was wearing a Patth robe.

With his back to us, his face wasn't visible. But I had no doubt that it was the Uroemm family's second assassin. "I didn't know Patth were so good at making friends," I said.

"I'm guessing he's been on Juniper for a few weeks," McKell said. "Working the underworld, passing out commarks, drumming up support. It's not like all the players didn't know you and Selene would eventually end up here."

"Our best efforts to send the hunt to Xathru notwithstanding," I said. "Here's the worse news: The Patth have already unlocked Mindi's entryway once. If the electronic tricks aren't working, it means the deadbolt's engaged."

McKell hissed out a breath. "Which means Mindi and Selene are still in there."

"Unless they've already sneaked out the back door," I said. "But I'd hate to count on that."

"Agreed," McKell said. "What's the Babcor's accuracy at this range?"

I was about to remind him that I didn't shoot people who weren't already shooting at me when I caught a sudden movement out of the corner of my eye. I spun that direction, my hand darting into my jacket—

"Thank the Gold Ones you're all right!" Bubloo exclaimed, bounding toward us like a happy puppy. Trailing a few steps behind him was Dr. Robin, looking like someone who'd been trying for hours to keep a hyperactive child under control and had gotten roundly tired of the effort. "I knew you would come for her."

"Is she in there?" I asked, pointing at Mindi's ship. "Selene. Is she in there?"

"I don't know," Bubloo said, his excitement flipping over into anxiety. "I can't tell." He looked up at the figures working on the entryway and brightened. "If you take me there, I can find out."

"Bubloo, please," Robin pleaded, huffing to a halt behind him. "It isn't safe here—I've told you that a hundred times. We have to leave, right now."

"He's right, Bubloo," I said. "There are bad people looking for you—"

I broke off. Robin's eyes had shifted to something behind McKell and me, and I now saw them widen slightly.

"—and you can't let them find you here," I continued, turning my left thumbnail into a mirror and raising my hand to eye level between McKell and me as if gesturing Bubloo back.

What had caught Robin's attention was a pair of rough-looking Saffi, moving stealthily toward us. Both were clutching Popper 2mm slug guns, a cheap weapon highly popular among low-rent criminals for its size and intimidation factor despite a bad tendency to misfire and a lack of serious penetrating power even when it worked properly. "Poppers," I muttered.

"Noted," McKell muttered back, studying the view in my thumbnail.

"Wait a minute," Robin said nervously, taking Bubloo's arm. "What are you—I mean—Roarke, they have *guns*—"

"Don't worry, we've got this," McKell said. "Roarke, play dead."

I gave him a microscopic nod, held my hand up another half second to give him a final ranging view...

Abruptly, I let my right leg collapse beneath me, sending me into a sideways crumple. Under cover of the movement I snatched out my Babcor, and as my right shoulder hit the ground I rolled over onto my back.

I needn't have bothered. With their eyes riveted on my sudden and inexplicable fall, the Saffi completely missed McKell's spin-and-draw. Even as I brought my own weapon to bear, he sent a low-power plasmic shot with casual accuracy into each of their weapons. An instant and a pair of soft but high-pitched yowls later, both Poppers were spinning to the ground, their erstwhile owners clutching at scorched gun hands.

Bubloo gave a little trilling squeak as I rolled back to my feet. "Oh, my," he said. "Friend Roarke—what did he *do*?"

"They'll be all right, Bubloo," Robin soothed. But he looked a little sandbagged himself. "Those guns are big enough to absorb most of the heat."

"But—"

"That's enough," I cut him off. Four of the nearest thugs, presumably alerted by the muted flash of McKell's plasmic, had turned to look at our little group . . . and while I was hardly an expert on Saffi expressions it was clear they didn't like seeing armed humans standing over a pair of their injured countrymen. "Doc, get him out of here. *Now*."

"Understood," Robin said, getting a fresh grip on Bubloo's arm. "Come on, Bubloo. We have to go."

"But Friend Selene is lost," Bubloo protested. "I cannot just leave—"

"Watch it!" McKell snapped. He fired off a shot, a higher-powered one this time, the hiss of his blast swallowed up in the louder *crack* of a slug gun. "There!" he added, firing a second shot that brushed back another Saffi. With his other hand he shoved me toward a squat power generator a couple of meters away. "You two, get out of here. Roarke, feel free to join in."

I nodded as I dropped into cover behind the generator and aimed the Babcor at a Saffi running toward us. A quiet corner of my brain noted the interesting contradiction that my weapon was smaller than the Poppers yet far more powerful.

Which led inevitably to the question of whether it was too powerful for me to use against street thugs with stars in their eyes and Patth promises in their ears. A proper bounty hunter with full body armor might be able to handle the impact of a Babcor rocket slug. An unarmored Saffi, not a chance.

On the other hand, maybe this was *exactly* the level of power I needed right now.

The Saffi braked to a halt, lifting his slug gun in a two-handed marksman's grip to point at me over the top of the generator. I lowered the Babcor in response and shifted my aim to the pavement a meter in front of his right foot and slightly to the side. Mentally crossing my fingers, I fired.

The material used for spaceport walkways was far less sturdy than the stuff they used for the landing pads. But it was still solid enough to send the slug from a normal firearm ricocheting off into the sunset.

But not the rocket slug from a Babcor. The rocket slug from a Babcor instead drove straight into the pavement, shattering the material, sending a spray of fragments into the Saffi's legs and torso, and burying what was left of itself deep underground.

The Saffi jerked violently, twitching away from the wave of shrapnel. He managed to hang onto his weapon, but any chance of returning accurate fire was now out of the question. He was still reeling when I blasted a second cone of shards from the ground beside his left foot.

This time he got the message. For a fraction of a second he seemed to dither over whether he should drop his gun, apparently decided it was too expensive to abandon, and took off at high speed for parts unknown.

Across the way, two more Saffi crouched into firing positions and brought their own guns up toward our shelter. I gave a mental sigh, wondering as always why some people seemed unable to learn from the experience of others, and brought the Babcor to bear.

And stopped at the sound of a muffled explosion. I crouched a little lower into cover and looked up at Mindi's ship.

While we'd been exchanging gunfire down here, the Patth and his minions had finished their work, retreated to the ground to stay clear of the blast, and triggered the explosive.

And as the cloud of smoke and dust cleared, I saw that the entryway hatch had been visibly warped. One more good explosive kick, and the Patth should be able to pry it open and get into the ship.

With Selene inside.

The ethical questions of taking the first shot abruptly vanished into smoke. I raised the Babcor, centered the crosshairs on the back of the Patth's hood—

"Here he comes," McKell said in my ear. "Cross your fingers."

I threw a quick frown around the area. There was no sign of Ixil, with or without any heavy weaponry. "McKell—"

"You're welcome," McKell said.

And with a roaring whine of thrusters, a small torpedo-shaped object shot into view, burning through the air a few meters above the ground. It cleared the end of one of the nearby ships and resettled itself onto a vector driving straight for Mindi's ship. It was moving too fast for me to get a clear look, but it looked vaguely like a trailblazer's bioprobe.

I caught my breath. No, not just *a* bioprobe. *My* bioprobe. Ixil had gotten into the *Ruth* and had turned one of our sampling probes into a missile.

But it was a missile without a payload. What did he think he was going to accomplish?

Two seconds later, I got my answer. Even as the Patth and Saffi started back up, the probe slammed full-bore into the zigzag where it met the entryway. With a horrendous screech, the zigzag snapped off the side of the ship and collapsed into a heap of twisted metal, scattering the Patth and the others across the pavement.

And with access to the entryway gone, so was the attack.

McKell tapped my shoulder. "Come on," he said, standing up.

I sent another quick look around. A couple of the Saffi were running toward the injured parties, moving in a sort of slow daze as they started to pull themselves together. But most of the thugs had realized that the operation was over, that whatever payoff the Patth had promised had evaporated, and that it was time to make themselves scarce. "What about the probe?" I asked.

"Sorry," McKell apologized. "It was hard enough to block the security cameras long enough to keep the badgemen from figuring out where it came from. There's no way we're going to be able to bring it back."

I sighed. Leaving one last probe from all the replacements Admiral Graym-Barker and the Icarus Group had bought for us over the years. From now on, Selene and I would be on the hook for everything ourselves.

But as my father used to say, *Beware of good-old-days nostalgia. Those days were never as good as you remember them, and these days won't be, either.*

"We need to go before the badgemen get here," McKell said as he headed toward the hauler's stern and the runaround we'd left on its other side. "Ixil says he has a surprise waiting in the *Ruth*."

"Selene?" I asked with a wary flicker of hope.

"He didn't say," McKell said. "But from his tone, I don't think either of us is going to like it."

It wasn't Selene.

And he was right. I didn't like it.

CHAPTER FIFTEEN

"She told me to come here," Mindi said wearily, rubbing her fingertips mechanically back and forth on the dayroom's foldout couch. Whether her subdued mood was due to her interaction with Selene or the fact we'd just dropped a few thousand commarks' worth of damage on her ship I didn't know. "She said she needed to draw attention away from someone, and that me calling her bounty post was the fastest way to do that. For the record, I didn't like it, and told her so."

"But she wore you down?" I asked.

Mindi's lip twitched. "You know how she is."

"Who was she trying to protect?" McKell asked.

"That alien friend of Roarke's," Mindi said. "Bubloo. She didn't go into details."

I nodded in sympathetic understanding. Trying to explain Bubloo and the reasons for the Ammei interest in him would dig way deeper into matters neither of us wanted to discuss with outsiders. "So she wasn't in here with you?"

"Not when I got here, no," Mindi said. "But she *had* been here earlier, before she called me. She said to tell you she'd left a note where only you could reach it."

I looked at Ixil. "Or where only someone I knew could?"

"I've got Pix and Pax running the air ducts," he confirmed. "If Selene hid something in there, they'll find it."

I turned back to Mindi. "Any idea where she is now?"

"I don't even know where she was then," she said. "We did that staged conversation with you and your Ammei friends from separate locations. Not sure what phone tricks she used to make that work." Her eyes narrowed. "So what exactly *did* you do to my ship? I only saw the beginning of the op before Ixil shooed me out of the bioprobe control room."

"The good news is that we kept the Patth from getting into your ship again," I said. I've been told that offering the good news up front could help soften the impact of the rest. In my experience, it seldom did. "The other good news is that you should still be able to get back in the same way you went out."

"How do you know how I got out?"

"Because we know the Patth can hack your entryway code," I said. "The only reason to try blasting it open would be if the deadbolt was—"

"They *blasted* it open?"

"Not all the way," I hastened to assure her. "Just remember that one's on them. On the Uroemm family, to be specific."

"So which one is on *you*?" she demanded darkly.

I raised my eyebrows at Ixil. "Don't look at me," he said. "Selene's the one who suggested using the bioprobes."

I braced myself and turned back to Mindi. "We sort of wrecked your zigzag."

"Lovely," Mindi growled. "Did you at least manage to take down the Patth along with it?"

"Unfortunately, he was close enough to the ground when the probe hit that I don't think he sustained any serious damage," I said. "Probably got some nasty bumps and bruises, though."

"Pity," she said. "That it wasn't worse, I mean."

From across the room came a sort of echoing squeak. I turned to see Pix's head appear in one of the air ducts, Selene's recorder clutched between his teeth. Ixil went over and pulled him out, then tossed the recorder to me. "I assume this is Selene's?"

"Yes," I said, craning my neck as I spotted movement deeper in the duct. "Hold on—Pax is there, too."

"Yes, I see," Ixil said.

"What's he's got in his mouth?" McKell asked, moving in for a closer look.

I spotted a metallic glint as the outrider came farther into the dayroom light. "Maybe an old lock washer?"

"It's not a washer," Ixil said, peering into the duct as he put Pix up on his left shoulder. "It's something very different." Pax stuck his nose out of the opening.

"What in blazes is *that*?" Mindi asked.

"Looks like a medallion of some sort," Ixil said, taking it from Pax and looking closely at it. "Gregory?"

I stepped over and took it from him. It was a thin disk, about four centimeters across, made from a silvery metal. In the center was a small hole the shape of a five-point star. One side of the disk had a sort of stylized face with lines of tiny letters engraved across it. The other side was a pattern of interlocking circles of varying sizes, looking like the aftermath of an explosion in a bubble factory.

I turned back to the front side, my throat tightening. The medallion was something new, but the script looked like the writing in the portal directory half that Selene had unearthed on Meima.

Which strongly suggested that the medallion was Icari.

I looked at Ixil. Clearly, he'd recognized the lettering, too. "Never seen it before," I said aloud, handing it back to him.

"Hopefully, Selene will tell us about it in her message," McKell said. He stopped and looked at Mindi.

Mindi gave a theatrical sigh. "And four's a crowd," she said, standing up. "Yeah, got it. I need to check in with the local Burke's rep anyway. Try to explain that I'm not *really* hunting. You got some place with a little privacy?"

"You can use my cabin," I said. "Second starboard hatch aft."

"Thanks."

She left and headed aft. McKell gave her a couple of seconds, then eased over to the dayroom hatchway and leaned out, watching her progress. Another half minute... "Okay, she's there," he announced, coming back in. "Hatch closed. Ixil?"

"Pix is on his way to watch her," Ixil said, nodding back toward the air duct. "If she leaves, we'll know."

"Good." McKell gestured to the recorder. "Let's hear it."

I nodded and keyed the device.

"Hello, Gregory," Selene's voice came softly from the speaker. "I'm sorry I have to leave this way, especially without having a chance to discuss it with you. But you've gone missing in the Ammei enclave, and your father says the best way to help you is for him to keep me as a bargaining chip."

I glared at the recorder. My father. I should have guessed.

"I know you automatically take everything he says as suspect," she continued. "But he's explained his reasons, and they make sense to me. Taking me to Nexus Six via the Mycene portal will put me under the protection of both First of Three and General Kinneman, and—"

"*What?*" McKell said, a sandbagged expression on his face.

I hit the pause button, feeling exactly the way he looked. *Kinneman?* What the hell was my father up to?

"He must be insane," McKell said into my thoughts. "If Kinneman gets hold of her he'll roast her alive."

"I don't think so," Ixil said thoughtfully, handing the medallion to McKell with one hand as he absently stroked Pax's fur with the other. "Given your father's presence on Juniper, I would guess Kinneman has tasked him with negotiating with either First of Three or Yiuliob."

"Negotiating for Selene?" McKell asked.

"Or for Bubloo," I said. "Or maybe for both."

McKell frowned at me. "Both?"

"That's the way it's starting to look," I said. "We know Bubloo has an extraordinary sense of smell—tracking us to Mindi's ship proved that much. We also know now that Daxtro and his clients in the Uroemm family have an in with the local underworld. A sudden bounty post on Bubloo might get all the locals looking for him, which would pull them off the search for Selene and hopefully give her a little breathing space."

"Except from the Uroemm family," McKell said.

"Right," I agreed. "*That* pair is certainly not going to be distracted by something shiny floating over Bubloo's head." I lifted a finger. "But it gets trickier. Back in the enclave it was the Ammei who caught me, but when Yiuliob came in for our little chat he brought Daxtro with him. That suggests an alliance, possibly one where Yiuliob put up the other half of the two-mil bounty on me. And we *know* Yiuliob doesn't want either of us dead."

"Selene, for obvious reasons," Ixil said, nodding. "You, because he thinks you can get her for him."

"Exactly," I said. "A goal disagreement that drastic would put any alliance on shaky ground."

"So why would distracting the locals do any good?" McKell asked.

"I'll give you a hint," I said. "Daxtro and his partner came looking for us armed with Babcor Seventeens. What does that suggest?"

Ixil and McKell exchanged looks. "They thought they might have to shoot through armored doors?" Ixil suggested.

"Or they thought they would have to shoot through armored hunters," McKell said, giving me a disbelieving look. "Are you saying the family put up half of the two-mil bounty on you hoping to lure a bunch of hunters into finding you so they could then move in for a poach? Why?"

"Because I have it on good authority that the Uroemm family is incredibly cheap," I said. "It would be just like them to let someone else beat the bushes and then try to snatch away the prize so they wouldn't have to fork out any actual money."

"How much of this do you think Yiuliob knows?" Ixil asked.

"I don't know," I said. "But I'm guessing their partnership is a lot more one-sided than Yiuliob realizes. Actually..." I frowned as another puzzle piece found its place. "Damn. Selene naming First and Kinneman in the same breath. I'm guessing that's my father's subtle hint that the two of them are running the same kind of deal on her bounty."

"Kinneman working with nonhumans," McKell said dryly. "That's one for the books."

"I doubt it's crazier than any other battlefield alliance," I said. "Especially when he has no choice." I grimaced as another memory popped up. "Cute. Back when we met my father on Mycene—probably during an intermission in his talks with First Dominant Prucital—he actually told us he didn't think either Kinneman or First could come up with a two-mil bounty."

"But together they could?" McKell shook his head. "He must have been a riot to grow up with."

I snorted. "You have no idea."

"So we're now running against two different consortiums, both of which are jockeying for control of you, Selene, and maybe Bubloo," McKell said thoughtfully. "Well, at least now we know who the players are."

"Some of them, anyway," I cautioned. "Bubloo, for one, is still a big question mark. Plus, we still haven't figured out who this Ammei Gold One faction is, where they're based, and how they figure into the rivalry between First and Yiuliob." I held up the recorder. "Ready?"

"Ready," McKell said.

I tapped the pause button again. "—he's sure that together they can resist any pressure Yiuliob and the Juniper Glory faction might bring against them. We were hoping we could bring Bubloo, too, but for whatever reason he seems intent on hiding from us."

"Or at least from my father," I muttered.

"So I'm going to have to rely on you and the others to find and protect him—"

"Hold it," McKell said.

I touched the pause. "Yes?"

"What did you say just then?" he asked. "He was hiding from your father? Why?"

"No idea," I said. "He apparently was fine when the Saffi handed him over. They were heading for the spaceport, and my father was talking to me, when Bubloo suddenly bailed."

"What was he talking about at the time?" McKell asked. "Yiuliob?"

"I don't think so," I said, searching back for the memory. "Wait. Yes, he was. Dad had just spotted some Ammei heading toward the spaceport and speculated that Yiuliob might be among them."

"Makes sense," McKell said, scowling. "If Yiuliob's the one who brought him to Juniper, I can see why he would be skittish about facing him again."

"That would make sense," I said. "Except that during my interrogation, Yiuliob asked me who Bubloo was. Why would he do that if he already knew?"

"Maybe to throw you off the trail," Ixil offered. "To make you think the two of them weren't connected."

"Why?" I countered. "Besides, he seemed genuinely curious. He even had his flunky look up the Pakenrill listing to see what they looked like." I frowned. "Though when he saw the entry his only comment was to hope they could find a better picture."

"Not much chance of that with a protected species," McKell said. "Relevant data is either vague or nonexistent."

"Did your father say anything else?" Ixil asked. "Aside from Yiuliob being on the move?"

I dug a little deeper into the memory. "After he mentioned Yiuliob, I asked him where Rozhuhu and Prucital were," I said. "He said not to worry, that they were aboard his ship—"

I broke off. "*Damn* it," I bit out. "*That's* who Bubloo was trying to avoid."

"Which one?" McKell asked.

"Rozhuhu," I said. "He's one of Yiuliob's people, and Dad was taking Bubloo right to him."

"Wait a minute," McKell said frowning. "I thought Rozhuhu was with First of Three."

"So did I," I said darkly. "Apparently, so does my father. But he's with Yiuliob, all right. Back in the enclave, just before they grabbed me, Rozhuhu came racing up with Overseer Quodli, one of Yiuliob's top people."

"If your father is negotiating with Yiuliob on First's behalf—"

"No," I cut him off. "Because when Rozhuhu got his first glimpse of me and realized who the intruder was, his first move was to try to hide his face. That tells me he wasn't supposed to be there, not as a negotiator or envoy or anything official. He certainly wasn't supposed to be consorting with the local leadership, and *absolutely* not supposed to be helping them catch a prowler." I swore again as one more piece clicked. "That's also why Yiuliob let me go so easily. He assumes I'm working for First and will link up with my father and run back to Nexus Six."

"Where Rozhuhu will be waiting," McKell said.

"Exactly," I said, digging out my phone. If I could catch Selene before they lifted—

"If you're trying to call your father, don't bother," McKell said darkly. "The *Median* lifted nearly an hour ago. They're long gone."

"I have to go after them," I said, standing up. "As soon as you and Mindi are off the *Ruth*—"

"Whoa," McKell said, holding up a hand. "How about we listen to the rest of Selene's message before we run off in all directions?"

Every nerve ending in my body was screaming for me to get after Selene *right now*. But McKell was right. Clenching my teeth, I again keyed the recorder.

"—until we can find a way to get him to Nexus Six," Selene

said. "The Mycene portal, the one we're heading for, is probably your safest route. Assuming, of course, that Prucital maintains his support of First and can keep Second Dominant Nibagu under control."

I scowled. A nice thought, and a fair assessment of the balance of power. And I was sure my father and Prucital thought they were on top of Nibagu and the rest of the Mycene enclave's politics.

But he had no idea Juniper Glory had an inside man aboard the *Median*. Add in any up-to-date instructions or insights that Rozhuhu might have brought with him for Nibagu and Yiuliob's other allies on Mycene, and Prucital could find himself on the short end of the stick without even a hint of warning.

"I hope Pix or Pax found the medallion," Selene continued. "It's part of a set of two that First of Three gave Sir Nicholas. The legend says they were left by the Gold Ones for the chosen one, the person destined to free the rest of the Kadolian people and bring them back home."

I stared at the recorder. Hadn't Bubloo said something along those same lines?

Yes, he had, back in Robin's apartment. He'd also claimed he'd gotten the word about the mysterious chosen one directly from the Gold Ones.

And I remembered thinking at the time that Bubloo seemed to believe that Selene would be the one to fill that role.

"We don't know how they're supposed to work," Selene continued. "Sir Nicholas says the writing on both of them is identical, and that he wasn't able to detect any mechanism inside. They're made of some variant of portal metal, similar to regular portal hulls but with some differences I've never encountered before. He gave them to me, since I'm the only Kadolian he knows, hoping I could figure it out."

The only Kadolian my father knew . . . but he might not know that the Patth also had one of that species close to hand. A young one, to be sure, but a Kadolian nonetheless.

Did the medallions require two hands or voices or souls in order to function? If so, we would need to somehow beg, borrow, or steal Tirano away from Nask. Or, more likely, come to some difficult and costly arrangement with him.

"On the theory that both are needed for whatever the Gold

Ones have planned, I thought it would be best to separate them," she went on. "I'm taking one and leaving the other with you.

"I know I'm not being much help, Gregory. But in truth, I think Sir Nicholas is mostly playing this by ear as much as the rest of us. I hope that once we're back together we can solve this tangle. Be safe, and I'll meet you on Nexus Six whenever you can get there."

The recording ended. "All right," I said. "*Now* can I get you and Mindi off my ship? I need to get to Mycene, and I need to get there ahead of the *Median*."

"You taking Bubloo with you?" Ixil asked.

"He's long gone," I said, focusing my mental power on the numbers running through my mind. The *Ruth* needed to be fueled; call that two to three hours of delay, minimum. "And to be honest, I'm not much worried. Doc Robin said he was always getting away from him. If you're right about Yiuliob bringing him here, it means he got away from the Ammei at least once, too. Don't worry, he'll stay hidden."

"Until he comes out to buy his street drugs?" Ixil asked. "If Yiuliob knows about that, he'll be waiting."

"Probably," I conceded. "Okay, so I'll get in touch with Robin and have him keep Bubloo under wraps." Once I was off Juniper and in hyperspace, I could run the engines to plus-twenty. That would mean two or three extra fueling stops during the eight-day run to Mycene, but if the *Median* was running on normal the additional boost to my speed should still get me there ahead of them. "He may just be a doctor now, but he's got the background and street smarts he'll need to keep them a step ahead of Yiuliob and the local thugs."

But no. My father was in a hurry, too. If he also ran his engines to plus-twenty, we would be right back where we started, with the *Median* holding at least a three-hour lead on me. If Rozhuhu and the Juniper Glory faction on Mycene were fast enough, they could have Selene before I got there. For that matter, they might have all of Nexus Six.

McKell might have been reading my mind. More likely, he'd simply run the same numbers I had. "You can't make it work," he said. "Besides, Mindi won't be safe in her ship until her entryway and zigzag are fixed."

"She's coming," Ixil warned quietly.

McKell nodded acknowledgment. "And since we're the ones responsible for that mess, it's on us to make it right. My suggestion is that you let her stay aboard the *Ruth* until her ship is fixed"—he gestured to the hatchway as Mindi came into view—"while you, Ixil, and I head to Mycene on the *Stormy Banks*."

"I—" I broke off at the sudden left-hand turn in the conversation. "What?"

"I second that *what*," Mindi said as she walked into the dayroom.

"The *Stormy Banks* is faster than the *Ruth*," McKell said. "We also have larger tanks, which means fewer fueling stops. It's our best chance of beating your father there."

"And who said Mindi's at all interested in hanging out in here?" Mindi demanded. "No offense, Roarke, but this isn't my idea of luxury accommodations."

"You could try a hotel," McKell offered. "Though with a Patth hit squad wandering around that might not be your best option."

"And sticking around Roarke's ship would be better?"

"I've got that covered," I said.

"Oh, *do* you?" Mindi said.

"Actually, yes," I assured her. "Right now, the *Ruth* is the safest place you can be on Juniper."

"Whether you stay or not is entirely up to you," Ixil said, reaching out a hand to the air duct as Pix trotted into view. "Jordan simply thought you might like an alternative while your ship is being repaired."

"At whose cost?" she asked pointedly.

"Mine," I gritted out, turning to the hatchway. I didn't like this, not a bit. But McKell made a good case, and arguing the point would just waste more time. "Wait here."

I hurried to the engine room, grabbed a spare plasmic and a phone from their hiding places, then dug into the heat insulation and retrieved one of Nask's hundred-thousand-commark bank checks. I opened the engine room hatch to head back forward—

To find McKell waiting for me in the corridor. "I thought you were with Mindi," I said, starting to brush past him.

"Ixil's with her," he said, stretching an arm out in front of me. "I have a question, a very important one. Do you really believe Bubloo can act as a substitute for Selene in getting Yiuliob's portal to work?"

"I don't know," I admitted. "But at this point, all that matters is whether Yiuliob or First of Three or anyone else *thinks* he can. Because that belief will be the driving force behind them hunting him down, finding him, and doing whatever they think they need to in order to get what they want. I can't let that happen to him if I can stop it."

"So you're willing to risk Selene's safety for his?"

"Not at all," I said. "But Selene seemed willing to go with my father. Either you trust your partner, or you don't. I do."

"And if she's wrong?"

"Then we crash and burn together."

A smile twitched at his lips. "Sounds like Alpha all over again."

"I suppose," I said, wincing a little at the memory of that gamble. "Hopefully, this one won't be nearly as dramatic. Or as literal."

"Hopefully." He lifted his arm out of my way. "Grab what you need, and you and I will head to the ship and start the precheck. Ixil will get Mindi settled in here."

Long experience had taught me the value of readiness. I ducked into my cabin, grabbed my go-bag, and headed for the entryway. McKell had gone on ahead and was standing by the open hatch.

Gazing outside with an odd look on his face.

"What is it?" I asked as I came up to him.

He nodded out the opening. "See for yourself."

Frowning, I stepped past him.

And came to a sudden stop.

"There!" Bubloo crowed excitedly from the bottom of the zigzag, jabbing a finger up at me and doing a little bouncing dance. "I told you he was here. Didn't I tell you he was here?"

"Yes, Bubloo, you told me," Robin said. He was also gazing up at me, looking more tired than ever.

"And I told *you* two to lose yourselves," I bit out as I walked down toward them. "Excuse me, Doc, but what the hell are you doing?"

"I wanted to see you, Friend Roarke," Bubloo said. "I told him you were here. Right here."

"Don't start, Roarke," Robin said, some anger trying to make it out past the weariness. "He's fast, and he's stronger than he looks. Anyway, with badgemen swarming all over the mess you left back there, the spaceport is probably the safest place in Pikwik City."

"I want to go home, Friend Roarke," Bubloo said, his excitement switching abruptly to a nervous sadness. "I don't like it here. Can't you please take me home?"

I reached for my info pad, remembering only then that it was still back on Yiuliob's desk. But if I was remembering correctly... "McKell, refresh my memory, will you? Belshaz."

"Probably way too far," McKell said, pulling out his own info pad and punching keys. "It's... yes. Twenty-four days from here, and in the wrong direction."

I nodded heavily. That was indeed what I'd remembered. "I'm sorry, Bubloo, but I can't," I told him. "I have an important errand elsewhere."

"But I don't *like* it here," Bubloo protested again. "Friend Selene would take me—I know she would. Can't you ask *her*?"

"Friend Selene isn't here," I said impatiently. We didn't have time for this. "She's gone to—"

And right in mid-sentence a strange thought suddenly flashed across my brain. Belshaz. Pakenrill. A minor Ammei enclave.

Maybe with its own Gemini portal?

It would be a gamble. A horrible gamble. If I guessed wrong, everything could collapse around Selene before I could ever get to her. She would become a pawn of First of Three and Nexus Six, or a pawn of Yiuliob and Juniper Glory, or possibly a sacrificed pawn that both sides agreed should be taken off the board to maintain parity.

But if I guessed right, it was my chance to intercept the *Median* and Selene in a way and from a direction no one would expect.

"Roarke?" McKell asked warningly.

"You're right, Bubloo," I said. "This is no place for you. Let me see if I can get you home. Do you have anything you need to get before we go?"

"I have other clothes and a travel case," Bubloo said, the sadness once again turning into excitement. "And radixiam. I can bring that, too."

"Let's just stick with the clothing," I said. "Is it back at your house?"

"Yes, yes," he said, doing the bouncing thing again. He grabbed Robin's arm. "And Friend Christopher, too. He can come too, can't he?"

"Actually—"

"Oh, please please please," Bubloo pleaded. "I need him."

I sighed. "Doc?"

Robin shrugged helplessly. "It would let me continue his therapy," he said. "And frankly, I'm about done with Juniper. If you're game, I'm willing."

"Fine," I said, fully aware that I'd just made what had already promised to be a very hard sell into something a hundred times harder. "Go get your things. I'll send you the ship's location along the way. McKell, who wound up with the medallion?"

"I did," McKell said, looking wary as he pulled it out of his pocket and handed it to me. I started to put it in my pocket—

"Ooh!" Bubloo gasped, darting out a hand and snatching it from my fingers. "Is this—? It *is*." He held it up for Robin's inspection. "See this? This is metal of the great twin globes."

A sudden chill ran through me. Bubloo recognized *portal metal*? I stepped toward him, reaching for the disk.

He twitched it away. Robin was right; he *was* fast. "See?" he said, again waving the medallion under Robin's nose. "Isn't it beautiful?"

"It's wonderful, Bubloo," Robin said, taking the medallion and handing it back to me. "We have to go now. Remember?"

"Oh. Yes yes," Bubloo said. "We go home. Come, Friend Christopher. There's a vehicle right back there—see it? Hurry."

He trotted off toward an unattended runaround. Robin gave me one last unreadable look, then followed.

"I don't know what sense you think this makes," McKell warned me quietly. "But even if you're thinking we go to Mycene first and then take them back to Belshaz when it's all over, all you're doing is risking both him *and* Selene."

"I agree with you completely," I assured him as I pulled out my new phone and punched in a number. "Which is why we're not going to Mycene at all," I added, watching the confusion on his face. "Don't worry. If this works you and Ixil will be completely off the hook."

The phone connected. "Who is this?"

"It's Roarke, Circe," I identified myself. "Sorry—had to get a new phone. What exactly was your mandate concerning me?"

"To keep you safe," she said warily. "Why?"

"Would that include taking me somewhere across the Spiral where I'll be safer than here?"

"Something wrong with the *Ruth*?"

"Yes—it's not fast enough," I said. "The place I need to go is twenty-four days away. I need to be there in six."

Out of the corner of my eye I saw McKell's mouth drop open. "Roarke?" he whispered.

I waved him to keep quiet. "Well?" I prompted.

"You know I can't take you aboard my ship," Circe said. "Non-Patth are forbidden passage on Talariac-equipped ships without special permission."

"Which you can grant me."

"Which would get me in a world of trouble."

"Not necessarily," I said. "I know you're here under the direction of Sub-Director Nask, so you may know about the couple of times he took three of us non-Patth aboard the *Odinn* for a quick trip from hither to yon."

"Those were when it suited his needs and his purposes," Circe countered. "*His* needs and purposes. Not yours."

"Agreed," I said. "May I submit in turn that, given his current mandate from the Director General, anything involving portals comes under that same heading." I paused, but she remained silent. "Furthermore," I continued, "I think the sub-director would feel that keeping First of Three and the Ammei from gaining supreme power over the Spiral—including the Patth—would be worth a little extra effort on all our parts."

"Roarke, are you out of your *mind*?" McKell whispered urgently.

I shook my head. "Circe?"

"Both points are well taken," she said reluctantly. "Where exactly do you want to go?"

"Belshaz," I said. "Northern mountain region. I'll get you details on the specific location en route. Oh, and there will be two more passengers besides me. I assume you can accommodate them."

Circe muttered something under her breath. "Sub-Director Nask was right. You *do* like pushing limits."

"I don't disagree," I said. "But I think he would also tell you that when I'm right, the end results are well worthwhile. Not just for me, but also for the Patth."

"This had better be one of those times," she warned. "All right, you've piqued my interest. When do you want to leave?"

"As soon as the rest of the party gets back," I said. "Which pad are you?"

She gave me the number. "One more thing," she said. "If this thing goes sideways, you *will* live to regret it. You'll live an uncomfortably long time regretting it. I trust I make myself clear?"

I sighed. "Perfectly," I said. "May I say in turn that if this goes sideways, you and Sub-Director Nask will have to get in line."

McKell was alarmed. Ixil was cautious. Mindi was intrigued, though clearly lost by the whole conversation.

But of the three of them, she at least didn't feel the need to talk me out of it.

"This is crazy," McKell said. "You have to realize that."

"Of course I do," I said. "But I don't see any other options. Do you?"

McKell and Ixil looked at each other, and I saw Pix and Pax do the little simultaneous twitch that indicated emotion in their Kalixiri host. "It's a gamble," McKell said, turning back to me.

"I know that, too," I said. "But it's the only way I can keep Selene and my father from walking into a trap."

"*If* your hunch is right."

"And I guess we'll find out about that, won't we?" I said. "I assume you've already checked on whether there's someone on Mycene you can contact to send a warning to my father before they land?"

"We have," Ixil confirmed. "Unfortunately, the only people we have numbers for are connected with Kinneman, the APA, or EarthGuard."

"All of whom would just kick Selene from Yiuliob's frying pan into Kinneman's fire," I said.

"At least she'd be among humans," McKell said.

"Not a huge selling point," I told him. "Yiuliob at least has to bring her out into the open to get what he wants. Kinneman could just lock her up and lose the key. Still open to other options if you have any."

Again, McKell and Ixil exchanged looks. "I wish we did," Ixil said. "I suppose all we can do is wish you good luck."

"Thanks," I said. "You can also try to find that full—that other thing," I amended, freshly aware of Mindi's silent presence. "I assume that Yiuliob confiscating the data stick wasn't the end of the search?"

"Not at all," McKell said, with a hint of malicious satisfaction.

"Pax's harness had a hidden backup built in that made a copy of the data before the Ammei got to it."

"I figured you'd done something like that," I said, heading for the entryway. "Actually, I'm a little surprised they didn't take it off him when they captured us."

"Probably thought the harness looked harmless but his teeth didn't," Ixil suggested.

"That's how *I* would have read it," I agreed. "Anyway, that should keep you and Ixil gainfully employed for a while. I'll let you know what happens."

"Assuming you live through it," McKell said.

"Always assuming that." I turned to Mindi, an odd thought suddenly striking me. "Mindi, does your entryway have security cameras on it?"

She nodded. "They're positioned *over* the entryway, but yes."

"Can you get me a copy before I leave? Mainly the parts that have Bubloo or the Patth, plus any of the crowd scenes."

"Sure," she said, pulling out her info pad. "I'll put it on your tab."

"What are you looking for?" McKell asked.

"I don't know yet," I said. "Something that doesn't fit. I'll know it when I see it."

Mindi shook her head, still working her info pad. "Anyone ever tell you you have a weird approach to basic detective work?"

"All the time," I said. "But I'm still alive, so I guess it works. Okay, I'm off. Have fun, and we'll get together for drinks someday."

"It's a date," McKell said. "Watch yourself. And bring Selene back safely."

A minute later, having sent Circe's pad number to Doc Robin, I was heading across the spaceport toward Circe's ship. Mindi was right, I had to admit. On the other hand, my intuitive ability to link random-seeming bits of information together had gotten me a long way.

But as my father used to say, *A strategy that always works is sometimes just a strategy that hasn't failed yet.*

Maybe the day for that crash had finally come.

CHAPTER SIXTEEN

—— ◆◆◆ ——

Back on the *Ruth*, Mindi had commented about four being a crowd. Here, on Circe's ship *Blaze*, the crowd was three times that number. Fortunately, most of the crew kept to the forward and aft ends of the ship: bridge, nav, and computer rooms in the bow, engine and hyperdrive areas in the stern. The hatches to those areas were sealed, and Circe explained in no uncertain terms what would happen to Bubloo, Robin, or me if we tried to breach either barrier.

For once, even Bubloo's fragmented attention span seemed to hold still long enough to get the message. Robin and I got it even faster. As my father used to say, *When someone takes great pains to heap threat upon threat onto you, he's either bluffing or deadly serious. Assuming it's a bluff almost never ends well.*

For the first two days, the three of us mostly kept to our compact but decently appointed staterooms, coming out into the common rooms only for meals or occasional brief conversation. Bubloo, in particular, seemed unusually subdued, though I couldn't tell whether that was the lingering effects of Circe's threats or because the level of drugs in his system was dropping.

Near the end of the second day, I asked Robin about it. He didn't know, either.

I saw Circe a few times during that period, mostly as she

traveled briskly into or out of the forbidden zone behind the forward hatch. I nodded politely to her each time we passed. Once or twice she even nodded back.

I spent much of my alone time poring over the security recordings Mindi had sent me before we left Juniper. Particularly interesting were the sections where up to a third of the image was washed out by some clearly artificial glow. It took a great deal of observation, analysis, and deduction before I finally figured that one out.

It was early afternoon on the third day, and the three of us were eating lunch in the dayroom, when Circe suddenly appeared and announced we would all be joining her that evening for dinner.

I hadn't expected the meal to be even slightly formal, given the somewhat ragtag nature of the *Blaze*'s passenger list. Still, my admittedly limited experience with Circe hadn't shown an overabundance of patience, and as we all sat down around the dayroom table I wondered what would happen if Bubloo decided to go off on one of his crazy tirades.

To my relief, for once he behaved like a civilized being. He was quiet and subdued but unusually sociable, answering questions posed to him and even occasionally inserting relevant comments as the four of us traversed the twisting conversational landscape of table talk. Even more surprising, a casual question from Circe about his home unlocked an eloquence I'd never suspected was there.

"...and the clouds are especially beautiful when they flow like a wispy waterfall over the mountain passes," Bubloo said, floating his hands over his water glass in demonstration.

The movements were twitchy, yet oddly graceful, and his facial tattoos seemed to carry a new sheen as if his reminiscences had literally awakened memories of sunlight in his face. But that latter might just have been the dayroom's lighting.

"More striking even than that," he continued, "is when the valley winds lift from an angle and blow them upward in midflow, thus creating an image like that of a waterfall's end-mist, but in midair."

I watched warily as he once again moved his hands in illustration. They were dipping perilously close to the edge of his water glass, and I winced at the thought that he might misjudge the distance and dump the contents into his lap.

But again, that fear was unnecessary. Though his hands came close to the rim, they never touched it.

Perhaps he was finally learning how the real world operated. More likely, with access to Juniper's street drugs cut off, his brain was starting to sober up.

"I've never seen clouds behave that way," Circe said. If she was impressed by the newly functional Bubloo, she didn't show it. "Maybe we'll be able to see that before we leave. Assuming your people allow strangers into their villages."

"My people are friendly," Bubloo said. He smiled at Robin and me. "We enjoy friendship." The smile faded. "But so few are willing in these latter days to visit us."

"That's because you've been given protected-species status," Robin reminded him. "The Commonwealth doesn't want random people coming in and disrupting your way of life."

"So you've told me," Bubloo said, his face and voice going a little sadder. "Though I still do not understand. But it wasn't always so. Once, many came to speak with us and watch our clouds."

"Have you lived there long?" Circe asked.

"Very long," Bubloo said, his eyes going distant. "Before the Kadolians came, we were there."

I felt a shiver run through me. *Before the Kadolians came?*

"Really," Circe said calmly. If Bubloo's declaration had hit her the same way it had me, she was hiding it well. "That long?"

"That long," Bubloo assured her. "One day, perhaps, they will return." He paused. "Or perhaps they will be gone forever."

"Perhaps," Circe said, turning to Robin. "How about you, Dr. Robin? Does your home have any natural phenomena that impressive? Or was there some species like the Kadolians that were also there before?"

"I'm afraid my homeworld's pretty boring," Robin said. "At least, the part where I grew up is. And I have no idea where humans stand on the universe's timeline, vis-à-vis the Kadolians or anyone else."

"It's not a contest," Circe assured him, eyeing Bubloo thoughtfully and then turning to me. "What about you, Roarke? You seen anything interesting along the bumpy road you've taken through life?"

I shrugged. The heavily populated worlds I'd traveled as a bounty hunter. The deserted and pristine ones Selene and I had visited as crocketts. The Icari portals. "I suppose that depends on what you consider interesting," I said. "For me, it all sort of blends together."

"Which tells us something about it right there, I suppose," she said. She gave me a final, speculative look, then stood up. "Thank you all for joining me. We'll have to do it again before we reach Belshaz."

"We'd enjoy that," I replied for all of us as Robin and I also stood. Bubloo remained seated, his eyes holding a wistful, faraway look, perhaps still wrapped in memories of cloud formations and intruding Kadolians. "Thank you for your hospitality."

Circe nodded acknowledgment and left the dayroom, heading into the ship's central corridor and turning right toward the bow.

"Well, that was interesting," Robin commented, stepping behind Bubloo and touching his shoulder.

Bubloo started and looked around. "Yes? What is it?"

"It's time to go," Robin said. "You ready to go back to your cabin?"

"Yes," Bubloo said, hastily standing up. "Yes, of course. I was just thinking." He looked at me. "A most interesting woman, Friend Roarke. How is it you know her?"

"We have some mutual acquaintances," I told him.

"That's it?" Robin asked, eyeing me closely. "Really? Just a friend of a friend? You never even met her, and yet she was willing to haul all of us halfway across the Spiral?"

"He didn't say they never met," Bubloo pointed out. "Perhaps one of their mutual friends introduced them?"

"That's basically it," I confirmed. "She and I *did* meet, but our time was brief. It's mostly the mutual acquaintance thing."

"Sure," Robin said. "I was just curious. Come on, Bubloo."

"You have truly been blessed with good friends, Friend Roarke," Bubloo called back to me as Robin led him from the room. "I am honored to be counted among them. Sleep well, and may the new day dawn with gladness."

"The same to you, Bubloo," I said. "Sleep well, Doc."

"Good night, Roarke," Robin said. "Come on, Bubloo, I'll walk you to your cabin."

I watched until they were out of sight, then returned my attention to the table. Normally, when it was just the three of us eating, I'd taken over the job of clearing up while Robin took charge of Bubloo. But given that it had been Circe's dinner party, maybe she'd arranged for one of the *Blaze*'s crew to handle that job.

But the crew had the ship to run, and as Robin had just reminded me, Circe was doing us a hell of a favor. Plus, I didn't really have anything better to do right now. Collecting the plates, I carried the stack over to the cleaner.

"You can leave those."

I spun around, my hand going automatically to where my holstered plasmic usually rode my hip. Circe was walking into the dayroom, an amused expression on her face, a bottle of Dewar's in her hand. "You always startle this easily?" she asked. "Grab a couple of clean glasses, will you?"

"Sure," I said, setting down the plates and selecting two glasses from the pantry. "And I prefer to think of it as part of a well-honed survival instinct package. Weren't you issued one of those when they gave you your Expediter's card?"

"Absolutely," she assured me as she resumed her earlier seat. "The very best money can buy. Ours just aren't as noisy as yours. You weren't in any hurry to get back to your cabin, were you?"

"Not at all," I said, returning to my own seat and setting the glasses down in front of her. "A little lonely up front with the pilot and your three Iykams?"

"With the *pilots* and the Iykams," she corrected, leaning a little on the plural. "No, everything's fine up there. It just seemed like a good time for the two of us to have a private chat." She lifted the bottle a little. "I'm told you like this brand."

"I do," I confirmed, watching as she poured a couple of fingers into each glass. "Not to excess, of course."

"You suggesting I might try to ply you with liquor?"

"No, I'm sure you'd never stoop to anything so sordid," I said. "Especially since it wouldn't work."

"You have a high alcohol tolerance?"

"I have a high respect for my limits," I corrected. "Unless you're planning to drug me, of course."

"If I wanted to do that, there are easier ways," she said as she pushed my glass toward me. "Not to mention cheaper ones."

"Yes, I imagine Dewar's *is* a bit pricey on the Path worlds," I said. "So what shall we talk about? Oh, wait—let me guess. Bubloo?"

"You *are* a clever one, aren't you?" she said. "Yes, let's start with him. You first."

"He's thought to be a Pakenrill," I said. "He's possibly tanked to the eyebrows with drugs, legal and otherwise. He's apparently a person of interest, at least to someone." I gestured. "Your turn."

"Hardly," she said. "Keep going."

"Keep going where?" I said. "You saw him at dinner, and that was the most lucid I've ever seen him. He's mercurial, unpredictable, sometimes spouts off with the strangest stuff, and socially is a loose cannon."

"I agree," she said, watching me closely. "Yet you wanted him along on this trip. What do you know that I don't?" She lifted a finger. "Correction. What do you know that you *think* I don't?"

"Cleverly put," I complimented her. "Tell you what. Since you probably already know everything I do anyway, let's cut to the chase by you telling me what *you* know." I lifted a finger. "Correction. By telling me what Sub-Director Nask has decided you need to know. After that, if he left any gaps I'll be happy to fill them in."

She took a sip from her glass, gazing at me over the rim. "You really are everything Huginn said you were," she commented. "Fine. First of Three and the Ammei on Nexus Six have cobbled together a bare-bones portal launch module, which they hope to use to find the...what does the Icarus Group call the big ones these days?"

"Full-range portals," I supplied. "And they call themselves the Alien Portal Agency now."

"Right," she said dryly. "I forgot. General Kinneman has no imagination whatsoever, does he? Anyway, First of Three hopes to use their makeshift module to find the full-range portal everyone assumes is hidden somewhere on Juniper."

"Which requires him to figure out the Juniper portal's address."

"Which he claims he already has," Circe said. "The sticking point is that for the final calibration they need the services of a Patth and a Kadolian." She cocked her head. "I'm also told they need some sort of ancient serum that's described in a book in *Imistio* Tower, except that a couple of pages from that book are missing. You wouldn't know anything about that, would you?"

"I just know what First told us," I said, a small burden lifting from the back of my mind. So First of Three and his minions *had* figured out they didn't have the full serum instructions. Hopefully, that meant they wouldn't mix up something potentially dangerous and inject it into someone. "Aside from the missing pages thing, of course. He didn't mention that part."

"Hardly surprising," Circe said. "But the question was more an inquiry as to whether you knew anything about the missing pages. Huginn thinks you may have absconded with them."

"Does he, now," I said. "Well, then, let me clear the record. Given that First of Three was planning to inject Selene with whatever the hell the stuff is, if I *had* found this book I'd have poured plasmic fire into it until it looked like the bottom of a barbeque pit."

"Interesting," Circe said thoughtfully. "Casual destruction isn't your usual style."

"Did you catch the part about them using it on Selene?"

Circe gave a small shrug. "Point taken. So: back to Bubloo. I understand he's got a terrific sense of smell."

"He does indeed," I confirmed. "Possibly on a par with Selene's. Current working theory is that he was brought to Juniper to test whether or not he could substitute for her in the Nexus Six portal calibration."

"And?"

"To hear Bubloo tell it, he escaped from them," I said. "Possibly before they finished their studies."

"Or they *did* finish, decided he didn't make the grade, and cut him loose."

"Or they finished, realized he *could* do the job, but then he escaped before they could secure him," I said. "Take your pick."

"You've asked Bubloo about it, I assume?" Circe asked.

"Numerous times," I said, resisting the urge to remind her that she probably already knew the answer to that. Though to be honest, if I had a group of potentially dangerous unknowns aboard my ship, I'd probably bug their living quarters, too. "He either can't remember or the memory is traumatic enough to send him into more of his standard scribble-talk."

"Any chance that he'll regain any of those memories before we reach Belshaz?"

"No idea," I said. "Doc Robin says he's steadily recovering from his old drug regimen, but how much of his mind and memory have been permanently damaged is still a big unknown. One additional conundrum: When I was in Ammei custody, Yiuliob wanted me to tell *him* about Bubloo. That would suggest he wasn't the one who brought him in."

"Or he was simply lying."

"Or there are things going on in the Juniper enclave that Yiuliob doesn't know about," I said. "After all, he's got Rozhuhu acting as his mole on Nexus Six. Why couldn't First of Three have one or two moles of his own on Juniper?"

"Like this whole thing wasn't complicated enough," Circe said. "What about before Bubloo was grabbed? That whole *before the Kadolians came, we were there* thing."

"Good question," I admitted. "It's entirely possible that I've got things backward. Maybe the original triumvirate was the Ammei, Patth, and Pakenrills, and it only changed when someone stumbled on the Kadolians and found out they were better at the job."

"Which is why we're going to Belshaz?" Circe asked. "To take a closer look at his people?"

"One of the reasons, yes," I said. "It's also possible that this is pure coincidence, the Pakenrills are nothing special, Bubloo got to Juniper some other way, and he's simply a crazy who's figured out that talking mysterious-sounding nonsense gets him attention."

"Glad we got that cleared up," Circe said with a hint of sarcasm. "What do you propose for our next move?"

"The fastest way to short-circuit the Ammei push would be to get to the Juniper portal first," I said. "And before you ask, no, I don't know how the Commonwealth and Patth would share the thing if we found it. Right now, I'm just focused on keeping it away from First and Yiuliob."

"Actually, there might be more of a problem than you think," Circe warned. "There's a small but determined faction among the Directorate that's all for the Patth and Ammei once again being undisputed masters of the Spiral."

"Then these starry-eyed dreamers need to sit down with First of Three and listen to him salivate over his hoped-for return to the glory days," I said grimly. "He didn't seem especially inclined to give either the Patth or Kadolians more than the barest sliver of the pie."

"Huginn agrees," Circe said. "His report has furthermore

convinced Sub-Director Nask to press the Director General to withhold all cooperation with First of Three and the Ammei."

I felt my eyes narrow. "I seem to hear a *but* in there."

"What you hear is the Uroemm family," she said. "They're focused on Conciliator Uvif's report, and he—"

"*Uvif?*" I cut her off. "Seriously? He's an incompetent loose cannon and a borderline traitor. Why is anyone listening to him?"

"Because he's one of the family."

I breathed out a curse. "Terrific. I should have guessed."

"Yes, you should," Circe said. "How did you think he'd managed to hold on to his conciliatorship after the public drubbing you delivered to him on Lucius Four?"

"*And* why did he think he could countermand your explicit orders in the field on Nexus Six," I muttered. "Who the hell *are* these people, anyway?"

"The biggest economic powerhouse in the Patth regime," she said. "Thirty years ago, when the Talariac Drive had finally been perfected and was ready to test, the Uroemm family had the foresight and resources to go all-in on the project. They threw everything they had into building the freighters and passenger transports they anticipated would be needed."

"And started recruiting pilots?"

"Indeed." Circe smiled thinly. "Plus, I believe they were the ones who first suggested that part of the circuitry be implanted in those pilots. With their massive investment, they wanted to make absolutely certain no one could steal the drive's secrets."

"A not unreasonable goal, actually," I said, thinking back to the Brandywine incident. The tech *could* be stolen, but not without a lot of effort, along with some *very* serious consequences. "And, of course, the family also happened to have a supply of young Patth who were ready, willing, and able to volunteer for the job?"

"*Volunteer* may be too strong a word," Circe said. "As you've seen, the family is run with a steel grip. But you're right. One way or another, they ended up with most of the ships and most of the pilots."

"How much is *most?*"

Circe took a long sip from her glass. "Current estimates are that the family runs between eighty-nine and ninety-two percent of all Patth shipping."

"Impressive," I said. "And all because they've got a monopoly on the Talariac pilot corps. I imagine they were quietly furious when our old boss Luko Varsi tried to make a private deal to get some of those face implants for himself."

"They were hardly quiet about it," Circe said. "The fallout in the Directorate . . . let's just say two sub-directors lost their positions, and a third lost his life."

"That sounds like the Uroemms," I murmured. "I take it they emerged from the dust cloud stronger than ever?"

"If not actually stronger, they at least didn't lose any ground," she said. "You can see now that we're not just talking clout, but a genuine stranglehold on the Patth economy."

"Understood," I said, forcing back the smile that wanted to pop onto my face.

Unfortunately, enough of it apparently got through. "What's funny?" Circe demanded.

"Nothing," I hastened to assure her. "Sorry. It was just that your complaint against the Uroemm family is exactly the same one the rest of the shippers in the Spiral have against the Patth in general. It just struck me as ironic, that's all."

For a moment she stared at me in stony silence. Then her face smoothed a little. "Yes," she said with only a slight edge to her voice. "Huginn said you had a tendency to see things through odd prisms."

"Not the first time I've been told that," I said. "Speaking of Huginn, is he all right? He was the one I expected to show up on Juniper, not you. No offense."

"None taken," Circe said, clearly still annoyed. "Hard though this may be for you to accept, you're not the center of the universe. Sub-Director Nask and Huginn both have other, more pressing concerns than you. I submit you're merely an interesting and occasionally useful afterthought to everyone's lives."

"Understood," I said. "Actually, that's not a bad position to be in. Being front and center can be unpleasant when the shooting starts."

"So it can," she said. "Tell me about Dr. Robin."

"Not much to tell," I said. "He claims he became a doctor to escape life in a street gang. He also claims he was on Juniper as a visiting xenopsychiatrist who'd been treating Bubloo for a few weeks for various mental problems, some of them probably drug-induced."

"And you don't believe any of that?"

"Oh, I believe most of it," I said. "Maybe even all of it. I'm also pretty sure there's more to his story."

"Such as?"

I shook my head. "You asked what I know about him. That's all I know. Everything else is speculation."

"I'm okay with speculation."

"I'm not," I said. "Not yet, anyway. Maybe later."

"Fine," Circe said. "Your choice. *Die gedanken sind frei*, and all that. *Thoughts are free*," she added at the puzzled look on my face. "Old German saying. You may have noticed Sub-Director Nask's fascination with Old Earth."

"I have," I said. "Comes under another old saying: *Know thy enemy*."

"Always a good idea," Circe said. "So let me see if I've got this straight. You're heading into the unknown with a Patth Expediter and two possibly untrustworthy companions with at least two different groups of Ammei chasing you."

"Plus, my partner is in deadly danger, and a powerful Patth family wants to kill me and everyone I've ever met," I added. "But yes, that about covers it."

"You *do* enjoy living dangerously, don't you?"

"I don't enjoy it at all," I said. "It's just how life seems to turn out for me."

"So it seems." Circe stood up. "I'll leave this with you," she said, capping the bottle and pushing it a couple of centimeters toward me. "Good that you know your limits on such things. Good night, Roarke. Nice chatting with you."

"Good night, Expediter," I said, also standing up. "Oh, and by the way, it *is* just the one pilot up there."

"I told you there were *pilots*, plural. Weren't you listening?"

"I was listening just fine," I said. "My eyes also work, and I've seen the pilot head aft a couple of times with his Iykam escort to check out something in the engine room. It's always the same one."

"That's because the other one stays on the bridge."

I shook my head. "Sorry, but the engine pitch changes noticeably when he heads aft, which I assume is the Talariac going into some form of standby when he and his implants get too far away from the engine sensor mechanism."

"It's an interesting theory, anyway," Circe said. Her expression hadn't changed, but I could see a little granite forming behind her eyes.

"It is, isn't it?" I agreed. "Also interesting is how everyone in the Spiral knows the Talariac Drive is four times faster and three times cheaper than every other hyperdrive in the Spiral, but no one ever mentions how *quiet* the thing is."

For another couple of heartbeats she continued to gaze at me. Then her lip twitched in the closest thing to a smile I'd seen yet from her. "Huginn really is impressed with you," she said. "Still wondering if I'll ever join in that opinion. Good night, Roarke."

"Good night, Expediter."

Once again, she disappeared out the hatchway. Huffing out a sigh, I picked up the bottle and my glass and headed back toward my cabin. As my father used to say, *The best interrogators already know the answers to most of the questions they'll be asking. Make sure your answers sound like theirs, whether they are or not.*

I'd tried my best to make sure all my answers matched Circe's questions. Whether I'd succeeded, only time would tell.

Probably sooner than I really wanted.

CHAPTER SEVENTEEN

———— ✦✦✦ ————

Three days later, we arrived at Belshaz.

"You've got two spaceports to choose from," Circe said as she and I sat together at one end of the dayroom table.

"Yes," I said, eyeing the row of bridge repeater displays that had been hiding behind the textured wood-grain siding on the forward bulkhead. I'd hoped I might get invited to the bridge for this part, since that was where all the ground-scan displays were. But the ship's designers had been one step ahead of me.

As to the landing itself... "I've changed my mind," I told her. "Let's try something in the—"

"What do you mean, changed your mind?" Circe demanded. Her tone had shifted to ominous, with the glare she turned on me a couple kilometers north of that. "The whole reason we came here was to check out Bubloo's people."

"And we will," I promised. "But first, I'd like to drop in on Rirto City."

"Would you, now," Circe growled, keying the display controls. The image shifted, zooming dizzily from Belshaz's northern mountains to the northeast edge of a large desert. "Let me guess. Rirto City has the planet's best barbeque?"

"You know me too well," I said. "But no, I just want to check out the Ammei enclave southwest of the city."

191

She shook her head. "There isn't any Ammei enclave on Belshaz."

"My father says otherwise," I said. "Though to be fair, he also said it was more like a neighborhood club than a full-bore enclave."

Circe was silent a moment, and I took the opportunity to study the aerial view of the region.

It wasn't very promising. Rirto City itself was pretty small—the data column alongside the image tagged its population as only about twenty thousand, most of them Zulians. The city ran nearly to the edge of the Suzem Desert, with the Ammei community nestled between the city edge and the desert. One interesting anomaly was that the desert section adjacent to the Ammei territory was a mottled green instead of empty brown, suggesting they had some irrigation farming going.

"Looks like the nearest spaceport to Rirto is four hundred kilometers north," Circe said. "Pretty long haul."

"What about private ports?"

"*Private* generally means the owners want to keep it all to themselves."

"Policies like that often bend under the weight of a sufficiently large amount of money."

"You have such a sum handy?"

"Actually, I do."

"From...?"

I hesitated. I assumed Nask hadn't mentioned to her that I was still holding a million commarks—nine hundred thousand, now, after paying off Mindi—of his private money.

But even if Nask hadn't, Huginn might have. Best not to even bring it up. "From a source who I think would consider this a reasonable expenditure," I said instead.

Circe snorted. "I'd love to be there when you tell Kinneman how you spent the Alien Portal Agency's money," she said. "Anyway, the point's moot. The nearest private port is even farther than the public ones."

I chewed at my lip. Even if we could find an aircar to rent, a trip that long would take hours each way, and I had only two days before Selene and my father arrived at Mycene. "All right, then, let's try this," I said slowly. "Technically speaking, the only reason we need a spaceport is for their repulsors and grav beams, right?"

"You mean the things that keep us from scorching the local real estate?" Circe countered pointedly. "The things that keep system patrol ships from raining fire and warrants down on us?"

"I'm pretty sure the *Blaze* can handle the fire," I said. "And your Patth registry can probably make the warrants go away."

"None of which will help the real estate."

"Unless you pick a spot where there isn't any." I gestured toward the display. "Such as all that empty desert."

She shot me a frown, then turned back to the display. I took advantage of her moment of silence to check the scale on the image and start searching for a spot that would offer the best balance between safety and proximity.

"You're a lunatic, Roarke," Circe said. "You know that, don't you?"

"It's been mentioned once or twice," I said. "But as my father used to say, *Madness and genius are two sides of the same coin, so be very careful when it comes time to flip it.*"

"The old Earth poets were more elegant on the subject," she said. "Okay. Cards on the table. What do you expect to find down there?"

I braced myself. "I'm hoping to find a Gemini portal that'll take us to Nexus Six," I told her. "It's the only way I can think of to get to Mycene in time to keep Yiuliob's people from grabbing Selene and my father."

"What do you mean, the only way?" Circe demanded. "This is a Talariac ship. The obvious way to intercept the *Median* would have been to chase after it. Hell, we could have spent another couple of days lazing around Juniper and still reached Mycene before they even popped out of hyperspace, let alone walked into the enclave."

"Does Yiuliob have any warships?" I asked. "If he does, he's certainly had enough time to set them up at Mycene. Does First Dominant Prucital have any?"

"I didn't know the Ammei had any warships."

"I don't know, either," I said. "That's kind of the point. Even if they don't, does Rozhuhu have orders to hijack the ship or even murder everyone aboard if something goes wrong? Is he alone, or are other passengers or crew also in Yiuliob's pocket?"

"No idea," she said. "Fine. Point taken."

"Thank you," I said. "We also don't know how much exception

either side would take to us poking a stick into their plans. Coming through a portal into Prucital's backyard is the only way I can think of to hit them in a way and from a direction they absolutely won't expect."

"And if there *isn't* a portal down there?"

My throat felt suddenly dry. "Then Selene and my father are prisoners," I said as calmly as I could. "Which means I'll just have to get them out some other way."

Circe's lip twitched. "I trust you realize how thin your logical ice is here. You're saying the Ammei figured out the Pakenrills might be a useful resource, traveled all the way to the northern mountains—and I don't see anywhere to park a long-range vehicle down there—grabbed one at random, hauled him back here on some kind of public transport, found a ship and stuffed him aboard, and sent him off to Juniper."

"I know," I said. "But if you substitute Yiuliob's people for the local Ammei I think it holds together."

"*If* Yiuliob even knows there's a portal here," Circe said. "It could very well be that he and the rest of the Ammei have forgotten about this place."

"Which would be pretty strange all by itself," I said. "If the portal links to Nexus Six, it's one of only twelve Geminis there. First of Three and his minions have surely checked out all of them."

"Maybe the Belshaz portal was buried and they decided it wasn't worth digging out," Circe suggested. "Or it opened up into a hostile area that didn't invite examination. All I know is that it's not mentioned in any of the records. In fact, as far as I know, your father's the only one who was able to unbury it."

"My father's good at that sort of thing."

"So I gather," Circe said. "Now let's make it a little worse. If there *is* a portal and you find it, I can't go in there with you. Not with the Uroemm family breathing down Sub-Director Nask's neck. If they find out an Expediter under his authority was working against the Ammei—especially after the Director General's push for complete noninterference—they'll have all our heads."

"Understood," I said. I'd hoped I could talk her into back-stopping me, but had been pretty sure this was the direction it would go. "I can handle it."

"Alone?"

"Unless you want to send one of your Iykams with me."

"That would still get Sub-Director Nask in trouble. So what's the plan?"

"I take the portal to Nexus Six," I said. "I know which of the portals there goes to Mycene, and I try to sneak across to it. If I make it, I head in and wait inside the launch module for Yiuliob's people to bring Selene and my father there. When they pop into the receiver module, while they're floating downward and mostly helpless, I nail them all with gas or vertigo darts. You *do* have both options available, right?"

"I have everything you're qualified to use," Circe said. "Plus some you aren't. What if you can't get to the Mycene portal?"

"Plan B is that I get captured," I said. "The Nexus Six Ammei haul me in front of First of Three and I hope I can dance fast enough to persuade him to send a squad to Mycene with me."

"Not much of a plan."

"It's not my favorite, either," I admitted. "But once it's dark on Nexus Six, I can hopefully sneak past the portal guards and get to Mycene. If I can, we're back to plan A."

"Which isn't much better than plan B," Circe said. "Not as a one-man show, anyway."

"You've already benched yourself and your Iykams," I reminded her. "Who else is there?"

"What about Doc Robin?"

"What about him?" I asked, Robin's stories about his criminal past flashing through my mind. "I can't tell him about the portals—big dark secret, remember? Anyway, I figured he'd need to stay here to watch Bubloo until I get back." I raised my eyebrows. "Unless you were planning to leave the minute I'm off the ship?"

"No, I'll stick around for a while." She hissed out a breath. "You can't do this alone, Roarke. Even given your ridiculously high opinion of yourself, you have to realize that."

"I'll only start alone," I pointed out. "Once I've got Selene at my side there'll be two of us."

"*If* you get that far."

"I will."

"Roarke—" She broke off, half a dozen emotions chasing each other across her face. If Selene had been here, the thought occurred to me, she probably would have been able to list the whole string. As it was, all I could tell was that Circe was wrapped in a big tangle of indecision. "I assume you're at least going to do a recon first?" she asked. "Make sure your hoped-for portal actually does take you to Nexus Six?"

"Yes, that makes sense," I said, running the timeline through my head again. Yes, I should have time. "I also need to figure out where the Belshaz portal is in the Nexus Six circle, and when it'll be nighttime. I've kind of lost track of their cycle."

"All right," Circe said. "I'll find us a landing spot and set down. You go do whatever prep you need to."

"Thanks," I said, standing up. "I owe you one."

"You owe me a lot more than just one," she said, her tone going dark. "You *do* understand, don't you, that when I said *all our heads* that yours was included?"

"I'm not worried about that," I said with a quiet sigh. "Between the Ammei, the Uroemm family, and Kinneman, I'm pretty sure mine's already spoken for."

Earlier, I'd hoped for a landing spot that balanced safety and proximity. Circe did me one better, adding in convenience and intimidation.

The convenience came in the form of a small, open-topped, and *very* high-end float car waiting at the foot of the zigzag. The intimidation came in the form of two Iykams standing guard beside the car, corona guns at the ready as they faced a group of Ammei curiosity seekers who'd gathered at the edge of the irrigated crop area.

"You ever driven one of these things?" Circe asked, gesturing to the float car as we walked down the zigzag.

"No, but I know the theory," I assured her, eyeing the vehicle. Float cars, riding high on compressed air cushions, were the rough-terrain vehicle of choice for those who liked comfort and could afford the finer things in life. Not being in the latter category, I'd learned to make do with high-clearance wheeled vehicles instead. "But I'll be starting on desert sand, so there'll be time to pick up the technique."

"Unless the locals challenge your right of passage."

"I don't think so," I said, surveying the silent Ammei. "The one in the fancy hat is probably their leader, and he's standing in a fairly exposed position near the front edge. If they were planning trouble, he'd probably take a more protected spot in the center."

"Maybe," Circe said doubtfully. "You might be surprised how quickly that can change."

"Actually, I probably wouldn't," I said. "Keys?"

She produced a pair from her pocket and handed them over. "Where are you planning to start?"

"I've found the best approach is to ask directions," I said, nodding toward the Ammei. "Let's see if Hat Man can speak English."

"Friend Roarke?"

I looked up. Bubloo was standing at the top of the zigzag, twitching in agitation. The *Blaze*'s third Iykam was standing half in front of him, keeping him back. Robin stood behind them, keeping a light grip on Bubloo's upper arms. "Where do you go?" Bubloo called.

"I'm just taking a little trip, Bubloo," I called back. "I'll be back soon."

"But you go without me?" Bubloo asked, the twitching increasing in intensity. "So near my home, and yet you go without me?"

I looked at Robin, noting his sudden surprised frown. "I thought you lived in the northern mountains with the other Pakenrills," I said.

"The others?" Bubloo asked, sounding confused. "There are others? Where?"

"In the northern mountains," I repeated.

"Where exactly do you live, Bubloo?" Robin asked.

"There." Bubloo pointed behind me. "Right there. In the mountains."

I turned around. Ten or twelve kilometers past the far edge of the Ammei enclave was a close-set collection of freestanding rock outcrops, a couple of hundred meters tall, the whole group maybe three hundred meters across. An odd image flashed across my mind: a clay model of a castle some giant toddler had started and then abandoned when he was called in to lunch. "*That's* your home?" I asked, turning back to Bubloo. "*Those* are the mountains you talked about?"

"Yes, indeed," Bubloo said with clear pride, the twitching momentarily slowing. "The Eight Sisters, they're called. My family has lived there throughout our memory."

I looked at Circe, saw my sudden horrible thought reflected in her face. "Bubloo, you didn't happen to find an interesting cave near your home recently, did you?" I asked carefully. "A cave that seemed—"

"The metal cave?" Bubloo cut me off excitedly. "Yes, indeed. I found the door." The excitement faded, the twitching increasing again. "And then I found the wrong door," he added in a subdued voice. "And then..." He brightened. "But I'm home now. You and Friend Circe have brought me home. Will you not take me home? I would like to show you my home."

Beside me, Circe made an ominous sound in the back of her throat. "This had better be a joke, Roarke," she warned quietly. "There had better be a *Surprise!* and a Category Six hurricane of laughter following behind it."

"I think all we're getting is the *Surprise!* part," I said, my brain struggling to adjust to this sudden revelation. After all my theories about Bubloo...all the conspiracies and multiple layers of Ammei plots toward him...could he really simply have accidentally walked into a portal and somehow found his way to Juniper?

I took a deep breath. "But ultimately, it doesn't matter," I told Circe. "Whoever he is, however he got to Juniper, Yiuliob and the Ammei are aware of him now. They know about his sense of smell, and if it hasn't yet occurred to them that the Pakenrills might be useful it will soon." I raised my eyebrows at her. "Unless you know something about him that I don't?"

"Not a thing," she said. "All I know is that he's a person of interest to the Patth. And no, not *that* person of interest," she added. "We didn't post that bounty."

"Maybe Sub-Director Nask didn't," I said. "But if it was the Uroemm family, would you even know?"

"Why would they post a bounty on him?"

"I've been wondering about that, too," I said. "Best guess at the moment is that they wanted to entangle him with my father and use that to get to me. It was Sir Nicholas's name on the post, remember."

"Sounds like a stupid plan, if you ask me."

"Personally, I have yet to be impressed by anything the Uroemm family does."

"Fair point."

"Friend Roarke?"

I sighed, looking up again at Bubloo. I didn't really want

him along on this trip. On the other hand, I also didn't want to spend the rest of the day poking around the desert and hills blind. "Can you take me to the metal cave?" I asked.

"Of course," Bubloo said, his anxiety shifting instantly to excitement. "And then we can meet my family?"

"We'll see," I said, beckoning to him. "Come on."

"And Friend Christopher, too?" Bubloo asked.

I looked at Circe. "Your decision," she said quietly. "Just remember what I said about doing this on your own."

"And the 'big dark secret' part?"

"As far as I'm concerned, you're welcome to let him in on it," she said. "Selene's just as valuable to the Patth as the portals themselves. If you need Robin to get her back, I can't see the Director General objecting."

"If you say so," I said. "As my father used to say, *When in Rome, speak Latin.* If you're giving me official Patth permission to reveal your deepest secrets to strangers, I'm game."

"And it's not like you can get into any deeper trouble with Kinneman," she pointed out.

"Yeah. Thanks for the reminder." I looked up and beckoned to Bubloo. "Okay, Bubloo. You and Doc Robin can come with me."

"Joppadeedoos!" Bubloo exclaimed excitedly, ducking past the Iykam and bounding down the zigzag. Robin eased past the guard a little more gingerly and followed. "That way," he said, pointing toward the rock outcrops as he hopped into the float car's rear seat.

"We're not going to your home, Bubloo," Robin reminded him as he reached Circe and me.

"I know," Bubloo said, peering ahead. "The metal cave is also that way."

"Nice car," Robin said approvingly. "Better than the ones I used to drive."

"You've driven float cars before?" Circe asked.

"A few times, yes," Robin said. "It was five or six years ago, though."

"Close enough." Deftly, Circe reached over and plucked the keys from my hand. "You're driving," she said, tossing them to Robin.

"Uh . . ." He looked uncertainly at me. "Roarke?"

"You heard the lady," I said, walking around the float car's rear and getting into the front passenger seat. "Let's go."

Robin climbed in beside me, ran his eyes and hands over the controls as if memorizing where everything was, and started the engine. The skirt filled with air and we were off, heading in a wide arc away from the ship and the Ammei onlookers. Briefly, I wondered if I should still talk to Hat Man, maybe get some idea whether they had any regular contact with the other Ammei enclaves. But the portal was our top priority, and we could always get a history lesson later.

"Ooh—look!" Bubloo exclaimed, pointing to our left as Robin took us around the southeastern edge of the enclave. "There—inside that pen. See? Animals!"

"Yes, I see them, Bubloo," I confirmed, a puzzle piece I hadn't realized I was missing dropping neatly into place. "See them, Doc?"

Robin glanced to the side, paused for a second look. "Those ferret things behind the mesh?" he asked, returning his attention to his driving. "Don't think I've ever seen one before."

"I can pretty much guarantee that," I said. "They're called tenshes, and the Ammei can telepathically control them."

"Really?" Robin asked, shooting me a startled glance.

"Really," I assured him. "Line of sight, I think. Not absolutely sure about that."

"Yes, it's line of sight," Bubloo confirmed cheerfully. "The Ammei use them to guard their crops and kill pests and scavengers. I used to like to come here and watch them." He made a rasping sound, like a hoarse chuckle. "They look so much like their masters that I once believed they were Ammei children."

Robin made a harumphing sound. "Don't see the resemblance myself."

"It's the fact they've all got the same armadillo armor," I explained. "You can't see the tensh armor as clearly at this distance. Actually, Bubloo, I wondered that myself when I first saw them. I'm guessing this is where they breed them."

"Yes, they're desert animals," Bubloo said. "I've seen them brought in. I like animals," he continued more quietly. "It's very sad when there aren't very many of them."

I nodded. The tensh breeding business had probably dried up around the same time the portal system went down, which might explain why this little enclave had all but disappeared from everyone's memory. Possibly the Ammei here didn't even remember what the Icari and their subordinates had used the animals for.

But if First of Three or Yiuliob reestablished their grip on the network, this place would likely undergo a major growth spurt. "How much farther, Bubloo?" I asked.

"Not far," Bubloo said. "Those three hills directly in front of us? The door is on the other side."

"Is this the *right* door?" Robin asked as he turned us toward the right-hand edge of the hills. "Because you also said something about a wrong door."

"This is the right door," Bubloo confirmed, reluctance creeping into his voice. "I don't want to use the wrong door again."

"We'll make sure you don't," Robin assured him. "So, Roarke. Is this the pot at the end of the rainbow you were hoping for?"

I stared at the approaching hills. Pakenrills to finish the Nexus Six launch module, tenshes to repopulate the portal control system. For First of Three and Yiuliob, Belshaz might well be that pot of gold.

For me, I just wanted to get Selene and my father out of danger.

"Could be," I told Robin. "I guess we'll find out."

CHAPTER EIGHTEEN

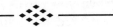

As was typical in my admittedly limited experience, the receiver module was buried under enough dirt and scrub grasses to somewhat camouflage the blatantly spherical shape. But in this case, the natural covering on the southern edge had eroded away sufficiently to leave a few square centimeters of metal showing. Probably how Bubloo had spotted it in the first place.

For all his talk about wrong doors, though, he was clearly excited to be back. Robin had barely brought the float car to a halt when Bubloo bounded out of his seat and ran over to the portal. "Here!" he called over his shoulder as he pointed to the metal. "Here is the door. Right here."

"Hang on," I said, climbing out and hurrying over to join him. "Wait for us."

"I don't see any handles," Robin said as he caught up with me. "You sure this is a door?"

"I'll show you," Bubloo said eagerly. He waited until we were flanking him, then pressed the release spot on the hatch that showed through the dirt. The hatch swung inward, disappearing inside and up.

Beside me, Robin muttered a startled curse. "Whoa."

"It gets better," I assured him, pointing into the opening as I stepped past Bubloo and gave the interior a quick visual scan.

The sphere was bathed in the usual soft glow, with no one visible. So far, so good. "Once you're inside you'll see that the hatch Bubloo just opened has folded up and melded itself up against the inner surface," I said, standing away from the hatch and turning to face Robin. "Now, here's the thing—"

I broke off as Bubloo put his hands on the edge of the hatchway and vaulted past me into the sphere. "Jumpadoo!" his voice floated back. "Come, Friend Roarke! Come, Friend Christopher!"

"I guess we'll let Bubloo go first," I continued, forcing back my annoyance. I'd planned to break trail on this one. "Here's the thing: There's an artificial gravity field inside that points radially outward. Okay? So when you get in—"

"What do you mean, radially?" Robin interrupted.

"As in from the center to the hull," I said. "Don't ask me to explain it, because I can't. When you get in, you need to give your inner ear a moment to adjust. Got it?"

"Sure," he said, clearly not getting it at all.

As my father used to say, *Experience is the best teacher, but he's pretty free with the demerits.* "Just watch me," I said.

I leaned my head and torso into the opening, waited for the vertigo to pass, then put my palms on the inner hull and pushed my way inside. For a moment I sat still on the edge, then pulled my legs the rest of the way in and stood up. "See?" I called outside.

"Yes," Robin said hesitantly. "Here goes. I guess."

"Come," Bubloo called. He was already halfway around the sphere to the interface and the launch module beyond. "The right door is in here."

"Hold up, Bubloo," I called after him. "Wait for us."

Obediently, he stopped, turning back to watch. Robin's head, arms, and torso poked through the opening, and I saw the momentary jolt of surprise and disbelief flash across his face. He took a deep breath, then mimicked my earlier push and got himself mostly inside. I grabbed his right arm as his momentum floundered and pulled him the rest of the way in. "You okay?" I asked.

"Yes," he said. "Whoa. Where the hell did this thing come from?"

"Long story," I said. "Short version is that an alien race we call the Icari built it a few thousand years ago." I gestured toward

Bubloo. "Follow Bubloo, and keep your eyes on your feet unless you want to fall on your face."

He ignored that advice, of course. The opportunity to gaze up at the alien sphere rising above him was just too great. But he managed to recover his balance before he lost it completely, so we could probably call that a win.

Still, for the rest of the walk to the interface he kept his eyes firmly on the deck in front of him.

We negotiated the interface and its opposing gravitational fields into the launch module—Bubloo and I got it on our first try, Robin made it on his third—and walked around the sphere to the extension arm. We grabbed hold, Robin silently following our lead, the local field switched direction, and we headed up.

Once again, the play of expressions across Robin's face was a source of private amusement. We reached the luminescent gray... our fingers brushed it...

Three seconds of blackness later, we were elsewhere.

I'd speculated earlier on how interesting Selene might have found tracing through Circe's string of emotions. Watching Robin's own kaleidoscope as he looked around the destination's receiver module would probably have been even more entertaining. For a few seconds his lips moved, forming unspoken words. Then, as the three of us started drifting toward the inner surface, he finally focused on me again. "And we're...?" He stopped.

"In the receiver module of a dyad-linked portal at least forty thousand light-years from Belshaz," I told him. "And you thought getting *into* the sphere was a fun ride."

He looked around again. This time, his mouth remained firmly closed, but I could see his throat working. "Okay," he said, his voice almost calm again. "Okay. I can't decide whether this whole thing is more surprising, exciting, or terrifying. You're serious about this? Instantaneous travel across multiple light-years?"

"We'll give you a quick peek outside once we're down," I said. "That should convince you."

"No," Bubloo put in nervously. "Not outside. It's not safe. There are more Ammei out there. Many, many more."

"I know, Bubloo," I said. "Unfortunately, we have no choice. We need to go out there and get to one of the other portals if we're going to rescue Selene and my father."

"Friend Selene," Bubloo murmured. "Friend Nicholas." He

huffed out a long, hissing sigh. "You speak bad choices, Friend Roarke." Another sigh. "Very well. If that is your wish and your need, I will show you. I will show you the wrong door."

I frowned. "What do you mean?"

"I will show you the wrong door," Bubloo repeated, a hint of impatience creeping into his nervousness. "Come."

I looked at Robin, got a puzzled shrug in return. "Okay," I said. "By the way, Doc, watch your landing. We pick up speed a bit at the end."

A moment later, we hit that final meter and dropped to the hull. Bubloo and I managed it more or less gracefully; Robin bobbled a bit but kept his balance. "Okay," he said. "Sure, why not? What now?"

"Bubloo?" I prompted, looking around the sphere. If this portal's positioning matched that of the others in the Nexus Six portal ring, the launch module being situated *there* should mean the likely exit hatches were . . . that group there. "You want to pick one of those hatches?"

"Not those," Bubloo called back. "Come."

I followed his voice. He'd gone an entirely different direction after landing and was now crouched over a hatch that was positioned well below the ground-level group I'd marked. "Here," he said, pressing on the release. "Here is the wrong door."

"Bubloo, there's nothing but dirt behind that one," I said. "The doors that go outside are up there." I started to point to my imaginary circle.

My hand froze halfway as Bubloo's hatch popped open to reveal open air.

"There is no dirt," Bubloo said with a mix of satisfaction and injured pride.

"What's that, a hole?" Robin asked, coming up beside me.

"Not exactly," I said, rerunning my calculations. If the hatches up there were ground level, then Bubloo's hatch . . . "The radial grav field's messing with your perceptions. That's not a hole, it's a horizontal tunnel."

"The wrong door," Bubloo repeated soberly. "Do you wish to travel into it?"

"Absolutely," I said. "But you don't have to go if you don't want to. You can stay here with Friend Christopher. Right, Doc?"

"If that's what he wants, of course," Robin said. "Personally, I'd like to see where that goes."

Bubloo seemed to draw himself up, an interesting visual given that he was still in a crouching position. "Then we shall go together," he said firmly. "I will show you. Then you will also know why it's the wrong door." He took a deep breath. "Follow."

He stretched out along the deck and slid his arms, head, and torso into the tunnel. A moment later, he'd pulled himself the rest of the way in and stood up. "Come," he said, and headed off.

"Doc?" I offered, gazing down at Bubloo as he apparently walked at right angles to gravity. Even after all my experience with portals, this one had my head spinning.

"You first," Robin said, an almost comical expression on his face as he also watched Bubloo. "I need to see this magic trick one more time before I buy it."

"Suit yourself." Positioning myself on the deck the way Bubloo had, I worked my way into the tunnel, wincing as the portal's artificial gravity gave way to the planet's real-life version. I stood up carefully, half expecting a last-second shift in direction.

But up stayed up and down stayed down. "Come on in," I called back to Robin. "The water's fine."

From inside the sphere, the tunnel's walls, floor, and ceiling had looked like plain dirt. Now, up close, I saw that it *was* dirt but that the surface had been heat-treated or otherwise glazed into a hard ceramic. Whoever had carved this thing had built it to last.

"How did you find this tunnel, Bubloo?" Robin called from behind me.

"I was looking for a way out," Bubloo called back. "This was the first door I found that did not lead into dirt." He looked halfway over his shoulder. "Friend Roarke was right about that." A shiver went visibly through his shoulders. "But it was the wrong door."

For the next few minutes we walked in silence. The tunnel's ceiling was at a comfortable height for people our size, though a pro baskethopper would probably have to walk stooped over. The walls were likewise comfortably spaced for single-file travel, but would present a challenge for a group who wanted to walk side by side.

Robin was clearly pondering the same thing. "You'd think that whoever went to all the trouble to dig a tunnel and fire-kiln the walls would have at least made it wide enough for two-way traffic," he muttered.

"I'm guessing ease of travel wasn't the builder's highest priority," I muttered back.

"What else would anyone want in a passageway?"

"Secrecy," I said. "Security. Ever notice how most Old European castle stairways circle upward to the right?"

"You've lost me," Robin said, sounding completely confused. "What do stairways have to do with this?"

"Security, medieval sword-fighting style," I explained. "If you're retreating up the stairs to the castle's inner keep, you want freedom of motion for your sword arm and obstacles for whoever's chasing you. Since most humans are right-handed, that's how castle spiral stairs were built."

"Truly so?" Bubloo called, again half turning toward us. "That is very clever. Are all humans so?"

"You mean are we all clever?" I shook my head. "Sadly, no."

"We're not all nice and trustworthy, either," Robin said. "You need to remember that."

For a moment, Bubloo seemed to digest the warning. "Do you speak of Friend Circe?" he asked.

"I don't know," Robin said. "I don't really know her. I just want you in general to be wary of humans. Sometimes they speak truth and encouragement. Sometimes they don't."

"I will remember." Bubloo pointed ahead. "The other side of the wrong door. Do you see it?"

I nodded. The glow from the portal we'd left had faded with increased distance, but I could see a faint sheen of metal ahead. Apparently, our tunnel ended at another portal.

I caught my breath as it abruptly clicked. Bubloo…the Belshaz portal…the wrong door to this tunnel…another portal beyond.

Could the wrong door have taken Bubloo to the Juniper Gemini portal? Was that how he'd wound up in the Ammei enclave? More importantly, were there more tunnels down here, specifically ones that would let me get from the Belshaz portal to the Mycene one without going overground on Nexus Six?

Because if there were, I suddenly had a brand-new plan A.

Bubloo was crouched beside the metal when we reached him. "Beware," he said. "There may be others inside."

"No problem," I said, making sure my plasmic was riding loose in its holster. "We're ready."

Bubloo nodded and pressed the release. The hatch swung

open, disappearing from view as it folded itself up against the sphere's interior. Bubloo ducked down and started to lean into the opening—

And gave a muffled yelp as I grabbed his collar and hauled him back into the tunnel. The movement simultaneously propelled me forward, and I reached into the sphere and slapped the hatch Bubloo had just opened. Obediently, it detached itself from the inner hull and swung back into place.

But not before I got a glimpse of another hatch swinging open far above me.

"What is it?" Robin whispered urgently.

"One of the other hatches just opened," I whispered back. "I got a glimpse of daylight as it started."

"Did he see us?" Bubloo asked, trembling with reaction and fear. "Did he see us?"

"I don't know," I said. "I don't think so. He was just poking his head in when our hatch closed."

"Has he come to travel?" Bubloo asked.

"I don't know that, either," I said, kneeling and pressing my ear against the hatch. Nothing. "I don't hear any footsteps. Can't feel any vibrations, either."

"Would you be able to hear or feel anything anyway?" Robin asked. "That metal looks pretty thick."

"Good point," I conceded, looking at my watch. "On the other hand, I *do* know how long it takes to get to the launch module and up the extension arm. I'll do a countdown, then head in for a look."

Robin grunted. "Better add twenty percent to your estimate," he warned. "He might be a dawdler."

The minutes ticked by. I added Robin's twenty percent, then added another ten just to be on the safe side.

And then it was time. "You two stay back," I said, drawing my plasmic. "I'll close the hatch behind me. If I'm not back in twenty minutes, go back to the other portal and Belshaz."

"You want me to come with you?" Robin asked.

"I'd rather you stay here and watch over Bubloo," I said. Turning back to the hatch, I reached for the release—

Once again, Bubloo was faster than expected. Stretching past me, he touched the release. "I brought you here," he said earnestly as the hatch once again disappeared inside. "I will come with you."

"Yeah, hold it," I said, pushing him back and peering inside. No one was in the receiver module, nor was anyone visible in the parts of the launch module I could see. "You need to wait here with Doc Robin, Bubloo."

"But—"

"Wait here," I cut him off sternly. "I mean it."

He gave a little whimper and huddled down on the tunnel floor. I holstered my weapon, pulled myself inside the module, and closed the hatch. Drawing my plasmic again, I headed around the curve toward the interface.

The launch module was indeed deserted. I rolled through the opening, studying the readouts as I walked to the extension arm. With full-range portals there were twin displays that lit up for a few minutes after each transit, one of them showing the address of the launching portal, the other the address of the receiving one. But with Gemini portals linked to only one other Gemini, there was no point in having any such displays and the Icari had therefore left them off.

There were probably more subtle ways to tell if a Gemini had recently sent a traveler on his way. Unfortunately, I didn't know what any of those clues were.

There *was* a way, though, to tell if this was the Nexus Six end of the Juniper module. Unfortunately, it would require me to do a quick trip across and back, and with the uncertainties inherent in such a trip I didn't want to try it and possibly leave Bubloo and Robin hanging.

Now that I knew about this back door, I'd make sure Bubloo and Robin stayed behind next time.

They were waiting nervously, the hatch already popped open, when I once again rolled into the receiver module and walked toward them. "All clear," I announced when I was close enough for them to hear.

"Was it a traveler?" Bubloo asked.

"I don't know," I said. "It could be the local Ammei are doing spot-checks of their portals. Given how many times lately some intruder has shown up in their backyard, I can't say I blame them."

"Great," Robin said tightly. "If they spot the open tunnel hatch back in the Belshaz portal, we're in serious trouble. Seems to me it's time to tuck tail."

"Not quite yet," I said. "Remember, we're assuming they

think that portal isn't of any interest. Not really much point in bothering with it."

"Yes, but—"

"You're welcome to go if you want," I cut him off. "Bubloo, did you find any more of these tunnels?"

"No, of course not," Bubloo said, shivering. "I had already found one wrong door. Why should I seek to find more?"

"You think there are others?" Robin asked.

"There are twelve Gemini portals in the Nexus Six ring," I said. "We've got a tunnel between two of them. Why shouldn't there be tunnels linking all of them?"

"Maybe this was a special case?"

"Maybe," I said. "But getting from one Nexus Six portal to another is a pretty easy overland stroll. The only reason I can think of to go to all this effort is to keep your movements out of sight."

"I don't want to find another wrong door," Bubloo said, his voice trembling. "But I also do not want to be seen. I will find one more door, Friend Roarke. One more. Then I go to my home. If you afterward wish others, you must seek them out yourself."

"Fair enough," I said, eyeing the open hatch that led back to the Belshaz portal and trying to extrapolate where the next tunnel in line would be.

Bubloo was already on it, heading across the sphere toward the group of hatches I'd tentatively tagged as the most likely locations.

And as he walked, I noticed for the first time that he was sniffing, quietly and rhythmically. "Bubloo?" I called as I caught up with him.

He stopped. So did the sniffing. "Yes?"

"Do the hatches hiding tunnels smell different from the others?"

He hesitated, looked at Robin, then back at me. "There are things that can be smelled in these metal caves," he said evasively. "I don't always know what those things are or what they mean. I'm sorry."

"No, it's all right," I said. "Sorry to interrupt. Please; continue."

He nodded and resumed both his walking and his sniffing.

There was a whisper of air as Robin came up behind me. "You thinking that whatever he's smelling Selene could, too?" he muttered.

"It's a thought," I said. "If so, it might make sense to hold off a full exploration until I get her back. Let's start by seeing what Bubloo finds."

"Here," Bubloo said, again crouching over one of the hatches. "It is here." He pressed the release.

And once again we were gazing down into a long tunnel.

"He makes it look so easy," Robin commented dryly. "After you."

I nodded and laid down on the deck. "No, Friend Roarke," Bubloo said, dropping beside me. "I found the door. I will go first."

"That's okay, Bubloo," I said. "I can—"

I broke off as he pulled himself into the tunnel ahead of me. "Bubloo!" I stage-whispered after him. "Come back."

I might as well have ordered the tide to reverse direction. Bubloo got to his feet and hurried into the fading light.

Rolling my eyes, I followed, Robin again bringing up the rear. We reached the other end, Bubloo again keyed the hatch, and again we found ourselves looking into a receiver module.

"Now I end," Bubloo said firmly, backing away from the entrance. "If you wish to continue, Friend Roarke—"

He broke off, his eyes widening. "He was here!" he said, fresh excitement in his voice. "Friend Nicholas—he was *here*."

"My father?" I demanded, squeezing past him to the tunnel mouth. If he was here...

But no. The sphere was empty. "When?" I asked. "How long ago?"

"Not long," Bubloo said, his excitement rising another notch. "Not long. Days. Perhaps weeks."

"Can you narrow it down any?" Robin asked. "Did he just come through in the past couple of days?"

"I don't think so," Bubloo said hesitantly. "Not so recently. Days or weeks."

"Bubloo—" Robin began.

"It's all right," I cut him off. "If he was here at all, this is almost certainly the Mycene portal. Thank you, Bubloo. You're free to go back to Belshaz."

"Yes," Bubloo said. "Come, Friend Christopher."

"You go ahead," Robin said, a hint of suspicion in his voice. "I'll stay with Roarke a little longer."

"Don't worry, I'm not going to do anything stupid," I assured him as I climbed into the sphere. "Just a little recon."

"And that doesn't qualify as something stupid?" Robin countered. "Right. Go ahead, Bubloo. I'm staying here."

"All right," Bubloo said. "Be safe, Friend Christopher. Friend Roarke." He squeezed past Robin and retreated down the tunnel.

"Just leave the hatches open for us," I called back to him.

There was no response. "I'm sure he will," Robin said as he followed me into the receiver module. "So we're doing recon?"

"*I'm* doing recon," I corrected as I headed toward the interface. "You're staying right here."

"Forget it," he said, falling into step beside me. "This whole thing's got my full attention."

"As do I?" I suggested.

He shrugged. "Sure. Whatever that means."

I hesitated. But we were going to have to have this conversation sometime. It might as well be now. "It means you want to keep an eye on the pot of gold at the end of the rainbow." I stopped and turned to face him. "Seeing as you're a hunter."

He was good, all right. No twitches or sudden catchings of breath, and the only thing that changed in his expression was a slight hardening of his face and eyes. "Excuse me?" he asked.

"You heard me," I said. "But don't worry about it. Right now I need someone at my side who's good at stalking, shooting, and running away, and I don't want you to pretend that all you've got is some imaginary street gang background to draw on."

For another few seconds he continued to stare at me. Then his lip twitched. "Actually, everything I told you about my life was true," he said. "I just left out the past couple of years of my job history. What gave me away?"

"Nothing you did or said," I said, breathing a little easier. The last thing I needed was for him to stubbornly pretend to be less competent than he really was. "Along with the air of competence we've already discussed it was your ability to quickly adapt to a changing environment. No matter what violent or outlandish things happened, you took everything in stride." I considered. "Plus, of course, the fact that I now know you staged the scene where we first met."

His eyes narrowed, just noticeably. "What are you talking about?"

"You weren't in the taverno because you were Bubloo's doctor and he kept running away from you," I said flatly. "In fact, I don't even think the two of you had ever met before that night. Bubloo certainly seemed confused by your presence and attention."

"Except that the POI bounty on him wasn't filed until a couple of days after that," Robin pointed out. "So why would I have even cared about him?"

"I don't know," I said. "Why don't you tell me?"

He sighed. "Fine—you got me. I've got a buddy at Bounty Hunter Central who keeps an eye on upcoming posts while they're being put together and vetted. He spotted the POI on Bubloo, knew I was already on Juniper, and sent me a heads-up."

"That's all?" I asked. "It's a big planet."

"He also fed me data on Bubloo's traveling habits," Robin said. "I was in the taverno to confirm he was the right target before I moved in."

"Very professional." I raised my eyebrows. "Only then Selene and I walked into your life."

"With your combined bounty of four million commarks," he said sourly. "Yeah, I should have known you'd pick up on that."

"So why didn't you switch targets?"

"Well, as *my* father used to say, *Why settle for a bird in the hand when you can have three of them?*" He smiled briefly, then sobered. "No, actually, he never said anything that clever. The truth is that by the time I realized who you were, I'd already locked myself into Bubloo and the story I'd first pitched to you. And vice versa—you saw how he grabbed on and clung to me like a wet handkerchief. I couldn't cut him loose without raising red flags. So I decided to hold off any action, keep all of you close, and wait for my chance."

"Seems to me you had several along the way."

"There were one or two," he agreed. "But like I said, this thing's got my attention." He shrugged. "Besides, I figured I could always turn you in for the bounty later."

"You could *try* to turn us in," I corrected. "Not necessarily the same thing. So why did you call those hunters down on us at your apartment?"

"Yeah, sorry about that," he apologized. "Bubloo was being suspiciously vague about where he lived, so I figured there must be something valuable there. Or at least something to explain why that POI was about to be posted on him. I figured an imminent threat might shake that information loose."

"I assume the fake badgemen weren't part of the plan?"

"Hardly," he said darkly. "The point is that whichever way you slice it—whether I'm all noble and helpful, or whether I just want to maximize my profits—you can trust me to help you get Selene back."

"I'll hold you to that," I said, resuming my walk toward the launch module.

Of course, as he'd already pointed out, once Selene was safely back there was a very real chance he would suddenly turn on us. But I'd face that one when it happened.

In the meantime, it wouldn't hurt to remind him that I had a hole card in this game. "Just bear in mind," I added, "that once Selene's here, she'll know if you decide to pull anything."

"Yes, that thought had crossed my mind," he said. "You happen to have a spare weapon I could borrow?"

"Circe can probably get you something when we get back to the *Blaze*," I said. "You shouldn't need anything right now. This is just a recon, remember?"

"Right," he said. "I'd forgotten."

CHAPTER NINETEEN

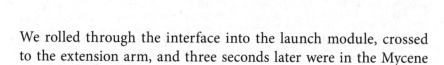

We rolled through the interface into the launch module, crossed to the extension arm, and three seconds later were in the Mycene receiver module.

Or at least that's where I hoped we'd ended up. If my father had been traveling between enclaves via portal before switching to his yacht, he could have left lingering scent through the whole system. In which case, we could be anywhere.

"Well?" Robin muttered as we floated toward the inner hull.

"Don't know yet," I answered. One of the hatches was open, but what little I could see from my current position didn't really tell me anything. "I'll take a look outside once we land."

"Make it a fast look," he warned. "I can't imagine it's much fun to race around to the big sphere with enemies chasing you."

I grimaced. "I *can* imagine it, and no, it isn't."

A minute later, we'd landed about a quarter of the way around from the open hatch. "If you want to go over to the interface and wait there—" I began.

"I don't," he cut me off. "Stop wasting time."

I nodded, and together we went the rest of the way around the sphere, doing the last few meters in a military crawl. We reached the hatchway, and I turned my thumbnail into a mirror and eased it up for a look.

It was Mycene, all right. Selene and I hadn't been close enough to see the portal during our recon a couple of weeks ago, but across the clearing that surrounded the portal was a paved, tree-lined path that looked very much like the other end of the one we'd started along from the export center. It was flanked by a pair of what looked like guardhouses, the clearing itself surrounded by tall and sturdy-looking mesh fences. Even if those two soldiers hadn't stopped Selene and me, I reflected, we wouldn't have gotten very far.

"Well?" Robin prompted.

"We're here," I confirmed, taking a closer look at the guardhouses. There were windows and gunports facing us, with presumably others pointed the opposite direction. Protection from all sides.

I was studying the fence when a group of armed Ammei strode into view along the path, marched between the guardhouses, and came to a halt.

"Company," I warned Robin, frowning. The soldiers were just standing there, holding formation, as if waiting for a signal to proceed.

"As in, we're getting out of here?"

"Agreed," I said. I started to pull my thumb back—

And froze. Emerging from the path was First Dominant Prucital, fancy hat and all. Walking close behind him were Selene and my father.

Behind them, all sunshine and cheerfulness, was Rozhuhu.

Rozhuhu. Trusted assistant to First of Three of Nexus Six. Secret spy for First Dominant Yiuliob of Juniper and the ambitious Juniper Glory. Strolling along behind Selene and my father, escorting them to their doom.

And there wasn't a damn thing I could do to stop him.

I swallowed hard, taking another look around. Two of us against the ten soldiers I could see, plus whoever was in the guardhouses, plus however many more Prucital or Rozhuhu could whistle up at a moment's notice. One plasmic and one spare power pack against a collection of lightning guns that could take out fully armored EarthGuard Marines.

My only chance was if Rozhuhu let Selene and my father enter the portal ahead of him and all the guards. In that case, I might be able to shoot enough of the rearguard and create enough chaos that we could get around to the launch module before we were likewise gunned down.

But as my father used to say, *Being a traitor makes someone evil, not stupid.* Even as I ran all the possible scenarios through my mind Rozhuhu said something to Prucital, Prucital said something back, and four of the waiting soldiers stepped forward and arranged themselves in vanguard position in front of Selene and my father. Another word from Prucital, and they all headed toward the portal.

Quickly, I pulled my hand out of view, stomach and heart churning. Selene...my father...

"We take the guards as they come in," Robin murmured. There was dark determination in his eyes, a layer of iced steel beneath the words. "Fast, quiet, before they can give the alarm. Strangle them, break their necks, crush their throats—whatever it takes. Got it?"

I swallowed. My hand-to-hand technique wasn't nearly up to the standards this job was going to demand.

But I'd once seen someone press a plasmic's muzzle hard into someone's chest before firing, and surprisingly little of the noise and light leaked out through his torso. If that was what it took to free Selene, I would just have to grit my conscience and do it. "Got it," I said.

Robin nodded, and I started a mental countdown. If they were maintaining the same pace as when they started, we had maybe thirty more seconds before the first soldier rolled in on us. I drew my plasmic and flicked off the safety...

"*Oh!*"

I twitched. The voice was Selene's but it was so distorted by pain as to be almost unrecognizable. I gathered my feet beneath me, ready to leap to her defense—

"What is it?" my father's anxious voice came. "Selene? What's the matter?"

"Something in...it's in the air," Selene answered, fighting the words out between gasps of breath. "I don't know what. Something...I can't breathe."

"Hang on," my father said. "She needs a clean room, First Dominant, like the one I showed you aboard the *Median*. Do you have anything like that here?"

"No, nothing that can be cleared quickly," Prucital said.

"What about the sampling module?" Rozhuhu asked. "That has vents."

"Not fast enough," my father said, his voice dark and anxious. "And she'll need her clothes cleaned, too. We have to get her back, First Dominant. Right now."

"Yes, of course," Prucital said. He didn't sound happy, but I couldn't hear any hesitation in his voice.

I smiled grimly, feeling the tension twisting through my body easing a little. And really, why *should* there be any doubt? They had Selene, and whether Prucital was planning to hand her over to First of Three or to join Rozhuhu in spiriting her back to Juniper, there was no way she could escape. A few hours' delay wouldn't mean much to them.

But it meant the whole Spiral to me.

"Come on, Selene," my father said, and I could visualize him helping her back toward the path and wherever he'd left the *Median*. I listened as the sounds of voices faded away, then caught Robin's eye and motioned him back toward the other side of the sphere.

A minute later, we were in the launch module. "What the hell just happened?" he asked, sounding confused.

"Selene happened," I told him. "She got close enough to smell me. Even better, she got close enough to smell my panic."

"And from *that* she figured out what you're up to?"

"Hardly," I said. "But in the middle of a crisis, your default goal is always to buy time. That's what she and my father have done."

"Nice," Robin said, nodding. "What now?"

"I need some things from the *Blaze*," I said. "You'll need to stand by here and watch while I go back."

"Can you tell me what you need?" he asked. "I mean, exactly?"

"Yes," I said. "But—"

"Then I'll go," he interrupted. "If something goes sideways and you have to improvise, you're the one she'll trust and synchronize to. What's the shopping list?"

I hesitated. I wasn't at all sure I trusted Robin this much, especially not with all our lives on the line. But he had a vested interest in keeping us alive and whole, and he was right about Selene and me working better together than the two of them would. "Fine," I ground out. "First is a weapon for you—something nonlethal like a vertigo dart gun would be good. Then . . ."

I ran the list for him. Fortunately, it was short. "Got it," he said, grabbing the extension arm and rising toward the center of the sphere. "Hang tight. I'll be back as quick as I can."

I watched until he hit the luminescent gray section and vanished. Then, with nothing better to do, I went back to the interface and settled down with my eyes and plasmic trained on the receiver module's open hatchway.

As my father used to say, *There will be times when there's nothing you can do but sit quietly and think. Use those minutes wisely.* And so I did.

It was an hour and a half before Robin finally returned. In that time, I died approximately a thousand deaths. Each time I heard voices or saw flickers of movement near the hatchway I tensed up, resting my chest on the edge of the interface, stretching out my arms into the receiver module with my plasmic in a two-handed marksman's grip, feeling the dueling gravity fields and wondering if it would be Selene or a guard who would come into my sights first. But each time the movements went away, and the voices faded, and I continued my lonely vigil.

It was almost a shock when Robin suddenly appeared in the center of the receiver module, a bandolier-style weapons belt wrapped around his chest and waist.

What was *definitely* a shock was that Bubloo was with him.

I waited until it was clear which part of the sphere Robin was drifting toward. Then, keeping a wary eye on the open hatchway, I rolled into the receiver module and hurried to intercept him.

"Got it," Robin whispered when he was close enough for me to hear. "Sorry about him," he added, nodding toward Bubloo, who was drifting toward another part of the sphere. "I mentioned that Selene was in trouble, and he insisted on coming back with me."

"Terrific," I ground out as I headed toward Bubloo. Bad enough to be dealing with the four-body problem of Selene, my father, Robin, and me. Bubloo had now added a fifth body to the mix. "This could be dangerous, Bubloo," I stage-whispered as he landed on the deck in front of me. "Let me send you back."

"Not with Friend Selene and Friend Nicholas at risk," Bubloo said in a shaking but oddly firm voice.

"I appreciate that," I said. "But there's nothing you can do to help."

"Of course there is something." And to my amazement, he drew himself to his full height, his shaking stopping. "You say the Ammei can use me instead of Friend Selene," he said. "If there is no other way to free her, I will offer myself to stand in her place."

I looked at Robin. He was clearly as flabbergasted as I was. "Bubloo—"

"There will be no argument," Bubloo insisted. "If you cannot free her, I will go with them."

It was clear there was no point in arguing the point further, especially since the neighborhood was about to get crowded. "We'll discuss it later," I said, taking Bubloo's arm and hurrying him toward the launch module. "Doc?"

"Ryuku plasmic, one," Robin said, tapping the muted-gray weapon holstered on his bandolier as he came up on Bubloo's other side.

"Good," I said. The same type of weapon Huginn carried, I noted. Standard Expediter issue, apparently. "And?"

"Airguns, two each," he said. "Spare vertigo dart magazines, four each."

"You sound like an accountant."

"Doctors like tidy lists, too."

"Right," I said. "The balloon?"

"Currently floating in the center of the Nexus Six end of the Juniper receiver," he said. "Circe didn't have any helium, so she electrolyzed some water and got you hydrogen instead. Good enough?"

I nodded. "Good enough."

"The balloon was very pretty," Bubloo offered as we reached the interface and Robin rolled through it. "What was its purpose?"

"To keep Yiuliob from sending reinforcements from Juniper," I told him. "Remember that when you travel through the portal it sends you to the center of the receiver?"

"Yes." Bubloo's face cleared as he rolled in behind Robin. "Oh. Yes, I understand. If something's already in that spot, it can't send anything else."

"Exactly," I said, following him in.

"Clever," Robin said, handing me an airgun and two magazines. "So what's the new plan?"

"We let them all come into the receiver module," I said. "As they walk along the curve, they'll hopefully spread out enough for us to target everyone except Selene and my father. While everyone is trying to see and aim straight, we nip back to Nexus Six, use the tunnels back to the Belshaz portal, then back to Belshaz itself. We hop aboard the *Blaze*, tell Circe to floor it, and are in hyperspace before the vertigo drug wears off."

"Sounds good," Robin said. "Also sounds wildly optimistic. Whatever happened to *no plan survives contact with the enemy?*"

"Sure," I said. "That's what plan B is for."

"And plan B is...?"

"Usually made up on the fly."

He sent me a look that was a mix of glower and dark amusement. "It really is remarkable that you've lived this long, Roarke."

"I find myself thinking the same thing on occasion," I conceded.

"I bet you do," he said. "Luckily, Circe had another clever idea." He pulled a flimsy plastic bottle from the back of his bandolier and tossed it to me. "She said you'd understand."

I caught the bottle, checked the contents label, and smiled. "She was right," I assured him. "Especially seeing as how I was the first one to come up with this trick."

His forehead creased. "Meaning?"

"It was a plan B I came up with on the fly a few years ago," I said, sliding the bottle into my jacket pocket. "Nice to know that Circe takes time to read the files when she's handed a job. But enough chatter. When Selene and I visited a few weeks ago, I spotted a pair of single-pad landing spots big enough for the *Median*. If they landed on one of those, they could be here any time."

"Got it," Robin said. "Bubloo, you stay back out of the way."

"Yes," Bubloo said, twitching again and sniffing the air. "They come. They come now."

I nodded and stretched out on my side by the interface. Turning my left thumbnail to mirror mode, I eased it above the rim.

"A little higher," Robin muttered.

I nodded and shifted my thumbnail slightly toward him. "Got it," he said, peering at the thumbnail and the image that both of us could now see. "When they come, you take the ones in back. I'll take the ones in front."

I nodded agreement. The seconds ticked by...

And then they were there.

I'd been right earlier about Rozhuhu not being stupid. The first four through the receiver module hatchway were Ammei guards, their lightning guns clutched close to their bodies as they rolled inside. As each got back to his feet he swiveled his gun around into ready position, and I saw the weapons were on shoulder slings. The soldiers stood in place for a few seconds, giving the sphere and interface a quick scan.

I tensed. But they were looking for intruders, not something as small as a single human thumb. They finished their survey, said something unintelligible, and Rozhuhu rolled into the module.

Followed by First Dominant Prucital.

"Roarke?" Robin muttered.

I gazed at the reflection, my mind churning. If Prucital wasn't on Yiuliob's side, shooting him would likely lead to unpleasant consequences down the line. But if he *was* part of the group plotting against Selene... "Shoot them all," I muttered back.

"Got it."

Selene and my father were next, followed by four more Ammei soldiers. The whole group took a moment to sort themselves out, then started around the curve toward us.

I let them get to the lowest position from our point of view where, as I'd predicted, they presented the most open formation we were going to get. I nodded across the interface at Robin, and in unison we rolled over, brought our heads and gunhands over the interface into combat position, and opened fire.

As my father used to say, *If you shoot fish in a barrel, don't expect to get any further use out of that barrel.* But in this case, sacrificing the tactic and the element of surprise was worth it. Unlike the flash of a plasmic or the flash-bang of a slug gun, the shots from our airguns made barely a whisper of sound and nothing visible at all, leaving our targets with no idea where the attack was coming from. Even better, as I started taking out the cluster of guards at the rear, Robin held off his assault on the ones in front for a couple of seconds, leading the Ammei to the conclusion that the attack was coming from their rear and the receiver module hatchway behind them. By the time the soldiers still on their feet turned, looked in vain for an enemy, and real-ized their mistake, it was too late. The last guard was just lifting his lightning gun toward us when Robin's dart sent him writhing on the deck with the others.

In the meantime, Selene and my father had threaded their way through the gunfire and carnage and were racing toward us.

"Get back!" I snapped to Robin, rolling away from the interface to give the fugitives room. Selene came through first, with my father two seconds behind her. "You all right?" I asked, giving both of them a quick once-over as they scrambled to their feet. To my relief, neither looked like they'd been hurt or mistreated.

"We're fine," my father answered. "What are we doing?"

"Getting out of here." I stuffed my airgun into my belt, pulled out Circe's bottle of naphtha, and twisted off the cap. "First we need to lock the back door." I dumped the liquid into the interface, and as it churned and spread out in response to the spheres' dueling grav fields I drew my plasmic and fired into the floating puddle.

And suddenly the whole interface was filled with roiling flame.

"Okay," I said, holstering my weapon and turning toward the extension arm.

To find Selene and Bubloo crouched together over a collapsed and semiconscious Doc Robin.

"What happened?" I demanded, hurrying over to them.

"I don't know," Selene said. "He's barely conscious, and his scent has gone all strange."

"I think it was something from the soldiers," Bubloo said, his nervous twitching back with a vengeance. "I saw him jerk right at the end, and then he went limp."

"Terrific," I muttered, getting my arm under Robin's shoulders. With my full attention on Selene and my father and their mad dash to safety, I'd completely missed whatever had happened. "Dad, help me get him up."

A moment later, we'd assembled at the base of the extension arm. "What are we going to do with him?" my father asked as we floated upward.

"I can take him back to Friend Circe," Bubloo offered. "She may be able to cure him."

"That's all right, Bubloo," I said. "We'll take him together. We're going that way anyway."

"Wait a minute," my father said. "I don't know about *your* plans, but Selene and I are due for a meeting with First of Three. *And* with Prucital and Rozhuhu," he added pointedly, "which now isn't going to be quite the friendly reunion I'd envisioned."

"I don't know about your envisionings, Dad," I said, "but you weren't going anywhere near *Imistio* Tower. Rozhuhu is Yiuliob's agent, and the only reunion you were headed for was you, Selene, Yiuliob, and a dark room somewhere on Juniper."

"You don't understand, Gregory," my father said, shaking his head. "We're all going to Nexus Six because—"

We hit the end of the extension arm, the universe went black, and we popped into the center of the Mycene portal's Nexus Six end.

"—precisely because no one needs Selene to sniff out the Juniper portal anymore. We have another, better way to find Nexus One."

"I'm happy for you," I said, keeping a wary eye on the hatchways as we floated downward. If one of the Nexus Six soldiers who'd been doing spot-checks earlier picked this moment to peek inside, we were in trouble. "I hope you can pull it off without Selene, because we're officially out."

"Would you please listen to me?" my father said, starting to sound irritated. "It's no longer a matter of *sniffing*. It's a matter of *reading*."

I frowned at Selene, floating alongside me. There was a calm sort of wariness in her pupils. "Reading what?" I asked.

"The medallion I gave you," she said. "Remember? We've studied the writing, and it turns out to be from an old Kadolian epic poem."

"Which First Dominant Prucital recognized as being similar to an equally old Ammei version," my father added. "*The path to freedom can only be found by the heart that sees the farthest.*"

"That's just as the Gold Ones said to me," Bubloo called excitedly from across the module. He and Robin had come through close together, I saw, with Bubloo holding onto his still-dazed companion. The two of them were aiming toward a landing near the open tunnel hatch, which so far Selene and my father didn't seem to have noticed, or at least hadn't focused on closely enough to realize it didn't lead to the Nexus Six surface. "The chosen one destined to free the rest of her people."

"Yes, I quote that poem all the time," I said. "I trust this is going somewhere useful?"

"It is, and it's arrived," my father said. "Prucital tells me there's a small percentage of books in the *Imistio* Tower library that are in Kadolian instead of Ammei. He thinks that if Selene can find the poem and decipher the clue, we'll be able to locate Nexus One."

"Really," I said, eyeing him closely. The others might not have caught the subtle pronoun shift of *he* to *we*, but I had. "And why exactly do we think that?"

"Because the medallions are part of a lore package that is supposed to help the Kadolians find their homeworld again," he said. "First of Three and the Nexus Six Ammei—"

"Wait a second," I interrupted. "What's this about a home-world? I thought the Gold Ones said it was about Kadolian freedom or some such."

"We aren't wanderers by choice, Gregory," Selene said quietly, an old ache in her pupils. "The location of our world has been lost."

"Oh," I said lamely. There was a soft thud, and I looked over to see that Bubloo and Robin had landed. "I didn't...you never told me."

"It's not something we speak of," she said. "And really, what would telling you have accomplished?"

"Probably nothing," I conceded. Somehow, such a scenario had never even occurred to me. I'd just assumed the Kadolians traveled around the Spiral because they preferred the nomadic life. And really, how do you misplace a whole planet?

I winced. With Icari portal technology, it was easy. All it took was forgetting an address.

"Whoa," my father said. "Where did Bubloo go?"

I looked across the module. Bubloo and Robin were nowhere to be seen. "Into that tunnel there," I said, pointing at the open hatchway. "It runs underground and connects to the Nexus Six ends of the Juniper and Belshaz Geminis. Bubloo stumbled on it when he fell into his hometown portal and couldn't figure out how to get back. I'm thinking that's how he wound up on Juniper."

"Interesting," my father said thoughtfully. "So you're saying that Yiuliob *didn't* deliberately bring him there?"

"I'm not giving up on any theories yet," I said. "Especially given Yiuliob's ambitions. But when you add in the fact that Yiuliob wanted me to tell *him* about Bubloo, the rabbit-hole theory starts sounding more plausible." Selene and I dropped the last meter to the hull and headed toward the hatchway. "But we can sort that out later. Right now we need to get to Belshaz before anyone can try to stop us—"

I broke off. From somewhere far away, like it was coming from a deep well, came a faint shriek.

"Come on," I snapped, breaking into a flat-out run. The only place that shout could have come from was the tunnel, and the only person it could have come from was Bubloo. I reached the hatchway, did a half dive, half roll inside and charged off into the dim light. A few seconds later, I reached the other end and looked through the opening.

Bubloo and Robin were already gone, presumably through the other tunnel back to the Belshaz portal. But even as I hauled myself through into the receiver module I saw that the other tunnel hatch was shut. Biting out a curse, I ran over to that part of the sphere. I reached it, dropped to my knees, and pressed the hatch release.

Nothing.

"Selene!" I called, moving to the next hatch in line and keying it. Again, nothing. "Come here—I need you."

"I'm here," she said, coming up beside me.

"Which one did Bubloo touch?" I asked.

She leaned over, her nostrils and eyelashes working. "That one," she said, pointing to the hatch I'd first tried. "Dr. Robin touched it, too."

I cursed under my breath. "Of course he did. *Damn* it. He's a hunter, Selene." I slapped the hatch again. Still nothing. "Is that the only one he touched?"

"Yes," she said. "Robin's a *hunter*?"

I nodded, staring down at the hatch. But how had he then locked it? I'd never heard of anyone being able to lock portal hatches. "I'm thinking he decided to cut his losses, faked whatever the hell that fit was supposed to be, and hauled Bubloo out of here for the hundred-thousand bounty on him."

"But he smelled strange," Selene reminded me, puzzlement in her pupils.

"Maybe he took something to help with the illusion," I said, still trying to work it out. "Okay. Maybe he didn't actually lock it, but just sealed it shut. Maybe a few plasmic shots around the edges—"

"Can you get it open?" my father asked as he came up behind us.

I squeezed the grip of my own plasmic. No, not plasmic fire. Icari metal was far stronger than that, especially with an entire receiver module to act as a heat sink. "Must be some sort of glue," I said. "Something he got from the *Blaze*."

"I repeat: Can you open—?"

"Yes, I heard you," I bit out. "No, I can't."

I looked up. The hydrogen balloon Robin had brought was still blocking any troops Yiuliob might try to send. But even at this distance I could see the balloon had been thrown together out of whatever Circe had on hand, and I doubted it would last more than a few hours at the most.

Meanwhile, we had a more urgent deadline waiting behind the fire barrier I'd created in the Mycene portal. The minute the naphtha burned itself out, the soldiers of an undoubtedly furious First Dominant Prucital would be coming down the rabbit hole after us.

Which left us just one option.

"Okay, Dad, you win," I said standing up and heading around the module's curve. "You wanted to go to Nexus Six and check in with First? You got it."

"Good," my father said as he and Selene caught up with me. "But there's something you should know before we—"

He stopped as, straight ahead of me, one of the hatchways opened to reveal bright sunshine beyond. Even as I braked to a halt, a pair of Ammei rolled through the opening and scrambled to their feet. They spotted us and in impressive unison swiveled their lightning guns in our direction.

And I felt a sudden chill run through me as I saw both were wearing the armbands of Yiuliob's soldiers.

"I was going to say," my father continued quietly into the sudden silence, "that you don't have to worry about First Dominant Yiuliob's people coming to Nexus Six."

"No," I said with a sigh. "Because they're already here."

CHAPTER TWENTY

The soldiers took their time disarming us and marching us across the open area to *Imistio* Tower. Once inside, they held us in one of the entryway rooms for nearly an hour. The soldiers remained silent the entire time, though the brooding looks they gave us spoke volumes. For our part, there didn't seem to be much to say.

Finally, the summons arrived. Still in silence, the soldiers sorted us out into the familiar Ammei formation of soldiers in front, Selene, my father, and me in the middle, and more guards behind us. Then we all marched along the ramps and up to the tower's ninth floor.

First of Three was waiting there, seated in the Chair of Authority with his fancy hat looking both awesome and, to my eye anyway, a bit silly. His armadillo scales seemed to have been polished, though I was vaguely disappointed to see they hadn't been painted gold the way Bubloo had described the Gold Ones. First Dominant Prucital stood on his left, looking just as formal and exactly as angry as I'd expected after the debacle in the Mycene portal.

Standing on First's right was First Dominant Yiuliob, looking like he owned the place. With his armbanded soldiers the only ones visible, maybe he did.

"We greet you, First of Three," my father said as we were

brought to a halt in front of the trio. "May I offer my apologies for the unexpected delay in our arrival."

Yiuliob snarled something before First could speak. First replied, and Yiuliob said something else.

"First Dominant Yiuliob asked the First of Three why Roarke of the humans is present," a voice murmured in my ear.

I half turned to find Rozhuhu standing beside me. "Excuse me?" I asked.

"He further said that for your actions you should at least be imprisoned, if not forthrightly executed," Rozhuhu continued, back to his onetime translation duties. "First of Three said that we seek knowledge and wisdom, and that you have shown a talent for uncovering truth. First Dominant Yiuliob said that you have shown only a talent for creating chaos." He stopped, and I noted a sudden stiffening of his expression.

Small wonder. While he'd been bringing Selene, my father, and me up to speed, First of Three and Yiuliob had halted their conversation and were waiting with clear impatience for him to finish.

I cleared my throat. "My apologies, First of Three," I spoke up. "May I suggest that continuing this conversation in English would save all of us time?"

"We have waited four thousand years for our triumph, disgrace of the humans," Yiuliob said tartly. Still, he *did* say it in English. "A few vanished minutes are of no significance."

"Maybe not for *you,* First Dominant," I said. "I submit that the Kadolians might disagree. After all, it's their long-delayed homecoming we're talking about."

I'd hoped to spark a reaction, something to show that the story my father had talked about in the portal hadn't just been textured smoke. But all I got from the three Ammei was silence.

"More to the point," First of Three said, "we seek the location of Nexus One, and only Selene of the Kadolians can obtain that for us."

Yiuliob said something—

"In English, First Dominant," First of Three said.

Yiuliob shot me a dagger-edged glare. "Does Roarke of the humans read Kadolian script?" he demanded. "Is he familiar with Kadolian poetry? Does he know the Kadolian people themselves? If not, he is useless."

"He *is* pretty good at solving puzzles," I pointed out. "Plus, Selene doesn't work very well when he's not around. She tends to worry. I submit that both of those are good reasons to keep him around."

"There's one other thing," my father said. "You, First of Three, are aware that General Kinneman of the humans wants both Roarke of the humans and Selene of the Kadolians to be handed over to him. Holding both of them, as you now do, will strengthen your bargaining position when discussions resume."

Yiuliob spat something vile-sounding. "You truly expect us to take your words at scale-value?" he demanded. "That you, Nicholas of the humans, point us to value against Kinneman of the humans' best interests?"

"My job is to guide negotiations so that the best value is obtained by both Kinneman of the humans and the First of Three," my father countered. "If you, First Dominant Yiuliob, choose to join with him, then you will also benefit when an agreement is reached."

"*I* will choose what is best for the Ammei," Yiuliob said. "What is best is that Roarke of the humans is unseen and unheard."

"That would be a bad idea," I said. "The medallion, for instance, the big clue that you're all so hot for. There may be more to it than you've considered." I gestured to the soldier who'd confiscated our weapons and other equipment. "May I have mine back a moment?"

First of Three considered, then gestured to the guard. The guard handed me the medallion, his expression stiff. "Thank you," I said, holding it up so that First and the others could see the face. "From what I've heard, you're all focused on the front and the Kadolian script. But have you taken a good look at the back?"

I turned it around so that the bubbled side faced them. "See all those circles? I've spent a fair amount of time studying them. As you can see, most of the intersections are of two or occasionally three circles. But there are eight places where *four* circles intersect."

"Of what importance is that?" Yiuliob asked impatiently.

"Maybe none," I said. "Or maybe this is a stylized map of the portal system, and those four-circle connections represent the various nexuses." I looked at my father. "Nexi?"

"Nexuses," he confirmed the plural, eyeing me closely.

"Nexuses," I repeated, looking back at First of Three. "Or if not the whole portal system, maybe just the local area."

"Even with a map, finding Nexus One will be difficult," Selene said quietly. "Like hunting for a needle in a tub of other needles."

"I agree," I said, feeling my heart speed up.

Because as my father used to say, *Only an idiot hides a needle in a haystack. The place to hide a needle is in a tub of other needles.* The *tub* part of that was an odd turn of phrase, and there was no reason Selene should reference that same quote in those same specific words.

Unless she and my father had worked out a plan during their flight to Mycene and she was trying to wave me off.

But I'd already started, and there was no way to back out without sparking even more suspicions than Yiuliob already had. All I could do was continue and hope I didn't stumble into their scheme and accidentally kick some piece off it.

"What I'm wondering," I said, "is whether those particular spots might be connected to the words or even just the individual letters directly behind them on the medallion's other side. Unfortunately, I don't have the equipment to obtain accurate readings. But surely, First of Three, you do."

"Yes," First said, gazing thoughtfully at the medallion in my hand. Not ready to buy into my theory, I guessed, but willing to at least take a closer look at it.

"In the meantime," my father said, "and while Selene of the Kadolians searches through the Kadolian books, may I suggest that Roarke of the humans be taken to Nexus One to familiarize himself with the problem?"

I frowned. Wasn't the whole point of this exercise to *find* Nexus One?

"Roarke of the humans may not go to Nexus One," Yiuliob insisted. "He will remain here, secluded and under guard."

"Why?" my father asked. "Where would he go? Especially since, as you rightfully suggest, he will be under guard. Rozhuhu and three or four of your soldiers would certainly accompany us."

Yiuliob looked at First of Three, then back at me. "Six," he said. "Rozhuhu and *six* guards will accompany you."

"Certainly, if you wish," my father said. "With your permission, First of Three, we will leave immediately."

"Permission is granted, Sir Nicholas of the humans," First

of Three said. He didn't look entirely happy, but that might just have been annoyance at how smoothly Yiuliob had taken control of the conversation, and how willing my father had been to let him. "You will return to *Imistio* Tower when you are finished."

"Of course, First of Three," my father said. "Oh, and we should take that with us," he added as the soldier who'd been holding my medallion stepped forward to reclaim it. "There might be a connection between it and the portal area."

"There is no such connection," Yiuliob said flatly. "We have searched for such throughout the centuries."

"As I said, I'm good at solving puzzles," I reminded him. "Who knows? Maybe I'll solve this one."

"We shall see." First of Three gestured. "Go."

Yiuliob selected a half dozen guards, chosen no doubt for their ferocity and overall distrust of Roarke of the humans. With Rozhuhu in the lead, we walked back down the ramps to the tower's ground floor, passed the two guards standing watch at the southwest entryway, and headed across the ring of greenery and through the circles of houses.

So far I'd pinned down the specifics of four of the portals in the Nexus Six Gemini ring: Belshaz in the nine o'clock position, Juniper at ten o'clock, Mycene at eleven o'clock, and the Patth base where the old Alainn portal had been taken at four o'clock. Somewhere in the mix, I knew, were the portals that connected Nexus Six to the Dulcet and Lassiter enclaves, but I hadn't had a chance to travel either of those.

Now, I could add one more to my list: Nexus One in the eight o'clock position.

"We travel in two groups," Rozhuhu said, staring at me as we all gathered at the extension arm base. "You and four soldiers first, I and Nicholas of the humans and two guards second. You will not try to leave the outglobe until all are present. Do you understand?"

"Yes," I confirmed.

"You need not worry, Rozhuhu," my father added. "Even if he left, where would he go?"

Rozhuhu's only reply was to shift his glare from me to my father. "Go," he ordered.

I nodded and took hold of the extension arm. My four Ammei

watchdogs did likewise, and we headed up. We made the transition, and began floating downward toward the receiver module's hull. My guards, I noted, were watching me closely, gripping their lightning guns in a way that suggested they were hoping for an excuse to use them. I made it a point not to give them that excuse.

We were about halfway down when Rozhuhu and the others popped in. My father seemed relieved at the sight of me alive and uncharcoaled, while Rozhuhu looked vaguely disappointed. But I suppose both of those conclusions could have been my imagination.

We reassembled into a single group and Rozhuhu led us to one of the hatches. He opened it, sent two guards out, then pointed to me. I rolled out, regained my balance, and looked around.

At a bare, windswept wasteland.

I stepped away from the portal, the guards staying with me like they were tethered to my hips, and gave the area a long look. The portal was the typical dome rising from mostly empty dirt, with only a ground cover of low grasses and a scattering of small bushes holding the soil in place.

I'd seen pictures of drought-spawned dust bowls that had ravaged places on a dozen Commonwealth worlds over the centuries. This place would have fit right in with those.

I shifted my gaze to the horizon. In one direction was a low ridge, maybe five meters high, with a range of mountains in the distance beyond it. Everywhere else the ground was flat, the dirt and scrub stretching as far as I could see. There were no trees, no rivers, no streams, not even any puddles. The wind wasn't intense but it was steady and had a dry feel to it.

I thought back to the wilderness area that pressed up against the Belshaz enclave. But that at least was an honest desert, with a proper desert ecology that included a variety of plants and animals. This part of Nexus One, in contrast, gave me the eerie sense that none of that had ever existed here at all.

"Lovely, isn't it?" my father commented, coming up beside me. "Mountains fifty kilometers away to the north. In every other direction, there's at least a thousand kilometers of this." He kicked the dirt, sending up a cloud of dust the wind quickly whisked away.

"You say *at least* a thousand?"

"At least," he confirmed, gesturing toward the ridge. "Come on. Prepare to be impressed. Not necessarily in a good way."

We walked up the slope. The ground cover here was noticeably thicker than that immediately beside the portal, which probably explained why the ridge had survived against the wind's efforts to flatten it.

Rozhuhu and the soldiers, I noted, didn't bother to follow. Whatever was up here, they weren't worried about us being alone with it. We climbed to the top—

I felt my mouth drop open. In a flat area below us, stretching out at least a hundred meters, was a junkyard.

For a long moment I just gazed at it, trying to take it all in. There was just about every conceivable type of high-tech equipment down there, ranging from hand-sized electronic components to shoulder-pad-shaped broken ceramic pieces to partially wrecked machines that might have been sections of ground cars or compact aircraft. Dozens of cylinders that looked like fuel cells littered the area, some looking relatively fresh, others covered with rust where their protective coating had worn away. Dust was everywhere, lying on protected surfaces or collected in wind shadows. The whole thing reeked of great age and, to me at least, a sense of desperation.

"Like it?" my father asked. "That, Gregory, is approximately three thousand years' worth of Ammei attempts to get to the Nexus One full-range portal."

I frowned. "You've lost me."

"A very appropriate turn of phrase," he said. "About thirty-five hundred years ago, the Gemini portal we just left—the one that used to link Nexus One back to Nexus Six—was taken out of the main Nexus One array and moved to this lovely little patch of real estate."

"Why?"

"Nobody knows," he said. "Or if they *do*, they're not talking about it. Theories range from judgment against the Ammei, Patth, and Kadolians for some unknown offense to a macabre joke played by the Icari on their way out."

"I see," I said, not really seeing at all. If the Icari had wanted to keep the denizens of Nexus Six from coming here, why not move the portal to orbit or the bottom of a lake? For that matter, they could just have filled the thing with dirt. There certainly was enough of it around. "So after they were kicked out of Eden, First of Three's ancestors set off to figure out how to find the portal array?"

"Oh, they know where the Nexus One portal array is." He pointed toward the mountains. "Five thousand kilometers straight that way."

I goggled at him. "Five *thousand*?"

"Five thousand." His lip twitched. "They think."

"They think that's the right distance, or they think that's the right direction?"

"Either," he conceded. "Both. But they're pretty sure."

"Yes, that's always so comforting," I said under my breath, looking at the junkyard with new eyes. Small, slender, cross-shaped things that might have been parts of drones. Sectioned vehicles that might have carried one or more passengers. Fuel cells to energize everything. Crates of food and water to sustain the work force. "But even with Ammei and Patth tech, that was too far a hike?"

"Way too far," my father said ruefully. "And it wasn't just the distance." He took a deep breath. "Okay. Start with at least a thousand kilometers of desert to the east, south, and west. We know that because that's as far as the drones and manned flights got before the Ammei gave up. No point continuing, because there's no water or food possibilities in any of those directions, which means no sustained travel."

"Seems to me humans have tackled worse situations," I pointed out.

"You're thinking about navigating Earth's deserts," he said. "But there the land has plants and animals that can be cultivated or harvested, plus oases where there's water. Here, there's nothing. On top of that are seasonal windstorms fully capable of bringing down any but the sturdiest structures."

"Which means no base camps?"

"Not unless you want to bring a prefab blockhouse with you," he said. "Plus, there are the limitations the portals themselves impose on such a project. Something living needs to trigger the extension arm, and only what that person is carrying goes through with him. You saw the massive logistics involved with getting a relatively simple bioprobe and its support gear onto Alpha."

He pointed toward the mountains. "You're probably wondering

why, if they think the portal array is to the north, they even bothered with the rest of the compass rose."

"The question *had* crossed my mind."

"Because travel directly toward the portal is even worse than trying an end run," he said. "First up is a field of deep crevices that start about a kilometer past that next ridge and run about twenty kilometers before they end. The center of the field also happens to be a groundquake zone, so the crevices shift over time in unpredictable ways. Once you're past the crevices and over the mountains, you finally hit life: a lush rainforest teeming with plants and animals, streams and lakes." He paused as if trying to remember something. "Oh, yes. And at least four species of very large, very nasty raptor birds that can take out drones with a single hit and play merry hell with larger manned vehicles. They especially like solar-powered ones for some reason."

"Convenient for someone," I said. "I assume ground travel is just as difficult?"

"No, it's way worse," he said. "Did I mention the lush forest and waterways? They come with a complete set of predators, stinging insects, oozing plant life, and everything else that's usually included in that ecological package."

"So no base camps there, either."

"Not for more than a few weeks, anyway," he said. "And if you get past that..." He waved again toward the mountains. "More mountains, a plain with lion-sized predators and more hunting birds, a large ocean or inland sea—there are conflicting stories—until the sheer distance takes you down. You reach a point where your drone or vehicle runs out of fuel, or runs into raptors and wind. I think they made it about fifteen hundred kilometers before they conceded defeat."

I nodded heavily. "Fifteen hundred out of five thousand."

"At least five."

"So what exactly do they think Selene can do for them?"

"That's an exceedingly good question," my father said, lowering his voice and giving a casual look over his shoulder. "The hope is to first get their makeshift launch module working. If they can, and if they can find Nexus One's address, they can go directly to the portal array from Nexus Six and bypass this whole kill zone."

"Yes," I said, thinking it through. When Selene and I had

first learned about the *Imistio* Tower portal, our assumption had been that First of Three wanted to locate the Juniper portal. But then Yiuliob had bragged about how gaining Nexus One would launch the Ammei into supreme power.

So did First want one thing and Yiuliob want something else? Was that the underlying source of their conflict? "So you don't think First has the address?"

My father shrugged. "He hints that he does. But he also hints that he has the serum he needs to feed a Patth and Kadolian to put the final touches on his launch module. So who knows? All I really know is that the legend says a Kadolian is going to free his people, and that Nexus One is the key, and that the clue to unlocking the door is somewhere in *Imistio* Tower."

"According to Bubloo, the legend also identifies the Kadolian hero as female," I said. "Seems to me that you had a saying about legends?"

"*Legends tell you more about the people who invented them than the people who are in them*," he quoted. "Applied to the current situation, it probably tags the Ammei as a species of wishful thinkers."

"Who can also get mean if their idea of what *should be* doesn't match with what *is*," I said, frowning. Something a few meters into the junkyard had suddenly caught my eye: eight of the abandoned fuel cylinders, standing on their ends in a loose group beside a section of broken solar wing and a large, rust-pitted metal plate lying at an angle on top of a small sphere of unknown purpose.

But my father had just said there were seasonal winds that blew things over. More than that, as I looked around the area I didn't see anything else that wasn't flat on the ground or leaning against something else. Everything in its lowest potential energy state, which was what normally happened when big winds came calling.

So why were those eight still standing?

I tensed. Eight cylinders in a group, just like the mountains on Belshaz that Bubloo had pointed out as being his ancestral home.

The place he'd named the *Eight Sisters*.

"You okay?"

Trust my father to catch even my subtlest reaction. "Sure," I said. "Just contemplating the future."

"Always worth doing," he said. "Head's up."

"But if the Nexus One address is hidden in that poem some- where, Selene *will* find it," I said, putting a double helping of confidence into my voice. "Take her to the Center of Knowledge and turn her loose, and it's as good as done."

"What do you speak, Roarke of the humans?" Rozhuhu asked as he came up behind us.

"Oh, hello," I said, as if I was surprised by his sudden appear- ance. "I was just telling Sir Nicholas that Selene is one of the smartest people I know. If there's a secret hidden in that poem, she'll find it."

"That may be," Rozhuhu said, eyeing me closely. "Do you still hold with your thought that the circles on the medallion are important?"

"I don't know," I said. "I merely offered that as an alternative."

Rozhuhu eyed me another moment, then turned away. "Fin- ish your observations, Roarke of the humans," he called over his shoulder. "We return in three minutes."

"We'll be there," my father called after him.

We watched as he reached the bottom of the ridge, passed through the line of guards, and continued toward the portal. "Doesn't look happy," I commented.

"He never does," my father said. "You *do* know he heard your comment about the Nexus One address, right?"

"Of course," I said. "I thought it was worth reminding him that they still need to finish their launch module before any of this works, and that they still need a Kadolian for that."

"Yes," he said quietly. "I just hope you know what you're doing, Gregory."

"I always do."

"You always know what you're doing?"

"I always hope," I corrected. "Come on. We don't want First of Three to get lonely."

We headed down the ridge, collected our guards, and joined Rozhuhu at the portal. Exactly three minutes, I noted, since his warning. My father's time sense had always been exceptional, as had his ability to find ways of annoying people without giving them any legitimate reason to complain. Both were abilities I'd gone to great effort to add to my own repertoire.

We arrived at *Imistio* Tower and were taken directly to the Center of Knowledge. Selene was seated at one of the six wide-topped desks, leafing slowly through a book with typical Icari-metal binding. Stacked on the other end of the desk were six more books, and across the room three Ammei were systematically pulling other books out of the racks, looking briefly inside, apparently checking the language they were written in, then returning them to their original slots. Presumably they would put aside any of the rare Kadolian ones to add to Selene's pile.

Seated behind her, close enough to watch what she was doing but far enough back not to be overly obtrusive, were First of Three and First Dominant Prucital. Pacing impatiently behind them was First Dominant Yiuliob, having apparently decided that sitting was a sign of weakness. Rozhuhu pointed my father and me to a pair of seats too far away to see much of anything, then walked over and took up a silent position beside First of Three's chair.

Distantly, I wondered if First had really been taken in by his act, or whether he knew where Rozhuhu's true loyalties lay.

We'd been there an hour when First called a halt. Selene, my father, and I were led away, down one floor and to the opposite side of the tower, where a dinner buffet had been laid out. Most of the food choices were ones Selene and I had sampled on our last visit here, but there were a couple of new additions that I found reasonably tasty. We were seated at the same table Selene and I had last shared with Huginn, which suggested this was the spot the Ammei had decided was the easiest one for them to keep an eye on.

They needn't have bothered. Aside from asking about Selene's search and briefly telling her about our visit to Nexus One, we didn't discuss anything at all related to portals, Ammei, or Gold Ones. Instead, my father spent most of the meal regaling her with stories of his past negotiations, focusing on ones where he emerged triumphant. If the Ammei *were* listening in on us, all they would take away was that Sir Nicholas of the humans was exactly the sort of person they wanted on their side.

Which, I had no doubt, was the reason for his performance in the first place.

After dinner, it was time for bed. I'd hoped the three of us would get to share a sleeping room, but First had apparently heard the human aphorism about eggs and baskets. Selene was taken out, presumably to one of the houses in the ring surrounding the tower, while my father was escorted to the upper rooms on the top floor where I'd once spent a few hours chained to a cot.

My bedchamber was much more Spartan than either of theirs. Rozhuhu personally escorted me down to the hermetically sealed storeroom where Huginn and his Iykams had been imprisoned when they first arrived at Nexus Six.

"You will be sent for in the morning," Rozhuhu said as his soldiers nudged me through the doorway.

"No need for a wake-up call, then," I concluded, looking around. The floor-to-ceiling shelves lining three of the walls looked the same as they had the last time I'd been here, though the specific packages had probably changed over the past few months. In the center of the room the Ammei had set up a cot, a chemical toilet, and a nightstand with a small light and two bottles of water. "All the comforts of home, too."

"We are gratified that it meets with your approval," Rozhuhu said sarcastically. "May you sleep well and long."

"I'm sure I will," I said. "Just make sure it's not the final and permanent sleep. You still need Selene, and if I don't wake up tomorrow she's unlikely to help you take over the Spiral. You *do* plan to take over the Spiral, don't you?"

"Yes," he said. "But only as the Patthaaunutth did before us. With the full portal system under our control, we will dominate all others in matters of transportation and economics."

"So, no violence?" I asked. "Not like, say, you were capable of thirty-five hundred years ago?"

For a long moment he just stared at me. "The Nexus One graveyard," he said. "You saw something there that you shouldn't have."

"I saw the remnants of Ammei technology," I said. "I also saw Shiroyama Island, where soldiers wearing Yiuliob's armband were imprisoned. It's just a matter of finding the correct dots and connecting them."

"I warned the First of Three that you were clever," Rozhuhu said. "He should have listened."

"I wouldn't worry about it," I soothed. "Just because broken pieces of armor and weapons are in the junkyard doesn't mean you still have the knowledge or skill to build them. There's also the fact that Selene and I are completely under your control, so neither of us is inclined to make waves." I considered. "Plus I wouldn't mind being on the winning side for a change. Plus your position will be even stronger once I give First Dominant Yiuliob the location of the Juniper portal."

Rozhuhu's armadillo scales seemed to turn a shade brighter. "You have its location?"

"Not yet," I said. "I will soon."

"*How* soon?"

"Very," I assured him. "In the meantime, it's been a long day. If you'll excuse me, I'd like to get some sleep."

"Of course," he said softly. "Sleep well, Roarke of the humans."

"You, too, Rozhuhu of the Ammei."

He walked out, passing the soldiers he'd left at the doorway, and headed off down the long corridor. One of the guards closed the door, and I was alone with my thoughts.

I would sleep, all right. I was tired, and I would sleep as deep and as long as I could before the Ammei came to haul me out of bed.

But before I slept, I had some hard thinking to do. I was pretty sure I had most of the pieces now, and knew where and how most of them fit.

So I stayed awake another hour, plotting and planning and scheming. And by the time I fell asleep, I had a plan. A plan I was certain would get me the last few missing pieces.

Provided it didn't first get Selene and me killed.

CHAPTER TWENTY-ONE

For the next three days, nothing happened. Nor had I expected it to.

Each morning, Rozhuhu unlocked my unofficial prison cell and brought me to the dining room for breakfast. Usually Selene and my father were already seated, though on the third day my father was the last of us to arrive. After we ate it was back to the Center of Knowledge, where Selene settled down at her desk in front of First of Three, Prucital, and Yiuliob, while my father and I were given seats in the distance where our chief duty was to be bored. Shortly after noon we broke for lunch, then it was back to work for Selene and back to tedium for the rest of us. Then it was dinnertime, and finally back to our designated sleeping areas for the night.

I noted that every morning there were one or two additional books on Selene's to-do stack. Apparently, First had his sorters working around the clock to dig out the Kadolian texts.

Unfortunately, the rigidity of the schedule meant that my only chance to talk to Selene was at meal times. Even more unfortunately, the close quarters and hovering presence of the Ammei servers also meant there was no privacy for any real exchange of information. Thanks to our personal code system I was able to confirm she was being treated well, and to assure her that I was likewise. But there was no way to find out if her studies had unearthed anything useful.

245

As my father used to say, *Everyone makes a last mistake. Sadly, they don't get to learn from that one.*

Early on the fourth day, Rozhuhu made his.

I'd already been sleeping with keyed-up nerves, so even though the latch was pretty quiet I was fully awake even before Rozhuhu swung the door open. "Roarke of the humans," he called softly. "Wake up."

"I'm awake," I called back, peering toward the sound of his voice. The corridor behind him was only slightly better lit than the pitch darkness of my cell, but there was enough light for me to see that there were three soldiers out there. One of them shifted position, and I caught the hint of an armband. Yiuliob's men, then. No surprise there. "What is it?"

"Nicholas of the humans calls for you," Rozhuhu said. "He has found something on Nexus One and requires your presence to decipher its meaning."

"Really," I said, blinking the sleep out of my eyes. So this was how he was going to play it. "What does he need me to do?"

"He requires your presence," Rozhuhu repeated. "Come with me. Now."

"Sure," I said, sitting up and snagging my shoes. "Anything for my father."

There were no guards at the outer door as Rozhuhu and his three buddies escorted me from the tower. Nor were there any at the Nexus One portal. "Everyone off-duty tonight?" I asked as I rolled into the receiver module.

"All are on alert elsewhere," Rozhuhu said as he joined me. "There is a threat from Kinneman of the humans."

"Ah," I said, nodding. As if my father, who was obviously mediating between Kinneman and First of Three, would be galivanting around Nexus One at a time of heightened tensions. "I can see how the First of Three would be worried about that."

"The First of Three is *not* worried," Rozhuhu snapped, pride momentarily superseding the internal logic of his story. "Humans do not worry the Ammci."

"Right," I said. "So where exactly are we going?"

"To meet Nicholas of the humans," Rozhuhu said. "Come. Hurry."

We went up the extension arm and were transported to Nexus

One. It was early morning, the sun about thirty degrees above the horizon and playing hide-and-seek with a layer of speckled clouds. The steady breeze from a few days ago was still there, though it felt marginally calmer. Rozhuhu led the way to the top of the ridge and stopped. "Nicholas of the humans is there," he said, pointing toward the far end of the junkyard. "Beyond that other ridge."

"I thought he'd be waiting at the portal," I said.

"He is beyond that other ridge," Rozhuhu said. "He requires your assistance. Go to him."

"Of course," I said, glancing over my shoulder. Rozhuhu's three soldiers were waiting at the base of the ridge, their lightning guns slung over their shoulders.

I frowned. *Slung*, not held ready to fire.

And now it was obvious. "So he's past the ridge," I said, looking back at Rozhuhu. "Somewhere in the crevice field, I assume?"

"He is there."

I nodded, gazing across the junk pile. Of course the soldiers' lightning guns were still slung. Even with loose dirt to bury me in, chunks of metal to hide me under, or crevices to drop me down there was always the chance that First of Three's people would find my body. One burn or stab wound on that body, and Rozhuhu's presumed story that I'd gone off exploring and had had an accident would instantly fall apart.

At which point any hope the Ammei had of Selene agreeing to find the Nexus One portal for them would be equally dead.

So the plan was for me to simply and conveniently fall into a crevice. Without Rozhuhu's help if possible; with his help if necessary.

And just because they'd prefer not to shoot me didn't mean they wouldn't if they decided it was necessary.

Still, a group of crevices also suggested places to hide. There was also all that debris laid out before of me, teeming with potential resources.

And then there were those eight standing fuel cylinders. It seemed impossible that such a formation could stand for centuries against Nexus One's winds, and highly improbable that there would just happen to be the same number of tanks as in the mountain home Bubloo had told us about.

Bubloo and Robin had disappeared behind a locked hatch,

reasons and aftermath unknown. Had Robin recovered from his fit, or whatever had happened to him, and found his way here? Had Bubloo? Had both of them?

Because the only reasonable explanation for those standing tanks was that someone had set them up as a secret signal to me. A secret signal for what, though, was also unknown.

I scowled across the landscape. If there was nothing there except a gloating note from Robin saying he'd collected Bubloo's bounty, I would be sure to reserve one of my last few minutes of life calling a curse down on him.

Meanwhile, Rozhuhu was waiting, and there were still three lightning guns at my back. "Then I'd better go find him," I said. Taking a deep breath, I headed down the slope.

In theory, as long as I was walking blithely into their trap, there should be no reason for any of the soldiers to shoot me. But my logic wasn't necessarily Rozhuhu's, and there could be any number of reasons why he would decide to take overt action against me right here and now.

For once, my fears were unrealized. I reached the bottom of the ridge and started across the junkyard, moving slowly and picking my route carefully. Not only did I have to worry about my footing—there could be any number of obstacles hidden beneath the dust—but I also had to make sure my path took me to the Eight Sisters without looking like I was specifically aiming for them. Multiple generations of Ammei had gazed balefully across this wasteland, and I couldn't have Rozhuhu noticing something out of position.

Halfway there. I pretended to stumble over something, and as I regained my balance I sneaked a glance behind me. Rozhuhu was still where I'd left him, two of the soldiers now flanking him on his right and left.

There was no sign of the third soldier.

I continued on, my brain running at high speed. If I'd been overseeing this operation, I'd have sent the third soldier back to the portal as a last line of defense in case the target evaded the trap. But he could also have stayed at the base of the ridge where he could see me if I came over the top, or he could have moved along the ridge into cross-fire position.

The Eight Sisters were just ahead. Once again, I pretended to stumble, but this time I overcorrected, staggering a couple of steps in the other direction. One final feigned trip, and I fell heavily to my knees between the tanks and the big angled metal plate. My flailing hand slapped across one of the fuel tanks, sending it toppling onto its side and rolling through the dust, hopefully drawing all Ammei eyes in that direction.

And there it was, half hidden under a thin sheet of rusted metal. Just as I'd hoped, just as I'd bet my life.

A Ryukind plasmic.

A surge of renewed hope shot through me. Whatever my benefactor's reasons for abandoning us midway through our rescue of Selene and my father, he'd apparently repented of that decision enough to shadow our movements to Nexus Six, find his way to Nexus One, and plant a wild card for me.

I rolled half to my side, putting my back to Rozhuhu. With his view of my hand now blocked, I retrieved the weapon, continuing my roll with the plasmic tucked close to my chest where it would be concealed as long as possible. I came back around in sight of the Ammei—

"Everyone freeze!" I called.

Too late. Even as I leveled my plasmic at the group, the two soldiers at Rozhuhu's sides dropped into identical crouches and started bringing up their lightning guns.

As my father used to say, *One invitation is a request, two is an order, three is a threat.* Unfortunately, it was clear that I wasn't even going to make it to two.

The first soldier's weapon was still pointed downward at a forty-five degree angle when I took him out. The second's was nearly lined up when my shot burned into the center of his torso and he likewise went down. I shifted my aim to Rozhuhu, standing rigidly—

A flicker of movement the edge of my peripheral vision was my only warning that the third soldier was targeting me from the far end of the ridge. Rozhuhu had indeed gone with the cross-fire option.

I was still lying on my side, with zero ability to move. But with that final roll I'd come within kicking range of the big metal plate. I bent my knees, swiveled a few degrees on my hip, and kicked the angled end upward as hard as I could. As I did so, I saw the distant Ammei bring his lightning gun up.

The metal plate was heavy, and my angle wasn't very good. But death was staring me in the face, adrenaline was pumping, and my desperate kick sent the plate lurching half a meter upward, just enough to briefly conceal me from my enemy.

If he'd waited another second for the plate to fall back down and give him a clear shot, that would have been the end of it. But he didn't. Either he was impatient, or else he didn't want to risk giving me time to line up my own weapon. Whatever his reasoning, the plate had just reached its zenith when he fired.

Even then, the shot nearly did the job. The top of the plate vaporized as the lightning bolt slammed into it, while the next few centimeters below the impact shattered as flash-heating met old and tired metal. A tingling jolt ran through me, both from the point of impact and from the debris around me as the plate conducted the residual current into the ground.

I blinked as the view cleared, wincing from a dozen tiny facial burns from flying droplets of vaporized metal. The lightning gun was still pointed at me, but the Ammei face behind it seemed oddly hesitant, and with sudden insight I realized that while the plate had blocked some of the initial flash from my eyes, the soldier's had taken the full brunt of the visual assault.

He was still trying to blink away the afterimage and reestablish his target when my shot ended it.

I turned my eyes and plasmic to Rozhuhu. He was still standing on the ridge, no doubt having lingered to personally watch my dramatic, violent, and hugely satisfying demise. Now, with his final champion lying smoking in the dust, he stiffened and spun around, clearly intent on getting back to the portal—

"Freeze!" I shouted.

Rozhuhu stopped short, his back to me. I scrambled to my feet and hurriedly retraced my steps across the debris field, keeping my plasmic trained on him. "Keep your arms out to your sides and your hands open," I ordered as I started up the ridge.

"Your weapon," he said, as he complied. His voice was calm, with a hint of dark amusement to it. "Where did you get it?"

"Tooth fairy," I said as I came up behind him and then circled around to his side. In profile, he looked just as unconcerned as he sounded. "Doesn't matter. What matters is that I'm armed and you're not."

"I disagree," he said, turning to face me. His expression was intense, his facial scales glittering. Reflexively, I took a step backward to put more distance between us, nearly tripping over one of the smoldering bodies as I did so. "So you are armed, Roarke of the humans. What do you do next?"

I opened my mouth to tell him...

And realized I had no idea.

I couldn't just haul him back to Nexus Six at gunpoint and hand him over to First of Three. It would be his word against mine, and I had no illusions as to which of us everyone in *Imistio* Tower would believe.

But I also couldn't just leave him here. There wasn't any place to hide him, and even if there was I didn't have anything to secure him with. Trying to take him back through the portal to Nexus Six, move him across open ground, and sneak him into another portal in the ring had even less chance of success. I didn't know how he'd contrived to move the guards off Nexus One portal duty, but I doubted he'd been able to send all the rest of the portal guards back home.

Besides, neither scheme would do anything but buy me a little time. Sooner or later Rozhuhu would be found, and then we'd be right back where we started.

Unless I moved him someplace where the Ammei *couldn't* find him.

Someplace, for example, like Alpha.

I could do it, I knew. Alpha was still hidden in the river that flowed past the city, loaded to the teeth with EarthGuard Marines. If the vac suits Selene and I had used during our first visit were still stashed away under the partial dock at the northwest edge of town, Rozhuhu and I should be able to get to the portal without drowning.

Of course, at that point I would have to face General Kinneman, which I wasn't exactly eager to do. But if it came down to that or killing Rozhuhu where he stood, I would just have to grit my teeth and do it.

"You see your problem," Rozhuhu said into my thoughts. "So end this foolishness. Throw away your weapon and return with me to Nexus Six. I will return you to your confinement, and no more will be spoken."

I snorted. "You don't seriously expect me to believe that, do you?" I asked. The critical question at this point was whether I could subdue him sufficiently to sneak him back to Nexus Six and stuff him into a vac suit. "The minute I'm out of earshot you'll go straight to First of Three and throw me to the wolves."

"You have no other options," Rozhuhu said flatly. "Return without me, and you will be severely punished. Return with my lifeless body, and you will be executed. Remain here, and you will be found."

"So I'm just supposed to trust you?"

"Surely you must recognize that it is in my own best interest to say nothing of these events," Rozhuhu said. "We must go. *Now.*"

"Yes, I heard you the first time," I said, a surge of annoyance rising over my uncertainty and dread. There was something about the word *must*, especially when repeated over and over, that had always irritated me. "How about you first tell me how you plan to cover up the deaths of Yiuliob's three soldiers?"

He smiled with an evil sort of smugness. "You make the assumption that there are *three* dead soldiers here."

My first urgent impulse was to turn around and see if I'd somehow missed with my last shot and find an injured but still living enemy coming up behind me. The vast majority of people would have a similar urge, I knew, and most of them would yield to it.

Unfortunately for Rozhuhu, I wasn't most people. Keeping my plasmic steady, I stroked my left thumbnail against my right wrist, then held up the mirror for a look. No Ammei soldier was walking, creeping, or crawling back there. "Nice try—" I began.

Without warning, Rozhuhu spun around, putting his back to me, and sprinted toward one of the two dead soldiers I'd shot in my first volley.

The soldier, and the soldier's abandoned weapon.

Mentally, I shook my head. A fair enough effort on his part, but ultimately pointless. My plasmic was aimed and ready, and the lightning gun was still two meters out of Rozhuhu's reach. Plenty of time for me, not nearly enough for him. I centered my plasmic's muzzle on his back—

And with a flash of horrified insight, I saw his plan. Of course he would die—he didn't know about Alpha and had therefore deduced that my only viable option was to kill him. He'd accepted that, and had decided to take me down with him.

Because all it would take to seal my own death would be for me to shoot him in the back with a foreign, non-Ammei weapon.

There was only one way out of the trap. Rozhuhu was going for one of the two nearby lightning guns.

The second was lying almost directly beneath my feet.

Thrusting the plasmic into my jacket, I dropped into a crouch and scooped up the weapon. For a second I bobbled the unfamiliar weight, then got it secure and brought it up into firing position. Rozhuhu was just leaning over, his hands reaching downward—

"Freeze!" I shouted.

He ignored me. Grabbing the weapon, he got a two-handed grip on it and started to straighten up. With no other option, I squeezed the trigger.

Nothing happened.

I squeezed the trigger again, my heart pounding. Still nothing. I rolled the gun a few degrees, first right and then left, searching for a switch, button, or slide that would mark a safety catch I hadn't disengaged. But both of the weapon's flanks were smooth and unmarked.

Rozhuhu was upright again. By now he'd surely realized I'd seen his trap and wasn't going to walk into it.

But hard on the heels of that thought would have come the knowledge that he'd unexpectedly been given a new chance at life. If he could beat me to the draw, he might still survive the next few seconds.

I watched him start into his turn, my mind racing. I'd once seen one of these things fired close-up, and frantically searched my memory for a clue. But again, there was nothing. There was no cover anywhere where I could buy time to think, and there was no way I could outrun a lightning gun bolt. I still had time to snatch out the plasmic and kill him, but that would only put off my own death by a few hours.

And then, almost too late, the logic of the situation burst like a solar flare in front of me. The soldier I'd shot had been preparing to fire, and had died too quickly to have activated any kind of locking mechanism. The safety that was blocking me had to be something that had kicked in when he let go of the weapon.

I squeezed the grip hard, felt a brief vibration, and pulled the trigger one last time.

And Rozhuhu, his own lightning gun now aimed, vanished into the glare of a brilliant flash.

Old habits sent me a quick couple of paces to my right in

case some dying reflex managed to send fire in my direction. But there was nothing. The afterimage faded away and I saw Rozhuhu crumpled on the ground, the center of his chest flickering with muted embers, the constant wind blowing foul-smelling smoke toward me.

I lowered the muzzle, a sudden weariness washing over me. I'd won this battle by the proverbial whisker. But the bigger war still loomed in front of me, and my life now hung by an even thinner thread than it already had. Setting the lightning gun down beside its previous owner's body, I trudged down the ridge toward the portal. I was halfway there when a strange and vaguely disrespectful thought occurred to me.

After all my history, and all my father's sayings, I *had* at least been able to give Rozhuhu two warnings.

CHAPTER TWENTY-TWO

The guards were still absent from the portal when I returned to Nexus Six, as were those who were supposed to be watching the *Imistio* Tower entrance. Apparently, Rozhuhu had wanted plenty of time to persuade me to kill myself.

I thought about trying to find Selene and maybe getting the hell out of here. If the Ammei had put her in the same house as before, I should be able to break her out. If they'd picked someplace new, though, my odds dropped dramatically.

Alternatively, I could go to the top of the tower and the upper rooms and see if my father had any advice to offer. But that seemed even less likely to be productive than hunting for Selene.

In the end, I wound up simply going back to the storeroom and settling in for the rest of the night. The morning light was likely to bring a massive load of trouble, and I might as well get some sleep while I could. Besides, there was always the possibility that if I was still locked up no one would connect Rozhuhu's disappearance to me.

No one, that is, except Yiuliob. Still, he would presumably have a hard time leveling any accusations without admitting his own complicity. At that point, First of Three would hopefully start asking questions, and if I was lucky the two sides would get so embroiled in their own local politics that they would forget all about me.

I was wrong on all counts. Half an hour before I was supposed to be taken to breakfast, Yiuliob and six soldiers burst into
the storeroom and informed me that First of Three demanded
my presence.

"...and without warning the soldiers suddenly turned on
Rozhuhu," I said with all the sincerity and regret I could manage. "It was bizarre. One moment everything seemed fine; and
then one of them said something, and all three of them turned
their weapons toward him." I paused, wincing with the supposed
memory of the tragedy. "I had no idea what was happening. But
Rozhuhu had been a friend and colleague, and my automatic
response was to try to help him."

"With the weapon you claim he gave you," First of Three
said, his face and voice utterly neutral as he gazed at me from
the Chair of Authority. It was, I noted with unease, the same
expression that was on Prucital's and Yiuliob's faces as they
flanked his chair.

My father's expression was considerably tenser as he and
Selene listened from a few meters to the side. Though some of
that stiffness might have been due to the armed Ammei grouped
closely around them.

There was also the fact that in a single night I'd not only put
myself in deadly peril but had also erased every gram of goodwill
he'd worked so hard to buy with First of Three and the Ammei
of Nexus Six. If I went down, it was a good bet that whatever
he'd negotiated with Kinneman would do likewise.

"Yes, it was that weapon," I confirmed. "In retrospect...well,
he never said anything, so I really don't know. But in retrospect
I wonder if he might have suspected they would turn on him
and wanted me there to back him up."

"Why would he expect you to take such action?" Yiuliob
demanded.

I gave a small shrug. "As I said: he was my friend and colleague."

His glare went a little hotter, his scales darkening a little. He
knew that was a complete and utter lie, but he couldn't denounce
it without inviting awkward questions.

"I was able to get the drop on all three of them," I continued
my story. "Though of course they couldn't have known I would

be armed. Unfortunately, one of them was able to shoot Rozhuhu before I could fully eliminate the threat."

"Which of the soldiers killed him?" Prucital asked.

"The one to Rozhuhu's right as he faced away from the portal," I said. I didn't know if the Ammei could tell which soldier had held which weapon, or which weapon had delivered a given shot, but the more truth I could ladle into my story the better.

Though whether that would help was looking increasingly problematic. Selene hadn't had a chance to speak since I was hauled in here, but I could see the tension and dark fear in her pupils. Whatever she was reading from First of Three and the others, I guessed that none of them was buying my story at face value.

On the other hand, I was still standing here and they were still asking me questions. That was something, at least, though part of that was probably First and Prucital trying to trip me up or find holes in my story.

Fortunately, neither of them was very good at the necessary technique, and I had my answers down cold. Best guess was that they didn't believe me, but were reluctant to take any irreversible action without solid proof.

We were an hour and a half into the interrogation when a soldier wearing both a fancy hat and a Juniper soldier armband arrived. For a few minutes he talked quietly with First of Three and the other senior Ammei, and I watched with growing trepidation as Selene's pupils went steadily more anxious. The private conversation ended.

And when First of Three turned back to me his earlier neutrality was gone. "This is the captain of First Dominant Yiuliob's guard," he said, indicating the newcomer. "He tells me that the soldier you accuse of murdering Rozhuhu was utterly incapable of such betrayal."

"Have you any further lies to speak?" Yiuliob demanded.

"Then perhaps it wasn't betrayal," I said, mentally crossing my fingers. I'd hoped I wouldn't have to play this card, but the jaws were closing around me and my only option was to go on the offensive. "Or rather, not the *soldier's* betrayal."

Yiuliob gave a small twitch. "What do you say?" he asked, a hint of wariness in his voice.

"Don't feign surprise, First Dominant Yiuliob," I said disdainfully. "I'm saying that Rozhuhu perhaps wasn't as dedicated to Juniper Glory as he pretended."

"You make no sense, Roarke of the humans," First of Three said, a different flavor of wariness in his tone. "Rozhuhu did not support Juniper Glory and First Dominant Yiuliob's ambitions."

"I think you'll find he did, First of Three," I said. "Or rather, that was the face he presented to First Dominant Yiuliob. I suspect he was killed because First Dominant Yiuliob's soldiers realized he had betrayed the trust their master had put in him."

First of Three turned a hard look on Yiuliob, the glare meeting an equally stony expression in return. I held my breath, preparing myself for the inevitable explosion.

"Enough, Gregory," my father spoke up loudly.

I looked at him, my stomach tightening. What the hell was he doing? I had them at each other's throats. Why was he interfering?

"With all respect, First of Three, this conversation needs to be brought to an end," my father continued. "Roarke of the humans is trying to sow discord among you. But such discord is now pointless." He gave me a cool look. "I can now definitely say that Juniper Glory is no longer relevant."

First of Three gave Yiuliob a final suspicious glare, then turned to face my father. "What do you say?" he demanded.

"I planned to hold off on this announcement, First of Three, until you and I had time to speak privately," my father said. "But circumstances dictate that I speak now."

He paused dramatically. "I've received a response from General Kinneman of the humans," he continued. "He has agreed to your terms and conditions. You will have the full cooperation of EarthGuard whenever you require it."

"Do you say this agreement includes passage to the outglobe of General Kinneman of the humans?" First of Three asked cautiously.

"Most likely, yes," my father said, his voice likewise going a little cautious. Clearly, whatever deal he was talking about wasn't as set in concrete as he'd implied. "Your specific requirements will need to be stated and defined."

"Then Nexus One is within our grasp," Prucital said, cautious hope in his tone.

"I don't trust Kinneman of the humans," Yiuliob growled. "Nor do I trust Nicholas of the humans to speak truth. I demand that we complete the *Imistio* Tower outglobe."

First of Three straightened in his chair. "The outglobe is

completed," he declared. "We await only the assistance of Selene of the Kadolians to reach the portals of Nexus One."

I stared at him. The launch module was *finished*?

My father had warned me that First of Three claimed to have the serum that was required to make that happen. But I'd assumed that was a bluff he'd pitched in hopes of convincing Kinneman he didn't need EarthGuard, the Commonwealth, or anyone else. If Kinneman thought he was about to be frozen out, he might make concessions he wouldn't otherwise consider.

But First of Three *couldn't* have the serum, at least not the correct one. Not with those two missing pages still tucked away inside my arm. Even if he'd managed to interpolate the formula around those lost instructions, didn't he still need a Patth and a Kadolian? Selene had already refused him once; was he counting on her to change her mind? And where was he going to find a cooperative Patth?

First of Three suddenly seemed to remember why we'd all gathered here. "We are not finished with you, Roarke of the humans," he warned. "You will return to confinement until a later time."

"Understood," I said, shifting my eyes to Selene. "May I ask how you will guarantee my safety?"

"You are in *Imistio* Tower, under the authority of the First of Three," he said. "The only danger here is that which you may bring."

"I appreciate that, First of Three," I said. "I merely point out that Rozhuhu was able to release me from confinement and take me to Nexus One without hindrance. What would prevent someone from doing the same thing tonight?"

"I have given my word," First said, sounding offended that his guarantee wasn't sufficient.

My father, at least, knew better. "I think Roarke of the humans is hoping for more active protection," my father said. "With your permission, I will share his confinement."

"How do you propose to protect him?" First of Three asked.

"It's not protection, but a question of risk and loss," my father said. "For whatever reason of good or evil, Roarke of the humans was taken from Nexus Six. If I am with him, anything that happens to him will likely also happen to me."

"And you perceive yourself to be more important than him?" Prucital asked with a hint of sarcasm.

"I know I am," my father said calmly. "It's through me that you deal with General Kinneman of the humans. My disappearance or death would bring confusion to the negotiations. It would certainly end any possibility of Ammei access to the Commonwealth's outglobe."

First of Three's reaction to that would probably have been interesting to see. But my full attention was on Yiuliob. From what I could read in his expression, it seemed my father's thinly veiled threat was of little or no concern to him.

So Yiuliob didn't care if First of Three got to use Kinneman's portal? Did that mean he'd already found the one on Juniper?

It was possible. Maybe even probable. My promise to find it for him should have kept me immune from any attempts on my life. The fact that Rozhuhu had launched such an attack strongly suggested that I was suddenly expendable.

"Roarke of the humans is under judgment for crimes against *Imistio* Tower," First of Three told my father. "You will not share his confinement."

"I assume that risk of my own free will," my father said.

"No," First of Three repeated.

"Then *I* shall," Selene said.

"Did you not hear my words to Sir Nicholas of the humans?" First of Three demanded. "If he will not be so permitted, neither will you."

Selene drew herself up. "Then the secret of the Nexus One portals will remain with me."

The room went suddenly still. Selene stood motionless, her calm demeanor in sharp contrast with the swirling emotion in her pupils. She was still missing several vital pieces of the puzzle I'd been working on, which meant her leap of faith was ninety percent trust in me.

"You have found the location?" First asked at last.

"I will spend the coming night with Roarke of the humans," she said. "In the morning, you shall have the portal array's location."

First of Three beckoned Prucital and Yiuliob to step closer and launched into a muted, rapid-fire conversation. I kept my eyes on them, studiously avoiding any kind of significant look at either Selene or my father. Yiuliob in particular was watching me closely, and I didn't want to give him the idea that there was any secret collaboration going on.

The conversation ended and the huddle opened. "Very well, Selene of the Kadolians," First of Three said. He was clearly not happy with the situation, but was apparently willing to accept it. "In the morning you will deliver the portal's address." He looked darkly at me. "And when you have done so," he added, "Roarke of the humans will be sent to learn if you were correct."

A flicker of emotion crossed Selene's pupils. But she merely nodded. "Very well."

"This meeting is over," First of Three said. "You and Roarke of the humans will be taken to the place of his confinement."

"What about meals?" I asked. "It's nearly midday."

"Your midday and evening meals will be brought to you," First of Three said. He gestured, and with a brush of displaced air a group of soldiers moved up behind me.

"I once again ask to join them," my father said.

"You will not," First of Three said flatly. "You will instead speak to General Kinneman of the humans. You will insist that we be offered passage through his outglobe."

My father pursed his lips, and I could tell he was tempted to counter with some comment that had an *or else what?* embedded somewhere in it. But he simply gave First of Three a small bow. "As you wish."

"Then depart," First of Three said, gesturing to the guards.

"One request, if I may, First of Three?" I asked. "I haven't had a shower since yesterday. May I have one before I'm returned to confinement?"

"You may not."

"It might offend Selene of the Kadolians," I pointed out.

"She may depart whenever she wishes," First of Three said. "Every decision carries a price. Sometimes that price is too high, and the decision is reversed."

"Understood," I murmured.

Unless it was a decision that *couldn't* be reversed. In those cases, the price had to be paid.

No matter how high that price turned out to be.

The storeroom looked the same as when they'd hauled me out that morning, with the usual amenities and still only a single cot. I wondered if they were going to bring a second cot for Selene before nightfall or if was going to have to ask. But I'd raised my visibility enough for one day, and decided I could wait until afternoon before saying anything.

First of Three was nothing if not a gracious host. With the noon meal came an extra cot and bedding, plus two additional bottles of water. The food was bland, as if the person who'd chosen the menu had taken careful note of our preferences and made a point not to include any of them. Still, it was filling and reasonably tasty.

I still wasn't offered a shower, though.

Selene and I had spent the morning searching the storeroom for bugs. I'd done a cursory check earlier, but since at the time I hadn't had anyone to tell any secrets to I'd been fairly casual about it. But now, with everything racing toward the make-or-break point, absolute security was vital.

The shelves and their supports went quickly. They were solid metal, the shelves starting a few centimeters from the floor and going all the way to the ceiling. There was no place to hide anything, certainly not without being obvious.

The food and supply packages the shelves were loaded with were another matter. There were dozens of them, and each had to be carefully examined.

The afternoon turned into evening. The evening meal was delivered, the selection as uninspired as the lunch menu, and after eating we resumed our task.

It was nearly nightfall, I judged, and time for the beacon to start its two-hour light show, when I declared the room secure. Pushing the cots close together, with me staying as downwind as possible in the ventilation system's gentle breeze, we were finally able to talk.

I went first, telling her the true story of what happened with Rozhuhu on Nexus One. "I don't like it," she said when I finished. "I've always assumed you were being held hostage to my good behavior. If they're willing to burn that card, they must not think they need me."

"Or it's just Yiuliob who doesn't need you," I said. "If he's found the Juniper portal—or thinks its discovery is iminent—he might figure he can do without both of us."

"Except that they still need me to find the Nexus One array for them," Selene reminded me. "Unless you think Yiuliob also has that address."

"Well, First of Three claims to have that address," I said. "Why not Yiuliob? But here's the more worrisome part. When he had me in his office he said that once he had Nexus One *'and all our goals have been achieved,'* even the Patthaaunutth *'will cower in fear before me.'*"

"Our *goals*?" she asked, zeroing in on the crucial word. "Plural?"

"Goals, plural," I confirmed. "Problem is, as far as I can tell, First of Three's only goal is finding the Nexus One array. If Yiuliob has others, he may not have shared them with his supposed chief."

"I'm more worried about the *cower in fear* part," Selene said. "I've seen Sub-Director Nask angry, gloating, and sullen. I've never seen him genuinely afraid."

"Not even with multiple weapons pointed at him," I agreed soberly. "Maybe he just doesn't show it. Yeah, that part worries me, too." I huffed out a breath. "Your turn. *Have* you found Nexus One?"

She shifted uncomfortably on her cot. "They were so insistent, Gregory," she said in a low voice, a quiet misery flowing into her pupils. "So impatient. I wanted them to think I was making progress, so yesterday I picked a random spot in one of the books and spent an extra minute staring at it. I thought it might make them ease up on the pressure. I shouldn't have done that, should I?"

"Probably not," I conceded. "I assume they *did* notice?"

She nodded. "All three scents changed. And once they realize there's nothing there..." She closed her eyes.

"Okay, but how will they do that?" I pointed out. "They don't even know what they're looking for."

"It doesn't matter what they see," she said. "They still expect me to give them an address tomorrow."

"So you'll pull a number out of the hat," I said with a shrug. "They still can't do anything until they get the launch module up and running—"

I broke off, a horrible thought hitting me. "First was lying, right? They really *don't* have it up and running, do they?"

"I don't know," she said, her pupils looking even more miserable. "They actually might. I hadn't told you yet, but there are two Path in the tower. The scent of the silver-silk in the portal room has also changed. It's similar now to what I smelled in Alpha when it was recovering from the crash."

I breathed out a silent sigh. This was not good. "These Patth anyone we know?"

"Conciliator Uvif is one of them. The other—"

"*Uvif?*" I demanded. "What the hell is *he* doing here? Huginn said—damn," I bit out, suddenly disgusted with both Huginn and myself. "Right. Huginn told me Uvif was unharmed. He never said he was in custody, and I never thought to ask for a clarification. Sounds like Uvif got away from Nask's attack force and stayed put."

"And renewed his deal with First of Three."

"*And* has delivered on his end," I said, my stomach churning. "Commas to commarks the other Patth is an engineer Uvif brought on board. But don't they still need a Kadolian to do the fine-tuning?"

"So they say," Selene said. "Maybe they've decided it's good enough as it is. At least good enough for a test run."

"This just gets better and better, doesn't it?" I muttered. "So they toss me into an untested, jury-rigged launch module and send me—" I broke off as the pieces I'd been assembling in my mind abruptly rearranged themselves. Yiuliob ... the portal ... Rozhuhu's attempt on my life ... "Oh, hell."

"What?" Selene asked, her pupils tense.

"They're not sending me anywhere," I said grimly. "That's why Yiuliob tried to take me off the board. He wanted me out of the way so that he could send one of his own people on this test run."

"But I don't have an address to give them."

"Maybe Yiuliob already has it," I said. "Nexus One's address, or—no, it can't be Nexus One's," I corrected myself, trying to think it through. "Even if he had that address, there's no way he could get back, not without a receiver module. No, it has to be the Juniper full-range. He doesn't have its physical location, just its address."

"So he gains the Juniper portal," Selene said slowly. "How does that terrify the Patth?"

"It doesn't," I agreed, scowling past her at the shelves. "You're right. There's something here that still doesn't track. Getting the Juniper full-range would be a big, fat triumph for him, maybe even leverage him into taking over as First of Three. But the likely Patth reaction is Nask trying to take it away from him."

"Maybe Yiuliob's just being overly dramatic."

I shook my head. "You didn't hear him. He was absolutely, positively convinced he was about to become master of the Spiral." I waved a hand. "But right now, the *how* of it doesn't matter. Whatever he's got up his sleeve, his first step is sending someone through that launch portal tomorrow. That means *our* first step is to keep that from happening."

"I assume you have a plan?"

"I've got three options," I told her. "Not sure any of them actually qualifies as a plan. One: We sneak in and sabotage the portal ourselves. No guarantee they can't fix the damage, though."

"Or that we'll live through the attack."

"There's that," I conceded. "Two: We find First of Three and raise the alarm. Maybe he believes us, maybe he doesn't. If he believes us but doesn't have enough troops on hand to counter Yiuliob's, he may be able to send to the other enclaves for reinforcements. Three." I braced myself. "We go to Kinneman and get him to launch an attack."

I could see in Selene's pupils that she'd been expecting and dreading that last one. But her voice, when she spoke, was calm enough. "You think you can persuade him to do that?"

"Depends on whether I can convince him that the future of the Commonwealth depends on it," I said. "Given that I'm having trouble convincing even myself, probably not." I rolled off my cot and got to my feet. "But of all the options, I think that's our best shot."

"I hope you're not planning to knock and ask nicely if we can leave," Selene warned nodding toward the door.

"No, I doubt that would be very productive," I agreed, crossing to the nearest set of shelves. "History refresher. Who did the Ammei have locked in here when we first arrived?"

"Huginn and his Iykams," Selene said, sitting up and watching as I crouched down and started feeling beneath the lowest shelf.

"And who were the last people who spent time here?"

"More Iykams," she said. "The ones who came in with Uvif and Conciliator Fearth."

"Who were subsequently rescued by Muninn and his commando force," I said, running my fingers along the back of the shelf. Someplace back here... "Can you see either him or Huginn ever being caught off-guard the same way twice?"

"No," Selene said, a growing anticipation in her pupils. "Tools?"

"Tools," I confirmed, retrieving a compact tool kit from behind the shelf and holding it up for her inspection. *"And..."* I pulled out a four-shot DubTrub slug gun and compact badgeman stunner that had been racked alongside the kit. "Weapons." Carrying my new treasures back to my cot, I laid them out and opened the tool kit. "Let's see what Muninn left us."

"Yes," Selene said, her pupils looking suddenly thoughtful. "Gregory, you said that Bubloo opened the hatchways that led into the underground tunnels. Did he open *all* of them?"

I thought back. "Yes. In fact, he made kind of a big deal about it. Neurosis or ego, not sure which."

"Did he use the same hand each time?"

"Yes, the left one."

"Where was his ring?"

I frowned at her. "Not a clue. Is it important?"

"I don't know yet," she said. "It might be."

"Well, hold on to that thought," I said, checking my watch. "In an hour and twenty minutes, the beacon out there will finish its nightly run and go dark. When that happens, we're out of here."

CHAPTER TWENTY-THREE

Getting out of our cell turned out to be easier than I'd expected. The storeroom hadn't been designed as a prison, and the Ammei had never bothered to retrofit it for that purpose. Muninn's tool kit included a set of slender, torque-enhanced picks that slipped easily into the gap between door and jamb and popped open the latch. The last thing the two soldiers on guard duty were expecting was a prison break, and I was able to silence them with the stunner before either could raise an alarm. The four guards at the tower's outer door were not only facing the wrong direction but had ridiculously slow reflexes and were just as easily put to sleep.

"So we're going to try Kinneman first?" Selene asked as I led us down the slope into the subway tunnel.

"Personally, I'd rather start with First of Three," I said. "But we don't even know where he sleeps, let alone what kind of security he has around him. Not to mention we're not exactly equipped to take on Yiuliob's soldiers." I gestured ahead. "But if our vac suits are still tucked away beneath the dock, we shouldn't have any problems getting to Alpha."

"And if the suits are gone?"

"Then we're in for a long, uncomfortable swim."

We continued along the tunnel in silence, and after a few

minutes we reached the ramps leading up to the Gemini portals. I strained my ears as we crept past, but heard no sounds of
reaction to our presence. We continued on, me trying to figure
out what I was going to say to Kinneman, Selene wrapped in
thoughts of her own.

We were nearly to the end of the tunnel when she suddenly
caught my arm. "Bubloo's here," she whispered.

I stared at her. Bubloo was *here*? "Where?"

"Somewhere up there," she said, pointing ahead toward the
incline that led to the surface. "Near the river, I think. I can't
pin it down more accurately from here."

"Well, that's awkward," I said, frowning into the starlight.
I could think of several good reasons why Bubloo might be on
Nexus Six. I could also think of several very bad ones. "How
does he smell?"

"Same as usual," she said, and I could imagine the question
in her pupils. "Why?"

"Just wondering," I said. So after all the detoxing he'd gone
through aboard the *Blaze*, his scent hadn't changed? That seemed
odd.

Unless he'd found a new supply of his old street drugs.

"*Just* wondering?"

"Mostly." I hesitated, then pulled out the the DubTrub and
pressed it into her hand. "Here. Just in case."

He was waiting right where I'd expected him to be, sitting
cross-legged at the end of the dock, gazing out at the starlit river.
"Greetings, Friend Roarke; Friend Selene," he called softly as we
came up behind him, his voice calm and steady. "I was hoping
you would find your way here."

"Why is that?" I asked, keeping my stunner ready as I threw
a quick look around. If Kinneman had found the vac suits, this
would be when he would spring his trap. But no flares went off,
no flash-bang explosions shattered the quiet of the night, and no
Marines rose triumphantly from the bushes.

"Because I need your help," Bubloo said. "I remember now.
I remember it all. I know what Yiuliob wants, how he plans to
obtain it, and the terrible power it will give him." He swiveled
around at the waist, turning his profile toward us. "And only
Selene can stop him."

❖   ❖   ❖

"That certainly sounds serious," I said, keeping my voice even. So not only was she the hope of the Kadolians, she was now also the protector of the Spiral? "What do you need us to do?"

For a moment he was silent, his eyes flicking back and forth between Selene and me. "You don't believe me," he said. His voice was still calm, but with a new edge of sadness and frustration. "I can hardly blame you. The way I must have sounded..." He shook his head. "But I assure you that I'm now whole. And I remember."

"What do you remember, Bubloo?" Selene asked.

"Conversations among the Ammei," he said. "Conversations they assumed I couldn't hear or wouldn't remember."

He pointed across the river. "Somewhere over there, in an area that was once an extended part of the Nexus Six complex, is an artifact called a *fiall*. It is that artifact that we must find."

"You're saying it was across the bridge?" I asked.

"Yes," he said, frowning briefly. "You know about the bridge? Good. Then you must also know there's a great deal of hilly forest in which such an artifact could be concealed. But Yiuliob is nearly ready, and time is perilously short. I need you, Selene, to find it."

"Interesting situation," I commented. As bait-and-hook stories went, I'd certainly heard more compelling ones.

Still, Selene and I *had* deduced on our own that there had once been a bridge here and that the riverside houses had been part of a defense grid. That added at least a layer of believability to his pitch. "How exactly to you expect Selene to find it?"

"She will smell it, of course," he said, sounding confused. "It's what Kadolians do."

"So this *fiall* thing is a portal?"

"I don't know precisely," he hedged. "But it *is* metal of the Gold Ones."

"Why do you need *me*?" Selene asked. "Can't you smell Icari metal yourself?"

He sighed. "That part of me is no longer," he said sadly. "It was the drugs they gave me, and now that is gone. You and you alone can find the *fiall*."

I looked at Selene. "What do you think?" I asked quietly.

"I don't know," she murmured back. "He doesn't appear to be lying."

"But he could still be wrong?" I pressed. "Misinterpreted what he heard, or just mixed it all up?"

"That's always possible," she conceded. "Especially with Bubloo. But you and I have already decided that whatever Yiuliob is up to has to be stopped. I see our choices right now being to go with Bubloo or to continue on to Alpha."

I scowled in indecision. And if Bubloo was wrong, we would waste a whole bunch of time traipsing through the woods and still have to face Kinneman.

But as my father used to say, *There will be times when you simply can't figure out which way to jump. When that happens, make sure to have a coin handy.*

And really, anything that put off my confrontation with Kinneman had to count as a plus. "Fine," I growled. "Come on, Bubloo. We're going for a swim."

It still struck me as odd that Kinneman had somehow missed the vac suits Selene and I had left under the dock a few months ago. But as we climbed into them, it occurred to me that the chore of checking out this strategically uninteresting stretch of river had likely fallen to McKell or Ixil. By the time Kinneman kicked them out of the Icarus Group, there would have been more pressing things on the general's mind than going over old ground, figuratively or literally.

Unlike the Barracuda scuba suits Ixil and I had used a couple of times, each vac suit had only a single breathing apparatus. Fortunately, there were also external oxygen lines designed for emergency repressurization of a companion's failed airseals. A minor tweak of the regulator, and I had the pressure cranked down to something that wouldn't blow out Bubloo's lungs with its first blast.

Twenty minutes after Selene and I reached the dock, the three of us slipped together into the river.

It was about as far from a professional dive as it was possible to get. We clung together like a bizarre three-headed sea creature, Bubloo hanging onto my tank while he breathed through my Mox line, Selene sandwiching him from above to hold him in place against my suit and to make sure he didn't lose his grip on the hose, the two of us kicking like crazy to propel us forward, Bubloo gamely but mostly ineffectually pushing at the water with his free hand. If Kinneman had any sentries watching this direction, they were probably laughing too hard to interfere.

Fortunately, the farther we went, the less likely that scenario became. A straight-line path from the dock to the far side of the river would take us right past the submerged Alpha, but with the current grabbing us the second we entered the water we were well downstream by the time we reached the portal's position. With the bulk of Kinneman's attention focused upstream toward *Imistio* Tower and its surroundings, he was unlikely to be paying much attention to anything happening down here. Certainly we weren't likely to show up on sonar as anything but a strangely shaped chunk of flotsam. By the time we reached the far shore, we were a good kilometer away from where we'd started.

"Where now?" I asked Bubloo as Selene and I stripped off our suits.

"All I know is that the *fiall* is here," he said. "Surely you're the experts at finding such things."

I raised my eyebrows at Selene. "Inland?"

She nodded. "At least far enough to be out of view of the tower."

"Agreed," I said, folding the suits together as best I could into a bundle that I could carry. If Bubloo was imagining this whole *fiall* thing, we would need them to get back to Alpha. "Let's go."

The reeds lining the river were stiff, but as we'd already seen on the other side they weren't too hard to push through. Past the reeds were more of the same type of bushes we'd encountered on our trip from *Imistio* Tower to the dock.

But where the bushes on the river's western bank gave way to a decrepit and long-dead cityscape, on this side they fed into a forest of short, wide-canopied trees.

"How much farther inland should we go?" Selene asked as we made it through the first stand of trees and walked toward the second.

I looked around. The farther into the forest we went, the better our protection from prying eyes, both those in the tower and those belonging to Kinneman's sentries. Balancing that was the likelihood that the deeper we went, the harder that travel—in any direction—was going to be.

At the moment, we'd reached a narrow, winding lane paralleling the river between the two stands of trees. It looked like a random gap that the larger flora just hadn't reclaimed yet, and it would probably peter out soon. Still, we might as well take advantage of it as long as we could. "This looks good," I said, pointing along the gap. "I'll go first, Bubloo behind me, Selene last. Watch for animals and anything else that could be trouble."

"I'm sorry I can't be of more assistance," Bubloo said as we set off. "Much of the recent past is still confused within my mind."

"No problem," I assured him over my shoulder. I'd have preferred to walk alongside him where I could see at least a little of his expression in the dim starlight, but the path was too narrow for that. Anyway, it was more important for Selene to read his scent than for me to read his face. "I do have a question, though. You said the Ammei gave you drugs that enhanced your sense of smell?"

"I believe that was one of the outcomes, yes," he said. "I was also given drugs they told me would increase my memory and ability to learn."

"That dysthensial stuff?"

"I don't know any of the names. I only know that they did little for me."

"Sorry to hear that," I said, a fresh knot forming in my stomach. If the Ammei had given him something concocted from the old Icari formula book before they realized there were two missing pages, the flawed dose could well have played havoc with his mind and memory. "But you say you're all better now?"

"I am somewhat better," he said. "I don't know if I will ever be fully whole. Some memories remain vague. Some may never return."

"Do you remember meeting us at the taverno?" Selene asked.

"I think so," he said. "I was there to ... I think I was to meet someone or do something. I don't fully remember. A human came to me, who I later learned to name Friend Christopher. And then you, Friend Roarke, joined us."

"So you're saying you didn't meet Doc Robin until right then?" I asked.

"He tells me I did," Bubloo said, sounding uncertain. "But I don't remember."

"Sure," I murmured. Bubloo's story meshed well enough with Robin's.

But there was still one crucial problem hanging over this

whole thing. Robin had told me he was stalking Bubloo because a friend in Bounty Hunter Central had given him advance notice of the upcoming person-of-interest post. Theoretically, I supposed, it was possible the scenario had played out that way.

But as a practical matter, it seemed ridiculously unlikly. Hunter Central employees were heavily bonded, with severe penalties for even the smallest breach of security. Mindi had taken a huge risk helping me out, and she was only working for a private tipster board. Robin's friend would have to be career-suicidal to pull a stunt like that, especially for the a miniscule hundred-grand payout.

I stared into the darkness, a sudden chill running up my back. A person of interest... but of interest to whom? Certainly not hunters, not at that point. But Bubloo was definitely a person of interest to Yiuliob and First of Three.

And anyone who was of interest to the Ammei would absolutely be of interest to the Patth.

I'd accused Robin of being a bounty hunter based on his competence and fine-tuned adaptability to new situations. It was looking more and more like I hadn't aimed my suspicions high enough.

"Gregory?" Selene called. Clearly, she'd caught the shift in my scent. "Are you all right?"

"Just great," I growled back, feeling like an idiot for not seeing it sooner. "Just having some minor revelations up here. Thinking how well Doc Robin would get along with our other friends, Huginn and Muninn."

"Oh," Selene said, her voice sobering as she caught the oblique message. "Are you sure?"

"Leaning that way, yeah," I said. No wonder Circe had tried to nudge me into taking Robin along on my foray into the Belshaz portal.

Still, he'd been a good enough ally, even ready to risk his life on that first and potentially disastrous incursion into the Mycene portal. Whichever director or sub-director Expediter Christopher Robin was working for, at least he wasn't working against us.

Or maybe he was, and I just hadn't spotted the hook yet. With Expediters, one never knew. "Bubloo, tell us what happened at the Mycene portal, will you?" I asked. "After you took Friend Christopher out through the tunnel. We heard you scream, and when we got there the hatch was locked."

"Did I scream?" he asked. "I don't remember."

"You don't?" I half turned and frowned at him. "I thought you were all whole now."

"So I also thought," he said. "But I see now there are still gaps in my memories. I'm sorry."

"Yeah." I turned back forward. "Me, too."

We continued on in silence. I'd made a private bet with myself that our impromptu trail would make it maybe a hundred meters before it breathed its last, but so far it refused to die. We reached the point opposite the dock, traveled another fifty meters past that . . .

"We're here," Selene said suddenly.

"Where is it?" I asked, turning to face her.

"There," she said, pointing inland. "That direction." I saw her brace herself. "And it's not just any Icari metal. It's a portal."

"Really," I said, an eerie feeling trickling through me. So the *fiall* was just another portal? So how was it also the key to Yiuliob's grand ambitions? "Well, at least now we know what we're looking for. Same marching order; let's go."

"Shouldn't Friend Selene be in front?" Bubloo suggested. "We don't want her to miss the *fiall* in the vagueness."

"If she misses it, we just backtrack a little," I said, frowning at him. A purely practical suggestion? Or did he suddenly feel the need to be behind her?

Or maybe to be behind both of us? "She's fine back there," I assured him. "On second thought, though, let's you and I switch positions. You can take point."

"Oh." Bubloo looked into the darkness again. "I . . . you will protect me?"

"Of course," I assured him as I set down the vac suits I'd been lugging and shoved them under the branches of a convenient bush.

"As you wish," Bubloo said, not sounding happy about it. "Straight ahead?"

"Straight ahead," Selene confirmed.

Bubloo nodded and started off into the trees. I fell into step behind him, making sure to stay close. The last thing I wanted was for him to suddenly rabbit on us.

The tentative conclusion Selene and I had reached about the dock having once been part of a bridge had made sense. But that theory had offered no estimate as to how far away our goal might be. It could be two rows of trees ahead, or it could be all the way up in the mountains.

We'd gone maybe four hundred meters when we arrived.

Not that that fact was immediately obvious. Every portal we'd ever seen had been a set of conjoined spheres, with whatever part happened to be aboveground always presenting as a smoothly rounded dome. The *fiall*, in contrast, was a flat slab, two meters by one and a half, looking like a section of slightly back-angled wall. It was peeking out from the base of a tree-covered hill, its surface largely hidden by a covering of what looked like tiny seed pods. In front of it were about three meters of open space filled with ankle-high ground cover plants and a partially decomposed section of hollow log at the far side. "You're sure this is it?" I asked Selene as she called a halt.

"It's the right metal," she confirmed, puzzlement in her pupils. "But the shape is..."

"Different," I finished the thought for her, crossing over to the plate. Up close, I could see that there were six dark circles on the metal, each about three centimeters across, arranged in a regular hexagon at about chest height. "Also seems to have come equipped with a combination lock."

"Let me see," Bubloo said. Out of the corner of his eye I saw him start toward me—

"Stop," Selene said quietly.

I turned as Bubloo came to a halt, his right hand frozen in midair halfway to the plate, his eyes on the DubTrub pointed at him. "What do you say?" he asked uncertainly.

"Yeah, I'll second that," I said, frowning.

Selene gestured toward him. "His ring. Look at his ring."

I focused on his still outstretched hand. The thick black ring was on the middle finger of his right hand. "That's the finger it was on when he stunned the fake badgemen at Robin's apartment," she continued. "He has weapons built into his hands, Gregory, with the ring as the power source. Like the Talariac circuitry built into Patth pilot faces."

I took another look at Bubloo's hand. Halfway to the plate, as I'd already noted. But also halfway to me. "I guess new twists are all the rage today," I said, leveling my stunner at him. "I don't think we've ever run into a nonhuman Expediter before. You can just drop the ring on the ground there, Bubloo."

"Friend Gregory—"

"On second thought, never mind," I said, gesturing with my stunner. "You want to pick a spot for your nap? Or would you rather just fall down there?"

He looked me in the eye, and I had the sense of a quick mental calculation going on. Then, abruptly, he erupted in a barrage of a language I'd never heard before. Or rather, it was a language I'd only ever heard bits and pieces of, and only then when Selene was especially stressed.

Kadolian.

I shot a look at Selene. At her present distance it was too dark for me to read her pupils, but I could see the sudden stiffening of her back. She unloaded her own rapid-fire staccato of Kadolian, and for a few seconds they spoke back and forth, their exchanges growing shorter and sharper. "Don't mind me," I said into the midst of the jabber. "I'll just stand here with my gun."

Selene broke off in what sounded like mid-sentence. "I'm sorry, Gregory." She took a deep breath. "Bubloo says he's—"

"No, no," I interrupted her. "I hate getting these things in translation." I lifted my stunner a little. "You say it, Bubloo. In English this time."

He threw a hooded look at Selene, then focused back on me. "I'm not an Expediter, Friend Gregory," he said calmly. "Nor any other agent of the Patth. Nor have I been the captive or tool of some imagined Ammei sect who name themselves the Gold Ones."

He straightened up, the last vestige of his half-crazy, half-innocent persona vanishing. "I am, in fact, a steward of the *true* Gold Ones."

He looked back at Selene. "The beings you call the *Icari*."

CHAPTER TWENTY-FOUR

$$\diamond\!\!\diamond\!\!\diamond$$

My first reaction was disappointment. After all the insane twists and turns we'd ridden since Bubloo stumbled his jittery way into our lives, proclaiming himself a vaguely defined steward felt like a letdown. "That's it?" I growled. "*That's* all you've got? Trotting out that tired gold-painted Ammei thing again?"

He shook his head. "You weren't listening. The Icari aren't Ammei, gold painted or otherwise. I've seen the pictures they left in the archives. They were a grand and glorious people, gold-haired and gold-skinned, just as in the legends. In many ways they remind me of the ancient Greek gods from the statuary of Earth."

"Pictures," I repeated, my disappointment starting to turn to anger. "So now *this* is the truth? Not your fancy story about busy little behind-the-scenes Ammei bees pumping you full of drugs and dropping you in front of us?"

He winced. "I know. I'm sorry I deceived you. Sadly, the truth is that the Icari are long gone from the Spiral. I and my brother Pakenrills are the last remnant of one of their client species, left behind when they departed, charged with cleaning up their final mess." He looked at Selene. "Their failure to return the Kadolians to their home."

"Right. Sure." I gestured to Selene. "Feel free to jump in any time."

"What do you want me to say?" she asked, her voice tense and tired. Maybe she was feeling let down, too. "Yes, that's what he told me just now. No, I have no way to confirm it."

"There are the ruins of one of our settlements on Alainn," Bubloo offered. "The one near the Seven Strands. We were the ones tasked with collectiong the silver-silk, handling the dealings with the Loporri and Vrinks and maintaining the bridges."

"All while living the rustic life," I said. "Sounds very homey. Also, like Selene said, impossible to verify. Tell me why you were going to attack me."

"You would not have been hurt," he promised. "Merely rendered unconscious for a time."

"Glad to hear it," I said. "Waiting for an answer."

He sighed. "I have a mission, Friend Gregory," he said reluctantly. "Sadly, you no longer have a part to play in it."

"I'm Selene's partner," I reminded him stiffly. "I have a part in everything she does, and vice versa. Try again."

"Go ahead," Selene said. "You said it to me. You can say it to him."

"Very well." Bubloo's back straightened into a sort of defiant posture. "Humans are a greedy species, lusting for money and power. The items in the *fiall* represent unlimited amounts of both."

"And you think I'm hot and eager to knock you over the head to get them?" I asked.

"I need one of those items if I'm to return the Kadolians to their home," he said, ignoring my question. "I cannot risk human greed possibly undoing that."

"I can sympathize," I said. "Lucky for you, I'm the only human on the scene, and my idea of greed is a plate of barbequed ribs, a Dewar's, and some friends to share it with."

"You expect me to simply trust your word?"

"Why not? We're trusting *yours*."

He shook his head. "No. Icari history demonstrates how easily trust can be betrayed."

"I wouldn't bring up betrayal if I were you," I warned. "Given that you're the one who's been lying about himself this whole time."

"It was necessary."

"The universal excuse," I said sourly, looking at Selene. She was standing quietly, waiting for me to sort through this impasse.

And I'd better do it fast. If Bubloo was concerned about

humanity misusing this *fiall* thing, it was for damn sure we didn't want Yiuliob getting hold of it, either. "Fine," I said. "You don't trust us enough for your plan to work? Then we'll just scrap it and come up with one of our own."

"Don't be foolish," he said. "There *is* no other plan."

"There's always another plan," I said, watching him closely. "Actually, now that I think about it, the simplest approach is probably just to let Yiuliob's plan go forward and hijack it somewhere along the way."

Bubloo's reaction was all I could have hoped for. He gave a violent twitch, his eyes widening, his mouth opening and closing in a violent-looking snap. "No," he said urgently. "No, you can't."

"Then it's your plan with the three of us," I told him. "You, Selene, *and* me. Your choice."

"You don't understand," he said, almost pleading now. "If First Dominant Yiuliob obtains the *fiall*—" He broke off.

"If you want Gregory's help," Selene said quietly into the silence, "you need to persuade him that Ammei possession would be a disaster for the Spiral."

"But I *don't* want his help."

"Maybe Yiuliob would," I said. "I should also mention that time marches on, and we have no idea of his schedule. If you don't decide quickly, we may lose by default."

"I know," Bubloo said, looking back and forth between us. "I just..."

"Why don't we ease into it?" I suggested. "Let's start with some history. Everything your archives have on your Icari friends—where they came from, why they built the portals, where they are now. Context, and all that."

He hesitated another moment, then nodded. "Very well. The story begins—"

"And you might as well be comfortable," I interrupted. "There's a log a couple of meters behind you where you can sit down if you'd like." I gestured with my stunner. "But let's first put that ring on the ground, shall we?"

He hesitated, then pulled the ring from his finger and placed it gently on a patch of dirt in front of him. As he backed up to the log and sat down, I stepped forward and retrieved the ring. "Go ahead," I said as I slipped it into my pocket.

"The story begins forty thousand years ago," Bubloo said.

"That was when the first Icari colonists arrived in the Spiral and began building—"

"Arrived from where?" I interrupted.

"From somewhere else," Bubloo said. "Another part of the galaxy, or possibly a different galaxy entirely. Sadly, the archives are badly fragmented. At any rate, they set up colonies, began dealing with and educating a few of the more promising local species, and started building a portal network."

"And buildings like the Erymant Temple on Fidelio to run the system from?" Selene asked.

"Yes," Bubloo said. "As far as I know, that's the most complete Icari structure left in the Spiral. About fifteen thousand years ago the building ended, and they settled down to enjoy their new home."

"Where do the Kadolians, Patth, and Ammei come in?" I asked.

"Very early in the process," Bubloo said. "At their original home the Icari had technicians and other client species to assist in building their portals. Here, those species weren't available to them. Fortunately, the Kadolians and the others could fill the necessary roles."

"But...?" Selene prompted.

Bubloo frowned. "But what?"

I looked at Selene, spotted the fluttering eyelashes. "She wants to know what you're lying about," I explained.

"I'm not—"

"Suit yourself," I said, stepping closer and leveling my stunner at his face. "We'll give your regards to Yiuliob."

"No!" he said quickly, cringing back a little. "Please."

"Then give us the truth," I said. "Now."

He closed his eyes. "It's not as bad as it's going to sound," he said in a low voice. "And it wasn't me. Remember that. It wasn't *me*."

He opened his eyes again. "I told you the Icari started working with the local species. They found that the Ammei, Patthaaunutth, and Kadolians had the raw abilities they needed. But those abilities weren't... quite good enough."

"Let me guess," I said, feeling my stomach tighten as I saw where he was going. "They did a little genetic manipulation to get what they wanted."

Bubloo winced. "Yes," he said. "Just a little, the archives say. But... yes."

"What about you?" Selene asked.

"You mean were the Pakenrills likewise manipulated?" Bubloo shook his head. "I don't think so. Really, there would have been little point. We were simple workers, with no special skills except loyalty and a willingness to serve."

"What kind of work did you do?" I asked.

"The menial jobs, as we did on Alainn," he said. "We liaised with species the Icari didn't want to bother with directly. Met with their leaders, set up trade deals—that sort of thing."

"So what went wrong?" I asked. "I'm assuming something went wrong."

"Of course something went wrong," Bubloo said with a sigh. "Chaos and entropy are the way of the universe. In this case, not for a few thousand years. But eventually, everything fades."

He paused, as if choosing his words carefully. "Understand first that the Icari weren't a monolithic society. The Overlords were the rulers who handled the portals and the various species who ran it. Below them were the professionals, then the greater-skilled, then the lesser-skilled. Families, clans, guilds—it was all very complicated."

"Like pretty much every other society," I put in.

"I suppose," Bubloo conceded. "The Overlords themselves were unified, but among the rest there was a wide range of philosophic differences. One group in particular, naming themselves the Principled, thought it was wrong for the Icari to control the portals when others performed the actual work of running them. They wanted the system to be handed over to the Ammei, Patthaaunutth, and Kadolians. Needless to say, the Overlords rejected that proposal."

"But the Ammei liked it and decided to make it happen?" I suggested.

"Some did, yes," Bubloo said, eyeing me thoughtfully. "You're oddly well-informed."

"I know a little of their recent history," I said. "Context works both directions."

"So it does," he said. "At any rate, that particular faction, naming themselves the Glorious, decided that if the Overlords wouldn't give the system to the Ammei they would take it for themselves. Over the next few hundred years they built an organization they hoped could challenge the Icari and seize control."

"Hold it," I said, frowning. "A few *hundred* years? How long do Ammei live, anyway?"

"Not nearly that long," Bubloo assured me. "Their life expectancy is about a hundred thirty years, similar to that of the Patthaaunutth. I don't know how long Kadolians live." He looked questioningly at Selene. But she was lost in her own thoughts, her eyes lowered. "I understand human life expectancy is currently at ninety-five," he continued. "The Pakenrill number, sadly, is only sixty-two. But you're right, the Glorious were working a multi-generational plan. While some focused on the military angle—planning, training, tactics, weaponry—others worked to gradually plant their people, their disciples, and those disciples' descendants in positions of authority within the operations hierarchy. Others worked to bring sympathetic Patthaaunutth and Kadolians into their ranks, the Patthaaunutth to create new weapons like the lightning guns, the Kadolians as trackers, hunters—"

"And assassins?" Selene cut him off, her pupils flashing dark anger.

Even sitting three meters away from her, Bubloo flinched. "I don't know," he said hastily. "There was nothing about that in the archives."

"Where are these archives?"

"Some are at my home on Belshaz," Bubloo said. "I can show them to you later."

"If you're sure you want to see them," I cautioned Selene.

She blazed a fresh glare in my direction. But already I could see the anger starting to soften. She might hate what had been done to her people, and she had every right to do so. But she was smart enough to know that unthinking rage was both foolish and dangerous.

Still, this would be a good time for a change of topic. "Let's see if I can fill in the next part," I suggested. "The Glorious stole the two halves of a full-range portal directory—"

"The Icari named those portals *omnis*."

"—and smuggled the right-hand half from Meima to Nexus Six," I went on, ignoring the interruption. "For some reason they couldn't immediately take the left-hand half through to join it, so they hid it away while they waited for another opportunity. The Overlords discovered the loss, tracked the right-hand half to Nexus Six, and started searching for it."

"But were unable to find it," Bubloo said, nodding. "The Overlords then declared the Glorious as rebels and arrested the leadership. Wishing to create a secure prison, they set up a set of twains—the dyad portals you name Geminis—linking Meima, Fidelio, and Popanilla."

"Like a transportation airlock," I said. "Anyone who got off Popanilla could only get to Fidelio and then would have to hoof it across a temple complex teeming with Icari before they could get to Meima."

"Exactly," Bubloo said. "Once that was ready, the Overlords sequestered the Glorious leadership there."

"Along with some of their soldiers," I said, remembering the armbands scattered around the island.

"Along with *most* of their soldiers," Bubloo corrected. "Everyone the Overlords could identify and capture."

"Why Meima?" Selene asked. Her burst of anger had faded, leaving a coldness behind. "Why that particular omni?"

"The archives don't say," Bubloo said. "I presume it was the one the Overlords had identified as the center of the trouble, or perhaps the one the Glorious had most fully under their control. Whatever the reason, the Overlords believed that was where the other directory half would be taken and set a trap. They evacuated all personnel from Nexus Six and then moved the omni from the center of the twain ring into planetary orbit. If the Ammei tried to smuggle the other directory half to Nexus Six, they would find themselves instead marooned in space. Without a complete directory in hand, they would be unable to reset the omni for any other location and would be forced to return to Meima."

"And of course, with no one left on Nexus Six to see what had happened and alert their allies, none of the Glorious knew about the trap," I said, another piece falling into place. "So they went ahead and launched their coordinated feint, moving soldiers from Shiroyama Island to Meima. While they attacked, the Ammei agents inside the complex set the omni for Nexus Six as planned and waited for the courier with the other directory half to show up."

"Only the couriers were caught in the middle of the battle," Selene said softly, a flicker of pain in her pupils. "They were killed and buried under the rubble."

"Yes," Bubloo said. "And since the trap was a secret known

only to a few of the Overlords, no one on Meima knew what might have been lost on the battlefield, and therefore no one bothered to search through the rubble. Those who *did* know about the trap most likely assumed the directory half had never arrived."

"So why was the Meima omni still set for Nexus Six when Jordan McKell stumbled onto it?" I asked. "Did the Overlords close down the Meima station after that?"

"Soon afterward, yes," Bubloo said. "The ferocity of the attack, combined with a growing disillusionment in the face of the growing disorder, brought the Overlords to a momentous decision." A shadow seemed to cross his face. "They decided it was time for the Icari to leave the Spiral."

It was obvious that this was where the story was leading. Even so, it still hit me like a slap across the face.

"They just left?" Selene asked. "No negotiations, no policy changes, not even any ultimatums? They just *left*?"

"It wasn't quite that instantaneous," Bubloo said. "Remember how long it takes to move people through omnis. It took over ten years to send all the colonists back home, which gave the local species time to adjust to the change. The Overlords also offered to return their Ammei, Patthaaunutth, and Kadolian servants to their homeworlds once the withdrawal was complete."

"I'll bet that went over well with the Ammei," I muttered.

"It went over very poorly," Bubloo said ruefully. "They had held supreme control over the portals for centuries and didn't want to lose that power. The Glorious were gone or scattered, but new Ammei leaders arose who petitioned the Overlords to give them the system."

"Which they didn't."

"To the frustration of the Ammei, yes," Bubloo said. "They refused relocation, choosing instead to gather in enclaves among other rising species. But adapting to life without the Icari and portals was more difficult than they expected. Between internal strife and outside enemies their numbers steadily dwindled. Eventually, they located and recolonized Nexus Six, where they could at least control those twelve twains."

"What about the Patth and Kadolians?" I asked.

"The Patthaaunutth believed that unchecked Ammei ambitions would be a danger to them," Bubloo said. "Fortunately, their worlds were largely unknown to any but themselves and the Icari, and they accepted the Overlords' offer. They returned home and mostly withdrew from the Spiral."

"Until they found and reverse-engineered the Talariac Drive," I said. "Then they made their reentry with a vengeance. And the Kadolians?"

Bubloo sighed. "Like the Patthaaunutth, they also feared to remain beneath the Ammei shadow. They were weary of the Spiral and asked to go home."

I looked at Selene. "Only the Icari had somehow lost its location."

"Not precisely," Bubloo corrected. "Their home is accessible via a twain, and the archives *do* mark where the Spiral end of that twain is located." He winced. "Unfortunately, it's in one of the Nexus One portal rings."

"And the Nexus One address *has* been lost," I said heavily. "Great. So now all you have to do is talk Sub-Director Nask and General Kinneman into letting you take a quick peek at their directory halves. How old did you say you were?"

"I didn't say," Bubloo said, frowning. "I'm thirty-eight. What does my age have to do with anything?"

"Because as my father used to say, *Beware of any adult who still believes in Santa Claus.* Seems to me Santa's the only chance you've got of prying those directory halves out of their owners' cold hands."

"But that's the point," Bubloo said. "I don't need a directory. I just need the location of the Nexus One omni. Not its *address*, but its physical location on the planet." He looked at Selene. "You *have* found that location, haven't you?"

"First things first," I said, giving Selene a quick warning hand signal. I could handle the talking. She needed to handle the sniffing. "What exactly is the *fiall*? Is it a full-range omni, or another twain, or something else? More important, if it is and Yiuliob has its address, can he just pop in any time he wants?"

"It's neither an omni nor a twain," Bubloo said. "It's a stand-alone inglobe, with no associated outglobe. You can travel to it from any omni, but the only exit is the hatch you see behind you." He made a face. "And yes. If Yiuliob has its address there's nothing to stand in his way."

"The Juniper portal," Selene murmured. "No wonder he's been searching so hard for it."

"And why he was so willing to let me go when I promised to get him its location," I agreed soberly. "So you can teleport in but not out? Sounds pretty limiting."

"And so it was deliberately designed," Bubloo said. "Those limitations protect the contents, as do the defenses that prevent anyone from breaking through the outer metal."

"Good to know," I said. "Lucky for us we have a key." I raised my eyebrows. "The ring *is* a key, right?"

Bubloo's eyes lowered to my stunner. "In a sense. But..." He stopped.

"We've already been through this, Bubloo," I reminded him as patiently as I could. "You wanted us enough to play crazy in the taverno to get our attention. You trusted us enough to let an unknown like Robin get close to you."

"*And* enough to post a bounty on yourself in a city full of trigger-happy thugs and bounty hunters," Selene added quietly.

"Very good," I said, nodding approvingly at her. "How long did it take you to figure that one out?"

"Not long," she said. "Your father and I concluded Bubloo wanted me back on Nexus Six to search the *Imistio* Tower archives, but couldn't risk using Yiuliob's portal. With the *Median* on Juniper, he decided to force a linkup with your father in the hope that I would follow. You?"

"A couple of days," I said. "Circe clearly knew things she wasn't sharing. It all kind of unraveled from there." I turned back to Bubloo. "So we're here, we've got what you need, and you really don't have any secrets from us. The only thing standing in our way is whether you're going to open the *fiall* or not."

"I will open it," Bubloo said. "Will you first please give me the Nexus One array location?"

"No," I said before Selene could speak. "We won't tell you, but we'll show you." I nodded back toward the *fiall*. "*After* we have whatever you need from inside."

"Friend Roarke—"

"Bubloo, this is becoming dangerously ridiculous," Selene said firmly. "Yiuliob could arrive at any minute. What is so horribly secret about this particular inglobe?"

Bubloo huffed out a sigh. "*Fiall* is a shortening of the Icari word *ultimate*," he said quietly. "It was to be the last hope for the Icari, should it be needed." He paused, and I had the sense that he was doing one final evaluation of Selene and me.

Whatever he saw seemed to convince him. Or maybe it just convinced him that he was out of choices. "The *fiall* is an armory. A repository of Icari weapons.

"And Yiuliob is right. Properly wielded, they could indeed allow him to rule the Spiral."

CHAPTER TWENTY-FIVE

$$\diamond\!\!\!\diamond\!\!\!\diamond$$

I looked at Selene. She looked back, fresh dread in her pupils. "Gregory?" she whispered.

"I know," I said grimly. The Ammei had driven the Icari from the Spiral. They'd refused to return to their homeworlds, instead clinging stubbornly to the memories of their onetime power.

And now they had ancient Icari weaponry within their reach. "All right," I said, forcing my voice to stay calm as I pulled Bubloo's ring from my pocket. "How does this—?" I broke off, lowering my gaze to his hands. "Of course. Tell us about your fingers."

"Yes; my fingers." Bubloo hesitated, then held up his right hand. "Selene was right about the ring powering the circuitry. But there's more to it than that." He touched his right forefinger with his left. "This one contains a de-aggressor. It calms down potential adversaries. You saw me use it on the gate guards at my Blackcreek home."

He shifted the pointing finger to the second right-hand finger. "Stunner. Used on the false badgemen at Friend Christopher's apartment." He moved the pointer to the third finger. "Confuser. That's what I used on him during the battle inside the Mycene portal. I still didn't know who he was or whether I could trust him, and I couldn't let him interfere with my plan to strand you in the Nexus Six portal so that you could be brought to *Imistio* Tower."

I felt my lip twist. Where Yiuliob had already set up shop . . . but maybe Bubloo hadn't known that. "What did you do with him?"

"I took him back to Belshaz," Bubloo said. "Friend Circe was happy to take him into her care."

"And then you sneaked over to Nexus One and stashed his plasmic for me?"

"Yes. I thought you might need it."

"And I did," I acknowledged grudgingly. "Thanks." I pointed at his hands. "So; three fingers, three separate weapons, and you don't want all of them running at the same time. So the ring doesn't just power them, but activates the one you want?"

"Yes." Bubloo switched hands, now holding up his left. "First finger: data and electronics hacking."

"Using the Patth backdoors, I assume?"

"Of course," he said, as if that should be obvious. "The Icari were, after all, the ones who instructed the Patthaaunutth in those techniques."

"Which is how you knew we'd been to Mindi's ship," I said. "No fancy Kadolian-level sense of smell, just you hacking into security cameras to see where we'd been."

"Yes," he admitted. "I apologize for yet another lie. But I needed you to believe I was of value to the Ammei if you were to remain interested in me."

"You underestimate your native allure," I said sourly. "Anyway, at that point we were just as interested in keeping tabs on Robin. Next finger?"

"The most important of all," he said. "It allows me to activate and control specialized Icari electronics." He nodded over my shoulder. "Such as the hatch into the *fiall*."

He stood up. "I still don't know if I can fully trust you, Roarke," he admitted. "Your species has the same obsession with power and control that the Ammei once had and that Yiuliob still possesses. But I have no choice but to accept Friend Selene's judgment."

"What's in the third finger?" Selene asked.

Bubloo looked at her. "Excuse me?"

"The third finger of your left hand," she said. "What does that control?"

"Nothing," he said, looking down at it. "It's a chef's equilibrium sensor. It allows me to create the proper spice and flavor balance when I cook."

"And that's there *why*?" I asked.

He gave me a slightly embarrassed smile. "I like to cook," he said simply. "My ring?"

I handed it to him, keeping my stunner ready. If he tried to put it anywhere on his right hand...

But he merely slipped it onto his left-hand middle finger and stepped past me to the plate. He touched one of the spots I'd noted earlier, held his hand there a couple of seconds, then moved to the next one in the pattern.

"You mentioned defenses," I said as he moved on to the third. "Just wondering what happens if you screw up the combination."

"There's no danger," Bubloo assured me. "It's not an ordered combination, but merely a matter of releasing all the restraints. And the defenses wouldn't endanger us anyway. At the first breach in the outer shell, the gravity inside reverses, dropping the contents into the center of the sphere."

"Effectively locking out anyone trying to use a portal," I said, nodding. "Clever. It does, however, mean that whoever brought a cutting torch to the party can still keep going."

"Not if he wishes to profit from his actions," Bubloo said. "As a breach lengthens, the reversed gravity's strength increases. By the time an intruder could create a large enough gap to enter, the equipment would be held in place by a field of over three hundred gravities."

I whistled softly. "Good luck finding anything useful."

"Exactly." Bubloo touched the final spot. With a rapid stutter of loud clicks, the plate swung open, revealing the familiar curve of portal metal behind it.

Bubloo exhaled loudly. "I've read so much about this place," he said quietly. "Both hopes and warnings." Reaching in, he touched the hull hatch, folding it inward to reveal the familiar glow. "Come." He leaned into the opening, did the usual twist-sit-roll, and disappeared. I gestured to Selene, who followed him inside. Bracing myself, I did likewise.

I'd seen military equipment dumps before, most recently on General Kinneman's private army base inside Alpha. Such gear was typically sorted by class: combat suits grouped together, light weapons and heavy weapons in their own orderly racks, combat explosives stacked elsewhere. Ammo magazines, ration and med packs, binoculars and star scopes—everything was neatly parked with its own kind.

The Icari did things differently. Instead of unified equipment stacks, there were racks spread neatly around the sphere, each holding a single, bright-yellow combat suit. Not just hanging there, as they'd be in EarthGuard storage, but set out like the old Da Vinci picture: legs separated and angled a little bit apart, arms stretched straight out to the sides. The suits were suspended a few centimeters above the deck, giving them the eerie look of warriors just about to touch down on the battlefield. Surrounding each rack, gathered together in neat piles, were the various weapons and support gear the suit's owner might choose to take onto that battlefield. The whole thing was impressive and pretty damn scary.

"*Imistio* Tower," Selene said suddenly. "I thought the name should be translated as *needle*. I was wrong."

I nodded, thinking back to that conversation. The Ammei word *imistio,* and the Kadolian version *imistiu.* Needle, point, arrowhead, or spear. "Not *needle*," I agreed. "*Spear.*"

"Yes," she said. "A weapon. *Many* weapons. There must be at least a couple thousand suits in here."

"Plus several times that many weapons," I said.

"Yes." She pointed upward. "And then there are those."

I craned my neck. Nearly a quarter of the hull arching above us was taken up by dark gray human-sized pods. "Bubloo?" I called. "What are those?"

"Compacted vehicles," his voice came from somewhere. I looked around, but couldn't spot him. "Sections of armored cars and small aircraft. Quick-open, quick-assemble. There are probably also remote-controlled observation and weapons drones."

"All the time and effort it took to bring the bioprobe equipment to Alpha," Selene murmured. "One of these pods could easily be strapped onto the back of someone wearing a combat suit."

"Bypassing the whole problem of having to have someone living in order to trigger the extension arm," I said grimly. "You give Yiuliob a full-range portal and access to this place, and he can move a whole army wherever he wants and be ready to go within a few hours."

"At least he doesn't have a directory."

"Maybe not yet," I said. "But Kinneman and Nask each have

half of one. How much destruction do you think Yiuliob would have to drop on the Spiral in order to persuade the Commonwealth and Patth to turn those halves over to him?"

"Or it may not take any destruction at all," Selene said soberly. "What do you think they would do if Yiuliob offered each of them an Icari combat suit in exchange for their directory halves?"

"Hinting broadly that the things could be reverse engineered?" I hissed out a breath. "I'd like to think they'd both be smart enough to turn him down. But I wouldn't bet money on it."

"They'd find themselves all the worse for any such deal," Bubloo's voice came.

I looked around again, and this time saw his head as he poked it out from behind one of the nearby suits. "It took the Patth decades to recreate the Talariac Drive," he continued, beckoning to us. "And the Talariac wasn't protected by weapons protocols the way Icari combat suits are. Come—I have this one activated." He touched something on the back.

Abruptly, the whole suit came apart. The arms slid a few centimeters outward on slender wires, each breaking in half longitudinally like very long metallic clamshells. The helmet slid upward, as did the neck, torso, and hip sections, each piece ending up a few centimeters away from the others. They didn't split fully apart the way the arms did, but the vertical seams on the right-hand side of each piece popped open, again like clamshells, offering quick and easy access for the potential occupant. The legs slid downward, stopping with the soles resting on the deck, then did the same longitudinal split as the arms.

"You see how it works?" Bubloo asked. "Very simple."

"I see how it opens, anyway," I said as Selene and I joined him. Up close, I could see a neat but bewildering array of push buttons on both forearms, the upper thighs, and the upper chest. Leaning sideways to look into the helmet, I could also see an array of displays above and below the visor. "I also see an awful lot of switches and readouts that would argue against these things being described as *simple*. Just how much of a learning curve are we talking about here?"

"None," Bubloo said. He moved to the next suit in line and popped it open. "Time is critical, and we have none to waste. But don't worry. I already know how to operate them, and you won't have to learn."

"Right," I said. "What are you going to do, attach tow cables to us?"

"In a sense, I am." He got a grip on the left-hand forearm of the suit he'd just opened and pressed a short sequence of buttons.

And suddenly the suit Selene and I were standing beside came to life.

Reflexively, I took a step back. Selene stayed where she was, gazing with fascination into the helmet. "You've slaved them," she said.

"Exactly," Bubloo said. "You'll control your own flight—choosing when you take off and when you land—but whenever you're in the air your suits will be tethered to mine. I'll have a beacon going, and you'll simply follow me."

"This is how you intend to get to the Nexus One array?" Selene asked.

"Exactly," Bubloo said. "Soaring far above the ground, with virtually unlimited range and complete protection from predators and other dangers."

"Ah," I said, a shiver running through me. And they would offer equal protection, no doubt, against EarthGuard Marines, Royal Kalixiri Commandos, Patth Expediters, and anyone else in the Spiral who had weapons and wanted to keep their freedom. No wonder Yiuliob and Juniper Glory were so anxious to get their hands on this place. "What happens if something goes wrong and one of us crashes?"

"You can't," he said. "Let me show you." He pointed to a thumb switch on the suit's right-hand forefinger. "This switch toggles between *fly* and *land*. Not *shut down*, but *land*. At that point the suit will take over its own operation and bring you to a safe and gentle landing. There are multiple redundancies to assure nothing goes wrong. Your suits also have radio beacons, so I'll know immediately if there's trouble and where to come fetch you. I'm the only one who'll be actively flying. You really will just be along for the ride."

"Great," I said. "And how many hours of flight time do you have?"

He shrugged, a little too casually. "None. But the instructions in its use were very detailed. Especially since, as I said, the suits largely operate themselves. Most of the complexity comes when you're in combat, and we won't need any of that."

He gestured to the first suit he'd opened. "Come, Selene. I'll set you up."

I smiled encouragingly at Selene as she stepped into the middle of the suit segments, noting the disturbed expression in her pupils. Probably wondering when I was going to drop the bombshell about her not actually having the portal array's location.

Nothing to worry about. If he was right about the suits having unlimited range, there was no rush. We could theoretically search the entire planet if we needed to, and pretty much at our leisure.

As for Yiuliob's hopes of popping across from *Imistio* Tower, I had an answer for that one, too.

It took about fifteen minutes, including a couple of false starts, before Bubloo finally declared Selene ready to go. The suit, I noticed, had automatically adjusted its proportions to hers while it was closing up, making for a snug but presumably comfortable fit.

After having her suit to practice on, it only took Bubloo five minutes to get into his own suit and an additional three to get me snugged into mine.

"Everyone all right?" he asked, his voice coming through a speaker directly behind my head.

"I think so," I said. "Selene?"

"Yes," she said.

"Good," Bubloo said. "Now. Here's how you take the helmet off." He indicated a pair of switches on opposite sides of his neck. "Hold them down together for about two seconds. Selene, you try it."

She did so, and I watched as the helmet split into a vertical clamshell and came free. She pulled it off and took a close look at the switches. "Seems straightforward enough," she said.

"Good," Bubloo said. "Once we get close to the portal, you can pop your helmet and see if you can smell the metal for the final run in." He looked at me. "Any questions?"

"Not yet," I said, taking a couple of experimental steps. The suit reacted instantly to my movements, its internal servos matching the speed and distance of the stride. I raised my arms and got the same gratifyingly quick response. On the helmet display opposite my left cheek, I noted, were charts of the arm, chest, and thigh switch arrays, with the buttons marked in Icari-style script. "I don't suppose there's a way to convert the readouts to English, is there?"

"I don't know," Bubloo said, his hand hovering over the thigh button arrays. "Let me see..." He found the button he was looking for, touched it, then held down another one. "English."

"Yes, Eng—" Abruptly, the labels flicked off and came back in English. "Whoa," I said, frowning. "Okay, this doesn't make any sense at all. How could the Icari possibly have programmed English into this thing when they disappeared from the Spiral three millennia ago?"

"I have no idea," Bubloo said, sounding as floored as I felt. "Nor do I know *why* they would do so. The *fiall* was never for the use of anyone except themselves."

"How far do StarrComm transmissions travel?" Selene asked.

"I—" For the second time in ten seconds I broke off in midsentence. "Not a clue," I admitted. "StarrComm messages cover the entire Spiral, and they're instantaneous. I've always assumed there was some signal boosting going on between the various stations, but StarrComm is pretty tight-lipped about how their system works. Are you suggesting the Icari might have eavesdropped from wherever they are now and decided to update their equipment?"

"I don't know what I'm suggesting," she said. "It was just a question that suddenly occurred to me."

"And an interesting one it is," I said. "And if it wasn't StarrComm specifically, maybe it was the Icari equivalent."

"But that's a mystery for later," Bubloo said. "Are your equipment labels to your satisfaction, Friend Roarke?"

"Hang on." I ran my eyes over the diagrams, located the section dealing with the suit's sensors. Infrared...light-enhancement... power usage. I found the latter control on my left arm and pressed it.

Abruptly, the view through my visor went a sort of dark purple. Against the dark was a scattering of brighter pink spots, three of which were clearly our combat suits. I touched the switch again, and the pink disappeared and the lighting went back to normal. "Seems to be working."

"Excellent," Bubloo said. "Then we're ready to head back to the twain ring and travel to Nexus One. I'll take us across the river by air to make sure the tethering is working properly. Come."

He went to the hatch and rolled back outside. As Selene sat down on the edge of the hatchway and prepared to follow, I stepped over to the nearest weapons cache and picked up something that looked like a compact laser rifle. It had showed pink on the power sensors, so presumably was still functional. All I needed to do was figure out how to use it.

Abruptly, a display that had been showing my suit's system status changed to a schematic of the weapon I was holding, identifying the trigger, safety, power level indicator, telescope sighting, and half a dozen other stats.

As my father used to say, *Sometimes the universe will decide to be helpful all on its own. If that ever happens, be sure to thank it.*

"Thank you," I muttered as I crossed to the hatchway.

"What did you say?" Selene asked.

"Nothing," I said. I tucked the weapon against my chestplate and rolled out of the armory.

"Come on, come on," Bubloo urged. "The night is fading—"

This time it was his turn to break off as he spotted my weapon. "Roarke?" he asked carefully.

"This'll just take a moment," I said, shifting the laser into a two-hand firing position. "A couple of steps back, please."

He hesitated, then reluctantly complied. "You too, Selene," I ordered, moving away from the armory's hatchway. I slid off the safety catch, adjusted my aim, and squeezed the trigger.

Sending a soft blue needle of light into the center of the flat metal plate Bubloo had told us carried the armory's defenses.

I wasn't fooled by the quiet, almost genteel blue light. The helmet's displays informed me that the bulk of the laser's energy was in the ultraviolet part of the spectrum, and that it was indeed delivering a massive assault.

But its target was Icari metal. I held the beam steady, noting that that part of the helmet's visor had automatically darkened in response to the additional light. Out of the corner of my eye I saw that Selene had removed her helmet, but with my newly darkened visor I couldn't see what her pupils might be telling me. I tried to imagine how she was reacting to the scent of hot, possibly burning Icari metal—

And suddenly there was a horrendous racket from beside me. I released the trigger and peered through the hatchway.

To find the combat suits, weapons, and support gear now

sitting in a massive ball in the center of the sphere, exactly as Bubloo had described.

"There you go," I said, gesturing toward the hatchway. "Now it doesn't matter whether Yiuliob gets an omni portal or not."

"Yes," Bubloo said, staring past my shoulder. His expression was invisible behind his faceplate, but I had the sense he was staring at my new toy.

As well he might. A functional, one-of-a-kind Icari weapon was an incredibly valuable commodity. Something Selene and I could barter for wealth, power, or protection from at least half a dozen species. For a pair of out-of-work crocketts with the Commonwealth, Patth, and Ammei all mad at them, it was something well worth holding on to.

"Not the way I would have done it," Bubloo continued. "But I suppose it *does* secure the armory. I need to seal the hatch now, so if you'll step back...?"

"Sure," I said.

But instead of moving back, I walked back to the hatchway. Resetting the safety catch, I took my weapon by the muzzle, leaned it into the opening, and let go. I watched it drop onto the general equipment jumble at the center, then reached in and tapped the interior hatch. It closed, and I stepped away. "*Now* you can seal it," I said.

For a moment Bubloo just looked at me. Then, stirring, he nodded and swung the outer plate closed. There was another stutter of clicks, and it was done.

"And now you're the only one who can get in," I said. "So. Nexus One?"

"Nexus One," he confirmed. He touched a key on his thigh, and I watched as the bright yellow of our combat suits faded into a dark, mottled nightfighter gray. "And may I apologize for momentarily thinking the worst of you."

"Not a problem," I assured him. "I already told you: Friends, barbeque, and Dewar's. Besides, bidding wars can be so tedious." I gestured in the direction of *Imistio* Tower. "Lead the way."

The soldiers guarding the Nexus One portal literally never knew what hit them. Focused on the possibility of ground action, either going into or coming out of the portal, they weren't prepared for dark, silent Icari combat suits to come to a hover above them and for one of those suits to deliver what was apparently a boosted version of Bubloo's confuser. We landed and made our way through the wandering Ammei, where Bubloo opened a convenient hatch.

A few minutes later, we were on Nexus One.

"Cheery place, isn't it?" I asked Selene as I popped off my helmet. "At least no one's shooting at us this time."

"I hope we can keep it that way," she said as she also removed her helmet. The steady westerly breeze caught her silver hair, sending it rippling like ocean foam.

"Seconded," I agreed, watching her pupils closely. "Hard to fulfill a prophecy when you're being shot at. Speaking of which, Bubloo—"

"Later," Bubloo said, looking around. "It's already midafternoon, but if we leave now we should still have four or five hours of light. We'll head due north—"

"*Not* later," I said firmly, still watching Selene. If I was right...

And there it was, blazing from her pupils.

"First, I want to know more about this prophecy," I said. "You told us the medallions were part of a package to help Kadolians find their homeworld, right? But how did the Icari know it would be a *female* Kadolian?"

"What are you talking about?" Bubloo asked, removing his own helmet and frowning at us.

"You told us way back when that the chosen one would free *her* people," I reminded him. "How could the Icari have known she would be a female?"

"They didn't," Bubloo said, an edge of impatience in his voice. "I added that part to help convince you."

"So what exactly *did* the lore say?"

"Roarke—"

"I have a right to know," Selene said, quiet determination in her voice and pupils. "These are my people we're talking about. This is my world poised in the balance."

Bubloo huffed out a breath. "All the package contained were the two medallions and a statement that they would point the Kadolians to their world."

"That's it?" I asked.

"If there was more, it was lost after the Icari left the Spiral. And no, there was nothing more in the archives, either."

"Leaving us with a wonderfully obscure—what was it again?"

"*The path to freedom can only be found by the heart that sees the farthest,*" Selene quoted.

"Right," I said. "Why don't these prophesies ever just say what they mean?"

"It's not a proph—" Bubloo broke off. "Please. I'll be happy to discuss such things later. But now, we have to leave."

"I'm sorry, but I can't," Selene said, lowering herself unsteadily onto the ground. "Not yet. I need to..." She closed her eyes. "I need to rest a while. Something in the air..."

"Are you all right?" I asked anxiously, kneeling beside her and taking her hand.

"Put your helmet back on," Bubloo ordered, hurrying over to us. "The suit has air filters."

"Too late," I told him. "Whatever's bothering her is already in her system."

"It's nothing dangerous," Selene assured us. "It's just...call it acclimation. I need to sift through the various scents and aromas, sort them out, and establish a regional baseline." She gestured. "You two go. I can catch up."

"Absolutely not," I said firmly. "Those guards we left wandering around Nexus Six could come to their senses any time. I'm not leaving you here alone if they drop in with friends." I looked up at Bubloo. "You go. We'll both catch up."

"You can rest while we travel," Bubloo said. His voice and face were agitated, and I could only guess what was happening to his scent. "The suits fly themselves."

"Which is why we can catch up with you," I reminded him patiently. "We're tethered, right? Besides, you know what the portal ring looks like from above. You might be able to find it yourself without having to rely on Selene's sense of smell. So go. When Selene's ready, we'll hit our little thumb buttons and you can reel us in. Okay?"

It was clear from his shifting expressions that it wasn't okay by any stretch of the imagination or the word. But eagerness and impatience won out. "All right," he said reluctantly. "Selene?"

I looked at her, holding my breath. If she hadn't caught on to my plan...

She had. "The array is six degrees east of due north," she said. "Distance approximately five thousand kilometers, plus or minus a hundred."

"Got it," Bubloo said. "As soon as you're able." He started to put his helmet back on—

"Which Gemini is it?" I asked.

He paused, the helmet halfway in place. "What?"

"The Gemini portal that leads to Selene's world," I said. "Sorry—the twain portal."

"Why do you need to know?"

"Why do you need to keep it secret?" I countered. "Come on, Bubloo. This is Selene's future we're talking about."

He looked back and forth between us, clearly suspecting there was something going on. "The inner ring, the one closest to the omni," he said. "Three o'clock position if due north is twelve."

"Thanks," I said. "Happy flying. We'll be with you as soon as Selene sorts all this out."

He gazed at me another long moment. But the time crunch was looming, and there was nothing in what we'd said or asked that he could legitimately call us on. "Be safe," he said at last, touching the key that turned our suits back to bright yellow. "That'll make all of us easier to spot," he added in explanation. "Top left chest button is the emergency switch. Signal if there's any trouble."

I put my helmet back on and checked the labels for confirmation. "I see it," I confirmed, taking the helmet off again. "Feel free to do likewise if you run into something you need help with."

"Thank you," he said with more than a hint of sarcasm. He sealed his helmet, hesitated another moment, then turned and launched himself into the sky. We watched in silence until he'd disappeared over the mountains to the north. "You okay?" I asked Selene.

"I'm fine," she said. "Bubloo's not happy with this arrangement."

"That much I know," I said. "The swoon act was inspired, by the way. I was wondering how we were going to get rid of him."

"Yes," she said, her pupils troubled. "But there was also... He's hiding something, Gregory. I don't know what, but I think it's something important."

"We'll figure it out," I assured her. "You ready?"

She nodded, her pupils going introspective. "It's odd, isn't it? Even people who know Kadolians the best—Ammei, Patth, even people like Bubloo—have blind spots they don't even know are there."

"That's kind of the way it is with blind spots," I agreed. "But you're right. Medallions, poems, secret clues, Kadolian books hidden in Ammei archives—everyone jumped to the conclusion it was the same kind of treasure hunt they would set up for one of their own."

"Instead of realizing the Icari would most likely go with the most straightforward clue a Kadolian would need."

"The metal the medallions are made of," I said, searching the sky again. Bubloo was long out of sight. "So. Where is it?"

"That way," she said, pointing southwest into the breeze. "About five kilometers away, I think."

"Closer than I expected," I commented. "Especially after all the centuries the Ammei have spent hunting for the end of the rainbow."

"They were hunting north," she reminded me. "The Icari legends said the portal array was that direction."

"And their searches in all other directions were handled from the air," I said, nodding. "They didn't find it because they weren't looking for it."

"The Icari didn't want them finding our world," Selene said quietly as she got back to her feet. "Not the Ammei, not the Patth. Only us."

"Only you," I agreed, peering into my helmet again. According to the beacon display, Bubloo was already a good hundred kilometers away. "Okay, he should be far enough. Let's go."

"Yes," she said, peering into the wind. "I wish we weren't slaved to his suit. It would be quicker to fly."

"I know," I said, taking her arm. "But that's okay. We already know how well these things fly. Let's see how well they run."

CHAPTER TWENTY-SIX

$$\diamond\!\!\diamond\!\!\diamond$$

We kept our helmets off on the grounds that our radios were almost certainly open, and there wasn't much point in skulking if we were simultaneously discussing our plans in Bubloo's earshot.

The suits turned out to be very good at enhanced running. Selene and I headed off at top speed, and the suits took the hint and keyed themselves to that standard, pumping the legs and basically carrying us along. Four minutes of that, and we were there.

It turned out that one reason the Ammei hadn't spotted the portal was that it was effectively invisible. There was nothing of the typical dome shape or even a distorted mound, but simply a spot downwind of a short, half-meter-high ridge. Like everywhere else in this part of Nexus One, a layer of dust had gathered in the ridge's wind shadow, covering the telltale sheen of the metal.

But the placement also allowed for random wind eddies that continually worked at the dust, opening and closing ever-changing patterns of tiny small gaps where the metal was almost clear to the sky. That was what Selene had smelled from the main Nexus Six portal, what the Icari had always intended for a searching Kadolian to smell.

"Okay," I said, peering into my helmet again. As far as I could tell from the beacon display, Bubloo was still driving his way north. "Let's go."

She nodded and tapped the hatch. It opened, dust spilling through the opening and reorganizing itself along the gravitic interface. A minute later, we were both inside with the hatch closed behind us. The size of the receiver module showed it was, as expected, one end of a Gemini dyad. We walked to the launch module, and a ride up the extension arm took us to the other end.

"I wish I could see Bubloo's face when our beacons suddenly show up five thousand kilometers ahead of him," I commented as we walked around the receiver globe toward a hatch whose edges showed faded markings. "Let's see where the Icari wanted you to go. Would you do the honors?"

Selene nodded and opened the hatch. It was set at a ninety-degree angle to the ground, a pretty standard configuration. "What do you see?" I asked, trying to look over her shoulder.

"I think we're on a cliff," she said. "The ground around us looks mostly flat, but I can see a vertical rock face about twenty meters back."

"Looks like a place where I should go first," I said, trying to nudge her aside.

I might as well have tried to nudge the cliff. She'd already dropped onto her rear and stuck her legs out the opening, and two seconds later was outside. Glaring at the landscape, I followed.

As Selene had said, we were on a wide ledge surrounded on three sides by tall, rocky vertical cliffs. Selene was standing at the edge of the fourth side, gazing out at what seemed to be a wide plain far below. "What do you see?" I asked, walking toward her.

She turned to me, a cautious hope sparkling in her pupils. "The way home," she said.

Bracing myself, I looked out onto the plain.

There it was: the Nexus One portal array.

I don't know what I'd expected. Something like Nexus Six, I suppose, a full-range omni surrounded by maybe three or four rings of Geminis.

From here on the ledge I could see the outer Gemini ring. I could see the ring inside it, and the one inside that, and three more inside that. The rest was obscured by a light mist drifting over the plain.

Selene murmured something reverent sounding in the Kadolian language. "How many are there, do you think?" she asked.

"No idea," I said. "I can't even see the omni in the middle, let alone the far end of the array. Bubloo's probably got a full count." I pursed my lips. "Speaking of whom, I suppose we ought to check in." Opening the helmet tucked under my arm, I slipped it over my head and fastened it in place. "Bubloo?" I called.

"*There* you are." His voice was tense and nervous, an echo of the crazy Pakenrill we'd first met in the taverno an eternity ago. "What in the name of—?"

"Easy," I soothed, taking a look at the positioning display. He was still flying mostly north, but had now shifted his angle a few degrees to line up with our current position. A bit west of north, I noted in passing, instead of Selene's impromptu east of north. "We're both fine. We found the back door your friends the Icari left us."

He was silent so long that I thought maybe his radio had broken. "So *that's* what it meant," he said, his voice under control again. "No mysteries, no clues, just medallions made of the proper metal to show what the shortcut portal smelled like. Are you at the array?"

"We're on on a high cliff overlooking it," I said. "Pretty damned impressive."

"I'm looking forward to seeing it," he said. "How high is this cliff? Can you safely jump, or do you need to wait until I get there and can fly all of us down?"

"We'll find our own way," I said. "Fly safely, and we'll see you when you get here."

"Roarke—"

I popped the helmet open and took it off. "I don't know how melodramatic the Icari were," I said to Selene, "but people who create instant teleporters aren't going to sacrifice convenience for spectacle. So where's the portal out of here?"

"Up there," she said, pointing at the cliff face behind us. "We go through that crack—it looks like a dead end, but I'm guessing the rock behind it is more a bend than a barrier. The portal should be two or three meters above our current position."

"Okay," I said, taking her arm and leading her away from the cliff. "Let's give it a try."

The crack was wider than it looked, and Selene's reading was right on the nose. Half a meter in, the passage took a sharp left-hand turn and became a narrow path angling upward. At the top was another sharp turn, this one to the right, and at the end was the curve of another portal. We went in—as expected, it was another Gemini—and a couple of minutes later we were standing on the ground somewhere inside the portal array.

"There," Selene said, pointing. "There's the omni."

I nodded. We weren't just inside the array, but right smack-dab in its center. Half hidden behind the Gemini we'd arrived through was the larger dome of a full-range portal. Surrounding us were the domes of other Geminis, though all we could see from here was the inner ring. Probably why the Icari had sent us first to the mountaintop, so that we could be properly impressed by the whole spectacle.

"The three o'clock position, he said," Selene said, looking around. "Do you have a compass? I don't see one on my displays."

"Yes, it's at—"

"Never mind, I found it," she interrupted. "North is that way. Which means...Gregory, I think it's this one right here."

I turned around. On the opposite side from the half-seen omni was the Gemini she was pointing to. It seemed much closer to us than the spacing between any of the other nearby portals.

Of course it was. "I think you're right," I agreed. "This little double hopscotch setup the Icari put together to keep out the Ammei and Patth wouldn't have been part of the original array. They had to shoehorn the extra Gemini in somewhere anyway, so they might as well put it as close to the Kadolian Gemini as possible."

"Squeezed between it and the omni," Selene said, nodding. "I'm surprised there was enough room."

"People who can lift an omni off Nexus Six and drop it into a perpetually stable orbit probably aren't used to taking *no* for an answer," I reminded her. "Are we going to just stand here?"

She looked at me, her pupils shimmering with hope, excitement, and quiet fear. "I don't know," she said. "Do you think we can?"

"Of all the people on this planet, you're the one who has the most right," I said firmly. "Am I invited along?"

"Of course," she assured me as she stepped over to the portal. With only a slight hesitation, she tapped the closest hatch.

After three to four millennia of disuse, a squeak or twitch would have been understandable. But like every other portal we'd ever encountered, it opened quickly and cleanly. We went inside and walked around to the launch module. "We should probably have our helmets on," I warned as we paused at the base of the extension arm. "There may be biotics out there our wide-spectrums aren't ready for."

"Good idea," she said, putting on her helmet and sealing it. "Though when the Icari were using the portals they probably transferred a lot of pathogens back and forth between worlds," she continued, her voice now coming through the speaker behind my head. "Maybe that's why wide-spectrums are as effective as they are."

"Could be," I said. "Still worth checking. The top-middle button on the left chest, if I'm reading it correctly."

"Yes, that's the one," she confirmed. "Do we ... ?"

"Yes," I said, taking hold of the extension arm. "We do."

The trip to the middle of the launch module seemed to take twice as long as it ever had before. I kept my eye on Selene, but her pupils were impossible to read through the helmets' visors. We reached the luminescent gray, felt the familiar tingle, and were once again transported somewhere across the universe.

"Nice place," I commented as we began our downward float. "Seems familiar somehow." It was a silly comment, but something in Selene's taut silence made me want to say *something*.

For once, my intuition was correct. Selene gave a small chuckle, and I felt the tension ease a bit. "Any idea which door we should use?" I asked.

"I doubt the scent from the last passenger is still available," she said. "We'll just have to keep going until we find one that works."

The first two she tried opened into dirt. The third opened into bright sunlight.

I took a deep breath. My protective instincts were screaming at me to roll outside first, to be ready to take the first spear if someone out there was inclined to violence.

I resisted the urge. Selene had the right to be the first one to stand again on Kadolian soil. I gestured, then stood back silently as she maneuvered her way through the opening.

I did, however, make double-damn sure to be close behind.

We found ourselves in a wide meadow, maybe a hundred meters across, with loose stands of tall, oddly shaped trees on all four sides. The blue-green ground cover was more like ferns than any grass I was familiar with and seemed springy beneath my feet. The trees were equally exotic, with bark composed of three intermixed colors and three different types of flowers lining the branches amid a spray of blue-green leaves.

In the distance, over the trees, I could see delicate spires of white metal or ceramic glittering in the sunlight.

"Gregory?"

Selene's voice seemed to be coming from far away. I looked over, to find she'd removed her helmet and was staring back at our portal. I checked my readouts, discovered that while I'd been gawking at the landscape the suit had declared the air safe to breathe, and popped my own helmet. "What do you think?" I asked.

"I think," she said quietly, "that we've been missed."

I frowned and turned around.

To find that the portal we'd just come through had been turned into a shrine.

The word had leaped unbidden to my mind. But as I gazed at the structure that had been built around the portal I realized my first instinct had been correct. A sort of wreath had been built around the dome, consisting of three different colors and textures of fabric interwoven together. Occasional tree branches were situated at artistically chosen spots, some with just leaves, others bearing the lines of flowers I'd already seen. Flanking the portal were two large standing stone slabs with words carved into them. "What do they say?" I asked.

"They say—" Selene broke off, a series of emotions flicking across her pupils. "The inscription on the left says, *In memory of the Kadolian lost, the ten thousand who gave themselves that we who remained might live in peace and freedom.*"

I winced. "The ten thousand being the ones the Icari took to help build their portals?"

"I think so, yes," she said. "The number matches our legends. The inscription on the right . . . it's almost the same as the other. The same thought, certainly. But the wording is different, as if it was written in an obscure dialect."

"Or maybe in the *current* dialect?" I suggested. "The first inscription in the dialect your ancestors spoke when they left, the other the way Kadolians talk now?"

"Yes," Selene said, her voice sounding a little distant. "That could be. I suppose I never . . . it's like coming to a place where you've never been, but where you hoped you'd be welcome."

"You'll be welcome," I assured her. "Those tree branches haven't been there for three thousand years, you know. The flowers on them are fresh. Someone's been tending them. Probably ever since you left."

"Maybe," she said, her pupils still concerned. "But—"

She broke off, her nostrils and eyelashes suddenly working the air. "We're not alone, Gregory. There's someone nearby." She raised her head and called something in her own language.

For a moment there was nothing. Then I caught a hint of movement at the edge of the left-hand slab and a young, silver-haired girl peeked around at us. She said something...

Selene glanced at me, and I caught a hint of sudden amusement in her pupils. She held her hand out to the girl and replied. The girl spoke again, and Selene answered. Another exchange, and the girl came hesitantly out from around the slab. With her hands now visible, I saw that she was holding a branch with faded flowers. "See?" I said quietly. "Continual upkeep and refreshing. What did she say that was so funny?"

"It wasn't really funny," Selene said, still holding out her hand to the girl. "It just struck me, somehow. She asked if I was a ghost."

"Can't say I'm surprised," I said. "After a few thousand years, I'd probably ask the same question. I'm also thinking she should probably call this in."

"She already has," Selene said, and there was no mistaking the quiet satisfaction in her pupils. "Even now, Kadolian children are taught proper responsibility."

"Yes," I said, thinking about the boy Tirano and his damaged social development. "So do we wait, or do we go back?" I hesitated. "Or maybe the better question is, do *I* go back?"

"We stay," Selene said. "Both of us."

She looked at me, firm determination in her pupils. "You're my friend, Gregory. You've shared in my fears and perils. It is only right that you also share in my joys."

We were sitting in a circle outside the portal with the girl, the girl's mother, and half a dozen officials who'd rushed in from the city spires I'd spotted earlier when Bubloo finally caught up with us. "Hello, Bubloo," I called, beckoning him over. "Join the party. How was *your* day?"

"Rather boring, actually," he said. He sounded cross, but with his helmet still in place and his expression unreadable that was only a guess. But it was probably a pretty good one. "You should have waited for me. Coming in cold wasn't a good idea."

"That's okay," I assured him. "Selene and I are used to dealing with bad ideas. Ours, and other people's."

"I'm certain you have," he said. "Well. What's done is done. But we need to get back."

"Agreed." I stood up, leaving Selene and other Kadolians still seated. "And we need to have a little chat."

"About what?"

"Of shoes, and ships, and something," I said. "I forget the rest. My father would know." I raised my eyebrows. "We can start with why exactly you're here."

"What do you mean?" Selene asked, looking up at me.

"Oh, I know why *you're* here," I told her. "I just want to know what's in it for Bubloo." I gestured at the portal. "But that can wait until he and I are back on Nexus One."

"All right," she said, standing up as well. "I'm ready."

"You don't have to come," I said quickly. If I was right, the upcoming conversation could be a sticky one. "Bubloo and I can handle it. You're welcome to stay here and get reacquainted with your people."

"There'll be time for that," she said. "Besides, the Elders need time to absorb all this and plan for our homecoming."

I grimaced. But to be honest, I'd prefer to have this talk with my living lie detector at my side. "All right, then," I said. "Say your good-byes and let's go."

"All right," I said when we were once again on Nexus One soil. "Take your helmet off, and let's have it."

"Of course," Bubloo said, popping off his helmet and tucking it under his arm. "Let me first say that if there'd been any other way I wouldn't have involved you at all."

"Thanks—that makes it so much better," I growled. "Get on with it."

"All right." He waved around us. "I needed the Nexus One ring to get to the Kadolian homeworld. But I didn't have the omni's address."

"No one does," I said. "That much we know."

"You also know that no one knows where the Juniper omni is," he said. "What you *don't* know is that First of Three and Yiuliob *do* have the Juniper's address."

"Okay," I said. "How does that help us?"

"Because I also have its address." He waved at the big omni behind him. "And when you use an omni...?"

I felt a shiver run up my back. "The launch module of your destination displays both addresses."

"Exactly," he said. "So now we travel to Juniper, get the Nexus One address, and start shipping the Kadolians home. And that's that."

"So it would seem," I said. "Selene?"

"He's telling the truth," she said quietly. "He's also wrong."

"No," Bubloo said, frowning. "I'm not lying."

"She means the part about that being that," I said. "By my count there are at least three loose ends that have to be dealt with before everyone can live happily ever after: Yiuliob, Kinneman, and the Uroemm family."

"I'm sorry, Friend Roarke," Bubloo said, wincing. "I hadn't thought about any of those. Perhaps we should remain here until we have a plan?"

"No need," I assured him. "I've got one."

I gestured to the omni. "Let's start by seeing what exciting stuff is happening on Juniper today."

After all we'd been through, we made damn sure to nail down the Nexus One omni's address as soon as we reached Juniper. Bubloo took pictures of the display, Selene sketched out the pattern in a notebook I found in one of my suit's external pouches, and I used every mnemonic I knew to memorize it.

It was only after the time had ticked to the end and the two addresses had disappeared that we set out to figure out just where on Juniper we were.

"I think I recognize this place," Bubloo said when we'd found a suitable hatch and were standing outside.

"Yes, I can see why," I said as I looked around. We were standing in about as pure and genuine a wilderness as I'd ever had the misfortune to encounter, with spindly trees looming over both the portal and the sea of bushes around it. Woven in and out of the bushes were thick branches of brown and withered thorn vines that even in death looked sharp and impressively nasty. "It's so memorable."

"Yes, it is," he said, completely serious. "See the mound over there?"

I stepped over beside him. From my new vantage point, I could indeed see there was a small hill in that direction. "And *that's* the part you recognize?"

"I think we're in a place called Thousand Tombs," he said. "A long cluster of low mounds that Saffi legend says is the burial site of their ancient heroes. You can see how the top of the omni looks like just another of them."

I took a closer look at our portal. He was right, I had to admit. Over the centuries enough soil had collected around and on top of the dome to transform it into a reasonable facsimile of a natural hill, complete with a crown of grass and a few flowering vines. "Close enough, anyway," I said. "Seems a pretty obvious place to hide a portal, though. Why haven't the Ammei already found it?"

"Mainly because the region is designated as a sacred wilderness area," Bubloo said. "The Ammei can't come in and explore without drawing unwelcome attention."

"And until Yiuliob found the *fiall's* address there wasn't any urgent reason to find it," Selene added.

"Yes—good point," I agreed. "Or maybe no one cared about it until Yiuliob came on the scene. Either way, they may only have been searching for the past century or so."

"Or possibly less," Bubloo said. "There's also the landscape itself to consider. You can see it's not very conducive for people to search through."

I looked at Selene, caught the confirmation in her pupils. "Though that would depend on who exactly is doing the searching," I said. "Which one?"

"Pax," Selene said.

I nodded and gave a soft whistle. "Pax? Here we are, boy. Come on, Pax."

There was a sudden rustle in the bushes, and the outrider emerged from beneath one of the bushes. He squeaked as he spotted us and broke into a full-on scurry. "Yes, we're fine," I assured him, dropping to one knee and giving him a quick scritch behind the ears. "You want to go tell Ixil we're here? We're going to need him and McKell on this one."

Pax gave another squeak and scurried back into the bushes. "And now?" Bubloo asked.

"We wait," I said, sitting down and resting my back against the portal. It had been a very long night, and we looked to be headed into an even longer day. "A short nap might be a good idea."

"Or you could stay awake and tell us your plan," Selene suggested.

"Sure," I said, bracing myself. They weren't going to like this. But then, neither did I. "It starts this way..."

With only half the team assembled, I'd figured I would have to go through everything twice. But McKell and Ixil joined us midway through the explanation, so I only had to repeat the first part.

Sure enough, all four of them hated it.

McKell got in the first objection. "Leaving aside the whole question of whether the Firefall portal is guarded," he said, "are you even sure your exit strategy will work?"

"Bubloo says it will," I told him. "It's just normally so pointless that it's never done. *My* question is how good your aim is."

"I'm pretty sure I can do it," McKell said.

"I'll need better than just *pretty sure.*"

McKell threw me a glower. "*Yes,* I can do it."

"Because if you miss by even a little bit—"

"Thank you; I *do* understand the physics involved," he cut me off. "I said I've got it."

"If that's settled," Ixil said, "I'd like to return to the Firefall question. The last information we had was that it was considered a research station, without any military aspects or connection to the Icarus Group. But that could have changed since Jordan and I left."

"Your father might know," McKell suggested. "Maybe it's time for you to call him."

"I'd rather not," I said evasively. I didn't know how much the two of them knew about my father's liaison work with Kinneman and First of Three, but it didn't seem like something that should be bandied casually about. "I'd hate to burn that communications channel for something like this, especially when he might not know the answer. Even more especially since Firefall going full military would mean there's nothing we can do about it anyway."

"Military or otherwise, they'll certainly have the receiver module blocked," Ixil warned. "If the Patth ever find another omni portal, they would certainly try to get Firefall back."

I looked at Bubloo out of the corner of my eye, waiting for some reaction. Nothing. I looked back at Selene, caught a flicker of something in her pupils. Something Bubloo knew or suspected? "No problem," I said. "Ixil, you've still got that Pax-sized vac suit, right?"

"Of course not," he said. "All our equipment stayed with Kinneman when he fired us."

"Of course it did," I said, wincing. "Sorry—wasn't thinking."

"Or you *were* thinking and thought we might borrow a few things on our way out?" McKell suggested.

"That's probably more likely," I said. That was, in fact, exactly what I'd been thinking. More crucially, it was what I'd been counting on. If that option was closed... "Okay. I guess I need a new plan."

"You could always use a small bomb," McKell offered. "Wrap it around something living and shoot it through to Firefall."

"If you make it just strong enough to pop the balloon, it shouldn't alert anyone in the portal area," Ixil said.

"Yeah," I said, again looking at Selene. "Problem is that we have to wrap it around something living."

McKell looked at Selene, too. "Oh. Well..."

The group went silent. Selene was all right with killing animals for food or if they posed an immediate threat. But what McKell and Ixil were talking about was a deliberate sacrifice. I could tell just by looking at her pupils that she wasn't comfortable with that idea.

For that matter, neither was I. "There has to be another way," I said.

"I don't see one," McKell said, his forehead wrinkled in concentration. "We've tried sending inanimate objects through. Doesn't work. All of them have presumably had bacteria and viruses on their surfaces, so we can't fudge things that way."

"What about something low on the animal spectrum?" Ixil suggested. "A spider or worm or something?"

"*Can* the trigger be that small and primitive?" McKell asked.

"What don't we ask Bubloo?" Selene suggested.

"Or ask him if there are other options," I added, that twitch in Selene's pupils when we mentioned the blocked Firefall now making sense. "I'm guessing he knows something we don't."

"I know many things you don't," Bubloo said, an edge to his voice. "But these are Icari secrets, and not to be shared with just anyone."

"This is the Kadolians and their homeworld we're talking about," I reminded him. "Your family's big mission in life, remember?"

"No," he said flatly. "It's not."

I frowned. "Come again?"

"My mission is complete," he said. "I have the Nexus One omni's address, and I have access to another omni I can use to send the Kadolians home."

"Can Roarke use that other omni?" McKell suggested. "We just have to keep Kinneman from getting Juniper's and Nexus One's addresses. If he travels from Juniper to that other omni and then to Alpha—"

"Then he'll have the other portal's address," Ixil said. "I presume that's unacceptable?"

"It is."

"Then I guess Selene and I are finished," I said, staring hard at Bubloo. "At this point it'll be a toss-up as to whether Kinneman, the Ammei, or the Uroemm family get to us first."

"At least Kinneman will probably only imprison us," Selene added, her eyes also on Bubloo. "Yiuliob is likely to kill us. The Uroemm family is certain to do so."

Bubloo huffed out a long, sibilant sigh. "There may be another way. There *may*."

"We're listening," I said.

For another few seconds Bubloo remained silent. "There's an old Icari legend," he said at last, the words coming out slowly and reluctantly, as if he'd had to grab each one and shove it out of his mouth. "An Overlord caught a spy in his inner court. In a fury, he killed the spy, cut him into twelve pieces, and sent one to each of those he suspected of the attack."

He stopped, and for a moment no one spoke. "Did he have to tie each piece to something living in order to send it through?" Ixil asked.

"The legend doesn't say."

"How soon after the butchery did he send the pieces?" McKell asked. "If he *didn't* need to attach any add-ons, how long did the pieces stay living? Just long enough for the portal's gatekeeper protocols to accept, or longer?"

"Again, that detail wasn't included," Bubloo said. "It probably wasn't very long, though."

Beside me, Selene stirred. "Does the legend identify the spy?"

Bubloo hesitated. "Not by name."

"That's not an answer."

He gave another sigh. "The legend says the spy was Kadolian."

"No," I bit out before anyone else could react. "We'll find another way."

"What if there isn't one?" McKell asked, his own expression a little unsettled. Whatever mixed feelings he had about me, none of that animosity spilled over onto Selene.

"Then we run," I said. "We have the *Ruth*, nine hundred thousand commarks of Sub-Director Nask's money, a couple of fake ship IDs, and thirty-five silver-silk strands we can turn into quick cash anywhere in the Spiral. We'll hide somewhere until it all blows over."

"It won't," McKell said flatly. "Not with that crowd."

"Then we hide until they're all dead," I said stubbornly. "Selene's not going to make that kind of sacrifice for this."

"It wouldn't have to be much," Bubloo offered. "A small piece of skin might do it."

"And if it doesn't?" McKell asked.

I took a deep breath. As my father used to say, *Sometimes the obvious solution is sitting right in front of you. Just remember that* obvious *and* pleasant *usually aren't synonyms.* "We'll give it a try," I said. "McKell, how fast can you and Ixil make us up that bomb you mentioned?"

"An hour or two," McKell said, his eyes narrowed. "And then?"

"We try Bubloo's trick," I told him. "We'll wrap the bomb in a little piece of skin." I braced myself. "But not Selene's. Mine."

CHAPTER TWENTY-SEVEN

—————— ❖ ——————

Eight and a half years ago, I'd lost my left forearm to a plasmic shot. In time I'd gotten used to my prosthetic, but the mental trauma of that fiery disaster still occasionally came back, usually in nightmare form.

Selene always knew when one of those nightmares happened. Emotional turmoil at that level left a lingering change in my scent that she was easily able to pick up the next morning.

The first few times it happened I deflected her questions. The next couple of times I reluctantly gave her the details. Now, she knew better than to ask.

None of those flashbacks was even close to the situation currently hanging over me.

It wouldn't be as bad as losing half my arm, of course. I kept telling myself that. A small slice of skin, pain and blood and a quick anesthetic bandage slapped in place, and it would be over. Quick, easy, and done.

But at least with the plasma shot I hadn't had to live with the knowledge that it was coming. It had been unexpected—a blast of fire followed by a surge of horrible pain. Then Selene had been shot, and the adrenaline had kicked in, and the pain mostly stayed in the background until we reached the hospital.

At least Selene was sympathetic. McKell, I could tell, thought

I was being something of a coward. Ixil was probably thinking along the same lines, though the fact that Pix and Pax were sitting this one out suggested that my offer had earned me at least a little understanding or respect in his eyes.

But then, neither of them fully grasped the situation.

Certainly we'd start with a small patch of skin. But if that didn't work, where did we go next? Did I offer the portal a finger? Two fingers? A hand?

My remaining arm?

Because the idea of running that I'd laid out earlier was nonsense. I could hand the Juniper portal to Kinneman and get him off my back, or I could likewise appease Yiuliob with the same gift. But making nice with either of them would leave the other still out for my head, and neither of them was a blood-oath enemy I could afford to have lurking in the background of my life. Kinneman had full access to EarthGuard resources; Yiuliob had access to Conciliator Uvif and his ambitions, with connections to the Uroemm family and *their* ambitions. Wherever we went to ground, one side or the other would eventually track us down.

Or rather, they would track *me* down. By then, Selene would be long gone.

No, unless I could make both Kinneman and Yiuliob disappear from my life, I was done.

And if that magic trick cost me my arm, that was just the price I would have to pay.

Ordinarily, facing something like this would have left me too keyed up to sleep. But the long night had left me physically drained, and when Selene finally persuaded me to lie down until McKell and Ixil returned with their bomb, I ended up falling asleep.

Two hours later, the bomb was ready. I checked out the olive-sized device, confirmed with McKell and Ixil that they were ready for their part of the plan, and Bubloo ushered Selene and me into the portal.

"I wish I could just let you hold on to this," Bubloo said regretfully as I finished stripping off the suit we'd taken from the *fiall*. "It would make things easier."

"I agree," I said. "But if Kinneman found it, he'd have a piece of genuine Icari combat armor to play with. I don't want that any more than you do."

"What are you going to do with the armor?" Selene asked.

"There's a place I can take it," he said. "Very secret. That's why I asked McKell and Ixil to wait outside. I'll travel there as soon as you've left for Firefall, and I can't have them peeking at the address."

"Understandable," I said, frowning at Selene. Keeping McKell and Ixil out certainly made sense.

So why had he let Selene stay?

I felt a flicker of embarrassment. So that he could collect her suit, too, of course.

I watched as she got out of her armor. "Thank you," he said. He did something to one of the controls on her suit, and it folded and collapsed, the arms and legs crunching up to the torso piece and forming a compact bundle. A similar tweaking of the controls on my suit, and it did likewise. He looked at the hatch, as if wondering if McKell and Ixil would suddenly decide to crash our party, then took off his suit as well.

"Into the outglobe," he said as he fastened the three sets of armor together. "You first, Friend Roarke."

I nodded and crossed the rest of the way to the interface, my heart pounding as I made sure the knife and medpack were in place on my belt. *The price I would have to pay,* I reminded myself firmly. I rolled through the opening and went over and crouched by the control board. It had been a long time since I'd had anything to do with the Firefall portal, but bounty hunters by necessity had very good memories. I punched in the address, double-checked it, and nodded. "Good to go," I said, standing up. Bubloo had in the meantime come in and was waiting near the extension arm, the linked suits on the deck at his feet.

Standing quietly beside him was Selene.

"Selene, you don't need to be here," I said. "Bubloo and I have this."

"What if it doesn't work?" she asked.

I frowned. "Excuse me?"

"What if it doesn't work?" she repeated. "You're not Ammei, Patth, or Kadolian, the only species we know the portal will recognize. What if it doesn't recognize a piece of human as living?"

I looked at Bubloo. He was just standing there watching. "It recognizes me fine when I use it," I reminded her.

"Because you're a living, breathing, sapient being."

"It recognized Pax, too."

She shook her head. "We can't risk it."

"Sure we can," I said, dread putting some bite into my tone. "If it doesn't work, maybe then we try you. But we try me first."

"You're not thinking this through, Gregory," she said quietly. "You need to be fully functional when you talk to Kinneman. You won't be if you're injured and have painkillers in your blood."

Bubloo stirred. "I agree," he said.

I spun on him. "Who asked *you*?" I snapped, suddenly tired of all this. From the very beginning he'd been standing on the sidelines, even as he manipulated the hell out of Selene and me...

"No one," he said, a dark calm in his voice. He pulled McKell's bomb from his belt pouch and held it toward me. "Here." Reflexively, I reached out and took it.

And in that instant of inattention, he stepped close and plucked the knife from my belt.

"Hey!" I snarled as he backed away. "Bubloo—"

"Selene's right," he said, still calm. "You're not going to do it."

"If you touch her—"

"*I* am."

"—I swear I'll—" I broke off. "What?"

"Bubloo, you weren't listening," Selene said, starting toward him. "I'm the only one we're sure can make it work."

I took a quick step toward her and caught her arm before she could reach him. "It's all right, Selene," I said, a flicker of shame running through me at my earlier unkind thoughts. "The portal will recognize him. Bubloo's not a Pakenrill emmisary.

"He's an Icari."

Selene stared at me, disbelief filling her pupils. "*What?* No. No, that's impossible."

"Maybe," I said. "But it's also true." I raised my eyebrows at him. "Go ahead. Tell her."

Bubloo hesitated, then sighed. "How did you know?"

"My father," I said. "Remember when you staged your own bounty and he picked you up? You were happy to go with him until he mentioned that Yiuliob was on his way to the *Median* and that First Dominant Prucital was already aboard. That's when you suddenly decided to bail and try a different approach."

"Why those particular two?" Selene asked.

Bubloo inclined his head to me. "Because they would recognize me," he said, turning to face her. "I was the one who went to Nexus Six seventy years ago, took the directory half and hid it, then disabled the Alainn portal."

"And hid the enhancement serum book?" I asked.

"Yes, that too," Bubloo acknowledged. "By then I knew First of Three had the Juniper omni address and Yiuliob had the *fiall* address. I couldn't let either of them obtain a fully-functioning omni."

"So why didn't you just destroy the book?"

"Because the serum would be needed if a flaw developed in the system and it had to be reset," he said. "I understand two of the book's pages were removed. Your doing?"

"Yes," I said. "Am I right in guessing you had help hiding it?"

"You are indeed perceptive," he said. "Yes. First of Three is highly vocal in his support of Ammei supremacy, but in truth he knows his people are safe and secure just as they are and has no interest in risking their survival by challenging the entire Spiral. He helped me hide the book and made certain none of the searches found it. May I have the pages back?"

"When all this is over," I promised. "Don't worry, they're in a safe place." Though given that the pages were coming with me, and I was going into a very *not* safe place, that probably qualified as a lie. "The point is that you didn't seem worried about running into younger Ammei—you *did* use the Juniper Gemini to sneak into Yiuliob's enclave from Belshaz, after all—but you had to steer clear of the older ones. After you claimed to us that you were only thirty-eight, the dots weren't hard to connect."

"But that doesn't make sense," Selene said, puzzlement in her pupils. "Surely they took pictures of you while you were on Nexus Six."

"Actually, they didn't," I told her. "I'm sure they wanted to, but they couldn't." I pointed at the silvery threads on his face. "Those tattoos aren't just decoration. They're some kind of fancy electronics that scramble photos and vids like crazy. Took me forever to figure out what the strange blotches were on Mindi's security recordings. Turns out they were you."

"We will speak more on this later," Bubloo said. "But now, there are tasks before us. Selene, would you prepare the necessary?"

"Gregory?" Selene asked, her pupils still uncertain.

"Go ahead," I said, watching Bubloo closely as I handed Selene the medkit. There was still the possibility this was all a scam, that he would pull a last-minute reverse and cut Selene instead of himself. Selene pulled a large anesthetic bandage from the kit and held it up. "Is this big enough?" she asked.

"Yes," Bubloo said. He stepped close to her and laid the knife blade against his left forearm. "Be ready, Roarke."

"I am."

He nodded and braced himself... and with a quick flick of his hand it was done. He dropped the knife and handed me the flap of bloody skin. "Take it," he said in a taut voice as Selene quickly but carefully sealed the bandage over the pulsing wound.

"Got it," I said, wincing as I took the flap and wrapped it around the bomb. Holding the package gingerly, I grabbed the extension arm with my other hand and floated upward.

"Hold it above your head," Bubloo called. "Arm it and touch it to the gray as soon as it's close enough. Don't forget to let go before it touches. By the time your other hand reaches the gray the bomb should have destroyed the Firefall balloon and you'll be able to transit without having to cycle through again."

"Got it," I said again, painfully aware of how many moving parts there were to this plan. If any one of them misfired... but there was no point dwelling on that. I held the bomb as high as I could, resting my thumb on the trigger.

And as it reached the gray section I gently squeezed the bomb's trigger and nudged the package the last centimeter to touch the arm.

I'd been prepared for the bomb to just float there, in which case I would have about a second and a half to get clear before it exploded in my face. Instead, to my relief, it vanished.

I took a deep breath. First moving part, successfully accomplished. I watched the gray section coming closer to my other hand, mentally counting down the seconds. The bomb goes off... the balloon deflates and drifts away from the center of Firefall's receiver module... I hit the Juniper trigger section and pop into the newly cleared area... I hopefully don't get immediately shot by whatever guards are on duty...

My hand hit the gray, and the universe went dark around me.

Sometimes, the transition passed quickly. This time, it seemed to drag as my brain ticked off the first couple of points and refocused on the parts still ahead. The blackness vanished.

I found myself floating in the center of a receiver module, bathed in the usual soft portal light, the remnants of a popped balloon rippling toward the deck a little ways above me. I looked around the sphere, bracing for a shouted order or the agony of gunfire.

But neither came. I was, in fact, alone.

I took a deep breath, a feeling of relieved scorn flowing across my mind. It was wonderful not to be shot at; but was Firefall's security *really* this lax? I turned myself around until I was facing the interface. I couldn't see anyone lurking in the launch module, either.

What I *could* see were about fifty cables coming out and snaking across the receiver module deck before disappearing out a hatch a quarter of the way around the sphere.

So the scientists and techs studying the portal had opted to do as much of their work as they could out there in the comfort of their lab instead of crouched in the disconcerting gravity and geometry of the launch module. With no one to watch over, and with one of Kinneman's magic balloons playing silent gatekeeper against unwanted intruders, they'd apparently also decided that stationing guards in here was a waste of effort.

It seemed a shame to intrude on their cozy misconceptions. Luckily, I didn't have to.

A portal landing was always a little problematic, noise-wise, and I winced a little as I dropped that last meter to the deck. For a few seconds I crouched there, listening hard. No raised voices, no sounds of hurrying footsteps. My arrival seemed to have gone completely unnoticed.

Hopefully, my departure would be likewise.

I hurried around the sphere to the interface and eased my way past the cables into the launch module. Emblazoned on the twin displays were Firefall's and Juniper's addresses, both of which would remain there for the next several minutes. A big part of the plan had been for me to do whatever was necessary to keep anyone from getting a look at the latter address, which would rob me of my one and only bargaining chip.

Now, with everyone here asleep at the switch, that wasn't going to be a problem. Dropping down beside the display, I started punching in Alpha's address.

And here was the final moving part. The last time I'd gone

through Alpha there'd been another hovering balloon in place as part of a strictly regulated access. But with all the traffic now presumably going back and forth between it and Icarus, it was a fair assumption that Kinneman had given up the idea of a rigid schedule in favor of leaving access clear. The fact that Alpha now presumably had a full garrison of Marines in residence also rendered other precautions superfluous.

But logical as all that reasoning was, it was still an assumption. If I was wrong, it would be back to keeping the Firefall contingent out of here until Juniper's address faded, and then waiting until such time as Alpha opened up again.

I finished punching in the address, started my double-check...

"Carol!" an urgent voice came distantly. "The balloon's gone!"

"What are you talking about?" a woman's voice came in reply.

I didn't wait to hear any more. I grabbed the extension arm and started up, completing my double-check of the address as I rose. The voices were joined by other, even more excited ones, and I could hear hurrying footsteps through the interface. I reached the gray area...

I got just a glimpse of a beard and a pair of eyes that were wide with shock and dismay as the portal sent me on my way.

Three seconds later, I was in Alpha.

I'd expected to find a Marine garrison. But as I floated in the center of the receiver module with a bird's-eye view, I realized the place looked more along the lines of a preinvasion staging area. The number of equipment racks I'd seen earlier had doubled, augmented by neat arrays of heavier weapons and what looked like siege equipment. There were at least fifty armor-clad soldiers in various stages of prep, about half of them Marines and the other half made up of elite multi-zone SOLA forces.

Plus, of course, an additional half dozen Marines lying on their backs on one side of the sphere, laser rifles pointed directly at me.

"Don't shoot!" I shouted, displaying my empty hands. "I'm Gregory Roarke. I'm here to make a deal with General Kinneman."

"What makes you think the general wants to make a deal with *you*?" a man wearing colonel's insignia shot back.

"Because he has a fondness for full-range Icari portals," I said, trying to ignore the fifty additional weapons now pointed in my direction. "I'm here to offer him a new one for his collection."

❖   ❖   ❖

The soldiers waited more or less patiently for me to float the rest of the way down, mainly because portal physics didn't give them any other choice. The colonel already had an escort squad waiting at my projected landing spot, and I was barely down before he sent the whole batch of us hustling around the sphere and into the launch module.

As we all floated up the extension arm, I noted with private amusement four techs busily photographing and transcribing the addresses on the display.

A minute later, we arrived in the Icarus receiver module. Five minutes after that, I was seated behind the table in a familiar conference room. The colonel waited until I was settled with half my escort grouped behind me and the other half at the door, then left.

I thought about asking my guards if there were any snacks available, decided that none of them looked like they had the right sense of humor, and kept my mouth shut.

Finally, a long half hour later, Kinneman arrived, my new colonel acquaintance in tow. For a moment the general stood at the doorway, just staring at me out of a face made of unpolished stone. Then, leaving the colonel with the door guard, he strode across the room and stopped across the table from me. For another moment he stared down at me with what I assumed was his most intimidating look. I stared back with my best innocent one. We held that pose a couple of seconds; and then, the corner of his lip twitched in what a charitable person might have classified as a smile. "You have *chutzpah*, Roarke," he said, his voice matching the stone of his face. "I'll give you that."

"Thank you, sir," I said politely. "Before we start, I'd like to ask a favor."

His eyebrows went up a millimeter. "A *favor*?"

"Yes, sir," I said. "Given the critical nature of our upcoming negotiations, I'd like to have a professional here to oversee everything. Specifically, I request Sir Nicholas Roarke."

I felt a touch of air on the back of my neck as one of the soldiers behind me shifted position. Kinneman's expression didn't even twitch. "What makes you think I even know where Sir Nicholas is?" he asked.

"Well, we can start with the fact that he's been negotiating with First of Three and the other Ammei on your behalf," I offered helpfully.

He tried hard. But even he couldn't hold an unreadable expression against that kind of revelation. "Oh—sorry," I said, shifting from innocent to contrite. "Was I not supposed to know that?"

He managed to bring his intimidation level up another notch. "So you've been to Nexus Six," he said.

"Yes, but don't worry," I assured him. "I didn't do anything to interrupt his work."

"Of course not," he said, without even trying to act like he believed it.

"On the other hand, that work may be rapidly coming to an end," I went on. "From the look of things in Alpha, I'd say you're preparing for the situation to go sideways."

"A good officer prepares for every eventuality," he said, his stone face back in position.

"As he should," I agreed. "A good officer also foresees imminent hostilities and pulls out civilians before they're caught in the crossfire."

"Unless that civilian's job is to keep those hostilities from happening."

"Of course," I said, nodding. "But as I recall, First of Three had ordered Sir Nicholas to contact you and demand Ammei access to Alpha. I can't see Sir Nicholas having a conversation of that sort over the radio. He'd want to have it face-to-face, which means he's currently somewhere in this complex. By the way," I added, raising a finger as if the question had just occurred to me, "how exactly are you hiding Alpha from them? Do you make Sir Nicholas walk a kilometer upriver before he hops in the water and swims back to the portal?"

For another moment Kinneman stared down at me. Then, with clear reluctance, he pulled out one of the chairs and sat down. "As a matter of fact," he said, "I think First of Three knows exactly where Alpha is. But our engineers tell me those lightning weapons won't work underwater. Our weapons will."

"Not to mention that throwing high-voltage discharges around a chamber filled with sensitive electronics is a bad idea," I said. "Another bad idea is wasting time you can't really afford to burn. I trust Sir Nicholas is on his way?"

"Colonel Rayburn tells me you claim to know the whereabouts of a full-range portal," he said, nodding back toward the colonel. "Where is it?"

"I really miss Sir Nicholas," I mused. "Great negotiator, Sir Nicholas."

"So I've heard," Kinneman said. "It's the Juniper portal, isn't it? That's where you came from."

"To be precise—and your techs have surely already confirmed this—I came from Firefall," I corrected. "Just between us, you might want to look into stepping up their security a bit."

"It's on my list," Kinneman ground out. "I'm prepared to grant you and Selene unconditional immunity from all charges pending against you."

"Very generous," I said. "Has Sir Nicholas at least been told I'm here?"

"I can also authorize a million-commark payment."

"Is that the million commarks you saved by not having to add it to the kitty with First of Three's million to make that two-mil bounty on Selene?" I asked.

His face went a little stonier. "I have no idea what you're talking about."

"My mistake," I said. "Anyway, I suppose paying me instead of a hunter will make the bookkeeping easier. I'd really like to see Sir Nicholas again. Always been like a father to me."

For a teetering moment, I thought Kinneman was going to lose it. His face reddened, and the tension in his jaw muscles showed his teeth were clenched firmly together. I sat still, waiting for him to run the calculation and come to the conclusion that his pride wasn't as important as getting hold of a new portal. "He'll be here in ten minutes," he said at last. A brief hesitation... "Would you like something to drink while we wait?"

As my father used to say, *Avoid kicking a man's pride. It's usually unnecessary, and it's never as fun as you expect.* "No, thank you," I said. "I'm good."

My father arrived about half a minute ahead of Kinneman's estimate. His voice and demeanor as he greeted Kinneman were one hundred percent professional, as was his greeting to me.

Which was all to the good. For the next however many minutes he was a negotiator, not my father. The minute Kinneman had any doubts as to his neutrality he would be summarily kicked out and the general would turn to more unpleasant ways of dragging Juniper's address out of me.

"You've heard my offer," Kinneman said when my father had joined us at the table. "A million commarks, plus immunity from all current charges. Your turn?"

"*Two* million commarks, plus immunity from all charges past *and* future," I said. "In return, I give you the Juniper portal's address."

"Address *and* physical location both."

"Once you have the address, its physical location should be easy enough to figure out."

"Let's back up a little," my father put in. "First of all, Gregory, I doubt General Kinneman can authorize that large a payment."

"Why not?" I countered, pretending he hadn't already given Selene and me his estimate of Kinneman's financial limits. "I'd guess the Icarus Group—excuse me, the Alien Portal Agency— has a pretty substantial budget. Don't forget we're talking about a full-range portal here, not another Gemini."

"Understood and appreciated," my father said. "But you must understand in turn that an organization like the APA has many other demands on its funds and resources. The amount you're asking is simply impossible."

I sighed theatrically, making sure my satisfaction didn't show on my face. My father knew me well enough to know that I didn't give a Hoover Dam about the money, but was simply trying to get Kinneman to look the wrong direction while I maneuvered to get what I really wanted out of him. "How about a million and a half?" I suggested. "Selene and I have expenses, too."

That earned me a snort from Kinneman. "One million," he said firmly. "And that future immunity thing is also out."

"That one *does* seem a little off the mark, Gregory," my father seconded. "You could go out and commit a murder and the badgemen couldn't touch you."

"Don't worry, I'm not planning any major crimes," I said. "I just don't want General Kinneman or the APA suddenly coming up with some bogus charge to nail me with. When this is finished I want us free and clear."

"I'm sure we can work something out," my father assured me, looking at Kinneman. "Say, one million commarks, immunity from past charges, and guarantees that no other charges pertaining to the APA or the portals in general are to be filed?"

It was a trap, of course, and as I watched Kinneman I saw

that he'd spotted it, too. My father had said charges from the APA, but Selene and I had started out working with the Icarus Group, which was technically not the same thing. Kinneman could happily sign away all APA hold on me, then turn around and find something from the old days he could throw at us.

Which, from Kinneman's point of view, was exactly what my father's position here was supposed to be: an officially neutral negotiator who was secretly on his side.

Out of the corner of my eye I studied my father's face, his neutral, professional expression, his supposed quiet support for Kinneman and his agenda. And for the first time in my life I realized that my father didn't just know me and understand me.

He also trusted me.

"I think I can agree to that," Kinneman said, joining in to the game. "But only if Roarke agrees to take a team through to the Juniper portal. No offense, Roarke, but I don't trust you enough to accept a few random numbers and let you leave before I can check it out."

"That sounds reasonable," my father agreed. "Gregory?"

"If you insist," I said, throwing some reluctance into my voice. "Just to clarify: You'll give me the money and an official document regarding our immunity, and I'll take your people through?"

"Correct," my father confirmed.

"What kind of timeline are we looking at?" I asked.

"I can have the documents drawn up in a couple of hours," my father said. "General, what about the payment?"

"I can't pull that much money together that quickly," he said. "But I can have it ready for you when the team returns from Juniper with their report."

In other words, once he got what he wanted I was to innocently walk back into his web for my money and whatever unpleasant surprises he was even now busily cooking up.

"Gregory?" my father prompted.

"I suppose that would be all right," I said. "But I want it in certified checks drawn on one of the major banks."

"Of course," Kinneman said.

Which was a mistake on his part. With a specific bank's certified checks in hand, I would finally have a clue that could point to Icarus's dead-secret location.

He knew that, of course. But since he wasn't ever going to

hand any of it over to me, he was fine with making a few empty promises in order to seal the deal.

"Then we're agreed?" my father asked, looking back and forth between us. "One million commarks, to be paid on completion of a successful transit to Juniper, plus a document of blanket immunity, to be delivered prior to that transit?"

"Agreed," Kinneman said.

"Likewise," I said.

My father held my gaze another second, perhaps concerned that I might have missed the trap he'd woven into the agreement. I gazed back, making sure not to do anything that might indicate in any way that he and I were, in fact, quietly on the same page. "All right, then," he said, standing up. "I'll get the immunity document drawn up right away. Gregory, you'll wait here until it's ready?"

"I think that's probably a given," I said dryly. "And you, General, will get started on those bank checks?"

"Of course," he said. "Are you sure you don't want something to eat or drink?"

"I'm fine," I assured him. "I wouldn't want any distractions that might make me forget Juniper's address."

Kinneman's lip twitched. Whatever mild drugs or confusers he'd contemplated dosing me with were now officially off the table. "Of course not," he said as he also stood up. "We'll be back soon. Until then"—he glanced at the guards still arrayed behind my chair—"make yourself comfortable."

He paused. "And be happy. You're about to become a very rich man."

"Yes," I murmured, my earlier confident words to Bubloo about ribs and Dewar's whispering through my mind. "I'm looking forward to it."

It took considerably longer than my father's promised two hours to get the immunity papers finalized. But when he and Kinneman returned four hours later, it was signed, sealed, and the proposal officially transmitted and recorded.

"All it needs is your signature," my father said, laying the papers and a pen on the table in front of me. "Feel free to read it first."

I did so. Slowly, carefully, and twice.

But there were no additional hidden traps. My father and Kinneman had been careful to keep all of those in strictly verbal form. I nodded, signed each page, and handed the stack back to my father. "We're good to go, then," I said, standing up. "How soon until your team is ready, General?"

"It's ready now," he said, beckoning. "Come."

"Great," I said. "You're coming too, Sir Nicholas?"

"Of course," my father said, studiously casual. "Wouldn't miss it for the world."

CHAPTER TWENTY-EIGHT

$$\cdot \diamond \cdot$$

The team, six Marines plus Colonel Rayburn, was waiting when we arrived in Alpha. All seven were dressed in light combat armor, complete with helmets and Bridgmine 6mm sidearms. Two of them also had Rolfkin over/under plasmic/10mm rifles slung over their shoulders. "Do Sir Nicholas and I get fancy dress-up suits, too?" I asked as we floated down to the hull.

"Sir Nicholas is only going as far as the launch module," Kinneman said. "As for you, you'll be going just as you are."

"Okay," I said, eyeing the Marines and wondering if I should feel slighted that Kinneman hadn't offered a more elite unit. Maybe he still suspected me of planning a trap and figured he might as well not risk his best troops.

Still, he *had* assigned a full colonel as my chief babysitter. Though that was probably only because someone had to operate the portals and the general was keeping Alpha's address strictly between himself and his senior officers.

And actually, I was just as happy that he was keeping his SOLA forces closer to home. The last thing I wanted were soldiers who'd been trained to react quickly to unexpected situations.

We rolled one by one into the the launch module, and they all stood around and watched as I punched in the Juniper omni's address. I double-checked it, nodded, and stood up. "There you go," I said, waving at it. "You know, it would save me a trip if I just waited here until my money was ready."

"It would," Kinneman acknowledged. "But you look like you could use the exercise. Colonel?"

Rayburn nudged me. "Let's go, Roarke."

Together we crossed to the extension arm. The Marines grouped around us, and we all took hold and started up.

"Right arm, Roarke," Kinneman warned. "We know the left one is artificial."

"Thanks for the reminder," I said, waving my left hand at him to show I was holding on with my right.

"And keep those knockout pills right where they are," he added.

"See you later, General," I said, enjoying this final bit of irony. He had no way of knowing it, but I was more than happy to do exactly as he'd ordered.

I was pretty sure I would never see him again.

We reached the top, and three seconds later I was back on Juniper. "Here we are," I announced as we started our downward float. "Juniper, exactly as advertised. Do you want to look outside first, or can we go back and get my money?"

"Why is that hatch open?" Rayburn asked suspiciously.

"Why do you think?" I countered, working my way partway around in midair. One of the hatches about forty-five degrees off the direct line to the interface was wide open, all right, just as I'd requested. "I left it that way. This portal can be confusing, and I didn't want to have to grope around for the way out."

The colonel didn't ask what exactly made this portal so special, which was just as well since I didn't have an answer. The eight of us reached our respective landing spots, reformed at Rayburn's order into a nice military clump, and headed for the open hatch. I looked around as we walked, as if confirming to myself that this was indeed the portal I'd been aiming for. We were nearly to the open hatch when I craned my neck and stiffened. "Wait a minute," I said, touching Rayburn's arm and pointing toward the section of sphere directly across from the launch module. "What's that?"

"What's what?" Rayburn demanded, signaling his men to stop.

"Wait here," I said, and started across the sphere.

Rayburn was suspicious, of course. There wasn't anything he could see that distinguished that section of hull from any other one, and he'd undoubtedly been warned about letting me out of his sight or possibly even out of his reach.

But he and his Marines were clustered around the only exit, he knew it would take several seconds for me to open another hatch, and it was a long way back to the launch module if my plan was to make a run in that direction. And until he confirmed that this was the right portal, Kinneman would take a very dim view of him prematurely shooting me in the back.

I had reached my target section and was peering intently down at the hull when I heard a soft *chuff* from above me.

I straightened up, looking back at Rayburn. He was staring at me, his hand hovering in midair, probably preparing to order his Marines to reel me back in. He opened his mouth—

And right on cue, a rope with a heavy weight at the end and a wide loop just above it dropped onto the deck squarely in front of me.

I'd warned McKell that a precise aim would be required. He'd assured me he could do it, and he'd come through with flying colors. The rope, fired from some sort of launcher he and Ixil had brought in, had passed perfectly through the center of the receiver module, from its own perspective flying first straight up and then straight down. Missing the center would have sent the rope falling in an arc that would have left it lying uselessly along the curved hull.

But McKell hadn't missed. I hooked my arm through the loop, and the colonel had just enough time to let out a single curse before I was yanked off my feet and pulled rapidly upward toward the launch module.

I'd passed the receiver module's center and was starting to fall toward the interface when I suddenly woke up to the fact that, barring divine intervention, I was going to come to a very abrupt and very painful stop against the winch currently reeling me toward it. I shot through the opening, hoping McKell and Ixil had anticipated this and come up with a solution—

And came to a slightly less abrupt and considerably less painful stop as the winch shut down and Ixil grabbed my legs, bringing me to a halt.

He let go as I started to topple over, landing me on the deck beside him. Pax, currently curled awkwardly around the shoulder anchor of Ixil's zero-g maneuvering vest, gave a sort of warning squeak, and I peered down through the interface to see Rayburn and four of the Marines making a mad dash around the receiver module toward us.

"Clear," McKell called calmly from beside the winch, his own vest wrapped securely in place around him. I took a long step sideways, unhooking my arm from the rope loop, as Ixil produced a large, flimsy-looking tube and broke it open over the interface. The liquid inside spilled into the opening and did the usual roiling splash as the spheres' gravity fields forced it into a thin layer floating in the interface. There was a flash from the side as McKell fired his plasmic, and the sloshing liquid blazed suddenly into a field of brilliant yellow flame.

"Vest!" Ixil called over the roar as I took two hasty steps back from the wave of heat blasting across my face. I held my arms straight out behind me, and he slipped a vest up my arms and onto my shoulders. I fastened it securely around my torso, grabbing the hand control with one hand and the extension arm with the other. A quick check of the displays showed McKell had entered the destination address correctly, and with him and Ixil beside me we headed up.

"How many at the hatch?" McKell asked.

"Two," Ixil reported. "The other five are probably—"

He broke off as a loud hiss momentarily eclipsed the sound of the fire and a section of the flame faltered. "The other five will probably try to get through before we leave," he finished.

"Or at least before the displays go dark," I said with a flicker of malicious amusement. For all the good it would do them. "We ready for the two at the exit?"

"We are," Ixil said. His voice was confident enough, but I couldn't help but notice the simultaneous twitches from the two outriders on his shoulders. Apparently, Ixil wasn't all that confident that this part of my plan would work. We reached the top of the extension arm, the universe went black, and we arrived.

Dead center in the Juniper receiver module, a grand total of thirty-five meters from where we'd started.

Bubloo had said a same-portal jump was possible but never used because it was pointless. But there were exceptions to every rule, and this was one of them. And I had to admit it was unexpectedly satisfying to watch from the other side as Rayburn and his Marines tried to use their suit's fire extinguishers to snuff out our flame barrier.

But there was no time to enjoy the view. The two Marines the colonel had left guarding the hatch were gazing across the sphere at their comrades' efforts, which put us above their line of sight as we popped into view twenty meters above them. We had to cross that gap before they spotted us and shouted a warning or, worse, got their Rolfkins into firing position.

McKell and Ixil were already on the move, using their vests' compressed air bottles to push them away from the module center onto an intercept vector with the two Marines. It took me an extra second of fumbling to get myself and my own air bottles properly lined up and follow.

Which put me in perfect position to see Ixil take one of his outriders in each hand and hurl them straight toward the door guards. They were nearly there when the movement finally caught the Marines' peripheral vision and they looked up.

I couldn't see their expressions through their helmet visors, but I could imagine it was somewhere between startled and contemptuous. The attack was totally unexpected, but wrapped snugly inside full combat suits they couldn't possibly feel threatened. Just the same, both of them flinched as Pix and Pax slammed into their shoulders, and I winced as I visualized the outriders' long claws digging through the small gaps between armor plates. McKell had assured me that the plates were thin enough for the claws to reach all the way through and pierce the skin beneath...

Without warning, both Marines abruptly dropped their rifles and collapsed onto the deck.

"Watch it, Roarke," McKell snapped.

I tore my eyes away from the unconscious soldiers, belatedly remembering that I was once again arrowing at increasing speed straight toward a collision with a hard object. I squeezed my hand control, sending a blast of compressed air ahead of me.

Too little, possibly too late. I was still blasting out air when McKell and Ixil, far more experienced with these things, slowed themselves and rotated a hundred eighty degrees to point feet forward. I started to shoot helplessly through the gap, still trying to slow down—

And was brought up short as each of them grabbed an arm as I passed, spinning me around and slowing me to their speed. We all hit the deck together, the impact jarring but not bone-threatening. "Thanks," I breathed.

"Out," McKell ordered, looking upward and drawing his plasmic.

I didn't need to be asked twice. I took two long steps to the hatchway, my back itching with anticipation of a blast from one of the Marines' slug guns, and dropped into the usual sit-roll-push of a ninety-degree portal exit. I landed in the narrow gap between the portal and the tangled zone of dead thorn vines McKell and Ixil had moved into position, nearly impaling my arm on one of the thorns, and peered back inside.

I'd hoped that, with the roar of the flames drowning out any sounds from our end of the receiver module, Rayburn's team might have missed the fact that we'd escaped our self-imposed cage. But the door guards had apparently had time to call in a warning before the outriders' claws delivered their dose of knockout powder into their bloodstreams. Rayburn and one of his men were still battling the fire, but the other three soldiers were again sprinting madly around the receiver module toward us.

My view was interrupted as Ixil appeared and rolled outside, Pix and Pax safely back on his shoulders. "That way," he said, pointing around the portal to my right as he drew his own plasmic. I nodded and headed that direction, being careful to avoid the thorns that continued their efforts to grab hold of my sleeve. I was about a third of the way around the dome when Ixil caught up with me, McKell right behind him. Ahead was a small gap in the thorn fence and I angled through it, Ixil and McKell again right at my heels.

And as we cleared the thorn barrier McKell fired a plasmic shot into the center of it.

When I'd first seen the dead thorn vines, they'd struck me as looking extremely dry. But I hadn't realized just how dry and flammable they really were. The blaze ignited by McKell's shot roared to life in both directions, creating a ring of fire around the portal that was perfect for hampering pursuit. Ixil brushed past me, heading through a set of bushes and between two trees. I followed, McKell again bringing up the rear. We pushed through another stand of bushes...

There, waiting on a relatively flat section of ground, were Selene and our car.

Thirty seconds later, the three of us were inside, me next to Selene with McKell and Ixil in the back, and Selene was maneuvering us along a violently twisty path through the vegetation. "Is everyone all right?" she called. "Did the knockout powder work?"

"We're fine, and like a charm," I assured her. "I'm thinking, Ixil, that you might want to remember that trick for the future."

"We'll add it to our repertoire," Ixil agreed. "How did the negotiations go?"

"About as expected," I said. "My father showed up, worked a scam on me that let Kinneman think he was still in control, and sent me on my way. Selene, were you able to get in touch with Yiuliob?"

"Eventually, yes," she said. "I don't think he was happy at being called back from Nexus Six for a phone call. But that changed when I told him you'd found the portal."

"Did he agree that I'd fulfilled my promise?"

"Yes, provided my information proved accurate."

"Good," I said. "And of course the Ammei did a track on your phone that confirmed the location?"

"He didn't say," Selene said. "But I assume so."

"I hope you took your phone's locator skew into account," Ixil warned. "Otherwise his numbers and yours won't match."

"I did," she assured him. "His track should bring him to within a hundred meters of the portal."

I looked over my shoulder at the thick smoke rising from the burning thorn vines. "I don't think he'll have any trouble pinpointing the exact spot now."

"I'd make a small wager on that," McKell agreed. "So what's next?"

"On the Kinneman and Yiuliob fronts?" I shook my head. "Nothing. It's over."

"What do you mean?" McKell asked, his voice frowning. "When they find out they've been cheated, you'll be back where you started."

"I didn't cheat anyone," I said. "I gave each of them the portal's location, exactly as I promised."

"You know what I mean," McKell said. "Even if you didn't promise exclusivity, they both certainly assumed it. I can't see either of them getting tripped up over technical niceties."

"You don't get it," I said. "Both of them have solidly anchored their personal and political reputations on getting hold of the Juniper portal. Neither is going to give it up without a fight."

"So they fight," McKell said, clearly puzzled. "They turn the portal into a localized war zone, sooner or later one of them wins, and the loser comes after you and Selene."

"No," I said, feeling a twinge of almost sympathy. "There won't be any winner. Yiuliob is working against limited manpower from his enclave. Kinneman is working against limited patience from his overseers. Add in Saffi fury at having their sacred wilderness torn up this way, and you're looking at a quick end to Juniper Glory and a major Commonwealth reassessment of the Alien Portal Agency."

"Yiuliob loses face and position," Ixil said quietly. "Kinneman loses his job."

"At the very least, both lose access to the resources they need to come after you," McKell said. "So that's the end?"

"With them, yes," I said. "There's still that other loose end. Selene?"

"They're here," she said. "And they've agreed."

"Good," I said, wishing I could see her pupils. Of all the facets of my plan, this was the one she'd argued the most strenuously against.

But right now she was keeping her full attention on her driving and our twisty path, preventing me from reading her. "Did you talk to Mindi, too?"

"No," she said, pulling my phone from inside her jacket. "I thought you should do that."

In other words, she expected Mindi to be furious with me and had no intention of getting in the middle of that. She was probably right. "Sure," I said, taking the phone. Bracing myself, freshly aware of McKell and Ixil sitting behind me listening, I punched in her number.

For a solid minute there was no answer. I could feel sweat breaking out on my forehead when she finally answered. "About time," she ground out. "I was almost starting to hope you'd been killed."

"Sorry to disappoint you," I said, breathing a little easier. Mindi angry I could handle. Mindi murdered was a burden I would have carried the rest of my life. "You still on the *Ruth*?"

"Like your creepy friend would let me go anywhere else," she growled. "You know you don't have a single package of decent French food?"

"There's plenty of Italian," I pointed out.

"Not the same," she said. "Can I assume from this call that I can finally get back to my own ship?"

"Almost," I said. "A couple more days at the most."

"Good," she said, her voice marginally less hostile. "Not that there hasn't been an amusing moment or two. I wish you had a better external monitoring system, though."

"I've been meaning to upgrade," I told her. "So she kept you entertained?"

"On occasion," she said. "The highlight was when the idiots decided to try a mass rush of the zigzag and got dropped one by one in a basically straight line pointed at the *Ruth*. Even among professionals there aren't many who take that much pride in their work."

"No, there aren't," I agreed, a shiver running through me. "I assume the aforementioned idiots were all local talent?"

"If you're asking if the two Patth were on site, no," she said. "Haven't seen them since you left. I think they figured it out early on and have been making themselves scarce."

"No doubt," I said. "Just out of curiosity, when was the last attack?"

"Three days ago," she said. "That was the *en masse* one. Your playmates may be running out of cannon fodder."

"Not going to shed any tears on that front," I said. "I doubt the Pikwik City badgemen will, either, though I imagine they have a whole raft of questions they're not going to get answers to. Anyway, I'm glad you're all right. I'll let you know when it's over."

"Do that," she said. "Oh, and Roarke...?"

I braced myself. "Yes?"

"Thanks," she said. "I owe you one."

I let out a relieved breath. "I think we're just back to being even," I said. "Hang in there, okay?"

"Sure," she said. "One more thing. The bounty posts on you and Selene have been cancelled."

"Really," I said, frowning. "*Both* of them?"

"Yes," she confirmed. "Selene's an hour ago, yours about two."

I nodded to myself. Selene's when she gave Yiuliob the portal's location; mine when Kinneman figured he had me safely by the throat. Both outcomes as expected, except for how fast the two parties had been on the cancellations. "Great," I said. "Let me know if you spot either being reinstated, okay?"

"I *do* have other things to keep track of than just you and Selene, you know," she said archly. "But I'll try."

"Thanks," I said. "I'll be in touch."

I keyed off. "You heard?" I asked Selene.

She nodded. "Yes."

"How about you two?" I asked, half turning toward the back seat.

"Mostly," McKell said. "I have to say, Roarke, that I still have reservations with this one. All you really need is to get them to admit they're breaking Patth law."

"I wish it was that easy," I said reluctantly. "But this is the Uroemm family we're dealing with. It'll take something more blatant to knock them back on their heels long enough for the Director General and the Patth legal system to get their act together and finally nail their shoes to the floor."

"Yes," McKell said sourly. "Go ahead and add that to the list of things I have reservations about."

"So noted." I gazed at my phone a moment, then put it away. "Selene, did Bubloo tell you when he'd be ready?"

"Two days," she said. "He said he'd meet us at his Blackcreek Street home."

Two days. I ran the timing. It would work. "Good," I said. "All we need now is to get to the nearest sizable city that has a major local communications center."

"Rosker's an hour's drive away," she said.

"That'll do," I said. "Thanks."

"What are we going to do there?" McKell asked.

"First, I need to track down a phone number," I told him. "After that, we're going to get a couple of hotel rooms and sleep until Bubloo gets back."

"We're going to sleep the whole two days?"

I closed my eyes. The adrenaline had dissipated, and two days' worth of fatigue was settling around my brain like a flock of vultures. "Probably not," I said. "But I'm keeping the option open."

CHAPTER TWENTY-NINE

Three days later, with all the pieces now on the board, we were ready.

On my last conversation with Mindi, she'd left me hanging a full minute before picking up. Daxtro, as was only fit and proper for a Purge assassin, answered on the second buzz. "Who is this?" he demanded.

"Gregory Roarke," I said. "Just wanted to check in and see how you and your associate were getting along."

There was a short silence. "We are well," Daxtro said, his tone cooling at least thirty degrees. "Where are you?"

"Back on Juniper," I said. "I thought we might sit down over a drink and discuss things." I hesitated, but couldn't resist. "Don't worry, I'll buy. I understand if you're a bit short of cash right now."

"Where and when?"

"You *are* short of cash, aren't you?" I persisted. "Hiring all those local thugs to kill Mindi has to have been expensive. Especially once the third and fourth batches found out what happened to the first and second and jacked up their prices."

"So it *was* you," Daxtro bit out. "You have been here the entire time."

"Oh, no, not me," I said. "I brought in a friend to play guardian angel. Sorry to have left you only one target, by the way. All the rest of us had to go elsewhere on business."

"Thank you for confirming both Mindi and the guardian angel are your friends," he said coldly. "Both can now be properly eliminated."

"Properly, maybe," I said. "Though so far you seem to be having trouble on that front. But legally? You know as well as I do that you and the Uroemm family are skating on very thin ice here as far as Patth law is concerned. But I think there's a way out, which I'd like to offer you. Interested?"

"Of course," he said. "Will your friend be there?"

"Which one? Mindi or Selene?"

"Your other friend. The guardian angel."

"Ah," I said. "Sorry, Nikki's not much for social events."

"Nikki?"

"The angel," I said. "Nicole Schlichting."

There was another short silence. A dark, very ominous silence. "Nicole Schlichting," he repeated, his voice gone flat.

I smiled to myself. It had been a toss-up as to whether he would recognize Nikki's name. Clearly, he did. "Now you know why all your hirelings failed," I said. "And why I know you won't try anything during our meeting."

"Where and when?" Daxtro asked.

"Traveler's Edge taverno," I said. "Eight o'clock tonight. I'll have a table for us when you arrive. Oh, and bring your partner. He's in on this offer, too."

"And Schlichting?"

"I already said she wouldn't be joining us," I reminded him. "Eight o'clock. Remember, it's your only way out of the mess you've gotten yourselves in."

I keyed off. "What do you think?" I asked Selene.

"I agree with Jordan," she said, her pupils haunted. "It's unnecessary and unwise."

"It may be unwise," I conceded. "But I think it *is* necessary."

She didn't respond. I mentally checked over everything one more time, then took her arm. "The players are in position," I said. "Time to bring this to an end."

I'd been in the Traveler's Edge for forty minutes and was halfway through a plate of so-so barbequed ribs when I felt the expected brush of air at the back of my neck. "Hello, Daxtro," I said without turning around. "You're right on time."

"I, in fact, arrived fifteen minutes ago," the Patth said quietly. "Do you really sit with your back to the windows? I might have simply killed you from outside."

"I don't think so," I said, cleaning the last bit of meat from my current rib and setting it down on the bone plate. "Without being able to see my face you couldn't be sure it was me and not some decoy I'd sent in my place. The Uroemm family's in enough legal hot water with the Director General and the Spiral legal system without you gunning down some perfect stranger. Plus, speaking of hot water, you're deep enough in your own private kettle to be looking for any straw to grab on to, even if it comes from someone like me."

"An interesting theory," he said. "Stand."

"Sure." I stood up, moving my arms a little away from my sides just to show I knew what was coming. It was impossible to hear the soft hum of a portable scanner over the conversational murmur coming from the diners filling the room around us, but his hand brushed against my clothing often enough that I could tell he was doing a tight search for hidden monitoring or recording devices. It was just as well, I reflected, that I'd rejected Ixil's offer of one of his leftover Icarus Group bugs. "Happy?" I asked when he'd finished.

"Sit," he said.

"I'll take that as a yes," I said, and resumed my seat. He circled the table and sat down in the chair across from me. His clothing choice was something of a shock: instead of the standard Patth hooded robe he was dressed in human-style tunic and trousers, with gloves and the hood of a sweatshirt concealing his telltale mahogany-red skin. "Interesting outfit," I said as he ran a palm-sized device over the table's origami centerpiece and the three small barbecue sauce dispensers in the center of the table. "Where's your partner? I thought I was clear about both of you coming."

"He will join us presently," Daxtro said. "Speak."

"Sure," I said. "Here's how I read your situation. With Selene and me having inconveniently disappeared, you decided you might as well knock Mindi off your list of Friends of Roarke while you waited for us to surface. She was a pretty small fish, so rather than bother with her yourselves you farmed out the job to some local thugs. Only they failed. Some of them spectacularly, others quietly. The point is, everyone you sent ended up dead."

"You need not belabor the point."

"Sorry," I said. "At that point your options were to take on the job yourselves or give up. But by now you were leery of putting your own skin at risk, and giving up would have kicked dust on your professional pride. So instead you simply kept going, hiring thug after thug, gang after gang, slowly but steadily draining your operating fund."

"It is hardly drained."

"Maybe not completely," I said. "But it's way down from where it used to be, especially since every failure prodded the next group to raise their prices."

"And your assassin continued killing them," Daxtro said harshly. "Multiple murders, multiple felonies. What if I were to swear out a set of charges to the Saffi badgemen?"

"For starters, you have no idea what she looks like," I pointed out. "For that matter, neither do I. She'll have had her face altered since the last time I saw her. More to the point, Nikki knows better than to open fire on someone just because he looks suspicious. She'll have waited until there was a clear and provable threat, at which point Saffi general self-defense laws kick in." I picked up the remaining slab of ribs and tore off the next one in line. "But don't take my word for it," I added. "Feel free to call the local badgeman office and ask. I'll wait."

He muttered something under his breath, a look of disgust flashing across his face. "You are barbarians," he ground out. "All of you."

"What, this?" I shrugged and took a bite. "Maybe. But don't forget, I was an unwilling guest of Sub-Director Nask for a couple of weeks a few years ago. I know for a fact that you eat stuff that's at least as bizarre as barbequed ribs, and not nearly as tasty."

"You said you had an offer."

"Right." Carefully, I set the rib down, swirled my fingers in the lemon-infused fingerbowl, then wiped them on my napkin. "I assume you're paid by the kill. Correct?"

"Yes."

"To be specific, in this case by the kill of anyone associated with me?"

"Yes."

"Then the solution is obvious," I said. "You take a shot at me outside, away from any witnesses, and we go our separate ways. You pretend you killed me and go back to the Uroemm family and collect your fee. Presumably it will be enough for you to repair your operating fund before anyone notices and still have some left over for you and your partner to split. You accept the family's thanks and move on to your next job."

"And the associates we were also directed to eliminate?"

"Vanished into the mists," I said. "You'll keep your eye out, of course, in case one of them turns up. But frankly none of them cared very much about me, and they're bound to forget me in short order. Mission accomplished."

"And when *you* turn up?"

"That's where my side of the deal comes into play," I said. "I still have a couple of false IDs, both for me and for the *Ruth*. I use one set to vanish into the aforementioned mists, and as far as my enemies and creditors are concerned I really *did* die."

"How is this better than my simply killing you?"

"One: I get to live," I said, my mouth going a little dry. I'd hoped he would at least *pretend* to have some enthusiasm for the plan. "Two: without a body to point at there won't be any way for the Saffi badgemen to charge you with my murder. Neither will the Director General. You and your partner can figure out on the trip home how you disposed of my body."

"You seem to have thought of all aspects," he said. "Except for two."

"Which are?"

"The first is as you yourself stated," he said. "Professional pride. I was directed to eliminate all memory of you from the Spiral. How can I return to the Paterfamilias Uroemm with such an absurd lie?"

"When the option is to open him up to serious legal charges back home?" I countered. "I'd say your primary duty to the paterfamilias is to protect him from that."

"No," he said. "Because your primary plan has now failed."

"How so?"

"You spoke at length of the presence of Nicole Schlichting, expecting such an implied threat to distract my thoughts," he said. "You hoped we would watch for her to the exclusion of all other precautions. But you forgot the Paterfamilias Uroemm has in the past interacted with Expediters Huginn and Muninn and that we know their faces." He nodded behind me. "Turn."

Carefully, I turned around.

There they were, in the second row of tables behind me: Huginn and Muninn, freshly arrived on Juniper as I'd requested. Seated behind them, his Babcor 17 held beneath a carefully arranged napkin on his lap, was Daxtro's partner, also dressed in a non-Patth outfit. Both Expediters had their hands flat on the table in front of them, chagrin and powerless anger in their expressions and body language.

"Ah—*there* he is," I said, nodding politely to the other Patth and then turning back to Daxtro. "So what happens now?"

"You hoped to lure me into a failed attack," he said, apparently not quite finished explaining how clever he was. "You hoped to survive as your Expediter associates disarmed us and took us to Sub-Director Nask for judgment." His shoulder twitched, and I had the sudden chilling sense that his own Babcor was now pointed at me under the table. "But you failed to recognize that Huginn and Muninn are *also* your associates. That makes them legitimate targets."

I took a careful breath. "You don't want to do this, Daxtro. Here in a taverno surrounded by witnesses? You really think you can kill three people and get away clean?"

"What witnesses?" Daxtro countered coolly. He inclined his head to the side, the gesture taking in the entire dining room. "These people break bread with you. All are therefore also your associates."

I felt my eyes widen. *This* twist hadn't occurred to me. "You can't be serious," I protested. "You're going to kill *everyone*?"

"You spoke of the fee for your death," he said. "Imagine the fee for the deaths of you plus thirty-two others."

I'd barely begun to imagine it when he squeezed the trigger.

I'd never heard a Babcor fired indoors. It was surprisingly quiet, almost civilized, the compact rocket projectile leaving the muzzle with a sizzle instead of a boom. An instant later the slug hit me, slamming into my abdomen with an impact that sent me jerking back and spinning me halfway around. I caught a glimpse of Daxtro's partner centering his weapon on Huginn's back—

And was therefore in perfect position to watch as Doc Robin rose from the table behind the Patth, one hand twisting the assassin's head backward, the other burying a dagger in his fore-arm at the precise spot to sever the nerves and tendons to his gun hand. Huginn and Muninn were already in motion, Muninn snatching the Babcor from the Patth's immobilized hand, Huginn snapping up a plasmic toward Daxtro.

He needn't have bothered. Even as I started to turn back around I heard the sounds of violence from the other side of the table, and by the time I was in view of Daxtro he was already flat on the floor, Circe's foot pinning his hand and weapon to the ground, a duplicate of Robin's knife poised ready in silent threat.

Which was something of a disappointment. I'd been looking forward to watching her take him down.

"You all right?" Robin's voice came from behind me.

"I'm fine," I assured him, looking down at my abdomen. My shirt and jacket were torn where the rocket slug punched through them, but the armored Icari chest piece hidden beneath them didn't seem to have even picked up a dent. "You know, they don't make things like this anymore."

"You will be exiled for this," Daxtro snarled from beneath Circe's cold gaze. "The human Roarke threatened me. I fired in self-defense." A frown touched his face as he belatedly realized I wasn't actually dead. "I fired in self-defense," he repeated.

"I wouldn't worry about it," I soothed. "By which I mean you've got way bigger problems than that. You got it, right?"

"We did," Robin confirmed. "Everything, including the part where he specifically named the Paterfamilias Uroemm."

"I'm surprised you were able to get him to do that," Huginn added, coming up behind Robin.

"Not my doing," I said as I picked up one of the ribs from the bone plate. "As my father used to say, *If you insist on gloating about how clever you are, never tell the other guy more than you know he can already prove.* I assume you also want the original recording?"

"I'll take that," Huginn said as Robin reached for it. "No offense, Robin, but a failed Expediter isn't considered a lawful courier for official documents."

I felt my eyes narrow. "A *failed* Expediter?" I asked carefully, frowning up at Robin.

"We can't all be Huginn," Robin said, some defensiveness in his tone. "I'm still good enough to be brought in on this operation."

"More like being obscure enough that no one knows your face," Huginn corrected, peering closely at the bone. "I *will* grant you that the bug was a good idea, though. People tend to ignore garbage."

"Thanks," Robin said. "You might mention that to Sub-Director Nask."

"Speaking of whom, is he here and available?" I asked, shaking away Huginn's casual revelation about Robin. I should have guessed he wasn't what he seemed to be, given that no one else around me these days was ever what they seemed, either. "There's a financial matter I need to discuss with him."

"I'll ask," Huginn said. "Go back to your ship. We'll contact you there. And I think it's safe to kick out your houseguest."

"Thanks, I'll let her know," I said, standing up. "And do thank the sub-director for letting you and Muninn play decoy."

"I prefer to think of us as mousetraps," Huginn said calmly. "Quiet and harmless until we aren't."

"Correction noted," I said. Circe and Muninn had the two Patth in restraints and were moving them toward the door. Most of the patrons were surreptitiously watching the procession, but the wide-eyed stares were fading and some of the diners were starting to return to their meals. "Looks like you have this well in hand. I'd better check in with Selene. She worries about me."

"As well she should," Huginn said. "You're one of the craziest people I've ever met."

"As we non-Expediter humans say, *If it works, it's not crazy,*" I said. "Thanks again, Huginn, and don't forget to ask Sub-Director Nask about a meeting."

"I won't," he said. "Just remember that he moves in his own way, and at his own pace."

"Understood," I said. "I'll be ready whenever he is."

Selene and Bubloo were waiting at one of the outside tables of a currently closed breakfast café a hundred meters from the Traveler's Edge. "I'm fine," I said as I approached them. "I suppose I don't really have to tell you that, do I?"

"No, we heard everything through the bug," Selene said. "But it's still appreciated."

"Any difficulties with the chest piece?" Bubloo asked.

"None," I said as I pulled off my jacket and shirt. "It held together just fine, and as you can see was more than up to the task."

"Excellent," he said. "As far as I know, individual pieces were never used this way, but only the armor as the whole."

"Well, you can add that to your library of ancient Icari knowledge," I said as I gazed down at the chest piece. "I don't suppose you'd let me keep this, would you?"

"Do you wish to become the bounty target of every human, Patth, and Ammei in the Spiral?"

"Point," I conceded. I opened the armor and handed it to him. "Though you're wrong about the Patth joining the chase for me. If they wanted one of these, they could have just taken it when you popped through to their new omni."

Selene turned to face him, but not before I caught the surprise in her pupils. "You took the other suits to the *Patth*?"

"Not *all* the Patth," I assured her, watching Bubloo's face. "He made arrangements with Sub-Director Nask to use his newly acquired full-range portal." I raised my eyebrows. "That's the one you're going to use to send the Kadolians home, isn't it?"

He hesitated, then gave a reluctant nod. "It is," he confirmed. "Sub-Director Nask has been most gracious."

"Yes, I've noticed," I said. "I won't bother to ask where the portal is now."

"In truth, I don't know," he said. "I and the Kadolians will be transferred to its location when the time comes."

"Assuming you can find them," I warned. "Nomadic people, and all that."

"They have two or three contact points," Selene said, still staring at Bubloo.

"Yes," Bubloo agreed. "I've already sent messages to the Elders explaining the situation and offering passage back to their home."

"Good," I said, feeling a surge of quiet relief. I'd been ninety percent sure I'd figured out that part of the puzzle, but it was always good to have these things confirmed. "I assume Selene will be getting a personal invitation?"

"Of course." Bubloo reached into a pocket and pulled out a data stick. "Here's the rendezvous location and contact information for Sub-Director Nask and the other Patth who'll be helping us. Once the transfer begins, I estimate it will take three months to complete."

"Does that transfer include the rest of the Pakenrills?" I asked. "The ones on Belshaz *are* other Icari, aren't they?"

He hesitated. "I suppose that depends on your definition," he said. "They are Icari blood, certainly. But over the centuries they've... *lost* is the wrong word. Perhaps it would be more accurate to say they've abandoned what made us who we truly are. Turned from the advances of our people and instead embraced the simple life they currently enjoy."

"You say over the *centuries*?" Selene asked.

"We're a long-lived species, Selene," he said, an odd hint of sadness in his voice. "I was here, though only a child, when the Overlords made the decision to leave thirty-five hundred years ago."

"So it wasn't whole generations of your family who were tasked with the job of sending the Kadolians home," I said. "It was just you."

He gave a small shrug. "At the start, it was also my father. But when he died a hundred years later, it was indeed just me."

I looked at Selene, wondering for the thousandth time why she'd teamed up with me in the first place. Had she voluntarily separated from her people in the hope that partnering with a wide-traveling bounty hunter might help them find their home? That would have been a daunting enough sacrifice.

But for Bubloo to have left his people for over three *millennia*?

"You want to know the real irony?" Bubloo continued. "By the time they left, the Overlords and the Icari elite had mostly stopped using the portals. Starships were comfortable and fast, and the passengers had plenty of leisure time, so they simply left the system to the lower classes and other species."

"So when they left, why didn't they close down the system?" I asked. "Did they keep it running just so the Kadolians could get home?"

"I know it sounds odd," he said. "But that is indeed the truth. And only because my father and a few others begged them to do so."

"So what happens to the portals once you and the Kadolians are gone?"

He eyed me with sudden interest. "I don't know. What do you *want* to happen?"

"Probably be best to leave them running," I said. "The Patth and the Icarus Group have put a lot of time and money into this. I'd hate for their consolation prize to be a collection of the Spiral's biggest paperweights."

"I don't know," Bubloo said hesitantly. "Things that are rare and valuable generate desire and conflict."

"Are the portals really that rare?"

"I was referring to the directory," he said. "As far as I know, the one currently split between humans and Patthaaunutth is the only copy left in the Spiral. If the system is shut down, that directory would become useless and therefore no longer a source of strife."

"True enough," I said. "But we'd also lose the potential the portals represent. Hopes and dreams are too valuable to just toss aside if you don't have to."

"The Ammei had hopes and dreams, too," Bubloo said. "Those dreams cost thousands of lives and threaten to cost more. Do you expect your dreams to be less bloody?"

"I don't know," I admitted. "But I'd still like the portal system to stay open."

"Very well," he said. "I'll trust your judgment, and hope that you find a way."

"Me, too," I said. "Well. It's been nice, Bubloo—"

"I have a question," Selene said.

"Yes?" he asked.

Her pupils hardened. "Why did you lie to us about being an Icari?"

Bubloo hesitated, then lowered his eyes. "I was ashamed," he said in a voice almost too quiet for us to hear.

"About what?" I asked. "The genetic manipulation?"

"About our entire history in the Spiral," he said. "We should have been more involved with the portals, more vigilant in monitoring how they were being used. Instead, we turned everything over to the Ammei."

He looked up at Selene. "And when we decided to leave, we should have worked harder to get the Kadolians home. Loneliness, machinations, misery—all because we became bored with our creation."

"Bored?" I asked pointedly. "Or comfortable?"

He frowned. "What are you saying?"

"I'm saying," I bit out, "that Selene and I have been wandering the Spiral together for well over a decade. You could have contacted us anywhere along the line and gotten this ball rolling. But you didn't. Not until you found out Yiuliob had the *fiall's* address and you suddenly had no choice but to leave your cozy Eight Sisters retreat and get back in the game."

"It wasn't like that," he protested. "I'm only one person, Friend Roarke. I can't see everything that happens in the Spiral. I didn't know about Selene, not until you found your way to Nexus Six. Up until then my full attention had by necessity been on the Ammei, especially once they began building their outglobe."

"What about the other Kadolians?" Selene asked. "You could have contacted them."

"And told them what?" he countered. "I had no way to locate the Nexus One array and their homeworld portal, not until First of Three found the medallions and turned them over to Sir Nicholas. Even then, as you saw, their true significance was lost on us."

"What about the combat suits from the *fiall*?" I asked. "You could have searched Nexus One on your own."

"The Overlords kept the *fiall's* location a closely guarded secret," he said. "Until Yiuliob found its address I didn't even know it was on Nexus Six."

I looked at Selene. Her pupils held frustration and dark anger, but I could see no indication that Bubloo was lying.

"But you're right," he said quietly, and I could hear fresh pain and guilt there. "I should have tried harder. I should have tried better."

He hesitated, then hesitantly reached out his hand. "I don't know whether you can forgive us, Selene. I don't know whether you can forgive *me*. Or, indeed, whether you even should."

I wanted to tell him that it was okay, that everyone made mistakes, and that it was all right now. But this wasn't my conversation to have. Certainly not my pardon to offer. I waited, hardly daring to breathe, watching the play of emotions across Selene's pupils.

Finally, she stirred. "Our life hasn't been easy," she said. "I can't say whether the other Kadolians can forgive the Icari, once they know the truth. I don't know if I can, either." She paused another moment, then stepped toward him and took his proffered hand. "But I can forgive *you*. And I do."

"Thank you," he said quietly. I could tell it wasn't what he'd hoped for, but that he also knew it was all he was going to get.

"I will return now to the task of assembling your people and preparing their way home," he continued, releasing Selene's hand. "Please accept my gratitude for your willingness to risk your lives that I might fulfill my promise to my father."

Briefly, I thought about telling him we'd done it for Selene's people, not him. But that would have just been twisting the knife for no reason. "You're welcome," I said. "After three and a half millennia, it's the least we could do."

"Then farewell for now," he said, bowing first to Selene and then to me. "I hope to see you again before I leave the Spiral." He looked at me, a flicker of old pain flashing across his face. "I'll leave the portals running, Friend Roarke, as you requested. I can only hope that you've thought through the consequences."

I felt my stomach tighten. "Yeah," I murmured. "Me, too."

CHAPTER THIRTY

I called Mindi on our way back to the *Ruth* to tell her it was safe to go back home. It turned out she was already there, though she was vague on why she'd jumped the gun instead of waiting for my call.

She also told me that Nikki had intercepted her on the way back to her ship to tell her she was glad she'd lived through the ordeal. The two women had had a brief conversation, then gone their separate ways.

She also said that Nikki told her she'd already been paid.

I puzzled about that the rest of the way to the *Ruth*. I'd been very clear in my original message that I would pay her when Mindi was safe, figuring I would hand over what was left of the million commarks I'd borrowed from Nask plus our thirty-five silver-silk strands. Squaring things with Nask afterward would be a challenge, but I figured I'd cross that one when I got there.

So how could Nikki already have her payment? Had Mindi found our stash and taken matters into her own hands?

We were a few meters from the end of the *Ruth*'s zigzag when Selene suddenly touched my arm. "They're here, Gregory," she warned as she sniffed at the night air. "Nask and Huginn." She sniffed again, her pupils showing confusion. "*And* Dr. Robin."

"*Robin?*" I asked, staring at her.

"Yes."

I frowned up at the *Ruth*'s entryway. Nask and Huginn I could understand, especially after Huginn's *in his own way* comment. But why had they brought Robin?

Unless he'd somehow gotten the drop on Huginn and taken them hostage? "Any trouble?" I asked.

"I don't think so," she said. "I need to get closer."

"Right." Taking her arm with one hand, I drew my plasmic with the other and we headed up to the entryway. "Well?" I prompted, doing a quick visual check of the area as she sniffed at the hatch. Nothing out here seemed suspicious.

"It all seems all right," she said. "You probably shouldn't be holding that when we go inside."

"Right." I holstered the plasmic and keyed the entryway. "Hello?" I called, swinging open the hatch and leading the way inside.

"No need to shout," Huginn called back. He was standing casually beside the dayroom hatchway. "You and Bubloo have a nice chat?"

"We did, thank you," I said, closing and sealing the entryway and ushering Selene forward. "I assume you're the one who settled up with Nikki on my behalf. What did you do, sneak in the back door last night while she was asleep and find my stash?"

He shrugged. "I thought it would save time. Yours *and* Nikki's."

"How does it save her time?"

"Because now she won't have to have her face changed again."

"She could have just veiled up for the occasion."

"She told me she was happy to help," he said. "Especially given her unintentional role in Mindi's injuries on Vesperin. Doesn't mean she ever wants to see you again."

"I can live with that," I said. "Thanks for persuading Sub-Director Nask to drop in."

"No persuasion needed," he said as he stepped back from the hatchway and gestured into the dayroom. "Just make it short. The sub-director is a very busy person."

Nask was seated on the foldout as we entered, looking much better than the last time I'd seen him. Robin was standing beside him, looking alert but calm. "Hello, Sub-Director Nask," I said. "Thank you for seeing us on such short notice. I'm glad to see your health continues to improve."

"Thank you," he said. "I presume this invitation was to discuss the million commarks I gave you some years ago?"

"Yes indeed," I said. "I see that Expediter Huginn has pre-empted part of that conversation."

"He has," Nask agreed. "But no fears. I came here to confirm to you that the debt is erased."

"Oh?" I said, feeling a partial lifting of the weight on my shoulders. Being that deep in debt to a Patth, even one I got along fairly well with, wasn't something I wanted to live with for the rest of my life. "Thank you. Thank you very much. And congratulations on finding the Niskea portal."

Nask's expression didn't change. Neither did Robin's, and I was sure that Huginn, standing behind us, also had his face under control. All of it wasted effort, of course. "Reaction," Selene confirmed.

"Thank you," I said. "I assume from what Bubloo said that you've already moved it?"

Nask shifted position slightly, his eyes flicking to Selene. "Yes, we have," he said. "How did you know?"

"There were several indicators," I said. "For starters, Huginn was all over the Yellowdune ruins when Selene and I were there, which meant the area was clearly of interest to you. Second clue was when I called from Juniper to warn you that the Uroemm family was up to their old tricks again and ask for help. I expected you to send Huginn. Instead, you sent Circe."

"I'm not at your beck and call, you know," Huginn put in from behind me.

"Granted," I said. "But given our history of working together, you should logically have been Sub-Director Nask's first choice. But you were busy with the new portal. Hence, Circe." I lifted a finger. "I'm not sure whether to be flattered or offended by her presence in my life, by the way."

"How so?" Nask asked.

"You'd already offered me an Expediter position," I reminded him, focusing on Robin. But if he was annoyed that I was on Nask's list, he didn't show it. "I'm flattered that you would go to the effort of throwing the extra enticement of a beautiful woman at me, but a little offended that you thought my decisions could be that easily swayed."

Nask shrugged. "There was, in fact, very little extra effort involved," he said without even a hint of embarrassment. "Expediter Circe was already in the Juniper area. And you'll admit that human males are susceptible to such inducements."

"No argument there," I agreed. "Getting back to the point, Huginn wasn't here because he was occupied with either excavating or moving the portal. Then there was Mindi telling me an unknown tipster posted that I'd been seen at Yellowdune. Petty and childish, but given the animosity between you and the Uroemm family it was the sort of poke in the eye I'd expect from someone like Daxtro."

I looked at Selene. "But the biggest indicator of all was when we were all on Niskea and you invited me to come to the *Odinn* for a chat." I paused. "*Me.* Not Selene and me."

"Yes," Nask said thoughtfully. "I wondered at the time if you would pick up on that."

"It took me a while and a couple more clues," I admitted. "But it fit perfectly with everything else. You could be reasonably sure that a brief visit wouldn't get enough secondhand portal scent on me for Selene to detect. But you couldn't risk bringing her aboard. Speaking of Selene, Bubloo tells me you're working with him to get the Kadolians back home. Thank you."

"You're welcome," Nask said. "But don't assume our motives are wholly altruistic. There are Ammei who still dream of conquest, a scenario the Director General considers unacceptable. Removing access to Kadolians will hamper their efforts in that direction."

"At least that's one thing he and the Paterfamilias Uroemm can agree on," I said. "With the family's current stranglehold on Patth shipping, I'm sure he hates the whole idea of widespread portal travel."

"He does," Nask confirmed with a hint of old bitterness. "At one point, in fact, he nearly succeeded in removing my mandate and closing down the project."

I nodded as one final piece fell into place. "The kidnapped Patth pilot you rescued," I said. "He was Uroemm, wasn't he?"

"Yes," Nask said. "The success of that incident forced the paterfamilias to drop his opposition." He inclined his head to me. "Indeed, your assistance in that matter is why I consider your debt to have been paid."

"Ah," I said. "Thank you. I'm glad I could help."

"Yes." Nask said. "It also inspired the Director General in an entirely different way." He looked up at Robin. "Expediter Robin is the result."

I frowned at Robin, noting the small, smug smile playing at his lips. "Meaning?" I asked.

"You're an anomaly, Gregory Roarke," Nask said. "With the Icarus Group, yet not with them. Receiving orders and instructions, but fulfilling them in your own way. It was your unique function within Admiral Graym-Barker's organization that induced the Director General to test whether or not such a pattern would work for the Patthaaunutth."

"And thus is born failed Expediter Doc Robin," I said, nodding. "Completely independent, officially unconnected to anyone in authority. A wild card the Uroemm family couldn't hang around anyone's neck." I raised my eyebrows. "Specifically, the Director General's?"

"Yes," Robin confirmed. "Officially cast aside; unofficially his eyes, ears, and hands wherever I was needed."

"In this case, to attach yourself to Selene and me?"

"Actually, I was only tasked with keeping a quiet eye on Bubloo," he said. "I was sent to Juniper knowing just that he was a person of interest. When you and Selene showed up—you also being persons of interest—it seemed like a good idea to bring you all into a single group and see what shook out."

"Which also happened to be Bubloo's plan."

"So it seems," Robin said ruefully. "Too much secrecy wrapped around too many separately spinning wheels. But that's the life we've been handed."

The life we've been handed. The words seemed to echo through my brain. *The life we've been handed.*

So that was it? None of us had any choice in the matter? The universe worked through our hopes and dreams to bring us to some convenient status quo? *Do you expect your dreams to be less bloody?* Bubloo had asked.

Maybe I did. Maybe I didn't. But at the very least I wanted them to be *my* dreams, not those of some random set of circumstances.

And with a universe-wrenching flash of insight, I knew what I had to do.

The others were staring at me. "The life we've been handed," I repeated. "Yes. I'm thinking it's time to bring part of that spinning wheel to a stop."

"Meaning?" Nask asked.

"Meaning I want to make a deal." I looked at Selene, feeling my heartbeat speed up. I should discuss this with her, I knew. Should get her thoughts and insights before I hit the point of no return.

But there was no time. We were here, Nask was here, and we had privacy. The time was now. "You have a new omni portal, and you have half of a portal directory," I said, still watching Selene. "What if I could get you the other half?"

Selene's pupils went stunned. "Gregory?" she breathed.

"Not as a gift," I added hastily. "I want something in return. Something big."

"You speak with strange calmness of an act of treason," Nask said. There was none of Selene's horror in his expression, just interest and suspicion. "How do you propose to obtain General Kinneman's half?"

"I don't need it," I said. "Selene and I made a copy before we turned it over to him."

The tension in the dayroom went up a few notches. Nask, two Expediters, and a strong hint that something the Patth desperately wanted was hidden somewhere aboard this very ship. "You haven't yet addressed the question of treason," Nask said.

"Huginn asked about our talk with Bubloo," I said. "Our resident Icari pointed out that you having half a directory and the Commonwealth having the other half would inevitably lead to contention and probably violence. I expect the current Juniper impasse to ultimately take Kinneman out of the picture; but what if someone even more aggressive takes his place? What if that person persuades the Commonwealth to launch a war against the Patth to get your half?"

"Such a decision would be the height of foolishness," Nask said coldly.

"I agree," I said. "And if a new Director General rose to authority and made the same decision?"

"It would never happen," Robin said flatly.

"No?" I asked. "Sub-Director Nask?"

"Expediter Robin is right," he said. But he didn't sound entirely convinced. "The treason charge could still be made against you."

"I know," I said. "But I've watched you and the other Patth work. You have your share of crazies and megalomaniacs, but for the most part you seem to be in this mainly for the money. All the security and communications system back doors you've put in place are there to assure your money flow isn't damaged. There are a lot of ways you could have used those resources to topple governments, incite wars, or otherwise meddle in other sovereign nations' lives. But you haven't. I expect you to use the portals with the same restraint."

I looked at Selene. Some of the horror was still there, but I could see she was following my logic.

"I should also remind you that you're buying a mystery box," I continued, turning back to Nask. "None of us knows where the portals go or which ones, if any, will be useful. You can only bring a limited amount of material through with each passage, so they'll be useless for large-scale cargo shipments. You can send passengers, but that'll be about it."

"Or explorers," Selene said quietly.

"Which is another point in your favor," I said. "I offered the Alainn portal to Kinneman as potentially useful. He refused on the grounds that using replacement parts from one of his other Geminis could lose him both. You, on the other hand, were willing to take that gamble."

I looked over my shoulder at Huginn. "Once upon a time, we humans were the bold adventurers, ready to say *damn the torpedoes* and charge off to explore the universe. Not anymore. I think the Patth have now taken over that role. If the portals lead to great discoveries, it's going to be you who make them."

"And if, as you suggest, a Director General rises to authority who wishes to put the Spiral beneath his foot?" Nask asked.

"Then I'll have gambled and lost," I conceded. "But it still seems less likely than that the Commonwealth and Patth will end up in a futile war."

Nask was silent a long moment, his eyes steady on me. "I accept your logic, and agree with your conclusions," he said. "Yet I am bound to remind you that I once threatened you and Selene with torture, as well as threatening the lives of Icarus Project civilians. How is it you can even think to trust me?"

I looked again at Selene. Still withholding judgment. "I understand now what you were doing," I told Nask. "I also note that while you kept promising torture, you also kept pushing back the deadline. So answer me this: If Tera had continued to stall, *would* you have moved on to torture?"

"Yes." He smiled slightly. "But not in the way you think. I would have isolated Selene in a different part of our facility and held her unharmed while telling you she was being tortured."

"So all the pain would have been self-inflicted in our own minds," I said. "Psychological torture. Nearly as devastating as the real thing, and you don't have to worry about your subject dying on you."

"It wouldn't have worked," Selene said. "We would have found a way to communicate the truth to each other."

"Yes, I believe you would have," Nask said.

"As for the Icarus Project civilians," I said, "you talked a good fight, but you were pretty quick to accept an alternative plan when I offered it."

"I had hoped you would do so," Nask said. "The more violent plan was Expediter Geri's, and I was relieved when I had reason to turn it down. Still, I must assume those issues remain at least partially between us."

"Don't worry about it," I said. "You won't betray us, because what I'm asking in return will also gain you something you desperately want."

"What is that?" Nask asked, frowning.

"I'm proposing to break the power of the Uroemm family for you." I took a deep breath. "In exchange for the directory half, I want the Talariac Drive."

Nask's eyes flicked over my shoulder to Huginn. "You wish the *Ruth* to be refitted?"

"No, I mean—what?" I interrupted myself, my intended line of conversation braking to an unexpected halt. "You can *do* that?"

"The retrofit is quite straightforward," he assured me. "It would take less than two weeks to complete."

"That's good to know," I said, my mind racing. The *Ruth* with a Talariac Drive... "I'll get back to you on that. But you misunderstand. I don't want *a* Talariac Drive. I want *the* Talariac Drive. All of it. The specs, blueprints, tech, the stuff implanted into your pilots' faces. Everything."

"The Director General will never agree to that," Robin warned.

"Why?" Nask asked, his eyes still on me.

"Because in and among all those threats of torture, you also laid out the Patth perspective on what the Talariac had done for the Spiral," I said. "You reminded me it had opened up possibilities previously undreamt of, and had made life better for billions of beings. I argued against it at the time, but I can now see your side of the argument."

"And you feel the Commonwealth would be better guardians than the Patthaaunutth?"

I shrugged. "As you said, I need to give them something to make the treason charges go away. More to the point, I want to live a safe and secure life. The Talariac is my ticket to that promised land. As for the Uroemm family, every non-Patth Talariac ship that comes onto the trade routes will erode their power a little more."

I stopped, stealing another look at Selene. There was growing understanding in her pupils, as well as cautious approval.

But there was also a hint of wariness. Unlike Nask and the two Expediters, she knew I wasn't telling the full truth.

"Your proposal intrigues me," Nask said, standing up. "I shall bring it to the Director General's attention."

"Thank you," I said. "Can you give me some idea of the timeframe?"

He smiled faintly. "If his response is no, it will come quickly. If otherwise, it will require thought and discussion."

"Understood," I said. "I'll just point out that we need to move before the Paterfamilias Uroemm gets wind of it. The fiasco we handed him at the Traveler's Edge an hour ago will distract him and put him on the defensive for a while, but that grace period won't last forever."

"I have no doubt the Director General will act as quickly as possible," Nask assured me. "Good night, Mr. Roarke." His eyes shifted to Selene. "Selene."

"Good night, Sub-Director Nask," I said. "Huginn; Doc. I'm going to move the *Ruth* a little farther from the Ammei enclave, but we'll stay close to a StarrComm office."

Two minutes later they were gone, the *Ruth*'s entryway hatch closed and double-locked behind them. "At least Mindi slept through Huginn's midnight robbery," I commented as Selene and I returned to the dayroom.

"How do you know she didn't wake up?"

"Because neither of them got shot." I braced myself. "So. What do you think?"

"I don't know yet," she said. "What is it you're not telling me?"

So I told her.

We'd been camped out in Rosker for a week when the word came through that the Director General had agreed.

CHAPTER THIRTY-ONE

To the casual observer, the group assembled aboard the *Median* on that cloudy day three weeks later wouldn't have seemed all that remarkable. Patth were a familiar enough sight, especially at spaceports, and Kalixiri and their outriders were somewhat more common. The two unfamiliar aliens might have sparked a raised eyebrow, but that would probably have been the end of it. Add in our handful of humans, and that hypothetical observer would most likely have completely forgotten the scene before he'd gone another hundred meters past it.

But to me, gazing at the group was like reaching the end of a long and twisty road.

For Selene, that road had been much longer and far more exhausting.

The Patth was Director Nask, of course, seated at one end of the *Median*'s conference table, resplendent in the robes of his new office. Huginn and Muninn stood on either side of him, presenting their usual deceptively calm watchfulness. A couple of steps back from them was Doc Robin, probably here on the Director General's behest.

At the other end of the table were McKell, Ixil, and two top-level hyperdrive engineers, one human, the other Kalixiri. Bubloo stood unobtrusively against the wall behind them, interrupting his work of overseeing the Kadolian exodus in order to witness this quietly historic occasion. He wasn't wearing his Icari armor, but I noted a small bulge under his tunic that suggested he thought it would be prudent to make sure everyone behaved themselves. Farther back from the table but close enough to keep an eye on everything was Admiral Sir Graym-Barker, the representative that the Commonwealth hierarchy who'd signed off on this deal had insisted on.

Overseeing the whole spectacle was the eminent negotiator Sir Nicholas Roarke, the man who'd single-handedly made the whole thing happen.

Or rather, was *ready* to make the whole thing happen.

I frowned as I ran my eyes around the silent room. The players were set, the script was set, and the air was filled with anticipation. So why hadn't the game begun?

I looked at my father and raised my eyebrows in question. He caught my look and flicked his eyes in the direction of the entryway. *Waiting on a late arrival,* he mouthed.

I gave the room a second look. Everyone I'd specified was already here. Had some high-ranking Commonwealth official decided at the last minute that the event needed someone of his stature and ego?

From down the corridor came the twittering of the entryway alert. "I'll be right back," my father announced to the rest of the room as he headed for the hatchway. "Our final participant has arrived."

He disappeared out into the corridor. I focused on Selene, watching for her reaction. I heard the entryway hatch open and a pair of muffled voices...

Abruptly, Selene's pupils went horrified. "Oh, no," she said. "Gregory—"

I didn't need to hear any more. There was only one person who could spark that kind of reaction who might still have enough clout to invite himself back into our lives. My hand dropped to my holstered plasmic; out of the corner of my eye I saw Huginn's and McKell's gunhands do likewise in their own guarded responses. My father returned, striding calmly and confidently into the conference room.

Followed by General Kinneman.

Or rather, Commonwealth civilian Kinneman. His fancy

EarthGuard uniform was gone, along with the rows of shiny medals, his outfit now a simple but expensive-looking tailored semiformal suit. He paused in the hatchway, his eyes sweeping the room and coming to rest on me. He flicked a dark look at Nask, then strode past my father toward me.

Reflexively, I took a step to put me between him and Selene. "Hello, General," I said, mindful of my father's dictum to always get in the first word. "I didn't know you were on the guest list."

"Roarke," he replied stiffly. "Did you honestly think Earth-Guard would let this travesty happen without having someone trustworthy"—his eyes flicked pointedly to Graym-Barker—"on hand to observe?"

"Don't know why you think it's a travesty," I said, passing over the *trustworthy* part. Given the messy political fallout from his part of the fiasco that was rapidly becoming colloquially known as the Juniper Tug-of-War, I was mildly surprised that EarthGuard hadn't taken away more than just his rank. "Sir Nicholas has papers that confirm the Commonwealth hierarchy has signed off on it."

"The politicians agreed on what was presented to them," Kinneman countered. "You and I both know what's really going on here."

"I'll be happy to hear your thoughts on the subject," my father said calmly as he came up behind the general. "But in the meantime, our other guests are waiting. Let me get things started, then I'll be more than happy to discuss it with you."

Kinneman inclined his head. "As you wish, Sir Nicholas. You're in command here."

My father nodded acknowledgment, then turned and walked to the table. He gave a small bow to each of the participants, then cleared his throat. "Welcome aboard the *Median*, honored guests," he said formally. "Shall we begin?"

The whole handoff procedure had been carefully choreographed, of course. Nask handed my father a data stick containing the Talariac plans, which he walked over to Ixil at the other end of the table. Ixil plugged the stick into their computer, and he and the two hyperdrive experts began poring over the documents.

My father caught my eye and nodded. I nodded back and crossed to his side, rolling up my sleeve as I walked. I popped open the compartment in my left arm, pulled out our copy of the directory half, and handed it to my father. He returned to the Patth end of the table and delivered the stick to Nask, who plugged it into his own reader. With Robin watching closely over his shoulder, he began scrolling through the pages.

There was a touch of air on the back of my neck, and out of the corner of my eye I saw Kinneman come up beside me. "That was the list?" he asked quietly.

"Yes," I confirmed.

"This supposed list of of twenty portal addresses Selene supposedly found in a book on Nexus Six?"

"If you please, General," my father said, taking his arm and gesturing toward the conference room hatchway. "There's a lounge across the corridor that would provide us more privacy."

Kinneman shook off his grip. "I'm not interested in privacy," he said tartly. "Furthermore, I was sent here to observe the proceedings."

"You're more than welcome to do so," my father said calmly, this time merely resting his hand on Kinneman's arm. "Shall we at least move a bit farther from the table?"

Kinneman hesitated, then strode past us toward the hatchway. He stopped beside it and did a neat parade-ground spin to once again face the table. "Happy?"

"Thank you," my father said as he and I joined him. "I gather you have some difficulties with the deal?"

"I have several," Kinneman said, his eyes flicking back and forth between Nask and Ixil. "Let's start with this so-called address list. When exactly did this convenient discovery take place, and why didn't First of Three ever mention it to me?"

"Of course," my father said. "As the documents explain, it was found after—"

"I'm not asking you," Kinneman cut him off. "I'm asking your son. You need me to repeat the question, Roarke?"

"Not at all," I said, feeling my heart picking up its pace. Kinneman had spotted the problem buried in the documents my father had given the Commonwealth, all right, and was clearly determined to run it to ground. The crucial question was whether it was the hook we'd hoped someone would find, or the one we'd hoped they wouldn't. "The book was found after EarthGuard invaded the Juniper full-range portal, ran into Yiuliob's Ammei, and the Saffi kicked both of you out of the whole Thousand Tombs area. You didn't talk to First of Three after that, so of course he couldn't tell you about it."

"What did you give the Patth just now? A copy of the book?"

"Only a copy of the relevant parts," I said, my heart kicking in a few more beats per minute. Kinneman had sniffed his way into the danger zone. "First of Three wouldn't let the book itself leave Nexus Six."

"I'll bet he wouldn't," Kinneman said, eyeing me closely. "Because there's more to it than that. A *lot* more."

"What exactly are you suggesting?" my father asked.

"Don't play cute," Kinneman warned. "I saw the documents you presented for the Commonwealth to sign. They saw what they wanted to see. I saw what was actually there."

He fixed me with a dark stare. "You gave the Patth more than just those twenty addresses, didn't you? You gave them something else. Something they were willing to bargain for, and something you were willing to commit treason for."

"I have no idea what you're talking about," I protested, my heart going at triple rate now. If he'd connected the dots...

"Do you think me a fool?" Kinneman snarled. "I *read* the damn document. Nowhere does it say the Patth are giving the Talariac to the Commonwealth. It says they're giving it to *you*."

I took a deep breath, the adrenaline that had been surging into my bloodstream starting to taper off. The general had found the hook, all right.

But he'd found the one we'd deliberately left for him. "Is *that* what you're worried about?" I asked. "I guess you didn't read *all* of the documents."

"We noticed that omission only a few days ago," my father put in. "We transmitted an addendum yesterday. The certification came through"—he checked his watch—"four and a half hours ago."

"Don't worry, I'm not keeping the drive all for myself," I assured him. "I'll admit Eternal Economic Dictator would be an impressive title, but it also sounds like way too much work. Trust me, I'll be turning it over to the Commonwealth the minute I get hold of it."

Kinneman was silent another few seconds. Then he stirred. "I would hope so," he said in a marginally calmer voice. "Because if you don't, the *eternal* part of that fancy title will be impressively short." He turned to Selene. "I'm told you rejected EarthGuard's request to return to the APA and continue your work with them."

"Yes," she said.

"Even now that it's being reformed as a civilian organization?"

She nodded. "Even so."

"That's a pity," he said. His words were directed toward her, but his eyes were back on me. "There's still half a directory out there for the taking."

"Did someone forget to tell you that RH is in the *Imistio* Tower library?" I reminded him. "Snugged away behind a ring of lightning guns?"

"*Probably* in the library, I believe McKell's official report said," Kinneman reminded me back. "Similar to *allegedly,* as in *allegedly* committing treason."

"You can think whatever you want," I said. With the danger that he would stumble on the truth past, I was suddenly tired of the man. "The Commonwealth signed off on the deal. You're getting the Talariac. What more do you want?"

"I want the truth," Kinneman said. "I want to know what game you're playing."

I shook my head. "I'm done with games, Kinneman."

"You'll never be done," he ground out. "I've dealt with people like you all my life. You think you've got a private handle on the universe and can do whatever the hell you want—*Hold* it," he snapped as Selene started walking toward Ixil's end of the table. "Where do you think you're going?" His arm shot out like a snake, his hand clamping firmly around her wrist. He took a step toward her—

And froze as he felt the muzzle of my plasmic press against his kidney. "Let her go," I said quietly.

"This is treason, Roarke," Kinneman snarled, ignoring my command. "Pulling a weapon on an official Commonwealth observer."

"Actually, it's more like self-defense," I corrected. "And as my father used to say—"

"Shut *up,*" he bit out.

"As my father used to say," I repeated, a little louder this time, "*Before stepping over the line, be sure the numbers are on your side.*"

Kinneman snorted. "You really think you have friends in this room?"

"Me?" I shook my head. "Of course not. No one here really likes me." Taking a step back, I holstered my weapon. "But *all* of them like Selene."

Kinneman frowned, his eyes flicking around the room... and I saw his expression stiffen as he saw that every eye was focused on him.

And none of those eyes looked friendly.

He looked back at me, anger and hatred digging lines into his face. But he'd lived his life as a soldier and he understood impossible odds even better than I did. He released Selene's wrist and dropped his arm back to his side. "Whatever you're up to, Roarke," he said softly, "you won't get away with it."

"Understood," I said. "Selene?"

"They're finished," she said. Turning, she continued across the room to Ixil.

My father stepped up beside Kinneman and touched his arm. "Come on, General," he said. "Let's step out for a moment, shall we?"

"I'm an official EarthGuard observer," Kinneman ground out. "As such—"

"Admiral Graym-Barker is the Commonwealth's official observer," my father interrupted, his voice calm but firm. "Please don't make me insist."

For a few seconds, the two men held each other's gaze. "This isn't over, Roarke," Kinneman warned. "For either of you." Spinning again in a crisp about-face, he stalked to the room's hatchway, my father close behind him.

"He's not wrong, you know."

I turned as Graym-Barker came up beside me. "Excuse me?" I asked.

He glanced around the room, probably making sure no one else was in earshot. "He's not wrong about you committing treason," he said, lowering his voice. "You didn't give Nask twenty portal addresses. You gave him *all* of them." He raised his eyebrows. "The ones you illegally copied from our half of the directory before you gave it to McKell."

I felt a hard knot form in my stomach. I'd hoped desperately that no one would pick up on that possibility.

In retrospect, I really shouldn't have been surprised. No one in the Commonwealth hierarchy knew the kind of devious mind I had, or how I looked at the universe. They didn't know about the trait I'd apparently inherited from my father of trying to make sure all sides of an issue came out ahead. Pulling wool over their eyes had been simply a matter of misdirection and obfuscation.

But Graym-Barker knew me. He'd seen me in action, time and time again. If I laid out enough dots, he would absolutely connect them.

"I have no idea what you're talking about," I protested. It was pointless, I knew, but I had to make the effort.

"Of course not," the admiral said. "You must have forgotten I was listening in with General Kinneman back at Icarus when you told your father that your philosophy is to first do whatever benefits you and Selene and after that what's best for the universe at large. Did I get that right?"

"Mostly," I conceded. "The trick is usually figuring out the latter part."

"No doubt," he said. "It's also a philosophy I tend to agree with, for whatever it's worth." He nodded toward Nask. "So tell me: Aside from theoretically gaining full control of the Talariac Drive, what do you and Selene gain here?"

"Nothing, really," I said. "It's the universe that gains."

"How so?"

For a second I considered giving him all of it. But Part One of the plan was going to be hard enough to swallow, and Part Two was likely to be worse. Better to drop them on him one at a time. "We start with an unpleasant truth," I said. "Nask already has the right-hand half of the portal directory."

Graym-Barker rumbled something deep in his throat. "Of course. There'd been hints...I assume it's the one we hoped to find on Nexus Six?"

"Yes."

"Unfortunate," he murmured. "Go on."

"Go on where?" I asked. "The Patth and Commonwealth each have half of a very valuable object, both of them useless without the other. That's a classic recipe for war. I wanted to find a way to keep that from happening."

"Classic doesn't mean inevitable," Graym-Barker pointed out. "I'd like to think cooler heads would prevail on both sides, that we and the Patth would work back and forth until we resolved the issue."

"Which is exactly what I just did," I said. "Only I got us there sooner. Plus, I got us the Talariac."

Graym-Barker was silent another moment. I focused on Selene, speaking quietly with Ixil and McKell. "I understand your reasoning," the admiral said at last. "But General Kinneman isn't wrong. Giving Nask LH *is* theft and treason." He gave a small shrug. "On the other hand, gaining the certainty of the Talariac in exchange for the ambiguity of the portals isn't an unreasonable trade."

"Not to mention preventing a war."

"Perhaps," he said, clearly still not ready to concede that point. "But I can't help thinking we've lost something intangible but precious. Free and instant travel across the galaxy, even if there's nothing useful at the other end, is the kind of dream that drove humanity to conquer the stars in the first place."

"It used to be, anyway," I said, feeling an echo of Graym-Barker's own sense of loss. "Sadly, I think humanity has lost that perspective."

The admiral shrugged. "Maybe. But I'd argue that the average person never really had much spirit of adventure to begin with. It's always been a small percentage of humanity who've struggled to propel us forward, and I don't believe they're all gone. There's a lot of galaxy beyond the Spiral's boundaries that the Talariac will now make accessible to exploration, and I'm confident there will be those eager to press against those new horizons." He favored me with a small smile. "You and Selene likely among them."

"Could be," I said, my stomach tightening. The fact that the Kadolians were heading home was a secret we hadn't shared with the admiral or anyone else in the Commonwealth. Whether she stayed with me or left with the rest of her people was a decision she had yet to make.

A movement at the corner of my eye caught my attention. Kinneman and my father, their private conversation over, had rejoined us. I studied Kinneman's expression, hoping for some clue as to what had gone down, but his face was encased even harder in stone than usual.

Hardly surprising. Sir Nicholas Roarke in quiet intimidation mode was already a sight to behold. Here, with the full backing and authority of the Commonwealth in his arsenal, I could only imagine the calm verbal brimstone he could rain down on the unfortunate. My father stepped up beside me and nodded toward Selene. "Consultation?" he asked.

"Or they're almost done," I told him. "She headed over on her own, so she must have picked up a change in their scent."

Kinneman rumbled in his throat. "This had better not be a scam," he warned. "If Nask is pulling a fast one, your fancy clemency guarantees go straight out the window."

"It's not a scam," I assured him. "Selene knows Nask well enough to have picked up on anything like that."

"Unless the Director General lied to him, too."

I shook my head. "No. There's a side factor on the Patth side that dovetails with the deal that I guarantee the Director General wants to see happen."

"A side factor?" my father asked carefully. "You said you told me everything. I *needed* to know everything."

"This is internal to the Patth," I said. "Completely self-contained. Doesn't affect the deal in the slightest."

"That's not the way negotiations work," my father insisted. "If I'm not aware of every aspect—"

"Looks like they're finished," Graym-Barker interrupted.

Selene and Ixil had finished their conversation, and as we watched he pulled a second data stick from the computer. His eyes flicked to me, and I could see him noting the presence of Kinneman, Graym-Barker, and my father around me. He made a final comment to Selene, then pressed the data stick into her hand. She nodded and walked back to us. "Well?" I asked.

"It's all here," she confirmed, handing me the stick. "The tech, the operational parameters, the platform matrix. Everything that makes the Talariac work."

"Great," I said, forcing my voice to remain calm even as my heart picked up its pace again. *Eternal Economic Dictator*... "Did Ixil say how hard it would be to adapt it to standard hyperdrive tech?" I pointed forward, toward the *Median*'s hyperdrive cutter array.

And with everyone's attention automatically turning that direction, I slid the data stick into my inside jacket pocket.

But not just into the pocket. In the same motion, guided by the hours of practice I'd put into the maneuver, I deftly inserted it into my phone's receiver jack and tapped the SEND button.

"I'll take that," Kinneman said brusquely, holding out his hand.

I took a quick step away from him. "That's all right," I said, pulling out my now empty hand. "I'd rather hang onto it until everything here is settled."

"I wasn't asking," Kinneman said, his eyes narrowing.

"I never said you were," I said, stalling for time. There was a *lot* of data that needed to wing its way across the planet. "But as you already pointed out, the Talariac is officially mine. *I'll* decide when you get it."

Kinneman bit out a curse. "I knew it. Damn you to hell, Roarke. I'll tell you right now—"

"Gregory!" Selene snapped a warning.

One of the handy things about fancy suits like Kinneman's was that a good tailor could cut it to conceal a small weapon without the conspicuousness of a holster. Unfortunately for the general, he didn't know how to carry himself so as to compensate for the additional weight. Even as his hand darted up beneath the right-hand suit flap, I took a long step to close the distance and locked my fingers around his wrist. "Please don't," I said. "Don't," I added more sharply as weapons suddenly sprouted in the three Expediters' hands. "It's under control."

"The Talariac is *ours*, Roarke," Kinneman snarled, trying to break my grip. "Whatever you traded him was *ours*, not yours." He sent a defiant look at Nask and the Expediters, shot another look at McKell and Ixil, at Graym-Barker . . .

His struggles against me abruptly stopped, his eyes returning to McKell and Ixil. "That's right," I said, hoping I was interpreting his suddenly frozen expression correctly. "They haven't drawn their weapons. They're not going to, either, because they know there's no point. It's done."

"What's done?" Kinneman demanded.

"This." With my free hand I pulled my phone from my pocket, maneuvering my fingers around the data stick still attached, and keyed it for speaker. "Tera?"

"I have it," her voice came into the sudden stillness of the room. "Last chance to change your mind."

I looked at Kinneman, then at Nask. Kinneman was confused and angry, Nask confused and thoughtful. I shifted my eyes to McKell and Ixil. Neither of them looked exactly happy, but neither looked like I should retreat, either. Selene's pupils held some nervousness, but also support and determination.

And finally, I looked at my father. His face was expression-less, just the way he'd trained it to be. But as our eyes met, he gave me a small nod.

I took a deep breath. "I understand," I said to Tera. "Send it."

There was a moment of brittle silence. "Sent."

"Thank you." I keyed off and pulled the data stick from its slot. "Here," I said, handing it to Kinneman. "It's all yours."

He looked at the stick like it was a trinket a stage magician had just urged him to take. Behind him, I saw Nask wave down his Expediters' weapons, the perplexity on his face now changed to understanding. Out of the corner of my eye, I saw Graym-Barker's expression heading the same direction.

Kinneman, though, was still lost. "What the hell did you just do, Roarke?" he demanded as he plucked the stick from my hand.

"That was Tera," I said, holding up my phone. "She's in a StarrComm booth a hundred kilometers away. On my instruc-tions, she has now sent the Talariac Drive data to every Com-monwealth governmental center and EarthGuard command base in the Spiral."

I threw a look at my father, noting the small smile on his face. He'd gotten it, too.

But then, he'd had advance notice. *And after that, what's best for the universe at large...*

I turned back to Kinneman. "She's also sent it to the Kalixiri, the Crooea, the Vyssiluyas, the Ulkomaals, the Narchners, the Bolfins, and every other starfaring species in the Spiral," I continued. "Also to every shipping company, shipfitters' asso-ciation, ship repair guild, and every other interested group we could think of."

And then, finally, he got it. The blood drained from his face... "No," he breathed.

"Yes," I confirmed. "I promised the Commonwealth would own the Talariac, General, and it does." I waved a hand. "So does everyone else."

I paused, but the room remained silent. "Our agreement had no exclusivity clause," I added quietly. "We were hoping no one would notice. They didn't."

For a long moment Kinneman stared at me. He shot another look at McKell and Ixil, then another at Nask, finally one at my father. "Did you know about this?" he demanded.

"Not a whisper," my father said calmly. "No, Gregory's Christmas gift to the Spiral was a complete surprise. I can't say I disagree with him, though."

"And if I tell your superiors that you *did* know?" he retorted.

"It'll be your word against mine," my father said, his tone hardening. "But I'd be very cautious about going that direction, General. Right now, I have more friends in the Commonwealth hierarchy than you do."

"You got what you wanted, General," I said. "What does it matter that the rest of the Spiral has the Talariac, too? Did you hope that the Commonwealth would have complete and total control? That it would be able to demand licenses and rentals from everyone else? Did you want humanity to become the Patth?" I looked at Nask. "No offense."

He inclined his head to me but remained silent.

For another moment Kinneman glared at me. But there were no words, and he knew it. He looked down at my hand still gripping his, and shook it off. For a second I thought he might still draw and fire out of sheer frustration. But it would have been pointless, and he knew that, too.

"You will pay," he said to me. "You will pay dearly." Spinning on his heel in yet another crisp about-face, he stalked to the conference room hatchway and disappeared down the corridor.

"Dad?" I asked, looking out into the empty corridor.

"There are EarthGuard Marines on his ship," my father said. "They'll look after him."

"He's not the one I'm worried about," I said.

"It'll be all right," my father soothed. "The moment when he might have done something impulsive is past. He won't do anything now."

"I should probably talk to him anyway," Graym-Barker said, looking at the hatchway. "Make sure those impulses don't come back."

"Thank you, Admiral, I'd appreciate that," my father said. "General Kinneman wasn't always this bitter and obsessive. Bad enough that he's lost his rank and his position in the APA. There's no need for him to lose his dignity and pension, too."

"Not to mention his freedom or his life," Graym-Barker said heavily. "If you'll all excuse me?"

We watched as he left the room and disappeared down the

corridor. "He really *was* a good officer once," my father said. "More's the pity."

I huffed out a relieved breath. That could have ended *very* badly. "Afraid I'm not as compassionate as you are."

"Which is why I do what I do, and you do what you do," he said. "So. What's next on your agenda?"

"Just got a couple of loose ends to tie up," I told him as casually as I could.

Because, really, the only such question was whether I was going to need a new partner soon.

I felt my lip twitch. No. Not *whether*. *When*. The Kadolians were heading home, and I could hardly expect Selene to stand beside me and wave good-bye to them.

"Loose ends," my father repeated, eyeing me closely. "Sounds interesting. Also sounds evasive."

I shrugged. "You taught me everything I know."

"To both my honor and my shame," he said, smiling. "Well, then."

And to my surprise, he stepped close and enveloped me in the kind of hug I hadn't gotten from him since my eighteenth birthday. My muscles reflexively tensed; and then I relaxed, wrapped my arms around him, and leaned into the hug.

We held each other maybe ten seconds. Then his grip eased, we let each other go, and he stepped back again. "Good-bye for now, Gregory," he said, his voice casually formal. My father was gone, the professional negotiator back in his place. "If you need anything, or if you just want to talk or split a rack of ribs, you know how to find me."

"I do," I confirmed. "Thanks, Dad. For everything."

"No problem." He gave a sort of secret smile. "And on behalf of the Spiral, Merry Christmas to you, too." He looked at the table. "McKell? Are we done here?"

"We're done," McKell confirmed as he, Ixil, and the two hyperdrive techs stood up. "We were just sifting through some of today's ramifications."

"And discussing how we can get the *Stormy Banks*'s hyperdrive upgraded," Ixil added.

"Director Nask told me once that it's a quick and almost painless procedure," I said.

"So we've likewise concluded," McKell agreed. "The question

is where we can go before the line gets crowded with everyone else who wants one."

"I can help you with that," my father assured him. "Come on back to my office and I'll make some calls."

"Thanks," McKell said. He looked at me and nodded. "Roarke."

"McKell," I said, nodding back. "I think that about covers it."

"Pretty much," he agreed. Stepping up to me, he gave me a quick but firm handshake. "Incidentally, the admiral is planning to talk to the new head of the APA about getting Ixil and me reinstated. You and Selene interested in coming back?"

"Probably not," I said. "Appreciate the offer, though."

"Let me know if you change your mind," he said. "Lots of portals still out there that the Patth don't have addresses for. Definitely a seller's market."

"We'll take it under advisement," I promised. Either he hadn't figured out what we'd done, or he was pretending he hadn't. I figured the betting odds were heavily on the latter. "Give my thanks to Tera."

"Will do." He smiled and nodded at Selene, then followed my father out of the room. Ixil paused long enough for me to give Pix and Pax a final scritch, and then he, too, was gone.

Leaving us alone with Nask, the three Expediters, and Bubloo.

"Mr. Roarke," Nask said, rising to his feet.

I braced myself. "Yes, Director?"

"I am satisfied that you have fulfilled your side of the bargain," he said in a formal tone. "On behalf of the Director General, I declare this matter resolved."

"Glad to hear it," I said, quiet relief flowing through me. The final hurdle, and we'd cleared it. "Best of luck with your new toys. I hope you put them to good use."

"We shall," he promised. "As to the other matter..." He turned to Selene. "I've met with the Kadolian Elders. They assure me that they will gladly accept Tirano, and that several families have already volunteered to take him in and continue his nurturing."

"Thank you," Selene said, a quiet pain in her pupils. "I only hope that it's not too late, that he isn't permanently damaged."

"If they can't help him, I doubt you could, either," Bubloo pointed out gently as he came up to us. "You've done all you can for the boy, Selene. You need to let him go."

I felt a fresh flicker of impending loss. Just as I also needed to let Selene go?

As usual, she caught the shift in my scent. "Gregory?" she prompted.

"Bubloo's right," I said. "No, I was just thinking about you. Whether you're going with Tirano, or...maybe staying in the Spiral a little longer."

"Of course I'm not going yet," she said, puzzlement in her pupils. "Did you think...? No. Did you think I was going to abandon you?"

"It's not abandoning," I assured her, wincing at the harshness of the word. "Things have changed."

"Things always change," she said. "That doesn't mean we always have to change with them."

"Doesn't it?" I took a deep breath. "Look. For years I've wondered why you teamed up with me in the first place. Now I know. You were looking for your home, and hoped my free-roaming lifestyle could help you find it. And that was fine. But now you've found it, and that's wonderful, and you don't need me anymore." I ran out of words and stopped.

"You really don't understand Kadolians, do you, Friend Roarke?" Bubloo said. "Selene hasn't been your partner all these years because she needs you. She's with you because *you* need *her.*"

I frowned at Selene. "Really?"

"It's not the way it sounds," Selene said, her pupils uncomfortable. "Bubloo doesn't mean he thinks you're somehow inferior or helpless."

"He can think whatever he wants," I assured her. "Anyone with brains knows that in a good team the members all have different skill sets. *Different* doesn't mean *better* or *worse.* It just means *different.*"

"I apologize for my assumptions," Bubloo said, eyeing me thoughtfully. "You speak of a maturity I didn't realize humans had."

"Apology accepted," I said. "And to be fair, I never said *all* humans thought that way."

"Then I can stay with you?" Selene asked.

"Of course," I said. "Though I think we're done hunting portals for the Icarus Group." I raised my eyebrows at Nask. "I don't suppose the Path would like to hire us?"

"You worked many years for Admiral Graym-Barker and EarthGuard," Nask pointed out. "Given that history, I doubt the Director General would accept you into important Patthaaunutth operations." He cocked his head. "Unless you're asking to become an Expediter?"

"Sorry," I said. "Not yet, anyway." I looked at Selene, a sudden thought occurring to me. "Selene, were you the only Kadolian wandering around the Spiral?"

"No, there were others," she said, her pupils gone thoughtful. "Perhaps a hundred in all."

"Would they have regular communication with the main Kadolian exiles?"

"Not normally," she said, her pupils stirring as she saw where I was going. "Are you suggesting we look for them?"

"Why not?" I said. "If they haven't already gotten the message, someone needs to tell them they can go home." I looked at Bubloo. "Someone who can guide them there even after the official exodus program shuts down."

"Yes," Selene said, a cautious excitement growing in her pupils. "All we need is to get to Nexus Six."

"As long as First of Three is willing to let us through to the Nexus One portal," I agreed.

"You won't need his permission," Bubloo said. "I'll unlock the private Icari tunnels for you before I leave."

"Then we're set," I said, nodding. "We have the *Ruth* and working money"—I nodded acknowledgment to Nask—"and even a couple of leftover ship's IDs in case Kinneman decides to come after us. Is that offer of a Talariac upgrade still on the table, Director Nask?"

"It is," Nask confirmed. "Before I reach hyperspace I'll transmit the name of a planet and a set of coordinates to you. The owners of that facility have already been informed to expect you."

"Thank you, Your Eminence," I said, bowing to him. "Congratulations on your promotion, by the way."

"Thank you," Nask said. He turned to Bubloo. "If we're finished here, the *Odinn* is ready to leave at your convenience."

"I'm ready," Bubloo said. He turned toward the hatchway—

"One more thing," I called.

He turned back, his expression wary. "Yes?"

"The title the Ammei gave you," I said. "The Gold Ones. Why?"

"It's quite simple," he said. "Also quite ridiculous. You've seen the Ammei and their hard, armored skins."

"Like Earth armadillos."

"Yes," he said. "What do you know about the properties of gold?"

I stared at him as it suddenly fell into place. Was he seriously suggesting...? "You're joking."

"Sadly, I'm not," he assured me. "Compared to the Ammei, Icari skin is soft. Compared to other metals, gold is considered soft."

"Sounds like a backhanded insult," Huginn said.

"I'm certain it was," Bubloo said, a distant sadness in his voice. "For all we gave them, for all we wished to nurture them, the Ammei never genuinely liked us." He shook his head. "But then, we hardly gave them reason to do so."

He paused, then seemed to shake the memories away. "Farewell, Friend Roarke; Friend Selene. I'm pleased to have met you, and honored to have known you."

"Farewell, Bubloo of the Icari," I said. "I hope we'll meet again."

"It's possible," Bubloo said. "But I fear it's also unlikely." He nodded and once again headed toward the hatchway, Nask and the Expediters following.

A minute later, Selene and I were alone.

I took a deep breath. "Maybe," I said quietly after them. "But as my father used to say, *Likelihood is just a way of measuring how surprised you'll be when something happens.*"

"Yes," Selene said, her pupils thoughtful. "And really, isn't continued existence itself unlikely?"

"Certainly the existence we've been living lately," I said. "And speaking of my father, assuming that he'll see McKell and Ixil off the *Median* before he comes back in here..."

Popping open my arm's elbow compartment, I pulled out the two pages I'd taken from the Icari serum book, folded and tucked unobtrusively beneath the data stick I'd given Nask. "Also assuming he'll continue to be involved in whatever talks the Commonwealth have with Nexus Six," I added as I unfolded the pages and laid them on the conference room table, "he might appreciate a little extra leverage." I tapped them in farewell and took Selene's arm. "Time to go."

We were outside and walking toward the *Ruth* before Selene spoke again. "Thank you for agreeing to this," she said quietly, her pupils brimming with a kaleidoscope of emotions. "Searching for scattered Kadolians won't be a very exciting a way to spend your time."

"I've had enough excitement lately, thanks," I assured her. "This will be just like bounty hunting, except that no one will be shooting at us."

"I'm still grateful."

"*I'm* grateful that you're staying with me," I said. "As my father used to say, *When you find the very best there is, whether it's a job, a partner, or a pizza, grab onto it and never, ever let it go.*"

"Yes," she murmured. "Is it just pizza? Or does the saying also include barbequed ribs?"

"Of course," I assured her. "*And* Dewar's."

I touched her arm. "And especially friends."

The End